WINTER S

MERLIN RADICAL FICTION

edited by
John Lucas

WINTER SOLSTICE
by
DOROTHY COWLIN

Introduction by
Gabriele Griffin

LONDON
MERLIN PRESS

Published in 1991
by the Merlin Press Ltd
10 Malden Road
London NW5 3HR
First published in 1942
by Jonathan Cape
Introduction © 1991 by Gabriele Griffin
Made and printed in Denmark by
Nørhaven Rotation
Viborg
ISBN 0 85036 408 6

INTRODUCTION

by

GABRIELE GRIFFIN

Winter Solstice, first published in 1942 by Jonathan Cape, is a curious and compelling novel, detailing a psychological drama dressed in twentieth-century garb against a social backdrop of decidedly Victorian fabric. Its protagonist, Alexandra Gollen, an orphaned young woman paralysed from the hips down, lives with and is cared for by her twin elder brothers who work from home as tailors. The text focusses on the unravelling of the mysterious nature and origin of Alexandra's paralysis, unquestioningly accepted by herself, her brothers and their neighbours as an unalterable, physically based condition until the successive, *deus ex machina* like appearance of two women, Miss March and Iris Young, who come to have suits made for themselves by the brothers, and demand explanations for Alexandra's state. Miss March suggests that Alexandra might be shamming, a thought shocking to her brothers who—because Miss March is perceived by them as a clever, rude 'Modern Woman' with 'masculine' shoulders, virile gait and knock, a hoarse voice,—very quickly forget her 'rather penetrating remarks as to the nature of their sister's malady':

> I'm not suggesting *deliberate* sham. There's such a thing as sub-conscious shamming, you know. But there—Freud might never have existed so far as the doctors are concerned. (28)

Iris Young's enquiry into the origin of Alexandra's paralysis, 'Was there no violent grief, or fit of temper—some trouble, that upset her mind so much that her body took refuge, or revenge, in this way?' (65), meets with a refusal on the brothers' and Alexandra's part to 'rake up the past'. They are convinced that Alexandra 'will never get better'. Iris' assertion that a shock 'can have queer effects on the nervous system' is not taken up: she, like Miss March, is dismissed on the grounds of being a 'masculine' woman.

Alexandra's total amnesia concerning the pre-paralytic period of her life and the absence of a specific medical condition indicate that she is suffering from a form of hysterical paralysis. (A good, recent account of views on treatment of hysterical women during the first half of this century can be found in Elaine Showalter's *The Female Malady*, London: Virago, 1987, esp. 121–64). In his *Studies on Hysteria* (Pelican Freud Library, vol. 3) Freud suggests that this phenomenon occurs when an individual in a state of extreme excitation due to some traumatic experience or event (e.g. the loss of a loved person) cannot adequately release the feelings associated with the traumatic event. The failure to *abreact* appropriately leads to a conversion of the emotions into a physical symptom such as paralysis. These so-called conversion-hysterias are accompanied by a loss of memory concerning the events related to the traumatic experience. The loss of memory is, however, not complete: the events are simply not accessible to the hysteric's consciousness. Under hypnosis, Freud found, hysterics could be brought to recall these events in great detail — a finding which reinforced his notion of the existence of unconscious ideas. He therefore talks of the *splitting of the mind* in hysterics who *repress* ideas inadmissible to consciousness (e.g. feelings, emotions, memories which are distressing). The inadmissible ideas persist in the unconscious and, in the case of hysterics, bringing them back to consciousness results in the immediate and permanent disappearance of the hysterical symptom.

In Alexandra's case the disappearance of the paralysis is precipitated not by the recovery of her memory of the circumstances concerning the onset of her illness but by the arrival on the scene of Iris with whom she falls in love. Iris, a female aviator *à la* Amy Johnson, awakens

Alexandra from her 'hardly-won [sic] content' with her talk of gliding making one feel in charge of oneself, 'It's a feeling of "I am master of my fate, the Captain of my—well no, not soul—but certainly of my body!"' (68). Alexandra's 'helpless docility' changes into discontent with her situation and gives rise to 'the growth of self-will [which] is a necessary stage in any mental advance' (69), mental advance being what her recovery depends on. Extrinsic events now begin to excite her curiosity and emotions to the extent that within a year of first encountering Iris she regains the use of her legs. The cause of her paralysis, however, remains a mystery.

The clues offered by the text for the resolution of this mystery are such as to arouse the suspicion, particularly in a reader of the 1990s which have seen an increase in the public awareness of child abuse, that Alexandra is the victim of some form of sexual abuse by her father. Indeed, Freud suggests that conversion-hysterias in girls, the onset of which occurs during puberty, most frequently have a sexual basis. Alexandra first became paralysed when she was twelve, i.e. during puberty. She has no feeling in the lower part of her body. At the beginning of the novel she cannot remember her father; when she eventually does, her memories are of a brutal, womanizing drunkard committing acts of violence against the mother, a character, in fact, familiar from Victorian melodrama. References to stories such as that of 'the "tragedy" of a little girl, found strangled and "indecently assaulted" under a canal bridge' (56), and Mrs. Tyler's comment, 'You with your pa the wair 'e was, me with mah Clifford, what 'e was—we knaw!' (48), increase the reader's sense of Alexandra's paralysis being related to some incident with the father. The recollection of memories related to the father is invariably coupled with suggestive comments such as 'Perhaps after all it would be as well not to stir the stagnant water of her memory, lest something worse than rats, some putrefying or obscene horror, should be disclosed.' (95) This is exactly what the reader comes to expect. It would explain the malevolent joy Alexandra remembers feeling at her father's death (115–6), her sense of 'nameless evil' associated with the father, her recollection of how, outside the pub 'The Railway Arms', 'he stood and leered at her. He seemed like a gorilla—made more horrible, more obscene, by being dressed in human clothes.' (140) Having been the victim of incestuous sexual abuse might explain Alexandra's initial falling in love with a woman which in turn may be a result of her—rather like the central character in Alfred Hitchcock's film *Marnie*—witnessing what might be termed *primal scenes* (Freud's description of the child's first observation of her/his parents having sexual intercourse, interpreted by the child as an act of violence perpetrated by the father against the mother—see 141-4 of *Winter Solstice*). Not until we are two thirds through the novel does the text's attention shift from the creation of this expectation to a more pronounced focus on the relationship between Alexandra and her younger brother Nick whose death occured two days before the onset of Alexandra's paralysis. The *dénouement* of the origin of the paralysis comes as a curious twist to the tale; the incest theory turns out to be a false lead.

The other major 'false lead' in *Winter Solstice* concerns Alexandra's infatuation with Iris who, in line with Havelock Ellis' definition of the lesbian or *invert* (*Sexual Inversion*, 1897), is described as a masculine woman in terms of appearance and manner, of superior social standing, and with outstanding talents that supposedly 'compensate' for her 'inversion'. In her assertiveness and directness Iris resembles Miss March, the 'Modern Woman' who, being 'hard, ugly, aping men's clothes and habits with disastrous and ludicrous effect' (29), is ridiculed by the tailoring brothers. But where Miss March in her outdated suffragette's attire of 1916 (25), being approximately fifteen years behind the times in terms of the novel's events which take place between 1931 and 1936, fails to impress, Iris Young does. Her striking, even if (this is a judgment made within the text) masculine, appearance, as much as her interest in Alexandra arouse a response in the latter.

The reader is led to believe that Iris is a lesbian, partly by her behaviour and manner, and partly by her suggestive invitation to take Alexandra out for a weekend which will include 'a night at an inn' with her. When they arrive at the inn the landlord and Iris appear to be on familiar terms with her asking if her 'usual room' is available ('All as usual you see, Miss Young!'), and the landlord wanting to know whether or not they will share it. The impression is given that Iris regularly conducts love affairs with women here. Alexandra is correspondingly aroused by the prospect of spending a night in a bed 'with the princess by her side' (137). The description of Iris' slow striptease as they go to bed—with Alexandra watching from the bed—leads the reader to expect the sexual consummation of the two women's relationship. However, apart from a peck on the cheek, an act of 'compassion for the child' on Iris' part, described however, from Alexandra's perspective, in erotically evocative terms as producing 'the delicious foam of sensuous pleasure' (144), nothing happens.

The night proves to be the turning-point of their friendship; Iris begins to find Alexandra's perpetual, jealous presence oppressive. It transpires that she considers her admiration an 'unhealthy "fixation"' (164) for which she feels responsible: 'I thought I could help her cramped mind to grow ... Now, I feel as if I'm *distorting* her mind instead'. (164) Later, Alexandra too comes to read her love of Iris in that way; describing her infatuation she maintains, 'I still like her, you know, but sensibly now—the other liking was out of all reason. I can see that now. I don't know what was the matter with me.' (216) Iris and Alexandra respectively are reassured about their 'normality' by the men they form relationships with who maintain that 'girls have these infatuations quite often' (216), and that these are 'quite a normal feature of adolescence ... especially female adolescence' (164). So much for that. A doubt, however, as to the adequacy of these explanations remains in the reader's mind, seeded by the suggestion in the text that Alexandra accepts this line of reasoning *simply* because she does not have 'an introspective nature:' 'She therefore accepted Donald's explanation meekly, as those who cannot generalize must always accept the theories of those who can.' (214)

It is worth pointing out that passing potential homosexual relationships off as fleeting immature infatuations is a line frequently taken in texts dealing with such relationships throughout the first half of this century as in Clemence Dane's *Regiment of Women*, A. T. Fitzroy's *Despised and Rejected*, Lillian Hellman's *The Children's Hour*, and Elisabeth Craigin's *Either Is Love*. The reasons for taking such a line are complex, encompassing a position frequently adopted in the sexological writings of the period that homosexuality constitutes a form of psychosexual retardation on the part of the homosexual person as much as being expressive of the social unacceptability of homosexuality. It is worth remembering that in 1921 an abortive attempt was made in Parliament to make lesbianism illegal (see Sheila Jeffreys, *The Spinster and Her Enemies: Feminism and Sexuality 1880–1930*, London: Pandora, 1985, esp. 113 onwards).

A further factor was, no doubt, the increasing visibility of women in the public sphere, facilitated and accelerated by the two world wars (the second one was raging when *Winter Solstice* was written). Ray Strachey's *The Cause: A Short History of the Women's Movement in Great Britain* (1928; rpt. London: Virago, 1978), esp. ch. 18 onwards, provides some useful information on this. Indeed, one of the conflicts delineated in *Winter Solstice* is between an 'old' static world ruled by men, embodied in the figures of Alexandra's father and brothers, and a 'new' dynamic world taken over by women, represented through Iris. Not only are she and Miss March, the two 'mannish' women, the ones who 'have the theory', i.e. know about Freud, but Iris, too, is associated with machines and motion. She flies a glider and drives a car, both objects of which the brothers are almost afraid and from which they dissociate themselves. This difference cannot be explained exclusively in terms of class; the brothers are unfamiliar even with those innovations of the early twentieth century which are available to them such as the cinema to which, typically for this novel, they are eventually introduced by a woman, Winifred, who comes from the same class background as the Gollen family. It seems as if brothers and sister alike have been petrified into stasis by the events of their childhood, which was governed by their tyrannical father, so that they do not wish to disturb the equilibrium achieved after his death. Change, for the brothers, can only be for the worse.

Where the father seems to represent the debauched, brutalized reality of the craftsman, driven to drink and despair by the advent of factories and mass production, translating his awareness of his degradation into the abuse of women, the brothers as adults seem to inhabit a life outside time which has a fairy-tale like quality about it. It is governed by attributes associated with the 'good' characters in such tales, e.g. simplicity, industriousness, cleanliness, regularity, order, sobriety, honesty, and compassion. The Gollen brothers personify 'poor but honest' artisans, the life not only of the fairy-tale but also of the nursery. Significantly the brothers, like many of the other characters, are presented as androgynous figures whose looking after their sister combines paternal protectiveness with maternal nurturance. Their profession itself, tailoring, is indicative of this androgynous stance; so is the fact that they operate as a harmonious, mutually supportive rather than competitive unit, even to the point of personal disadvantage. When both fall in love with the same woman, Winifred, one asks for her hand on behalf of the other. Winifred is repulsed by this without quite knowing why: 'It wasn't *natural* to do that ... I think I felt like I do with a cripple—or somebody with a horrid birthmark—sorry and yet disgusted—*repelled* by them somehow! Do *you* think it was a natural way for a man to act?' (157–8) Winifred's conception of manliness does not include the notion of their co-operation or, indeed, selflessness, especially where affairs of the heart are concerned.

She would, for the same reason, probably not take to Donald Yates, the youth who becomes interested in Alexandra in the last stages of the novel and whom Alexandra likes precisely because she can 'talk to him as if he were one of her brothers' (192). He embodies most strongly, perhaps, the man who seeks to redress the balance between the sexes, the imbalance of which is epitomized by the unequal power structure governing the relationship between the Gollens' parents. He has 'the quality, rare in boys, and rarer still in men, of wordless divination of the moods of others' (215). This feminine sensitivity is coupled with two other significant symbolic gestures he makes: he offers Alexandra his breeches which she finds easy to wear because 'her long illness [has] rendered [her] innocent of the fussy sexual self-consciousness that cheapens a good many relationships' (199), and he not only maintains that it is a pity that 'women have to give up their names when they marry' (216) but also says, 'I'll adopt *your* name if you like.' (219) He, as much as the Gollen brothers, is a cousin of Gregory, a character in Olive Schreiner's *The Story of an African Farm*, a similar androgynous figure.

Winter Solstice explores androgyny in terms rather similar to those adopted by Virginia Woolf in *A Room of One's Own* where the term stands for the harmonious co-existence within the individual of masculine and feminine qualities, symbolized through the image of a woman and a man getting into a taxi together and vanishing into the stream of London traffic. Vehicles, especially the railway, as emblems of movement, change, progress both feared and desired, are familiar from Victorian fiction; *Winter Solstice* offers a re-reading of this symbol, linking the locomotive with the idea of androgyny in a conversation between Iris and Gordon whose supposedly humorous tone denounces what is conceived of as con-

ventionally feminine and masculine in equal measure:
'Gordon began one of his characteristic extravagances,
upon the locomotive and its essential maleness. "Look
at its flat bosom for a start . . . the emphasis on locomotion—the restless seeking after movement for movement's sake, rather than living for living's sake, betrays
the male. And the absurd self-importance of the creature!
. . . Oh, but surely that scream was feminine," protested
Iris . . ."Definitely feminine! Dangerously and perpetually on the verge of hysteria!" . . . So they disputed . . .
in the fashion of those who, in love with one of the
opposite sex, are temporarily out of love with their own.'
(165)

Winter Solstice seems to lose the courage of its convic-
tions as it progresses. The lesbian relationship is interpreted as an intermediate state, post-dating infancy and
pre-dating maturity; Alexandra's paralysis is explained
by Donald as resulting from an over-developed 'maternal
instinct' (213), and essentially self-inflicted. The novel
has much to say about female masochism, and women's
internalization of guilt, whether justified or not, but does
not explore the conditions which give rise to such a
disposition other than to suggest that it is not good for
'little girls from poor homes lugging babies about, nearly
as big as themselves' (213–4). Economic and social conditions, especially urban slum life, are cited as playing
a significant role in the individual's psychological make-
up. It is at this point that the modern psychological
drama and the Victorian background intersect.

The descriptions of the Gollens' hometown's nether
region, Colebridge's slums (e.g. 111–5), discovered by
Alexandra in her quest for her past, are Dickensian
rather than Orwellian (compare, for instance, *David
Copperfield* or *Little Dorrit* with *Down and Out in London and
Paris* or *The Road to Wigan Pier*). The same is true of the
opposition of craftsmen versus the alienated workforce
in a factory as commented upon by Iris (139). The
socio-economic critiques offered in *Winter Solstice* seem
themselves 'anachronisms' in the context of the period

when the novel first appeared, during World War II, and the context in which it is set, the early 1930s, when the after-effects of the Great Depression could still be felt. But the novel does not suggest that its main preoccupation is the general conditions in which the Gollen family live; rather, as one of the brothers says when measuring a fat man for a suit, 'it's the unusual figures that make our work into an art' (39).

Dorothy Cowlin creates a number of unusual figures in this novel, unusual because—to use terms from Woolf's *A Room of One's Own*—they are 'man-womanly' and 'woman-manly'. To what extent the transformation from work into art, from, perhaps, documentation into imaginative invention turns the story into not only an aesthetic object but also an artificial one, thereby (deliberately?) undercutting the credibility of the central characters, is left open to debate and individual readings of the text.

Winter Solstice's unusual figures are matched by the novel's unusual and asymmetrical structure. It is divided into a prologue and three parts of uneven length. The prologue details a night in Alexandra's life. Part One describes one week in March from Monday to Sunday— 'a dip at random into the life of Alexandra Gollen between the ages of twelve and twenty-one' (58)—which is representative of her life during those years. Part Two begins with the spring of 1933 and the appearance of Iris in Alexandra's life, ending with Alexandra's recovery from her paralysis in the November of that year. Part Three begins in January 1935, 'a little more than twelve months after the inception of her miracle' when Alexandra has 'ceased to be grateful for it' (86). Having regained her ability to walk she has not only to rediscover the past but also find a future. This she does in the following twelve months during which the events of Part Three take place. Structurally, the novel thus operates in ever-widening circles of time, moving from the description of one night to that of one week, six months, and a year, gradually encompassing more and more of Alexandra's past and future until the former is fully revealed and the latter has taken a clear shape with the potential marriage between Donald and Alexandra in sight, and her decision to learn dress-making and enter the family firm.

This movement through time is paralleled by Alexandra's development from a state of infancy to one of maturity clearly mapped out in the text. In the prologue she is presented as an infant in its cot, content and cared for. She and her tailoring brothers live a fairy-tale existence as orphaned siblings keeping house together with no sense of past or conception of change in the future. The 'unreality' of this life, which in its perpetual sameness, has a quality of timelessness, is symbolized by Alexandra's relationship to 'firelight', her 'shadow-showman', with the help of which she entertains herself by inventing stories. The image of Alexandra watching the fire and fantasizing bears a direct relation to Plato's cave myth (*The Republic*, BK VII, 514–21). Like Plato's prisoners in the cave Alexandra has to be led from illusion to reality/truth, from darkness/night into light/-day. The cave myth surfaces again in slightly different form when Alexandra first goes to the cinema and is confronted with the need to distinguish between the world on the screen and the world outside (122–7).

Unpleasure promotes the desire for change. When Iris appears, Alexandra experiences discontent with her situation (Part Two) — like the central character in Hans Anderson's fairy tale 'The Little Mermaid' (5, 23) Alexandra now longs for 'mortality and legs', i.e. entering time and becoming independent. *Winter Solstice* here makes use of the same images as H.D. in *Her* (1927; London: Virago, 1984) where Anderson and the mermaid (as well as Freud) are also evoked in the description of a woman's finding a sense of self that makes an interesting comparison to this novel.

Part Three details Alexandra's maturation, her re-learning to walk, learning to name objects like plants, and her re-discovery of her hometown and her past.

Iris' friend Gordon describes this process by analogy to 'certain kinds of fish who live in the Arctic Sea' and who 'are able to survive a winter frozen into a block of sea-ice, and when it melts, are able to resume their physical processes where they left off' (164–5). Hence the title of the novel, *Winter Solstice*, which—denoting the 21st December when the sun is furthest from the equator—signals the turning-point when the sun, moving towards the equator again, leads to a gradual melting and increasing of light.

The title highlights the symbolic use of language which dominates the novel, giving it a poetic quality and indicating the consciously crafted nature of the text. Symbols provide the interface between experience and reflection upon it, between the unconscious and the conscious, between one episode and another. As a narrative device they are particularly appropriate for *Winter Solstice* as Alexandra's search for her past, which surfaces fragmentarily in images (e.g. 112, 114–5) and dreams (e.g. 75–6, 178–80), is mirrored by the reader's attempt to unravel the mystery of her paralysis and the trauma behind it. Direct references to the work of Freud (e.g. 86) indicate to the reader the possibility of a psychoanalytic reading of the novel as the analyst, too, relies on narrated memories as the key to the origins of the individual's behavioural and linguistic patterns. One example of Alexandra's traumatic history which may have fed into her paralysis is hearing her mother scream in the night, going down to find her mother being dragged about by the hair by her father, and Alexandra taking scissors to cut the mother free. Alexandra's heroic deed results in the mother siding with the father against her (142–3). One conclusion the reader is left to draw is that Alexandra's later self-infantilization (being confined to her cot after the paralysis) is a way of her claiming the attention and mothering she was denied as a child.

A relationship is established between text and subtext, the consciousness and the unconscious of Alexandra, from whose viewpoint the third person narration mainly proceeds, which is signalled through a series of images that repeat the idea of continuous active processes going on beneath the surface. Their negativity is indicated through phrases like 'fragments of those blank thirteen years began to be vomited from time to time into her present memory' (114), and through images such as Alexandra's sense that there is another room 'behind' the room she is familiar with (horribly described as 'a green putrefying corpse dressed in a pretty pink frock' 117), the polluted river into which Iris finds Alexandra staring (173–5), and Donald's story of the history of Eyam (193–4). Through these vivid images the novel becomes intensely atmospheric, not in a vague, indeterminate fashion but in the visually actualized manner one associates with the medium of film, made possible through the specificity and particularity of concrete tangible objects employed as symbols in the text such as the recurrent bird images (e.g. 5, 75–6). At the same time the text abounds with imaginative descriptions such as:

> Piled in terrace after terrace, tumbled and tilted madly at all angles like the walls of some lunatic's multiple castle, were more houses than she had dreamed existed in the world . . . Here and there a tower or a chimney shot out of the plum-coloured mist like the naked arms of sooty-skinned swimmers. (105)

or;

> A sluttish version of a traditional April shower had just ceased . . . the wet pavement was slimy with combined soot and rain, shining like the skin of black slugs, and the usual litter of tram-tickets and chip-papers and cigarette packets had been swept in sodden puddings over the grids of the gutter. (109–10)

The use of alliteration, and the rhythmic structure of the sentence give this last description, of which there are many more instances, its poetic quality. This combines with the constant personification of objects (the tram, for example, '[grinds] its teeth like an exasperated dragon' 90, and '[shudders] epileptically' 91) to create a literally animated world, at times akin to the world of the nightmare or horror film. The reader is led through this nightmarish world of Alexandra's horror of what might be hidden beneath the surface. Here a continuity exists between dream world and reality (e.g. 177–86) which Alexandra (and the reader) must to learn to distinguish and unravel.

About the author: despite the fact that she wrote many novels, eight of which at least were published by Jonathan Cape (*Penny To Spend*, 1941; *Winter Solstice*, 1942; *The Holly and the Ivy*, 1950; *The Slow Train Home*, 1951; *Rowanberry Wine*, 1952; *An End and a Beginning*, 1954; *Draw the Well Dry*, 1955; *The Pair of Them*, 1956), it is very difficult to find any information about her—a fate not untypical for women writers (see Tillie Olsen, *Silences*, London: Virago, 1980; Joanna Russ, *How to Suppress Women's Writing*, London: Women's Press, 1984). According to *Contemporary Authors: The International Bio-Bibliographical Guide to current Authors and Their Works* (Detroit: Gale, 1962) Dorothy Cowlin was born 16 August 1911. She gained a B.A. at the University of Manchester in 1931. On 12 April 1941 she married Ronald Harry Whalley, a schoolmaster. She had one daughter.

PROLOGUE

ALEXANDRA GOLLEN lay contentedly on her left side watching the firelight. Sometimes she liked to be put on her right side to watch the night-clouds silently outpacing the steadily climbing stars. But generally she preferred the firelight to the starlight.

Firelight was her personal friend, her shadow-showman, a sort of inarticulate Hans Andersen, who, from common things like pokers and chairs and tables and coal-buckets, could invent the most fantastic shows imaginable; sometimes terrifying, sometimes comical, sometimes homely, sometimes beautiful shows, performed always in the same medium, flat, wavering smoky-edged silhouettes, upon a glowing screen of tangerine, yet infinitely various.

To-night the chief character on this screen was a giant bird with clumsy shawl-like wings, beating ponderously but silently upon a sky made of golden marmalade. A terrifying creature, very erratic in movement. Now he would seem to soar very high, gathering in his pomponed wings close to his amorphous black body; now he would pounce down upon her bed, spreading and spreading until he blotted out the whole wash of golden marmalade, and all the world was black wings. Yet though Alexandra sometimes held her breath at these swoops, her fright was luxurious, a make-believe fright, for she knew that this giant bird was really only the frill along the mantelpiece, as seen through the fanciful eyes of her shadow-showman, the fire.

The bird lasted for about half an hour. After that he became very obviously only a pomponed mantel-frill. The character of the drama changed to one of those domestic, chit-chat stories beloved of the real Hans Andersen and the fire Hans Andersen alike. A couple of very homely characters came on the screen, a windsor chair, with a high intellectual forehead, and a gas-bracket with a long coy neck wobbling unevenly, an obvious simper in dumb-show. These, with the pomponed mantel-frill as chaperone, were flirting. They were trying very hard to put their heads together in order to whisper what Alexandra believed were known as 'sweet nothings'.

5

It was comical to see the windsor chair, in daylight so stiff with pride, shooting eagerly up the wall, and bending himself across the middle at the ceiling. It was funnier still to see how the gas-bracket, at the precise moment of this wooden bow, would bob aside her head with that little simpering movement, so that he invariably failed to reach her after all. At last, worn out with his efforts, he sank back below the picture-rail in a sulk. Whereupon the gas-bracket began, it seemed, to regret her coyness, and reached out her neck to him quite tenderly. But it was too late. He refused to bend his dignity again, and at last she too shrank back to her own place on the wall.

Alexandra closed her eyes, which were tired by the coloured screen. She was not yet ready for sleep however. Being compelled to lie or sit inactive all day, she was seldom in need of a really strong draught of forgetfulness at night. Her sleep was always shallow, like that of a wild animal. Usually it was four o'clock before she was ready even for this puff-ball slumber. And until this time she habitually lay and watched, or, when the firelight failed, listened.

She began to listen now. She listened to the invisible body which came and sat down in the worn basket-chair, settling back in it and making it creak as the firelight darkened. She listened to the fire licking its lips after its recent meal. She listened to the periodic bump on the ceiling, which meant that Sam was turning over in bed. Sam — not Peter. For if Peter turned, as he presumably did occasionally, he would do so noiselessly. All that Peter did was neat and noiseless, whereas nearly everything that Sam did made a clatter.

She stopped listening at this point, to meditate on this strange need of Sam's — and perhaps of Peter's — to turn over in bed. For her part she was always perfectly content to lie all night on whichever side Peter had laid her.

Her mind resumed its listening. Footsteps came along the street. By their sound she knew that the passer-by was a little light-footed woman in high heels, rather nervous at being out alone so late.

It certainly was late to be out, thought Alexandra, who was an expert in guessing Time, as well as in the interpretation of footsteps, and knew that it was after two o'clock, a time when Finn Street echoes were usually undisturbed.

After this there was utter silence. Or rather, there was no specific noise, though there still continued that indeterminate, almost inaudible hum which seems to rise from towns even at the absolute nadir of sound, even when trams, cars, buses, voices and footsteps have ceased for one day and not yet begun the next. But Alexandra had heard no other, and thought of this as utter silence. She was not ready for it yet. She still was not tired enough for sleep. She was glad when Sam bumped the ceiling. She was glad too when she heard the thin, peevish, strangled wail of a cat.

'I wonder if that's our Neb?' she thought anxiously. But opening her eyes, and lifting her head as much as she could, she saw in the triangle between her thigh and her body, a coiled shadow, darker than those the moonlight was making in other hollows of the bed-clothes. Then it was not Neb wailing out there. Neb was having a night in to-night. She could not feel him down against her thigh. Below the hips she could feel nothing at all. Still, it was comforting to know that he was there.

In imagination she began to stroke his beautiful black glossy fur. She could not reach him actually. But whenever the strange cat outside lifted up its voice, the image of Neb became instantly vivid to her. She could feel the tingling electric warmth of his fur against her palm; she could feel the live thrust of his backbone against her hand as he responded eagerly to her touch; she could feel the needle pains of his scratches; see the graceful loop of his body as he leapt up to her bed; hear the velvet thud of his deliberate departure; picture his wet, pale nose, marked like a little hot cross bun, and the pinky-beige lining of his ears, so sensitive to a touch that they would often turn inside out; she even thought once that she could hear, and feel too, his rumbling gratitude for her imaginary stroking.

At last the cat outside was silent. And then the image of Neb faded too. She nearly fell asleep.

But just as she was about to slip into those shallow reaches of Lethe which were peculiarly hers, another wail stroked the silence. This time it was not the wail of a cat. It was a wail slightly husky, high-pitched, evenly drawn out, nostalgic, yet peculiarly impersonal.

7

'A Train!'

Alexandra picked out from her brain the correct ticket for this sound, in the manner in which a well-taught circus dog might pick out the correct ticket from a box — that is, without the slightest knowledge of its significance.

She did not, however, realize the poverty of her response to the sound.

She did not know that to other people this sound would be immensely more than a clue to a name. When she heard that husky, sagging cry, she did not visualize a long, jointed, worm-like creature with lighted squares along its side, and a gallant curled ostrich plume of grey and flame flying back from its funnel as it rushed on, on, along faintly gleaming lines, between fields coloured indigo by night. She did not hear, in imagination, the dry metallic shuttle-rattle of its wheels. She did not feel the bumpetty rhythms of its carriages lurching over points. She could not see the great coupling-rods, so human in their suggestion of a boney-joint, so inhuman in their implacable movement. Nor above all, did she feel the faintest pang of that nostalgic yearning which the sound inflicts upon those who have from their earliest childhood, rightly or wrongly, associated it with disturbing words like Adventure, Change, Travel, Speed, the Unknown.

This poverty of response was not due to any deficiency in her powers of visualization, as was proved by the vivid character of her response to the sound of the cat. It was due to the fact that she had never, to her knowledge, seen a Train, and certainly never travelled in one.

Many of the words she could use were little more than tickets, empty of association, valueless therefore as the dummy chocolate boxes used to decorate sweet-shop windows.

After the railway train had passed, Sam in the room above seemed to discover the ideal posture. He bumped no more. The fire gave one last creak as it settled its dry exhausted bones into the cold grate. Moonlight swung silently round the room that had been lately washed with the golden marmalade of the firelight.

Alexandra slipped at last into her shallow lake of sleep.

PART ONE

CHAPTER I

IT was Monday, with a hard, cold, windy light in the room. Some feet scuttered past the window, and voices, low, sullen, Monday voices, blew along the street with the wind. People were going to work.

The window jiggled. The empty chimney blew deep soft notes like a huge bamboo pipe. The postman came. Alexandra, screwing her head round with some pain, could just see the tips of his cold purple fingers poke through the letter-box for a second. Then they jerked nervously back, and the letter they had held swam into the room like a pale flat fish, sank to the shiny linoleum, and slid across it to the kitchen door. There certainly was a strong wind, thought Alexandra, pleased because, never having to her knowledge experienced the discomforts of a bitter March wind, she looked upon it as a frolicsome show designed solely for her amusement.

She lay impatiently waiting for the day to begin.

Presently it began. A heavy thud above her head shook down a small flake of whitewash on to her forehead. A series of lighter thuds followed, back and forth across the ceiling, as if a large rabbit was lolloping excitedly up there.

Then something soft slithered down the stairs, landing on the black mat at their foot. One of Sam's shabby brown slippers!

A second later, both figuratively and literally hard on its heel, came Sam, thrusting his big toe into the fugitive almost before it had settled on the mat, and bending in the next stride to pick up the wind-swum letter.

'Morning Al!' he cried in his high cheerful voice; and padded across to her, thumped her pillow, and turned to clatter the fire-irons.

The next moment his curly head was haloed with a nimbus of ashdust, for he rattled the poker in the grate as vehemently as if he were a boy who had just discovered the delights of a stick and a tin-can. One cinder flew out towards Alexandra, but before it reached her Sam caught it with his left hand and returned it to the grate, without slackening in the least the savage and complex tattoo he was making with the poker.

When the fire was snapping its fingers, surprisingly soon, considering the contempt with which Sam threw the wood, the paper and the coals into the grate, he padded into the kitchen to prepare the breakfast.

Alexandra put her nose on the alert, to smell which of the two ancient Household Gods — eggs or bacon — was to reign to-day. These humble deities were both acknowledged, in this household as in all other British households, to hold unchallenged sway over the domain of breakfast — but for reasons of economy they had to reign in turns. Sam refused to be bound by rules concerning which day was to be devoted to which god, and thus converted every morning into an olfactory question mark for Alexandra.

Cascades of hardware were now falling in the kitchen (which was strange, for so far as she knew they possessed only three saucepans and a kettle; but then, Sam had the knack of making much, so far as sound went, out of little); the gas exploded, then hissed venomously like a nest of vipers or a box of sparklers; water rushed in fountains as if the pipes were burst; and presently there came drifting out fine elegant tendrils of pale violet smoke. These were followed by a luscious smell, opening in the cold air like a large, warm, velvet-petalled flower.

Alexandra smiled happily, knowing from these signs that it was a bacon morning.

When the efflorescence had opened so sumptuously that it filled the room, in padded Sam again, with cups, saucers and plates clinging to all his ten fingers as if he had coated his hands with glue and then dipped them into a crate of china. A cup slipped off his little finger as he came round the corner. Alexandra held her breath. Disaster at last! But no, the cup, like everything that Sam handled, seemed to bear a charmed life. Sam merely put out one foot, the big toe of which protruded through his broken slipper, and the cup obligingly alighted on it, upside down, and spun round gravely once. When it was safely balanced, Sam crouched cautiously, and inserted his little finger into the handle again.

Alexandra began to laugh helplessly, whereupon he looked at

her somewhat startled, for to him this performance was as natural as sneezing.

He would have made an excellent circus clown. Extravagantly deft, he concealed it, like a clown, under a clever pretence of stupidity — not, in his case a conscious pretence. All his antics were as natural as a bear's. Moreover, like every good clown, whatever happened to him, his face remained an obstinately good-tempered mask of pink and white.

Alexandra lay shaking the bed.

'You shouldn't make me laugh so. It hurts when I'm hungry!' she told her brother weakly.

'I don't make you laugh!' retorted Sam, rushing back to his bacon, which was sizzling and popping with some urgency.

And now there came a new sound on the stairs, a quick evenly spaced patter, like the footsteps of a neat-footed little girl. Peter was coming down, at the exact moment when the bacon was being transferred to the plates. It was his instinct to time everything perfectly; never to hurry, never to be late. He had the same exaggerated deftness as his brother, but in his case concealed by no clownish awkwardness. Thus, though he was not in the least feminine in build or face, he gave a feminine impression. He and Sam were twins, and when people met them separately they always declared that this was obvious. But when together, though it was plain that they were closely brothers, they seemed not like enough for twins. Peter then looked like an image of Sam seen in the back of a vertically held spoon — having precisely that effect of elongation, elegance, and remoteness which only a convex metal mirror can give. Besides being slimmer, paler, graver than Sam, his hair was less crisp, a shade darker, his hands were longer, whiter and much finer, and his smile, though quite as cheerful, was more rare. He moved twice as leisurely as Sam, yet usually got there before him.

Their father had once explained their divergence thus:

'Ower Sam were toombled into t'world seven howers after t'other. Ee's bin toomblin ower 'imsell ever sin ter catch oop!'

But this theory was long forgotten by the Gollen brothers, as indeed were most of his sayings, for the Gollen brothers took their gentle revenge upon certain unpleasant memories by a cold neglect.

Peter smiled cheerfully at his sister, but gave her no greeting.

He was as economical with words as with movements. Silently he came to her, pulled her up into a sitting position, inserted under her knees the bolster without which she could not remain upright, and hung over her shoulders her red knitted shawl. His hands were cool and certain, never hurting and never fumbling, and he had her ready at the exact moment when Sam came hurtling recklessly in with her breakfast on a tray.

They began to eat, in a gay mood. Sam and Peter, no less than Alexandra, liked windy days. Besides, the letter which had swum into the room contained a cheque from one of their favourite customers.

The fire danced in high spirits, roaring up the chimney in a fine baritone voice; the window jiggled merrily; two starlings chuckled on the roof opposite, the bacon was triumphantly crisp; Peter hummed snatches of tunes between mouthfuls, and Sam drummed with the handles of his knife and fork.

They did not waste time over their breakfast, however. There was too much to do.

Firstly, there was Alexandra to wash and dress. As she had had a complete bath on Saturday, it was only necessary to bring her a basin of warm water, and she could wash her own face and neck.

Our limbs are more interdependent than we realize — a relic perhaps of that geologically distant period when we were four-footed. Alexandra's inability to move below the hips hampered even small movements of her upper half to a surprising extent. Very often Peter had to finish for her this task of washing her face.

But to-day she was feeling well, and slowly, feebly, continued to the end.

Peter then brushed her hair for her — a task always beyond her strength. Her hair was very long, very heavy, black, straight and glossy. Every morning and every night Peter brushed it with long careful strokes that never pricked her scalp or rasped her ears, until it hung like a shawl of black ring-velvet about her shoulders. Then he plaited it into two thick ropes, one over each shoulder, tying the ends with tape. She liked the process. When he divided her hair into three parts his knuckles touched her neck just under her ear, and this gave her a very pleasant, but indefinable sensation along her spine. When Sam plaited her hair, the same touch irritated instead of pleasing. The strange thing was that though she had never spoken of these sensations, the brothers had insensibly fallen into the habit of dividing the work so that Peter had all the more delicate care of Alexandra, while Sam had the cooking and the heavier housework.

When the plaits were finished Sam came back from the washing of the pots and lifted Alexandra into a chair. Though Alexandra was twenty, and heavy for her age and invalid condition, he did this with ease, being stockily built, with strong thick arms. The brothers together then turned her mattress and remade her bed. Then, as it was a windy day, they propped her up, with the bolster under her knees, so that she could watch the street.

It was still only half-past eight. But now the day's work began for the Gollen brothers.

Carefully Peter laid out on the wooden trestle table which served them as dining-table and work-table, a little crescent consisting of these objects: a reel of thread, a ball of wax, a needle, a pair of small glittering scissors, a thimble, a card of black trouser-buttons, and a pair of spectacles with steel frames and side pieces like golf clubs.

Meanwhile Sam was juggling with exactly the same objects. They were seven in number, but dropped extravagantly, caught in his teeth or with his toes, trampled on in confusion with Neb's paws, tossed behind his head and caught miraculously in his coat-collar, these seven small objects seemed multiplied to seven-and-seventy.

Nevertheless, by the time Peter had taken a pair of navy-blue trousers from the pile on the machine, and drawn himself up, backwards, on to the table, landing neatly, with legs crossed, in the middle of his neat crescent, not one object of which was thereby deranged, Sam was at his side. His landing was by no means neat. Reels and needles and buttons and scissors seemed to fly out from his descending behind like the spray from the stomach of a bad diver. Yet when they had settled again, there they all were — within workmanlike reach of Sam.

And there, side by side, cross-legged, spectacled, their eyes cast-down but crinkled with thirty-two years of laughing, their chins rather pointed, their heads small, neat, with crisp short hair, and pale rather outstanding ears, sat the two brothers, like a pair of lepre-chauns, not hammering fairy shoes, however, but sewing buttons and making buttonholes on four pairs of very mundane trousers.

It was when they sat at work like this that they looked most like twins. Sam's preparations might be clown-like. But once that spluttering hoop-leap on to the table was taken, the clown dis-appeared completely in the tailor.

Though his fingers were reddened and roughened by housework and cookery, and were by nature a fraction shorter and a fraction thicker than Peter's, he could sew at the same speed, and with identical and precise gestures, so that they looked like a pair of oriental dancers making patterns with their hands.

For half an hour they scarcely lifted their eyes, never their heads. Sewing by hand in a world practically given over to the machine, they had to work fast and long in order to live at all. They depended often upon Alexandra to report the news of the Finn Street world to them while they sewed.

For a while Finn Street was empty. Those of its inhabitants who had breakfasted early had long since scuttered by. For the remainder it was still breakfast time.

But Alexandra sat and stared at this empty and entirely ugly street, not in discontent, but in confident expectation, as an experi-enced playgoer will stare at a stage, when the curtains have risen upon an empty scene.

Alexandra's scenery consisted, and had always consisted, she thought, of a flat façade of dim mulberry-coloured brick marked off into four and a half separate dwellings by brown doors, approached each by a flight of yellow-ochred steps, set flankwise to the house-walls, and protected by buckled balustrades of rusty iron. Four chimneys flew diagonally-blown flags of yellowish smoke above this façade. A black cat distinguished one balustrade from the other by lying uncomfortably balanced along the top-rail, its fur rising along its back in little puffs whenever the wind blew.

And that was all.

But Alexandra waited, like the veteran playgoer she was. And she was not disappointed.

Suddenly the third door flew back, shivering flimsily like a canvas stage-door, and out rushed Mrs. Wragge with a table-cloth.

'Oh look! Sam — Peter!' cried Alexandra, and the two crinkled faces lifted just in time to see Mrs. Wragge go into total eclipse beneath a suddenly tempestuous table-cloth. A passionate struggle followed, and when Mrs. Wragge finally conquered, and (reversing Caesar's order), saw again, her dark hair was seen to be powdered with breadcrumbs and crowned with half an egg-shell, absurdly tiny, like a comedian's hat.

Her audience laughed heartily, for their taste in humour was very far from sophisticated.

'Oh! Oh dear!' said Alexandra weakly, when Mrs. Wragge had slammed the door indignantly upon the wind. 'That was a lovely bit, wasn't it?'

'You might say the table-cloth turned the tables on her!' remarked Peter, who was inclined to make puns and to play harmlessly with conventional metaphors.

Almost immediately after this incident, two starlings arrived on Mrs. Wragge's roof, waddled up to her chimney like a couple of old tramps in baggy overcoats and battered bowler hats, and thrust their noses inquisitively into her chimney to smell what she had eaten for breakfast. They then leaned back and began to exchange low stories in a guttural, clicking, barbarous-sounding language. Every now and then, however, the guttural clicks were interrupted by a long, sweet, upward slurring 'oooo-ou-ee-ee-ee!'

'Peter — do you think the starlings talk in French?' said Alexandra. 'There's a word they keep saying, just like that Frenchman did that once came here for a suit. I wish I could understand French!'

The brothers laughed. Most of Alexandra's remarks, in their opinion, needed no further answer than this sign, in friendly recognition that she had spoken and they had heard. In this they were perhaps akin to certain tribes of negroes and other friendly, simple beings.

The next entertainment now came by — a squat little woman, slightly hump-backed, in a long purple skirt and a black satin-covered hat like a coal-bucket, six inches too wide for her head, but kept suspended over her by invisible cords. She had bright glassy eyes like a rabbit's, a suggestion reinforced by the soft brown fringe of whiskers on her chin. She shuffled past with a huge black bag clutched in front of her in a pair of squirrel-like paws, resting its chief weight on her stomach.

'I wonder what she carries in that bag?' mused Alexandra.

Peter pushed his spectacles up his nose, in order to give them the fun of sliding down to the tip of it again, and said dreamily:

'Is this the thousandth time that Al has been told that Miss Hope is carrying a bag of hats from a factory, to take home and bind the brims?'

'No — it's the thousandth and fifth!' said Sam, not looking up.

'Oh — you spoil all my stories!' said Alexandra without heat. 'I'm certain — for all you say — that Miss Hope is a witch. In that awful bag she collects horrible bits and bobs to put in her cauldron to brew spells!'

Then suddenly she dropped her make-believe.

'Poor Miss Hope. Mrs. Tyler says her work is little better than "sweated work". Do you think she is very unhappy?'

This time Sam answered, 'She isn't paid as much as she ought to be paid. But then, neither are we. Some people might say *our* work is "sweated" work. But the fact is we *don't* sweat, and we are happy. So what does it matter what they call it?'

'That's right!' laughed Peter, snapping off the thread of his fifth button-hole.

But Alexandra stared out of the window, sobered for a moment, and wondered vaguely about Miss Hope. For though in most ways her mind had remained a child's mind, something about that absurd little trotting drudge had quickened her imagination with sympathy that was adult.

However — the next moment a new sound distracted her attention. Miss Hope was as if she had never been.

The coalcart was thundering along Finn Street.

The coalcart horse was a massive black shining monster with muscles like a giant athlete's and a temper straight from the Devil. She was cunning too. Waiting until her master was bowed under a sack of coal, she would then begin to stamp viciously and to jerk the cart zigzaggedly across the road. When her master, rid of his burden, came running to seize her bridle, she would draw back her thick upper lip to expose long hideous fangs, that seemed to Alexandra to stretch right back to the roof of her skull.

All horses seemed fantastic to Alexandra. Although she knew nothing of prehistoric monsters, had never even heard the word 'prehistoric', she nevertheless perceived in the horse that element of cumbrous fantasy which betrays, more than in other mammals, its ancient lineage — its ultimate kinship with those incredible fantasies the giant reptiles.

But of all the horses she had seen, this seemed to her the most grotesque, with its huge black buttocks like rolling waves of hot viscous tar, its massive hooves, more like pedestals than feet, and its long stupid, hanging face, not terrifying, despite the rolling blue-black eyes and the hideous yellow fangs, but merely stupid.

The giant and its pygmy master rumbled out of her frame of vision.

Some boys shambled by as if they were afraid of their boots falling to bits if they lifted them off the ground. Then a girl with lank, greenish-coloured, uncombed locks, passed leaning maternally over a meat pie. Another smaller girl with a red beret clinging like a burr to her sheep's fleece of ginger hair, came by with a newspaper parcel whose steam found its way through the letter-box, and whispered 'Fish and Chips!'

Alexandra decided that she was hungry.

'What's for dinner to-day, Sam?' she asked.

'Shepherd's pie and rice pudding,' replied Sam — looking up and contorting his face about the eyes and mouth, in the clown-like way which preserved his individual character, even when his hands were admitting themselves to be the twins of his brother's hands. His grotesque face, and his high, abrupt, snapped-off voice, made the answer sound like the solution of a nonsensical riddle.

After dinner Alexandra's spine and heels ached so that she could not endure to sit up any longer. Peter removed the bolster, and laid her with her face to the window. Then he and Sam mounted their table again, and bent their spectacles diligently over the buttons and buttonholes. The afternoon was very quiet. But Alexandra, after such an eventful morning, was content to lie and use one sense instead of two.

Perhaps it would be truer to say one and a half senses, for she could still see the upper half of her world.

Over the four slate roofs with their four pairs of grimy-crowned chimneys went the grey herds of the clouds, moving reluctantly before their compelling herdsmen. Once an untidy company of rooks went by — blowing helplessly like a company of black woollen shawls wrenched from their owners, protesting hoarsely all the while.

Occasionally the head and shoulders of a passer-by bobbed along the base of the window. But for the most part she had to rely on her ears for news of Finn Street. She made a little game of this limitation of her senses. Whenever she heard a sound, she had to guess what had caused it, before the clock had ticked four times.

That afternoon she guessed in time old Miss Perne's squeaky bicycle, which was very easily confused with the rag and bone man's donkey; the dignified *largo* paces of the policeman; and the chipping heels of the afternoon postman. She even detected in a long and elaborate expectoration the subtleties which distinguished it from three other similar performances, and marked it as the work of 'Uncle Andy'.

Towards tea-time a number of women's voices were hung across the street at many angles, like a tangle of telephone wires — as taut, and as shrill, as if the wind, and not human, female voices, sang in them. Gossip in Finn Street was always conducted from the top of each woman's steps, and no lungs so far had proved themselves unequal to the demands made upon them.

Alexandra had some difficulty in distinguishing the separate wires in this tangle of voices. All were high, rasping as cats' tongues, and piercing as a radio soprano. But Mrs. Cuthbert's shriek was a laughing shriek, Mrs. Duke's nasal, Mrs. Pollit's shrewish, Mrs. Darwen's plaintive and Mrs. Matthew's pure shriek.

She could occasionally distinguish words — or phrases, such as:
'Fred 'e reckons . . .'
'I said to doctor . . .'
'Our Meooriel . . .'
'Wuuping cough . . .'
'Went ter t' pictures . . .'
'Ole devil . . .'

But she was not interested in piecing the meaning of these exchanges. She was only concerned with the correct identification of sounds. And so absorbed was she in this effort that she scarcely spoke for two hours, though once she laughed aloud, at a certain sound, a sudden hurtling and reckless tumbling of metal, it seemed.

'What?' said Sam eagerly, for the Gollen brothers were always eager to be admitted to a joke.

'I was just thinking how that tram sounded just like you clearing out the ashes!' replied Alexandra, and Sam laughed, as loudly as a clown at his own discomfiture, but, unlike the clown, sincerely.

The wind had dropped, and the March dusk sifted quietly down into the raw little street of bricks and cobbles.

The children came home from school, and though their feet and tongues were shod with iron, they were free now to play, and they therefore added to the effect of evening quietude. Some women's heads passed by, dark but sprinkled with grey flecks of cotton-wool. Mill 'girls', these were. It was time for tea. Sam put the kettle on. Peter's neat crescent and Sam's Lucky Dip of tools were swept aside for a brown teapot, three white and gold cups, a plate of white bread and butter, a saucer of jam and a plate of Sam's 'buns', massive, curranted, shapeless objects with a surprisingly subtle flavour.

After tea, when the firelight made Finn Street look the colour of bacon smoke, the gas had to be lit, for there were still three hours' work to be done before the Gollen brothers could relax.

Alexandra disliked gas. Its colour was crude yet muddy; it smelt; and it breathed as though it had adenoids. She was always a little sulky during this interval between tea and eight o'clock.

At last the day was over. As the last stroke of eight quavered out from the old grandfather clock, Peter took off his spectacles and sprang lightly off the table.

'One more buttonhole — but it must wait till to-morrow!' he cried in a curious tone, as if he were a gentle but inflexible old lady reprimanding the buttonhole for a vulgar and childish impatience.

Work was cleared away, by Peter, as if he were a prestidigitator, by Sam as if he were the prestidigitator's comic assistant. The red and purple damask of leisure was spread on the trestle table, and a jar of humbugs set honourably in its centre.

As Peter stepped upon the windsor chair to reach down a celluloid whistle from behind a shelf of eight or nine books, Alexandra raised her head. 'Oh — but it's *not* music to-night!' she protested. 'It's *Three Men in a Boat*!'

'So it is! — I was thinking it was Tuesday!' apologized Peter, and he replaced the celluloid whistle, and reached down from the shelf instead a tattered paper-backed book, obviously the property of Sam, to whom he gave it.

Then he popped a humbug in his mouth, and sat down in the windsor chair, with one leg crossed horizontally over the other, like the Lincoln Imp.

Sam stretched himself in the rocking chair and began to turn the pages over with the hands of a faithful, but no longer very reverent lover — more like an affectionate husband perhaps, for he had read aloud from this book every Monday night, ever since Alexandra could remember. Yet his pleasure in it was as fresh as ever, and so, for that matter, was that of his audience.

There was one incident which he had never in fact been able to finish reading, so much did he appreciate it.

This was the incident in which the nameless narrator, leaning 'with careless grace, in an attitude suggestive of agility and strength' over the prow of the boat, for the benefit of some photographers in Hampton Court Lock, hears someone bawl, 'Look at your nose!' and thinking that they are insulting his own handsome organ, continues to lean over the prow, not realizing that this is what is referred to, and that it is caught under the edge of the lock, so that the boat is gradually tilting as the water rises.

Whenever he reached the word 'look' in this passage, his voice expired in a falsetto shriek, and he collapsed on the rocking chair in a series of convulsions, threatening to somersault the chair, so that Peter had to snatch the book and finish the passage for him.

However, it was not this passage to-night, but 'The Maze in Hampton Court'. Though Sam's face became creased and scarlet like that of a baby preparing to yell, he managed to stagger through to the end.

After culture came hygiene — Alexandra's bedtime wash, hair-brushing, and tooth-brushing.

And after supper and some fragmentary talk by the fire, Alexandra was laid down, and the brothers ran upstairs to bed, leaving her to the starlight and the gentle consolatory noises of the fire at her back.

For some time she watched drowsily the wind-tremulous stars unobtrusively creeping across the dark window in a diagonal curve.

She did not know the traditional constellations. But her fancy shaped the haphazard clusters of light into pictures of things familiar to her mind. Perhaps it is a world-wide human habit to do this. Educated people abandon their own fancies for the traditional fancies. But Alexandra was almost completely uneducated. Or, rather, perhaps it would be more true to say she had been half-educated, and then, by her peculiar circumstances, *dis*-educated. In stars her fancy could run free.

There was a group of eight which she called 'Neb', for they suggested very clearly to her the body of a great elegant cat, elongated and bowed earthwards in the act of yawning. There was another group which she called 'the singing kettle', because on very clear nights such as this she could detect a faint puff of star-steam issuing from its spout. There was a third group — low over the chimneys, which she only saw in winter. This she thought was like a clock, an old-fashioned clock with the pendulum and weights hanging naked.

She sighed lightly. It had been a nice day, very full — and now this starry ending made her feel a little more sleepy than usual. She thought she would probably sleep about three o'clock instead of four o'clock.

But she slipped so gradually into her shallow Lethe that she did not know at what time came her final immersion.

CHAPTER II

ALEXANDRA had scarcely noticed, but when she closed her eyes on Monday night the stars were beginning to be smudged by a faint scum, creeping over them like a cataract over bright eyes.

When she awoke this pearly scum had thickened into a great feather-bed of cloud. The light in the room was soft and muffled and warm. And gradually she became aware of an unemphatic but incessant thrumming. Looking vaguely at the window she saw that a veil of rain blew and wavered against it, making this gentle sound.

Alexandra's moods moved very easily to the weather, despite the fact that weather was merely scenery to her, with no tactile meaning.

Thus, whereas on Monday she had listened eagerly for the day's drama to begin, on Tuesday she lay still and allowed sounds to drift idly through her ears.

Everything seemed muffled by her own passivity. Even Sam's antics, which were never really influenced by the weather, seemed less boisterous. And Peter moved about her like an accurate ghost.

The sounds of Finn Street were like under-water sounds, slow, viscous and, though clear, slightly muted.

The wet rubber of tyres on the wet cobbles made a stealthy rippling sound as if someone were tearing up secret documents. The milkman's horse trotted as one of Little Claus's river horses might have trotted; the wheels of his cart turned like waterwheels. Footsteps reminded her of Sam slapping the batter for the Sunday Yorkshire pudding.

Some mill girls passed. Usually they went hatless, but to-day their heads were covered in grey wool shawls, out of fashion long since, even in this remote Lancashire town, except on wet days. In these shawls, willow-grey in colour, their heads looked like cats' heads, small, neckless, sloping immediately to the shoulders.

In her prone position she could not see the school children. But she knew how they would look. The very poor ones would have pulled their shining wet jackets over their heads; the less poor would look like misproportioned dwarfs, their heads and legs enlarged in sou'westers and wellingtons.

None of the Gollens spoke very much. The brothers were absorbed in the final pressing of two finished suits. The hot vapour from their pressing cloths muffled their spirits, and clouded the window still more.

Alexandra could not be bothered to sit up even after her wash. She lay relaxed on her back and watched her four sooty chimneys twist and waver behind the veil of rain as if they were *made* of smoke instead of merely conducting it to the sky. And as she watched, her mind blurred and wavering as the glass itself, strange broken pictures rocked and swam in the shifting waters of her thoughts. Amongst them were some faces, nameless and meaningless, but momentarily vivid — a child's face with large brown eyes; a man's face, heavy-jawed, with a sloping forehead like a gorilla's; a woman's, with soft long hair; and others even more elusive than these three. She paid scarcely any attention to these scraps, however, as they bobbed and swirled under and bobbed out again like scraps of bright shell or seaweed.

In the afternoon she read *The Little Mermaid*, poring over it for over an hour, for her reading speed had remained at the level of a child of eleven, and shedding tears of luxurious grief at the troubles of the faithful sea-creature who, having immortality, longed for mortality and legs.

When she had finished brooding on this lovely tragedy, and turned her clarified eyes to the street again, she saw that there had come a change.

The rain had been thrumming dreamily, mutedly, like a rain out of eternity. But now it was flurried, as if it had suddenly become aware of earthly time and the transitoriness of all material things. It came in agitated rushes at the window, alternating with sudden doubts. It was collected into larger, more passionate drops, and these made on the glass a pattern like flung grains of transparent rice.

Before this vehemence people were cringing, as they had not cringed in the gentle veil-rain of the morning. They hurried along with their shoulders hunched, their heads shrinking into their necks, their eyes screwed up, their hair clinging to their temples like wet paint, their eyelashes silvered with little granules of water.

'Do you know — I don't think people *like* rain!' said Alexandra, with an air of a great discoverer proclaiming a new land.

The two tailors laughed. 'You don't say!' remarked Peter teasingly, and continued the slow rhythmic march of his cutting-out scissors, his pointed chin working in sympathy with their jaws. Sam however paused as he knotted the string of a parcel, glanced curiously at his sister and then at Peter, and said, 'Don't you *really* know how it feels?'

'No,' said Alexandra, in a tone of curiously shifting texture.

'But you've been out many a time in a downpour!' persisted Sam.

23

'Have I? I suppose I have. You should know!' said Alexandra — still in that ambiguous voice.

'But don't *you* know?'

'No! I don't remember!'

Amongst other elements in that tone was one of thin, but impenetrable defiance. Sam detected it, but was too unskilled in the shade-card of tones to name what he heard. He made a low puzzled grunt and looked anxiously at Peter as if for enlightenment. And Peter, without looking up, responded: 'How many rainy days can *you* remember from your childhood, Sam? *I* can't remember *one*! They must disappear down the grids! All my days then seem to have been either snowstorms or burning sunshine!'

Sam was not convinced. 'But she can't remember any sunny days either!' he persisted, in a low intimate tone, as if he were a doctor discussing the condition of a semi-conscious patient.

And indeed, so he was. Alexandra was not interested in this problem of her loss of memory, which she had heard discussed so many times without advantage. She never had shown any great interest in it, even at its inception — rather indeed she had shown a faint cloudy sort of antagonism to its discussion.

She was now once more absorbed in watching the rain. It was making a passionate but toneless music on the wet, iron-grey cobbles. Little silver tops bounced up from the road. Brown coffee lees surged along the gutters, falling down the grid at intervals with a loud gulp.

Then, abruptly the rain's passion ceased. The coffee lees still surged down the gutters, and were gulped down the grid; the houses opposite still glittered with a thin veneer of wet; but the silver tops were still, and the whole world seemed taken aback by the sudden quiet.

Then Alexandra saw a row of silver beads along the underside of each railing. She laughed with delight as she watched these living beads elongate themselves, swim silently along the rail, and drop, unexpectedly as falling stars, to the steps below — lovely creatures, incalculable in their birth and in their death, gradually turning from crystal, through pale amber, to the colour of butter, and so causing her to become aware that a length of sky above the chimneys had cleared to a watery gold.

'Sam!' said Alexandra suddenly, descending from visual pleasures to a consciousness of her interior.

'Isn't it time for tea yet?'

After tea Alexandra became fully conscious for the first time that day, and asked to be propped up to look out into the street, darkening and greening now in the light of the gas-lamps.

Scarcely was she arranged when a somewhat puzzling head and shoulders passed by the window, in silhouette against the green gaslight.

The shoulders of it were masculine in character, but a large knob distorting the line of the head proclaimed a woman. Yet this feminine 'bun' was surmounted by a hat which Alexandra identified with the straw boaters of *Three Men in a Boat*.

Then a knock shook the door. Again the evidence of that bun was contradicted.

Sam was doorkeeper. He quitted the table with one of his paper-hoop tumbles, and pulled back the shuddering door.

'Good evening!' said a voice, neither male nor female in quality, but most like that of a boy pretending desperately to be manly.

Sam bowed and stood aside, and the ambiguous creature walked into the room.

It was a woman. But what a woman! Alexandra's experience of humanity was narrow, confined in time by her loss of memory, and in space by her loss of the use of her legs. But she had a very extensive knowledge of fashion plates, of which her brothers possessed a large number, extending back to about 1900, and she was therefore able to recognize this strange woman's costume for that of about 1916. It was made of greenish tweed, rough, and woven in a chevron pattern. The jacket was masculine — a 'Norfolk' style jacket of 1916. But the skirt was long, gored and placketed like the skirt of a suffragette. In fact, her black and white striped blouse, high collar and tie, shallow straw boater yellow with age and secured to her lapel with a black cord, and her wispy 'bun' made her seem an animation of certain caricatures of these creatures that Alexandra had seen in an old volume of *Punch*.

She tramped into the Gollens' room as if she were storming the last remaining outpost of masculinity.

Alexandra's bed trembled in response to her feet. She then

25

stopped, abruptly, planted them defiantly astride and cried hoarsely, 'You are the Gollen brothers, I presume?'

Sam grinned and ducked his curly head by way of assent, and Peter removed his spectacles as a mark of courteous attention.

'I'm told you make ladies' suits here as well as gentlemen's?' pursued the attacking party, threatening Peter with a pair of knife blue eyes.

'Oh yes — certainly,' Peter assured her — made nervous by these weapons.

'I was also told that here I should find a tailor whose work was not *utterly* stereotyped. I can't endure all this Mass-production!'

'Oh well — we — we certainly try to cut our coats according to the — the customer!' said Peter, a little mischievously, as if in his own mind, his words carried a double meaning.

'Excellent!' responded the woman, in her absurd deep voice.

'Now let me tell you what I want. I wish you to make me a suit exactly like the one I am wearing. A perfectly plain, sensible, ordinary suit! I *detest* frills and furbelows. And I absolutely decline to be one of the herd of silly sheep following every whim of fashion. A plain well-fitting jacket with no nonsense about it — and a skirt of a respectable length — just above the ankles, please! I don't approve of this craze for exposing the knees. It is neither healthy nor aesthetic. Oh — and a waistcoat, please. And can you find me a tweed of approximately this colour and pattern? I'm not asking for the same quality. This has worn for quite ten years. They don't make 'em to wear ten *months* nowadays.'

They laughed, protestingly. '*We* don't go in for that sort of trash!' declared Sam, and Peter said:

'We can guarantee you five or six years' wear at any rate!'

'I'll believe it when I've worn it!' grunted the woman.

'However — I'm prepared to give you a trial. March is the name. *Miss* March,' she added belligerently, as she saw Sam bring a little notebook and pencil from the machine drawer.

At this precise moment Peter had conjured out a tape-measure from somewhere, and now stood before Miss March, ready to take her measurements. Sam stood just behind him, with his feet apart and his pencil hovering and quivering alertly over the notebook like the tail of a dog waiting to be thrown a stick.

Long practice had made the brothers as perfect in this collaboration as a pair of music-hall trapezists. But to-night there was an awkward pause before they began. Peter was hesitating before Miss March, like a youthful and inexperienced amateur actor required to kiss the heroine. Miss March, for her part, was standing stiffly on the defensive — like an equally inexperienced actress, terrified of the absurd figure she will cut while being kissed, but determined that all the timidity shall seem the unfortunate wooer's.

'Well! Begin man!' she cried, very unfairly, since it was her own attitude which was holding him off. So blushing faintly, Peter advanced, with a look of desperation, and put his hands gingerly round to the back of her waist, sliding them hurriedly to the front where the ends of the tape-measure met.

'Twenty-two,' he called over his shoulder to Sam.

The first bridge down, the measuring went rapidly, a trifle more hurried, but as accurate as usual. Throughout the ordeal Miss March stood rigid, her straight mouth tightly folded, her eyes stabbing the air like blue steel hatpins. When Peter came to take her bust measurement she lifted her arms with a sort of stern abandonment, as if defying the conventions, coldly, on principle, against all her instincts.

At last the task was done. Miss March replaced her jacket, refusing Sam's assistance, and remarked unchivalrously to her late antagonists, 'You don't have many women customers, I can see!'

Peter and Sam laughed simultaneously in the unfinished way that means embarrassment. She thereupon dealt another unchivalrous blow.

'You don't have to treat *me* any differently from your own sex. I don't believe in either chivalry or false modesty!' she informed them. They laughed in even more embarrassment.

Miss March glanced at them with eyes that plainly despised them as foes, and stalked suddenly to the fire. They looked at her like a pair of startled deer as she passed. But it was only to warm her gloves and to blow into them.

'There was a perfect sunset to-night,' she remarked over her shoulder as she stooped to the fire. 'It was like a sheet of beaten gold behind the Viaduct — with long streaky clouds in the most exasperating tones of lavender and smoke and mauve! I paint, you know! And that Viaduct and the skies behind it, are my challenge and my despair!'

'That's right!' said Sam, shamelessly uncomprehending. The jerks of Miss March's mind were too much for both brothers, and certainly too much for Alexandra, who had not even the advantage of knowing what a viaduct was — nor even a sunset, for her only window into the world faced south.

Miss March gave up the attempt to make mental contact with a pair of palaeolithic survivals.

'Well — good evening!' she cried abruptly, like a sudden twang at a double bass string, then as she strode to the door — 'Is that your sister?'

It was the first sign she had given of being aware of Alexandra's silent presence.

'Yes, that's Allie!' replied Sam eagerly, thankful to be able to reply at last to a comprehensible remark.

'Thought so — same sort of eyebrows and forehead, though the chin and eyes are quite different. What's wrong with her?' said Miss March, her curiosity unwarmed by sympathy.

'She is paralysed. She has been like that for seven years now!' Peter told her, in a lowered, reverent voice — containing a curious note — almost of pride.

'Oh — wouldn't think it to look at her! Appears in almost disgustingly healthy condition!' commented Miss March, staring with lively but stone-cold interest at Alexandra. 'Sure she's not *shamming* dead?'

The faces of the brothers stiffened as if at some blasphemy. 'What would she want to do that for?' said Peter, very coldly indeed.

Sam's indignation, however, spurted out piping hot.

'Four doctors and a specialist we had to her when it happened! But though they couldn't agree *what* had caused it, not one of them suggested it was a sham!'

'Oh — I'm not suggesting *deliberate* sham. There's such a thing as sub-conscious shamming, you know. But there — Freud might never have existed so far as the doctors are concerned. Donkeys are not more hide-bound! — Oh well, it's not *my* funeral! Good evening!'

She strode abruptly to the door, opened it herself, descended the three steps into Finn Street, and was heard spurning its pavement with her nailed brogues — long before Peter and Sam had even begun to grapple with her remarks.

Dazedly Sam closed the door on her diminishing footfalls. 'Phew!' he remarked, after a long pause, a tentative grin beginning to smooth over the furrows of his recent anger. 'These Modern Women!'

Then Peter smiled. And the discomfort left behind by Miss March began to creep out of the room.

'Yes,' he agreed. 'Give me the old-fashioned sort every time!' But Alexandra frowned doubtfully.

'Do you think she *was* a Modern Woman, altogether!' she suggested diffidently. 'Her *clothes* weren't, you know. Why, they must have been made in 1916 at the very latest!'

'Oh — clothes!' said Peter with contempt; and who should know better than he the value of clothes as a guide to real character?

The brothers laughed obstinately. They were quite sure they were rightly judging Miss March. From newspaper evidence of ten years ago — itself ten years behind the times, and even then formed on superficial grounds, they had grasped the notion that the Modern Woman was rude, clever, hard, ugly, aping men's clothes and habits with disastrous and ludicrous effect. Miss March had been rude; they had scarcely understood a word she said, therefore she must have been clever; she was absurdly ugly, and her clothes were ludicrous. Therefore she must be a Modern Woman.

Their prejudice, being founded on no personal experience of women whatsoever, ancient or modern, was quite impregnable. And accordingly, Miss March's rather penetrating remarks as to the nature of their sister's malady was forgotten as soon as their anger was dead. And anger, with the Gollen brothers, was insect-like in the brevity of its span.

CHAPTER III

ON Wednesday it was raining again when Alexandra wakened. It was still raining in the afternoon when Winifred Bell called with the washing.

Winifred Bell was the daughter of a Mrs. Bell in the next street who washed the Gollens' linen. She was about Alexandra's age, and had known her for longer than Alexandra remembered. She was made up of three parts of sweetness, two parts of mischief, and one of reserve. She had a body which seemed to ask for a billowing, eighteenth-century dress of muslin, decorated with ribbon bows. She had a face that seemed to need a long fat ringlet over one of her rounded shoulders, and a graceful and utterly useless hat of pink straw, wide-brimmed, with cherries and ribbons trailing from it.

But being of the 1930's, she wore instead a short cramped skirt reaching to just below her knees, and a woollen jumper, pretty, but not quite in tune with her character. Being poor she seldom wore a hat at all; and not being in the least independent in mind she turned her warm brown locks into a neck-chignon, or into top-knot sausages, or bobbed them, or crimped them, or transmuted them to corrugated copper, whatever all the other girls of her age thought fit to do. But her hair knew better. Whatever she did to it there was always one large fat curl which escaped and clung to her left cheek, trying hard to lie over her shoulder in the eighteenth-century manner.

Alexandra caught the sound of her footsteps on the wet pavement long before she arrived. They sounded rather like the delicate light trot of the rag and bone man's donkey. And so did her three playful triplet knocks at the door:

'Titty tum, titty tum, titty tum!'

'Open Sesame!' she called, in the light, ringing voice which made the name of 'Bell' so perfectly appropriate to her.

Sam somersaulted off the table instantly. 'Sesame' was her nickname for him, in his capacity as doorkeeper.

As the door was flung open she sprang on to the top step, then turned and fluttered her umbrella up and down outside the door to shake the drops from it. When she did this it was as if she shook part of herself, as if she were a bird, daintily and vigorously shaking a shower from its wings.

'How are you, Sesame?' she said over her shoulder as she did so.

Sam laughed excitedly, and as she turned with her furled umbrella, looking round with quick turns of her head, like a finch, to see where to put it, he lurched forward to take it from her hand.

He was an instant too late. Peter's hand was on the handle before his.

Alexandra and Winifred Bell began to laugh — for Sam's disappointment was ludicrous to see. It really looked for a moment as if he might cry. But Peter saved him from this disgrace. With a look of self-sacrifice almost as ludicrous as Sam's chagrin he surrendered his prize.

'Here!' he said, his voice thick with martyrdom. 'Here! It *is* your turn really. I forgot!'

But Sam snatched his hands indignantly behind his back, and his already scarlet face turned brighter still, like a red apple in the rain. 'Don't be a fool!' he cried. 'Do you think I don't know how to lose? There's no "turns" about it. It's first come, first served!'

'Why! You know very well we agreed . . . you know we said after that last . . . Here! Take it! Take it, you fool!'

Peter moved round the room after Sam, who retreated backwards, bumping every possible piece of furniture, his hands obstinately behind his back.

Winifred leaned against the door in her dripping mackintosh and laughed helplessly, while Peter, who rarely lost his temper, and rarely changed colour, began to turn faintly pink with anger.

But when Sam had narrowly avoided sitting in the coal-bucket, Winifred roused herself, and intervened. 'Peter! Don't torment poor Sesame! If *you* don't put that umbrella away to dry, *I* shall!' At this threat Peter instantly halted, hurrying without another word into the kitchen, whence he returned immediately, terrified of missing Winifred's next command.

'Aren't they a couple of idiots?' she was remarking as he returned, at the same time going to the table to put down her parcel, which she had forgotten in her amusement at the umbrella controversy.

Again the brothers rushed simultaneously for the same honour. Winifred Bell must never, by their creed, be allowed to put down or take up any object herself.

Their hands gripped the parcel simultaneously. They paused, like two opposing players who have simultaneously grasped a rugby football, while their expressions changed rapidly from fanatical devotion, through chagrin, to equally fanatical self-sacrifice. Simultaneously they decided to relinquish the parcel. And, rather naturally, it fell to the floor!

The antagonists looked at the object in astonishment, then at each other in perplexity, then at Winifred with a faint appeal.

Then Peter bowed slightly. 'Yours I think, Sam!' he said with stiff yet courtly intonation, like an old-fashioned tennis player to his lady partner.

This time Sam accepted the sacrifice, and bore away the parcel to the kitchen.

Winifred Bell removed her blue rain-sleeked mackintosh and, to prevent further rivalry, hung it up herself on the door. 'What a dull world it would be without male chivalry!' she remarked as she did so. 'And that reminds me,' she continued, 'though why I can't imagine — I've become an auntie since I last saw you! An auntie! Isn't it awful? I've felt nearly a hundred years old ever since I heard!' She laughed, in a manner which consciously contradicted her own assertion, and stood pushing back her escaped ringlet with a hand which, though born to the gesture, was as yet only half-conscious of its charm. 'Well!' she added, with a curious little shrug of one shoulder only, 'there's *one* comfort. It won't begin to *call* me auntie for another two years yet. I shall be able to more or less ignore the tragedy!'

While she spoke Sam and Peter had been stealthily approaching the two easy chairs that stood by the fire. Now they stood, Sam with his hands on the back of the rocking chair, Peter with his on the back of the cushioned windsor chair, silently offering her their rival comforts.

Winifred affected to see neither (though a mischievous kink at one corner of her small mouth betrayed the dreamy slanted innocence of her eyes) and went to perch on Alexandra's bed. The two brothers were thus left with their empty chairs foolishly in their hands, looking like people who try in vain to coax a truant bird into its cage.

'Do you know, Allie?' said Winifred, taking Alexandra's hand and playing with her fingers, a trick she had with almost anyone she talked to, though never with Peter or Sam. 'Do you know, Graham, that's my new nephew (ugh!), is awfully like your brother — lovely big brown eyes, you know — somehow not like a baby's eyes, as if he knows more than he ought to!'

Alexandra's eyes moved instinctively to Peter's face. 'Sam and Peter both have grey eyes — not brown!' she protested.

'Oh, but I don't mean *them*! I mean your little brother, Nick! Surely you remember Nick's eyes?'

'Oh — *Nick*!' cried Alexandra, taken off her guard. Then, after a perceptible pause, 'Oh yes — Nick had lovely eyes, hadn't he?' Her voice was eager, a creditable imitation of a suddenly returned memory. The truth was that even now she had no genuinely visual remembrance of her brother's eyes. She had indeed no real visual memory of any part of Nick's person. But, ashamed of this inability to recall her own brother, she carefully collected all data concerning him and stored it in her clear, if scantily furnished mind, in order to deceive people into thinking that she *could* recall him. And usually she succeeded in doing so. She now made a mental note of the colour of his eyes, a detail which had not been previously brought into her stock of data.

But Winifred was shrewder than her dreamy, slanted eyes would have you believe, and detected immediately the falsity of Alexandra's reply. However, she made no comment upon it. She believed the subject of Nick to be dangerous. And though, like a daring bird, she would sometimes swoop down to dip the tip of her beak in the dangerous waters, she had no intention of falling into them, or of seriously stirring up their mud. She hopped neatly to another subject.

'But if you want to see some *really* lovely eyes!' she cried, turning to Sam and Peter, 'do go and see Katherine Hepburn. I saw her in "Morning Glory" last night. She's a marvellous creature, don't you think? — Oh, I forgot. You never go to the pictures. You don't miss much as a rule — but, honestly, you'd adore Katherine Hepburn.'

'I doubt it! We're not so fickle as some!' retorted Peter, smiling the swift, unguarded smile that was only for Winifred.

'Oh! Oh!' cried she at this, dropping Alexandra's hand and leaning back with a pout which was charming because it was obviously not sincere. She knew well that the accusation was true to some extent. Where film-stars were concerned she was like a schoolgirl; that is, her passions were all very hot, but all very brief. Concerning real people, she was at any rate extremely light-hearted, though perhaps hardly light enough to be called fickle. Like many pretty girls she obtained social admiration so easily that she felt no very deep gratitude for it in return. It is the ugly and the awkward who desire admiration most passionately and who repay with the deepest gratitude anybody who feeds them with even the tiniest crumbs of it.

Winifred could afford an artificial pout, therefore, and also an artificial laugh, both as attractive as the unconvincing flowers made of pearly sea-shells, as she protested her innocence.

'You have no grounds for that aspersion, Peter Gollen! I defy you to prove it!'

Peter opened his mouth to do so, but Sam tumbled into the affair now.

'I'll bet you anything you like, from a trouser-button upwards, that you didn't go to the pictures last night with the same young man as the one last week!' he challenged her.

'It wasn't a young man at all!' she retorted, buttoning her nose at him so that it turned momentarily as white as china.

'Oh! An old man's darling is it now?' teased Peter. Winifred tossed back her curl, so that it bounced against her cheek. 'It *is* a clever Peter!' she replied mischievously.

'Will you have three shies at his name? I'll give you a few clues. A little tubby man he was — with a moustache that only his wife can see as an embellishment (yes, he's a married man — that makes it worse, doesn't it?) and a funny little bent nose — Fred to his friends, and Dad to his daughter!'

Peter burst out laughing, not the short, unfinished laugh that meant either embarrassment or non-comprehension, but a rarer, leprechaun-like laugh reserved chiefly for Winifred Bell.

'Has his daughter the reputation of being fickle?' he said, thus neatly bringing the banter full circle back to Winifred, who broke into a brief merriment like a cherry tree, and pretended to collapse over Alexandra's knees.

She 'came to' instantly however, and sitting upright again, and swivelling her face round to all three of her audience, instituted a new subject.

'You remember my faithful swain — of our infant school days, Allie?' she said.

'*Which* faithful swain?' said Alexandra, frowning in genuine perplexity, but causing by her remark a fresh outbreak of leprechaunish laughter from Peter, and artificial pouts from Winifred.

'Why!' cried the latter, "you know very well there was only one (then!). Surely you remember Loonie Willie? You know — the "lump of misery" as Miss Britton used to call him, poor lad, always in trouble; being poked with the "Poking stick", or being smacked with the "Dusting Stick", or having to lie under Miss Britton's table for her to put her feet on him, and dig her high heels into, the nasty old cat; and once, do you remember, being made to drink what she pretended was a bowl of ink?'

'You know,' said Winifred, interrupting herself, the mischief popping into her weather-house of a face, and the sweetness which was its other tenant popping out of it. 'You know, I used to laugh at Loonie Willie, like we all did at the time, kids being so heartless. But now when I look back, I think that woman ought to have been put in irons for her cruelty to that boy — and other children. It was nothing but torture, mental torture, for a sensitive child! Poor Loonie Willie! It's no wonder he wasn't quite all there when *she'd* finished with him. It's a wonder any of us are — well — as I was going to tell you ...' (Mischief came out of the little weather-house again here.) 'Loonie Willie's deserted my memory at last. My only faithful follower has gone and got himself married. And to the weirdest creature, Allie! Honestly, she's a cracked cup herself! It's very unkind of me, but I can't help wondering what the chips will be like!'

She laughed, momentarily as heartless as water, and jumped up from the bed so suddenly that Alexandra was bounced several times.

She did not appear to have noticed the strange look on Alexandra's face during and after this reminiscent chatter — a look of incomprehension struggling hard to disguise itself, and of something furtive behind this incomprehension that tried still more frantically to hide itself, something — was it of terror, or of defiance? But she had noticed it, and had cut her chatter short intentionally, fearing that after all she had stirred the mud of those dangerous waters over which she preferred merely to skim.

She stood now with her back to Alexandra, twisting back in vain the independent curl into the coil on the nape of her neck, and smiling teasingly at the brothers.

35

'I suppose I can't persuade either of you to take me to the pictures to-night? I get a little tired of being my old Dad's darling!' she said.

The brothers looked like shy youths who long to dance, but do not know how.

'Oh — we — we don't care much for the pictures, you know!' said Sam; and Peter, more honest, pretending to mock at himself — 'We're too old-fashioned. We can't adapt ourselves to these modern amusements!'

Winifred shook her head at them. 'Aren't they a couple of old mummies?' she asked their sister, rhetorically. 'It's incredible really! Two young men, of only thirty odd, living in the nineteen-thirties, and never setting foot in a picture house all their lives. Why, you must be unique specimens!' she said, then, sensing that they were hurt, made swift amends. 'But they're a couple of dears all the same!' she added. She did not know, shrewd though she was, that the amends had wounded, in its way, as much as her light mockery had wounded.

When Winifred Bell had gone there was an enchanted quietness in the room, such as falls sometimes when a bird whose song has seemed part of the evening, suddenly ceases, leaving its empty twig to bounce faintly, in memory of its recent tenant.

None of the three broke through this enchantment with speech. Their thoughts bounced, gently, meditatively, a little wistfully, upon the memory of the recent visitor.

Or rather, Sam's and Peter's thoughts did so. Though they sat, as before the interruption, cross-legged, spectacled, their thimbles clicking briskly, their crisp heads bent, there was something different about them, something that set them apart from each other. Close though they sat, and identical as their heads and movements were, their thoughts walked stealthily down two garden paths, parallel, exactly alike, yet screened by clipped arched hedges so that in either path you could be totally unconscious of the existence of the other.

Meanwhile Alexandra was wandering not down a neat path screened by clipped archways, but in a tangled 'wilderness'. In this wilderness, in the enchanted stillness left behind by Winifred Bell, she was conscious of presences, beings behind the ragged tumble of nettles and seeding herbs, which peered out at her but never allowed her to catch a glimpse of their persons.

Wind-snatched footfalls, broken scraps of voices, were all that betrayed the presence of these creatures, and even these furtive scraps fled whenever she turned her eyes their way.

Names too — not heard and not seen, but elusively just-not-remembered — seemed to haunt the green-seeded quiet of the wilderness. It was as if there lay, hidden in the ranks of nettles, old gravestones, with carved inscriptions crumbled and time-bitten to such an extent that they were almost polished smooth again. Yet, in the centuries in which they had stood there, these inscriptions had printed themselves invisibly upon the still air.

Idly, yet with a vague sense of strain and distress, she wandered in this nettled quiet-run-wild, trying in vain to read the invisible, inaudible inscriptions printed upon the mouldering air.

'Well — who says tea?' said Sam, quietly enough, yet causing Alexandra's nerves to leap convulsively. And the next moment all the green, nettled quiet was dissolved. Back came the room that was her whole reality — the faded, but still pretty wallpaper, mauve, pale blue, pink, and pale green, like a flowered tobralco; the scrubbed trestle table; the worn coconut matting, the treadle-machine piled high with tacked garments; the pomponed mantel frill of faded green plush; and the red, teatime firelight.

Nothing haunted this room.

When Peter took off his spectacles and smiled, it was plain that his thoughts, as well as Sam's, no longer dreamed along his secret alley with its clipped screen of privet.

The after-quiet of Miss Bell's visit was spent.

CHAPTER IV

THURSDAY afternoon, as often happened, was somewhat thick with customers, for a good many of the Gollens' clients were shop assistants, whose only free half-day was on Thursday.

On this afternoon the first clients were two young men with hair like wet black paint, low, cat-like foreheads, and waists bent a little as if in permanent expectancy. They came for black coats and pin-striped trousers. They were assistants in a draper's shop, so Peter said. They amused Alexandra on account of the profusion of 'thank yous' in their speech, and the way they jerked forward from the waist at the 'thank' and up again at the 'you' as if the movement set in motion some mechanism which produced the sounds. They did this not only when receiving, but also when presenting.

After they had gone, Alexandra made Neb pretend to be a draper's assistant. She held him up on her knees and jerked him forward, saying the 'thank you' for him in careful imitation of the cere-monious sounds she had just listened to.

At length, however, even the good-natured Neb rebelled. Snatching his paw out of her grasp, he inflicted a spiteful scratch on her wrist, accompanying it with a 'miew' that seemed to be a sarcastic echo of her last 'you!' She released him, and he thudded very deliberately to the floor, where he sat, with his hunched shoulder sulking at her, licking his paw as if he were tasting in memory the sweetness of his revenge.

Alexandra laughed and turned her eyes to the street. Presently a chubby, pink-faced gentleman in a bowler hat passed by, looking anxiously at the window.

'A new customer!' said Alexandra, who was something of a Holmes in her own narrow world.

She was right. The next moment there came a rapid trill of knocks like a badly performed drum-roll. And in response to Sam's inviting duck of the head, in walked one of the fattest creatures that Alexandra had ever seen, and without exception the shyest.

He stood on the doormat for an aeon of his own agony, prodding nervously in a semicircle before him with the ferrule of his umbrella, as if he suspected quicksands in the linoleum. Then he became aware that he had not removed his hat, and, removing it, blushed deep cyclamen, prodding one of his own toes in his agitation.

Fortunately, by this time the brothers had perceived his distress, and, skilled in the handling of nervous customers, set themselves to soothe the frightened animal.

Before the cyclamen had cooled, Sam had juggled away his hat and umbrella, thereby reducing his social problems considerably, while Peter had introduced him into the windsor chair.

'I don't think we've had the pleasure of your custom before, Mr.——?' he said, but in such a way that he sounded as though the name had merely slipped his memory for a moment.

Like a skilful doctor drawing out from an embarrassed patient the symptoms of an indecent disease, Peter gradually elicited the cut, colour and quality of material desired by Mr. Woolsey. Presently he was even persuaded to remove his coat in order to be measured.

The Gollen brothers darted nimbly about him, reducing his apparent bulk by their neat and rapid footwork, as the size of the globe is reduced by the rapidity of modern transport, and reassuring him all the while with cheerful platitude and friendly laughter.

There was one awkward moment when Peter, trying to take his hip measurement, found his hands would not meet behind Mr. Woolsey's posterior. But he was equal to this crisis. With a flick of his right wrist he flung the tape-measure round, lasso-wise, and caught its end with his left hand.

Mr. Woolsey, however, was not deceived even by Peter's sleight-of-hand. Cyclamen of the deepest dye, he stammered:

'I'm — I'm awfully sorry to be so — er — so abnormal.'

Peter laughed. 'Oh — I shouldn't call you that, sir. Well-*covered* perhaps! But we'd be lucky if we never saw a worse case than yours.'

Sam added, more honestly yet somehow more comfortingly, 'If God made everyone the same, where would *we* come in?'

'That's right,' affirmed Peter, 'it's the unusual figures that make our work into an art!'

Mr. Woolsey was almost self-possessed as he took his leave. Nor would his self-possession have suffered any deflating if he had paused to eavesdrop instead of tripping instantly down the street. No laughter broke out even when he was not present to suffer from the sound of it. Unsophisticated as their humour was, the Gollen brothers saw nothing inherently humorous in corpulence. They saw Mr. Woolsey's figure in two aspects only — as a source of pain to its sensitive owner, and as a challenge, as Peter had quite truthfully said, to their art. And Alexandra, in this as in many things, accepted their outlook as her own.

After tea, staring idly through her window into the world, Alexandra saw a strange figure standing on Mrs. Wragge's top step

39

— strange in the sense of eccentric, for he was new neither to Finn Street nor to her.

He was a small man — so small, so thin, so fleshless under his loose black suit that he reminded Alexandra of a wish-bone penwiper she had once been given. His suit was disgracefully shabby, the trousers baggy beyond redemption in the knees and in the seat. Had it not been for his clerical collar you would have imagined him to be one of the unemployed. He had a dark semi-clerical hat, which he was using to emphasize his speech, whacking it on the iron balustrade in an awkward, unrhythmic manner.

Watching the mouthings, twitchings, pursings, gapings, snappings of the Reverend Revell's profile, yet cut off by the plate of glass from the aural result of all this vehemence, she suddenly thought of the goldfish in a glass bowl that a customer had given her last year, and how she had strained her ears in vain to hear what the creature had been mouthing at her as it swam round and round in its transparent prison. The absurdity of human speech became suddenly apparent to her. 'How silly we must all look to people who are deaf!' she thought; 'Or even to animals! No wonder Neb looks so scornfully at us sometimes!'

Gradually, step by step, mouthing ceaselessly in this absurdly noiseless fashion, slapping the balustrade babyishly with his hat, the Reverend Revell retreated backwards down Mrs. Wragge's steps as if she were royalty, then, after a pause, during which he flapped his own thigh helplessly with his hat, like a penguin's flipper, he darted suddenly across the road, ran up the Gollens' steps and knocked at their door.

Alexandra gathered herself together with anticipatory pleasure, for the Reverend Revell, though not a frequent visitor, was a favourite of hers, chiefly because his personal peculiarities provided her with endless amusement.

'Good evening, good evening, good evening,' he said in his soft, reflective, but rapid manner, like the trebly repeated notes of a meditative thrush, as he came darting to the centre of the room. 'This is *not* a professional visit!' he announced, nodding separately to all three of them. 'At least — not on my part — on *your* part, yes!'

'Oh! — are you going to have a new suit?' cried Alexandra.

40

The parson laughed. 'Your incredulity is well deserved!' he said, with a stiff little bow of mock-humility.

'I think I must be the worst dressed man in England — even the worst dressed clergyman. But even *I* draw the line somewhere. I believe my more ribald friends have for several years been making bets upon the probable date when my suit will fall from me in rags. As a clergyman I can hardly give my sanction to such indecent speculations! Hence this visit!'

He finished with one of his typical, treble, rather breathless laughs. He had a habit of repeating his words and noises thrice — perhaps due to the unconscious influence of the triple nature of the God he preached and tended.

By this time Peter and Sam were ready with notebook and tape-measure. He delivered himself into their hands — rather in the manner of a lively minded child being undressed by its nurse. While allowing them to raise and lower his arms, turn him about, lift his chin, turn his head, and unbutton his waistcoat, his mind was busy on its own much more important matters, his eyes were independent and distant, and his tongue jumped nimbly all the while, like a squirrel, from thought to thought.

Once Peter recalled him momentarily to the object of his visit. 'Another two days, Mr. Revell,' he remarked, with the air of old-ladyish severity which occasionally visited him. 'Another two days and both knees would have been through!'

'What? — through *what*? Oh — yes! yes! yes! I expect so! Professional wear and tear, you know! Wear and tear — wear and tear!' he repeated vaguely — for already his mind had leaped to another tree.

'The last time I was measured for a suit here,' he was saying dreamily, his eyes moving about the room incessantly, 'was in your father's time. That would be — let me see now — six — or seven — or is it eight years ago since he died?'

'Eight,' said Peter very curtly.

'Eight years! Dear me, dear me — eight years! I was just thinking, what a remarkable change you have made in this room since his death. I remember — but perhaps I had better *not*. There are things better forgotten, better forgotten — *much* better forgotten!'

None of the three answered him, Alexandra because there was

nothing she *could* say, the brothers because there was nothing they *would* say, on this subject.

He showed no sign of feeling the very palpable chill his words had made, but pursued nimbly his own thoughts. 'I often wonder if he was of Welsh extraction — he had to my mind a definite look of the Welsh — those heavy, harsh eyebrows, angular you know; and something about the brow-ridges; and then of course certain — shall we call them "propensities"? (Well, never mind those.) Then, a certain sibilance in his speech — definitely a celtic sibilance, though there were people, unchristian people, pharasaic people, who would put it down to the — shall we call it "propensity"? to which I was referring. They were wrong. I studied his speech from time to time. I dabble in such matters, you know. And whether — how shall I put it? — whether he was in a normal condition or an *ab*-normal condition, that slight sibilance was always there. He called himself, always, if I remember rightly, "Gothlan", not Gollen, as you do. That points most definitely to a Welsh origin. 'Don't you think so?'

Peter forced himself to answer, markedly distasteful of the subject: 'I don't know. He *spelt* it as we spell it. We prefer to say it as it's spelt!'

'Oh quite — quite — yes quite! Still, actually that is only fresh evidence for my theory. The double "l" is the traditional method of writing that half guttural, half sibilant sound peculiar to the Welsh language,' persisted the Reverend Revell.

Silence answered him. It became clear even to him that the subject was not welcome. Still he clung to it, for it fascinated a lively curiosity as to origins, heredities, ancient lineages, which had made him something of an amateur in anthropology.

'There were curious streaks of likeability in the man,' he persisted, almost as if pleading for the elder Gollen. 'The women certainly liked him. Though I don't know that their famous intuition is much to be trusted when it concerns a man! I am,' he added, with a sort of professorial roguery, 'rather a favourite with the ladies myself!'

The chill remained unthawed. He abandoned the unwelcome subject at last. By this time the measuring was well over, and after some further squirrel-like gossip, he took his leave. Before he went he knelt by Alexandra's bed, and offered up a prayer for her recovery.

Alexandra stared the while at his bent head, scantily covered with grey tufts of silk. She enjoyed being prayed for, but with no very passionate interest in the subject of the prayer.

The same indifference was shown by the brothers.

'Thank you very much!' they said cheerfully as he rose, much as they might have thanked him for a cigarette, or a free ticket for a theatre.

He flapped his thigh thoughtfully, gazing down at Alexandra's unruffled face. 'I cannot say that I see any sign of the efficacy of prayer in *this* instance, if I may be pardoned an apparently blasphemous doubt!' he said at last, in a curiously unprofessional tone of distrust. Then, remembering his trade, he added, but in a perfunctory manner: 'But it is not for us to question the motives of the Almighty, nor the manifestations of his power. Perhaps his answer is in the cheerful courage with which Alexandra has always borne her affliction.'

He did not sound very convinced by his own piety, and before they could respond to it, he slapped his side briskly to dismiss the subject, and began to back his way to the door.

'I shall see you, I know, in the choir on Sunday evening!' he said to the brothers. 'And you, Allie — I shall be round again sometime soon, and then we must have a real talk!'

Brought up violently by the door, he turned in astonishment, opened it, flopped his hat to his head, nodded thrice, and sprang down the steps into the muddy green dusk of the street.

The brothers returned in a peculiar silence to their work. It was not the silence of enchantment, such as had held the room after Winifred Bell's departure, but an uneasy, disagreeable silence.

The tailors sat on their table, their faces bent over their work, their mouths straight and obstinate, their cheeks bonier looking than usual, and their black comedian-shaped eyebrows pulled well down. Alexandra watched them with idle wonder. What were they thinking about? She knew it was something disagreeable, and she guessed it had to do with their father — and hers. She had noticed that they were always like this when their father had been mentioned. Yet somehow she had never cared to ask why.

As for her, what the parson had said had conveyed nothing. Like the school she had apparently attended once upon a time, like the young brother she pretended to remember but could not remember, her father was non-existent in her real memory. Such scraps as she had heard about him she had pieced together, but without any great force of curiosity. She knew that he had died eight years ago, that he had been a tailor and had taught Peter and Sam his trade, that he had had two wives, one of whom was Peter's and Sam's mother, the other her own mother. But, beyond a confused notion that he had in some way been disagreeable she had no picture of him at all — nor of either of his wives. Black eyebrows — Mr. Revell had said. She tried to picture a face to fit the eyebrows — but her mind baulked at it, and she was left with a pair of immense bushy black eyebrows *in vacuo*.

'Something always gets in the way,' said Allie to herself. It was a feeling invariably experienced by her whenever her mind reached back in time beyond the past six years — and particularly in connection with her father.

Changes in the room, too, the Reverend Revell had mentioned. She stared at the walls, the floor, the ceiling. The room obstinately remained the same. It had never been otherwise than it was, she felt. And yet — the parson remembered it otherwise, and if she read his face aright, remembered it in less pleasant aspect than its present one. She gave it up, as she had given it up dozens of times before.

CHAPTER V

THURSDAY had had no individuality as a day, apart that is from the visitors it had brought. But Friday was a personality, from the moment Alexandra opened her eyes to see the window delicately crusted with Frost — that mysterious substance which appeared so rarely and so capriciously that it never failed to delight, which was so frail in pattern, yet so firmly fixed to the window that certainly Alexandra's strength was not sufficient to rub it away.

She lay and marvelled at it — brilliant, brittle, stiff-textured, yet pliant in design, grown like a fresco of sugared ferns half-way up the window, so that she could see above them a rinsed and hard-dyed sky of sugar-bag blue, and one curl of the extravagant white wig of a cloud.

She put up her hand timidly and held four finger-tips on the ice-cold, granulated window. After a time she could feel that the granules of ice had disappeared beneath her warm skin. She removed her fingers; in their place were four little peep-holes through which the dark mulberry complexion of the bricks opposite could be seen. This magical disappearance of Frost at her touch gave her an obscure sensation of destructive power, and of pleasure in that power. She would have liked, despite her wonder at their beauty, to have ruined the whole frieze of sugared ferns. But her hand was not big enough.

However, what she could not do, the fire did for her. When it had been lit for an hour or so, the ferns, silently as they had come, rolled themselves off the window, beginning at the top. By nine o'clock the window was polished clear of them.

And there were the dim mulberry brick façade, the muddy ochred steps, the rusty balustrades, the chocolate-coloured doors, and the little lace-curtained windows, more hopelessly themselves than ever. This disenchantment, Alexandra had noticed, was the invariable sequel to Frost on the window.

One remnant of gaiety remained however. The dark roofs opposite were powdered lightly as if with flour, and this reminded Alexandra what day it was — Baking Day — Mrs. Tyler's Day.

She laughed aloud with pleasure. The day, after all, was to be very far from flat, even though the frieze of white ferns was gone. 'Peter — Sam!' she called to her brothers, who were shaving in the kitchen, preparing for their weekly round of visits to customers who, though not too proud to make use of a pair of cheap and skilful tailors, were too superior to be seen in Finn Street.

Sam came to the door with his pink face looking through whiskers of soap like a Father Christmas mask.

'Well?'

'Somebody is going to bake cakes on the roofs to-day!' she said, nodding at the view from the window.

'Good heaventh, ith that all!' said Sam frothily, and retired in good-natured contempt.

But the similitude continued to please Alexandra, until the pre-

45

sence of Mrs. Tyler herself drove it from her mind. It was seldom that she looked at her street while Mrs. Tyler was about.

Mrs. Tyler was large, shapeless, heavy and damp-looking, like a 'sad' cake, her flesh, wherever visible, the colour of raw pastry. She was probably very strong-minded, Alexandra concluded, for whereas Mrs. Bell, Winifred's mother, wore skirts not appreciably longer than her daughter's, Mrs. Tyler persisted in ankle-length skirts that swung heavily like plush curtains, and creaked nearly as loudly as those of two nuns who sometimes walked down Finn Street. From her window-gazing, and from fashion books, Alexandra calculated that Mrs. Tyler was at least ten years behind her times. Yet somehow she failed to seem old-fashioned and certainly failed to be ridiculous.

There was another anomaly about Mrs. Tyler. Looking as she did, like a huge image made of half-cooked pastry, she ought to weigh at least half a ton. Yet she contrived to blow about the room as lightly as a balloon escaped from its moorings. You scarcely noticed the effort of her feet — hardly *saw* her feet in fact, and if by chance you did, you were amazed at the minuteness of her black high-heeled court shoes, of patent leather with little bows on the instep, the only note of frivolity in the whole of her person.

But what mystified Alexandra most of all was the peculiar rigidity of her bust. Sometimes she thought that Mrs. Tyler must wear corsets extending up to her neck; sometimes she thought she must wear a sort of stiffened shirt-front of cardboard; or had Mrs. Tyler some terrible deformity which necessitated a permanent breast-plate of plaster of Paris? She even wondered, in her most fantastic moods, if Mrs. Tyler had only one breast, huge, hard as iron, covering her whole chest. She had read somewhere about giants with only one eye. So why not one breast?

But apart from all these fascinating problems, there was endless pleasure merely in watching Mrs. Tyler at work. To see her kneading the dough, for instance, folding it over upon itself, pounding it, slapping it, pommelling it, so rapidly that it was hard at times to distinguish the dough from her dough-coloured hands, gave Alexandra a most peculiar pleasure; fierce, almost savage, half-sensual pleasure, as if, vicariously, she were punishing an ancient but now helpless enemy.

46

While the dough, battered, but with unconquerable soul, was put down in what Mrs. Tyler called the 'Bread Moog' to rise, she would turn her hands to the pastry.

It was a wonder ever-fresh to see those hands, which had seemed while pommelling the dough to partake of its stubborn, heavy, elastic quality, become so marvellously light when 'crumbing in' the lard. Now they rose and fell buoyantly, like two soft putty-coloured birds; and as the flour sifted through them, it seemed like showers of small creamy feathers loosed from their breasts.

When the pastry, a sticky, flour-powdered mass, was being squeezed remorselessly out into a thin pool, Alexandra felt a mild return of the same sensuous cruelty as she had felt as the dough was punished.

But the converting of this pale shapeless pool into tarts and pies was the prettiest sight of all. One moment the skirts of limp pastry would be drooping over the edge of plate, basin or dish, frumpish as Mrs. Tyler's own skirts. The next minute, the silver lightning of the kitchen knife was playing among them. And in the third minute, like the little old woman in the nursery rhyme, there stood the dish or the basin or the plate with its skirts cut up to its knees. In the fourth minute it would be edged with loops of pastry, neat as tailor's binding. In the fifth the prongs of the kitchen fork, hopping all round each circle like the toes of a silver bird, made a charming border with its footprints. Then came the scarlet jam, or the golden treacle, to lie richly on the soft cream of pastry laps. And lastly, came the cross of white laid over like a holy spell to keep the jam or the treacle within their lawful home.

All these things Alexandra would watch in silence. She was too enthralled ever to wish to speak.

As for Mrs. Tyler, as she worked, you could almost fancy that all the life in her had drained into her hands, so still was her long, oblong, pasty-coloured face, with its deep folds of fat about the chin, the cheeks and the mouth, with its Lancashire-shaped lower lip, heavy, thrust forward beyond the top teeth, its steep forehead, and its thin, pale brown hair. She looked as likely to speak as a statue, and her eyes, cast down to the table, the lids fringed by almost invisible lashes, assisted in this impression.

If, once in a while, Alexandra ventured to speak, this blank-eyed statue would slowly open its mouth, as if worked by some ponderous machinery, and, deep, slow, harsh, like the cries of rooks, would come forth sounds of reproof.

'For t'Lord's sairke, oosh Allie! Dawn't *mither* me!'

But this was only until the bread and pastry were in the oven. Once Mrs. Tyler was begun upon the more frivolous task of cake-making she would unbend a little, and would then treat Alexandra to the news of the neighbourhood, in particular the obstetric news, the deathbed news, the matrimonial news and the unemployment news.

'Ye knaw that pooer Mrs. 'Awkins — Prin*cess* Street — third owoose fra t'little shop at t'carner?' she suddenly said to-day without lifting her eyes or interrupting the dance of her hands.

'Yeess!' Alexandra replied doubtfully, for she knew the streets beyond Finn Street only by proxy.

'Ad a miscarriage — there's *soom* auld cats as carl it soomat worse! But as to that ah wouldn't like to sair!'

'Oh dear!' responded Alexandra knowing from experience that a miscarriage was something you responded to with an 'Oh dear!' but otherwise very baffled by the information.

'Ee!' Mrs. Tyler continued. 'What oos women do 'ave to put oop wi! S'easy to see as God Arlmighty were a mahn! Troost a mahn to 'and t'women t'dirty end o't stick!'

Mrs. Tyler, Alexandra understood, had once had a husband, now either dead or missing. He seemed to have some connection with her recurrent resentment against the male sex in general. Often she would say '*We* knaw them! You with your pa the wair 'e was, me with mah Clifford, what '*e* was — *we* knaw!'

'Yes — that's right!' Alexandra would say, with an inappropriate cheerfulness due to the fact that she did *not* know them.

There was much in Mrs. Tyler's talk that she failed to understand. Interesting words, like 'Roopcher', 'cahncer', 'stawnes', 'deooaw-deenal', 'pahles', and many others came slow and hoarse from her mouth, as intriguing, and as incomprehensible as the language of rooks. After Mrs. Tyler had gone, Alexandra tried to find the words in an old tattered Webster's dictionary, but as she could not spell, and as Mrs. Tyler's phonetics were hardly orthodox, she had little success.

When the oven door was slammed upon the last cake-tin, Mrs. Tyler became quite gay, breaking into snatches of *The Merry Widow* (in a deep graveyard tone and at funereal pace it is true), and clattering the basins, tins and spoons almost in Sam's fashion.

While she washed these to the strains of her *Merry Widow* dirge, Alexandra looked out of the window for the first time since Mrs. Tyler's arrival. There was very little to look at this morning. The street looked dry, as if that cat that was strolling across the road had just licked it clean with its rough pink tongue.

How different cats and dogs were, she thought, in their street behaviour. Dogs — like that batter-pudding-coloured one there, for instance — never seemed to know what they had come out for. Aimlessly they would rush about, sniffing here, lifting a leg there, barking fatuously at nothing in particular and scratching for a flea of whose existence they were not quite sure. Cats on the other hand always go out on some secret little matter, of a slightly sinister nature, the details of which they have planned beforehand with the utmost precision, and over which they gloat quietly as they trot. Cats tread as if the whole street were made of something fragile. Dogs tear about as if they would like to scratch the whole world up for bones.

The cat passed out of sight, and with it passed her thoughts on the nature of cats and dogs. They returned to Mrs. Tyler.

What a strange ugly woman she was! How well her ugly speech fitted her face. It was as if those heavy, folded, colourless cheeks and lips were expressly formed to make the sounds that came out of them. Yet somehow the essence of Mrs. Tyler, you felt, was *not* ugly. The essence of Mrs. Tyler was as good and as beautiful as the smell of mingled cakes, bread and pastry that was beginning to creep out of the cracks of the oven — a rich, motherly, kindly sort of smell. She was comfortable and comforting. Even when you did not require comfort for any particular sorrow (and Alexandra, so far as she knew, had never had need of comfort for any particular sorrow), she seemed to draw you into a circle of snug warmth and good-baking smells.

Yes — Friday was a lovely day, especially when to Mrs. Tyler was added Frost.

FRIDAYS, Saturdays, and Sundays were the days most steadfast in personality in Alexandra's life; Friday being filled with the scent of baking and the sight of Mrs. Tyler, Sunday being distinguished by bells, Mr. Bell, and the absence of work, and Saturday being dominated by the weekly bath.

So much indeed was Saturday dominated by its special ritual that it did not really begin to exist until the moment when Sam came staggering in from the kitchen with the zinc bath clasped to his bosom like a female robot. For this was the opening scene of a long series of luxurious delights, opening in vistas one from the other like the chambers of a glittering palace, of which Alexandra was the queen.

Those who are born into the age of bathrooms and running hot water for nearly all, can never believe the luxury of bathing in a zinc bath on the hearthrug before a blazing fire — for the bather that is. Those who have to superintend the bath do not of course find it a luxury at all.

However, the Gollen brothers were never heard to complain. Though for Sam it meant the lifting of many crushingly heavy objects — the zinc bath, the huge eighteen-inch saucepan in which the water was heated, and finally Alexandra, he seemed only one degree less delighted than the invalid herself.

Peter provided the smaller details such as soap, soapflakes, sponge, talcum powder, warm towels, clean underwear, a nightdress, and a pair of nail-scissors. These he brought reverently, arranging them in a traditional pattern.

Mrs. Tyler, accepting and centralizing the ministerings of the two men, seemed like a priestess, accepting the assistance of the novices who hand the bell, the book, or the sacrament at the precise moment ordained by the god. When all was ready she would bend over the bath water to test its temperature as if she bent over the steaming entrails of a sacrifice to examine the omens.

For Alexandra the ritual meant peace and sensuous pleasure for every sense in her body.

To her ears came the manifold music of water; the hollow roar of the cataract of hot water from the saucepan; the cracked-bell notes as Mrs. Tyler mixed the hot and the cold waters, and frothed the lather; the flat metallic plunge when Sam let her down into the water, as gradually as he could, but with an unavoidable flop at the end which set the water swinging irresistibly, until it gradually lessened of its own accord to a quiet low 'wap-wop' against the ends of the bath; then the whispering stealth of the lather all about her thighs, whispering its own death-song; and the pretty sledge-bell tinklings when Mrs. Tyler dipped in her hand or squeezed the sponge to rinse her.

For her eyes was the feast of the sparkling foam, white as frost in the mass, but really composed of hundreds of little polished opals of pink and green; the queer green-grey of the water when the foam was all dead; her own body, white as freshly cracked nuts out of the water, but a pretty pink where the water had touched it.

To her nose came the warm faintly peppery smell of soapy water, the thick smell of singeing towels; the crisp smell of the clean starched sheet being tucked into her bed, and the playful teasing smell of the talcum powder with which she was dusted, as a sort of flower-dance conclusion to the ceremony.

And lastly, for the delight of her skin was the warm tickling of the water as it lapped up her sides and stomach; the fire beating on her naked side with its great outspread palms; the strange shrunken-ness of her body when dried; and, last inner shrine of luxuries, the sensation of lying, small, soft, velvet, warm, and exquisitely clean, between stiff new sheets.

By the time the room was cleared of the bath and the rest of the paraphernalia, she would be almost asleep, and had to be roused in order to be given her supper.

Saturday night was the only night of the week on which Alexandra slept before midnight. For bathing was the only exertion she underwent which tired her body sufficiently to put her in need of the amount of sleep required by most of mankind.

Sunday mornings always suggested to Alexandra the image of a cat, lying in the sun, with its front paws doubled neatly under it, its eyes gently blinking, and a smile of conscious virtue on its prim little mouth of velvet.

Not all Sunday mornings were sunlit. But when they were it seemed entirely fitting that they should be so. Moreover, March sunlight, on a Sunday morning, could somehow seem no thinner in quality, no less rich in benignity, than the very loveliest June sunshine.

Through its clear meshes came sifting the voices of more distant and less distant bells, pure and cool and thoughtful. Most distant was a two-note chime, like a lazy cuckoo not bothering to attain the proper interval. Nearer was a single bell, 'cerlang! cerlang!' very measured, almost cautious sounding. Nearer still was a lovely jangle of eight, repeating endless variations twice each, the rhythm slightly and charmingly drunken, like the steps of children just learning to run. And nearest of all, a tottering, rather cracked trio, saying 'ray *me* doh', over and over again.

There was no work done in the Gollens' house to-day. But this Sabbath observing was not of the self-righteous variety. It was as natural and as regular as sleep, or the hibernating of inoffensive woodland creatures, or the fall of leaves. After a breakfast in which both of the British household gods were given equal due in honour of the day, Peter shaved himself, even more deliberately than on other mornings; and as he scraped he hummed 'All creatures of our God and King', for to him all Sundays were as Easter Sunday.

Before the bells had quite finished their superimposed patterns he would be ready, in his well-pressed navy suit, unfashionably narrow in the legs because he had looked after it too well, carrying a pair of knitted woollen gloves, and a shining bowler hat, exactly in time to reach St. Joseph's, the church whose cracked bells said 'ray *me* doh', and to whose choir Peter lent his alto voice every Sunday morning and evening.

While he was away, Sam, as if inspired by the now silent challenge of the bells, rang recklessly all possible changes on his pots and pans. Sunday dinner required from Sam the jongleur his utmost in its honour.

Through the din could be heard snatches of Sam's whistling, like a thrush heard in snatches through a thunderstorm. Outside, the sunshine dilated and contracted in gentle caprice. One or two dogs barked in a good-natured, make-believe spirit. People began that mysterious and objectless hammering which belongs peculiarly to

Sunday mornings, and which seems with some men to be the only possible substitute for religious exercises.

Yet despite these noises, a devotional peace seemed to wash to and fro in Finn Street.

Alexandra leaned back against her pillow, stroking Neb, and sniffing with deep rapture the bunched nosegay of smells that came thrusting from the kitchen, efflorescence of the roast mutton, Yorkshire pudding, cabbage, roast potatoes, and rhubarb and custard which was in preparation there.

Because the morning was homogeneous it had seemed a very short time when Peter came home, took his shining greenish bowler up to its tissue paper, and came running lightly down again to lay the table.

On Sundays they had their clean table-cloth. It usually stuck together at the folds owing to the generosity of Mrs. Bell's starching. Alexandra loved to hear its little reverent whisper as Peter pulled its clinging folds apart.

Sometimes on a week-day Sam's cookery was eccentric. But never on a Sunday. They ate his dinner voluptuously, not insulting its perfection by speech. Speech was for after dinner, for they did not in this household relapse into that reptilian torpor which is one of the lingering relics of the Victorian Sunday.

'I saw a sight for a king coming home from church!' said Peter, when the last spoonful of his rhubarb was transposed into the past.

'Oh!' said Sam — his teeth still rough with his, for though he appeared to eat hurriedly he ate more slowly than Peter.

'Yes! Mr. Wyatt's set his crocuses *in* the lawn this year. I've not seen that idea before — they're not in rows, you know — but in bunches, scattered about as if they had pleased themselves where they grew!'

Mr. Wyatt was a town councillor, with a big house on the main road and a very public and ostentatious garden. Peter, however, did not perceive the ostentation, but was merely grateful for the result of it; neither envious nor critical of a state of affairs which allowed one man to own the means for such pageantry, and all others merely the right to look on.

'What are crocuses like?' asked Alexandra, who was almost as ignorant of flowers as if she had been born on the moon.

53

'Well,' said Peter, closing his eyes to picture them. 'They're little flowers — the golden ones are smaller than the white ones, and the mauve are the floppiest of all; and in shape they remind me of those little flares that jump out of coal — especially the gold ones. It looked as if the lawn was puffing out little bunches of flames!'

'Oh Peter — why didn't you pick me some?' said Alexandra, stirred to covetousness by this description.

'What — out of a private garden?' cried Peter, who was as reverent of others' property as only the unpossessing can be.

'Were there many cyclists to-day?' asked Sam, cutting into this dialogue. He was not very interested in flowers.

'Oh — hordes of them! I should think nearly everyone in Cole-bridge went out this morning!' laughed Peter.

'I *can't* understand what they see in it — tearing along in all that dust and stink of petrol, with their shoulders hunched up, and their chins pushed out, and their eyes screwed up, and their faces as sticky with sweat as fly-paper, and their white coats flapping behind them like flabby balloons! What *can* they see in it?'

Sam shook his red face. 'It beats me, Peter,' he said cheerfully.

It beat them both regularly every Sunday. They were content not to understand, for not to understand allowed them to feel cheer-fully superior to these peculiar young men and women who found their Sunday pleasure in turning the wheels of a machine.

In the afternoon it was Sam's turn to see the world, while his brother stayed in to attend and entertain Alexandra. As usual, the entertainment was performed upon his celluloid whistle. This instrument was nearly twenty years old, so yellowed by his fingers that it looked like old ivory.

Alexandra liked to see his fingers dancing on the holes, and was never tired of listening to his tunes, however old they were, for every time he played a tune it was dressed in new frills and flourishes.

He played a new tune to-day however. It was very sweet and fresh, with light frills and fluttering ribbons of sound that somehow made Alexandra think of Winifred Bell. She asked Peter what it was called. But as usual he did not know.

'I picked it up in the big house we went to on Friday. But the young lady's words were very bad. I couldn't hear *one* of them.

Pretty though, isn't it?' He began absently to play it again. Whenever he had a new tune it was hard to part him from it.

At six o'clock the brothers went out together to sing in the St. Joseph's choir. So that they might do so, Mr. Bell would come to sit with Alexandra.

He was rather late to-night. When he arrived and saw them standing in the middle of the room, bowler hats and knitted gloves in their hands, he began to laugh.

'Luke as if yu was wairting for t'king to coom by!' he said, and as they began to pull on their gloves somewhat feverishly, added: 'Sorry t'king's lairt! S'matter of fact, ower Ned fra *Manchester* come over this after' in 'is car; and tuke uz arl fer a ride. Fair treat it was! Roons like clockwork! Better! Coz yu dawnt 'ave to wind it oop!'

The brothers looked at each other in humorous, wilful mystification. 'Well,' said Peter, 'I hope you showed more signs of enjoyment than the folks *I* saw this morning riding in cars — looking as if they were riding to their own funerals! And perhaps they *were*!'

Mr. Bell scratched his lamb-like curls. Like his daughter he maltreated his hair, cropping it unmercifully half-way up the back of his head. But his hair, like Winifred's, knew better, and very soon after each cropping a small grey curl or two like little snails' shells would cluster about his ears and temples. He scratched a cluster of these now and laughed at the brothers.

'Ever *bin* in a car in your lives?' he inquired.

The brothers shook their heads and impatiently put on their hats, for it was high time they were off to church.

'Next time ower Ned coom's over from Manchester I'll get 'im to pick you oop! Ye'll *never* oonderstand what the thrill is till ye've felt it fer yerselves!' said Mr. Bell.

They laughed deprecatingly. 'I'm afraid we're not made for these modern pleasures,' protested Peter, as he opened the door.

Mr. Bell scratched his head harder than ever.

'Ye're a pair of anacreons! That's what yu are!' he shouted after them, as the door slammed and they ran down the steps. But it was doubtful whether his shot reached them. Mr. Bell came and settled himself in the rocking chair facing Alexandra.

55

'What is an anacreon, Mr. Bell?' inquired Alexandra, as he drew out his Sunday paper from his pocket.

'Someone as is born out of 'is time — owd-fashioned — ante-deluvian!' defined Mr. Bell promptly. Like Humpty Dumpty he always knew exactly what he meant by the words in his vocabulary. Alexandra added the word silently to her own rather meagre vocabulary.

Meanwhile Mr. Bell was searching for something suitable to read to her. ''Ere we are!' he said joyfully, after a short hunt. ''Ere we *are*!' and he began to intone, in that jerky, aitchless monotone produced by his generation of elementary schools, a story of a newspaper parcel in a cloakroom, which 'attracting attention' as the report delicately put it, was opened, and discovered to contain a human forearm, two big toes, and a hand.

This absorbing tale was followed by the 'drama' of a coloured doctor who was being tried for an unmentionable operation, and this in turn by the 'tragedy' of a little girl, found strangled and 'indecently assaulted' under a canal bridge.

Though Alexandra was acquainted, through repetition, and some questioning, with the theoretical meaning of the terms of these strange reports, they had no practical reality for her — no correspondence with the details of her own life at all. Read to her in Mr. Bell's one-toned voice, jerked out of him woodenly like the cluckings of a mechanical hen, the tales were to her a sort of sordid, grimy, thousand and one Arabian Nights — tales of a fantastic land that never was, whose inhabitants were exclusively occupied in murder, assault, sexual misconduct, abnormal births, burglaries, suicides and divorces.

Yet, though totally inhuman, incredibly grimy, extravagantly morbid, the tales gripped her. For they nosed out from somewhere within her a recognition of their fundamental, if distorted truth. Somewhere in her, locked down under strong hatches, she carried, she felt obscurely, some disreputable, some evil-smelling cargo, which if she should ever be able to bring it to the light, would enable her to comprehend the criminal inhabitants of this grimily fantastic land of Mr. Bell's Sunday paper.

Sometimes, when Mr. Bell had gone home, and her brothers lay upstairs in bed, and the firelight made caricatures of the furniture on the coloured screen of the ceiling, this evil-smelling cargo seemed to stir and waver and murmur uneasily, as if it might possibly be dreaming of breaking loose.

But as the firelight ripened and then died, even this dream-far mutiny was quelled. Sunday night always ended, as Sunday morning began, with a sensation of impregnable content, symbolized by the image, very frequently in her mind, of a black cat, its golden eyes dilating and contracting with the sunshine, its velvet paws doubled snugly under its warm, purring chest, and a smug smile on its little velvet mouth.

She fell asleep stroking her Sunday.

PART TWO

CHAPTER I

THE foregoing pages are a dip at random into the life of Alexandra
Gollen between the ages of twelve and twenty-one. It is at random
because any other seven days in that period would have been equally
representative of the whole.

It is possible that but for a certain visitor in 1933, she would have
lived the rest of her life in a similar fashion. On the other hand, it
is possible that the seeming miracle which now temporarily
startled the small world of the invalid was no more a miracle than
the birth of a velvet-clad, gorgeously-coloured moth out of a fat,
white, disgustingly comatose larva; that the apparently sudden
metamorphosis was really only the last phase of a long train of secret
and invisible development in her pathological condition; and that
there was no need of the stimulant which was the apparent cause of
the miracle.

In human affairs it is always very difficult to disentangle causes
and motives. But whether it was the ultimate cause of the miracle
or not, the visitor who came in the June of Alexandra's twenty-
second year was certainly a contributory fermenting agent. For it
was observed that, after that day, she became a different creature.

It had been a day of classic beauty, rather windy, but with a sun
which melted through the glass and lay like a warm shawl over her
shoulders.

Over the chimneys there were great piled clouds, like eighteenth-
century wigs, or white leghorn hats, delicately shadowed with blue
on their undersides, as if by reflections from the deep, matt, wedgwood blue of the sky. A flock of pigeons looped the chimneys,
flashing silver and then dark, like a dancing dazzle of lights thrown
from a revolving mirror.

Such flashing freedom of wings, such magnificent clouds, breed
thoughts of escape. Schoolboys and girls, schoolmistresses and clerks
and housewives, all who are condemned to sit indoors at some dull
toil on such a day, are driven mad with a yearning to be free — free
to run to the top of a hill, to watch cloud shadows sweep from dis-

tant hills to near hills, to follow bird-shadows, most free of all libertine things, to hear the air sifting in the full trees, to hear the careless feet of running water, and to forget that work was ever invented.

Alexandra never ached with such yearnings. She was like an animal several generations of whose ancestors have been born into captivity, so that it accepts captivity as the natural order of things. She did not even regard the free as eccentric madmen. She was so wrapped in her own comfortable narrow world that she did not even realize that others *were* more free than her.

Once in the first years of her illness, a kindly customer had lent the brothers a long invalid's hand-carriage, thinking to lighten her lot with an occasional outing. The carriage had been used once — and the expedition had evoked so little gratitude from Alexandra that the brothers came to the conclusion that it had not been worth the tremendous expenditure of effort required to transport Alexandra down the steps to the carriage waiting on the pavement, to push her considerable weight about the town, and to lift her out at the end of the journey and carry her up the steps again — not to mention the time lost from their work.

They would have been willing to repeat the effort if it had seemed to give Alexandra any particular pleasure. But she never spoke of the expedition afterwards and when asked if she would like a second outing, obstructed the idea with a sort of cheerful, cunning obstinacy. The carriage was therefore never borrowed again.

On this afternoon in June Alexandra sat looking rather like her favourite Neb, her face smug, without speculation, surveying the world with the indifference of the completely comfortable, utterly content to survey so small and so mean a portion of it as Finn Street, utterly incurious as to what lay beyond Finn Street.

The sky with its soft, massed clouds and its glitter of birds was beautiful to her, but quite without that poignance which quickens beauty for those who are conscious of its frailty, of its rare occurrence, and of the brevity of their own lease on earth.

Into this small smug world there walked that afternoon the being who shattered it for ever — or, at any rate, whose advent coincided with its shattering, and seemed to contribute at least some of the vibrations which finally cracked the neat little edifice.

It is perhaps melodramatic, but it is nevertheless true, to say that the shattering began with a knock on the tailors' door.

Alexandra had never before heard anything quite like the accomplished virility of that knock. Her interest was therefore quickened even before she set eyes on the visitor.

When she came into the room Alexandra thought immediately how well she matched her knock. She was tall, with long straight thighs which, swinging freely as the limbs of a lioness, brought her in four easy strides to the middle of the room. There she stopped, quite still, again with the easy, uninhibited power of a wild animal, and looked all about her, unsmiling and inquisitive. Her eyes swept superbly across and across the room, and when they swept across Alexandra's line of sight, she saw that they were of a brilliant, yet curiously insubstantial blue-green, and that they were unusually small.

Having inspected the room at her leisure, the confident creature announced her business. 'I want a costume making on the lines of this one that I'm wearing,' she said, in a voice which, though rough, was agreeable to the ear, as a rough towel is agreeable to the cheeks. 'I want plenty of room in the skirt, and the lapels must button up to the neck for warmth. But otherwise I leave you fancy-free! And this is the material.'

She put down her parcel on the table and untied it rapidly with large but skilful fingers. The material was a mixed blue and green tweed, the twill pattern of which produced at a distance a shot, peacock effect. The costume she was wearing was golden-brown and, though very worn, was well cut.

Evidently, thought Alexandra, despite the indifference with which she spoke of the details of her costume, she had an eye for clothes, both for their colour and their line, and she knew too what suited her.

While this unusual customer was being measured, a process which she suffered in silence and absolute indifference, Alexandra stared at her, with an interest quite different in quality from her usual lazy curiosity, an interest intense enough to increase the speed of her heart perceptibly, and to cause a definite constriction in her breathing.

Why did this woman so powerfully affect her?

Certainly her looks were in a category of their own. Alexandra, at any rate, had seen neither man nor woman in the least like her before. Her hair alone would have distinguished her. Dull copper, with firelight gleams at the temples, perfectly straight, it hung in front in a thick fringe level with her eyebrows, and at the back was cut in a straight line level with her ears, behind which the side locks were pushed back. It seemed to fit her head like a helmet. She held her head as if it supported the weight of a bronze helmet, yet supported it with ease, even with pride.

Her face was equally individual. It had the directness, the simplicity, yet the smooth polish, of a face carved in wood. Broad in the cheek-bones, with long eye-sockets, slightly concave cheeks, and a square chin, its general outline was almost rectangular, powerful for a woman, yet not masculine in effect, on account of the smoothness of the modelling, the silky polish of the pale, white-wood-coloured skin, and a curiously flexible sweetness about her long upper-lip.

Except for the darting blue eyes, it was a face exceptionally well controlled. After that first glance round of measured curiosity, it had expressed nothing of its owner's thoughts. Yet you felt that the helmeted head was no mere empty casque.

As Peter knelt to measure the skirt length, she turned those restless eyes to the window. There they stayed, almost still, but with a gauzy vibrant effect, like the whirring of the transparent wings of dragon-flies, for several seconds. Then the wide, short upper lip lifted, with a curious effect of buckling along its length.

'What a perfect day for flying!' she said.

Peter rose to his feet, and stared first at her, and then at the window at which *she* stared. Sam stared fixedly at her. And Alexandra stared at all three. The room was all alive with startled wits like a disturbed rabbit warren.

At last Peter recovered his speech. 'Flying?' he echoed, rather breathlessly, and again, unable to proceed further than this ejaculatory response, '*Flying?*'

The woman was compelled to laugh at their thunderstruck expressions. Her laugh, Alexandra thought, was even more agreeably rough than her speech.

'You look as a fish might if I said to it, "What a perfect day for a walk!" ' she said, but with some power of sincere sympathy which

61

robbed her rather insulting simile of offence. 'It's extraordinary,' she continued, 'how little the idea of flying has got into people's consciousness. I suppose you two have never been in an aeroplane in your lives?'

'Good heavens! No!' cried the brothers simultaneously, as they might if she had said, 'I suppose you have never been up in Elijah's fiery chariot in your lives?'

She looked at them, her long face tilted, considering them with the intense curiosity which was her most vital characteristic.

'And never *expect* to go in an aeroplane in your lives?' she pursued.

'No — I don't suppose so!' answered Peter, cheerfully indifferent to this privation.

'Oh well! I suppose after all nine-tenths of the world is the same,' she remarked, with a sort of impatient tolerance. 'In time everybody will fly, of course — but to me it's such a glorious sensation that I'm impatient for everybody to try it immediately!'

'Can *you* fly, then?' asked Alexandra, speaking for the first time since this unbelievable creature strode into the room, and even now unable to free her voice from a childish, husky awe.

'Oh yes!' said the woman, matter of factly, yet with a certain pride in her ability to be matter of fact. 'Not a plane. I can't afford that. And if I could I doubt if I would care to. But I can fly a glider.'

The three stared at her in dumbfounded silence. After a pause, looking at them with the slightly ashamed amusement of an adult who perceives she has been talking above the heads of an audience of children, she laughed and said, 'But it's very ill-bred of me to brag in this fashion. Forget it! Now! When will you want me to come to "try-on"?'

'We're rather busy just now. Say, a week to-day?' suggested Peter.

'Right!' said she immediately. And this settled, she took her leave as she had entered, that is in perfect ease — with the long, swinging, confident steps of an animal which knows itself to be in perfect hunting health.

During the following week, the tall red-helmeted figure was seldom out of Alexandra's mind. 'Forget!' she had commanded. But Alexandra at least could forget neither her looks, nor her voice, nor her words. These lingered in her memory as the words and voice of the serpent must have lingered in the memory of Eve, with as tremendous, though ultimately not so catastrophic result.

'Iris Young,' was her name. She had said it herself, in that rough deep voice that seemed to leave a tingling behind like the tingling after a scrubbing with a rough towel.

'Iris Young.'

Alexandra heard the name a thousand times during those next seven days, in the exact tones in which its owner had pronounced it. And always it acted like an incantation. At the sound there came striding into the room the vivid ghost of its owner.

Once Alexandra woke up convinced that the name had just been spoken in the room. The room was drowned in the transparent darkness of a June midnight. No one could have spoken the word. Yet the tones of it hung still in the dark air — and they were the rough-textured tones of Iris Young herself.

On the day when she was to come again, Alexandra woke up earlier than usual. As soon as Sam's broken slipper slithered down the stairs, Alexandra called out, 'What time is that Miss Young coming?'

She would not arrive, it seemed, until five o'clock.

Alexandra settled herself down to wish the day away. Anticipation, particularly impatient anticipation, was a new experience for her. Hitherto her mind had always been content to jog along at the side of Time, at its own ambling pony-speed; content to watch the changing of her small world, never wishing to change it herself, or to hurry the tempo of its changes.

Now, for the first time, she was *riding* Time. In the manner of all who ride, whatever their mount, she was instantly seized by the devil of impatience. She wanted to whip and goad the ambling little creature into her own speed. Yet, despite its gentle looks, and small, dust-muted hoofs, she found Time remarkably obstinate. The more she fretted the slower it went. Several times during the day she caught Sam or Peter looking at her with a reproachful expression, and realized that she had been petulant more times in one day than she had been in all the time she remembered.

At last five o'clock arrived, and, almost simultaneously, Iris Young. Alexandra was delighted to find how well she matched the memory of herself. It was as if Alexandra had been singing a song, mentally and silently, all the week, and the visitor had joined in exactly at the point she had reached. The helmet of gold, the lean thighs, the curiously unsubstantial blue of her eyes, were all exactly as she had thought. A week's brooding upon her first impressions had not distorted them.

Flying was not mentioned on this visit, perhaps because the day was so still, so vapid, a hot blue day without clouds or wind.

Iris Young by this omission seemed somehow more earthbound, less remote, more human than before.

While the brothers fitted gingerly over her shoulders the frailly-held, sleeveless coat, marking it with chalk where its fit displeased them, she divided her attention between this business and Alexandra, whom she had before merely included in her preliminary survey of the furniture and personality of the room.

Now her blue gauzy eyes hovered continually upon Alexandra, in definite curiosity. Presently, sandwiched between two suggestions about the pockets of her suit, which she required large, for use, not for show, she asked whether Alexandra's convalescence was nearly ended.

Peter looked up — mildly amused. 'Convalescence!' he remarked. 'I never heard of a convalescence lasting nine years!'

Iris Young looked incredulous. 'You don't mean that your — sister is it? — is an *invalid?*'

Alexandra, looking her most complacent, began to enumerate her signs and symptoms. The visitor listened, with that irrepressible air of distaste which is usual in the impregnably healthy when forced to listen to accounts of sickness, but with a genuine curiosity which caused her to ask many questions; thus prolonging the very thing that was causing her own distaste.

'And you say there was no actual stroke?' she inquired at last, when she had been told every detail Alexandra could remember.

'No — They say I just woke up one morning to find I couldn't get out of bed. And I never *have* since!' replied the invalid, in a tone of unmistakable pride.

Miss Young disregarded this, and seized upon the other curious point in this reply. ' "They say"? Do you mean that you yourself don't remember how it began?'

'No!' declared Alexandra, as indifferently as a child might confess to ignorance of some incident which happened so early in her infancy that it has left no imprint upon her brain.

'But don't you remember anything at all that happened which might have caused your illness?'

'No!' said Alexandra again, and now there had crept into her voice that faint suggestion of resentment usual to her when people pressed too closely into her past.

Peter broke in, remarking that Alexandra had forgotten a good deal of her life previous to her paralysis.

Iris Young turned her inquisitive eyes to him therefore. 'But *you* have not forgotten,' she said eagerly. 'Was there no violent grief, or fit of temper — some trouble, that upset her mind so much that her body took refuge, or revenge, in this way?'

Peter laughed dryly. On the faces of both brothers there now appeared a certain set, cold, stubborn look.

'*Some* trouble!' he said. 'There was nothing *but* trouble, all our lives, till then!'

Most people, embarrassed at having stirred up the mud of settled and clarified sorrows, would have murmured shamefacedly some polite regrets, and abandoned the subject. Iris Young still clung to it however. 'But was there no culminating trouble which might have caused this — well, *call* it paralysis?' she persisted.

Peter was showing signs of impatience, holding out to her the loosely tacked skirt of her costume, and waving his hand quite tyrannically towards the screen behind which customers retired to 'try-on'. Iris Young appeared to see neither skirt nor screen, but waited in an insistent silence, which at last forced him unwillingly to answer:

'We *did* think, at the time, that it had something to do with the death of our brother Nick. He died two days before Alexandra became ill, in a street accident. But the doctor pooh-poohed the idea. As he said, other girls' brothers die, but they don't become paralysed with grief!'

'That was very unintelligent of him — besides being cheaply cynical,' retorted Iris Young. 'Doubtless it is true on the whole. But surely your sister is different? Might not all this other trouble you speak of have so undermined her resistance that the shock of this brother's death was too much for her? A shock, you know, can have queer effects on the nervous system.'

There was an antagonistic silence, sensing which, in her forthright way, she remarked, 'It's very queer. The invalid was very eager to tell me all her symptoms. But all of you seem to resent any inquiry into the cause of it all!'

'Well,' said Sam, 'what's the *good* of raking it all up again now? Some things are best buried. It's plain Allie will never get better, after all this time. And she's quite happy. And so are we. What's the sense of remembering the time when we were *not*?'

'Perhaps your sister's cheerfulness is only one more symptom of her sickness!' suggested Iris Young.

But as to them this suggestion seemed so paradoxical that it must be nonsense, they did not reply.

She abandoned the problem, and seemed to concentrate her whole mind henceforth on the costume-fitting.

This visit left a rather different sediment behind it. As by the first visit of Iris Young, Alexandra was intensely stimulated, so that the image of that copper-helmet, the memory of that agreeably rough voice, and the leonine movement of those long lean thighs, haunted the room almost in physical form.

At the same time there was another, far less pleasant residue, a feeling of resentment, of petulant disappointment, which came from the realization that this brilliant creature had not admired her as she was used to being admired for her courage under her nine-year long affliction.

The only other person who had, like this Iris Young, expressed any disbelief in the genuineness of her paralysed state, was a queer woman with a voice like an adolescent boy's, and a hat like *Three Men in a Boat*, and a skirt down to her ankles.

Alexandra pretended to herself to see likenesses between that rude uncouth woman (named, she thought, Miss March) and the lovely, red-helmeted creature called Iris Young.

'I don't approve of women trying to look like men!' she told herself, recalling a sentiment of her brothers. And, silently, she mimicked and caricatured the deep masculine voice of Miss Young — urged by the instinct which people usually feel, to abuse the

66

object of their worship if that object seems to despise or to neglect them.

When Iris Young came for the third time, however, all this childishness, this humiliation, this petulant revenge, were forgotten in the intense pleasure of watching her again.

The day was another one of wedgwood blue skies, and piled masses of soft, wig-like clouds. And, as on her first appearance, Iris Young seemed remote, free of earthly trammels, her eyes wandering constantly to the window, as naturally as blue smoke spirals to its native element.

Suddenly Alexandra became conscious of the fact that in a few moments she would probably lose her, for ever.

In a sort of mental paralysis, she watched her in the new suit, pulling at the lapels, tweaking the skirt, striding to measure the width of its hem, looking down her shoulder and along her stretched-out legs, plunging her hands into the pockets and buttoning and unbuttoning the collar, then, satisfied, retiring behind the screen to take it off.

More and more frantic within, more and more paralysed without, she watched Sam bundling it — first in tissue paper and then in brown paper, watched his fingers play Hamlet with the string, but bring it all too soon to a triumphant knot.

More and more feverishly she searched the while for something to say which would keep Iris Young here a little longer — even a minute longer; but could think of not a single word, except the words 'Iris — Oh Iris! Don't go away!' These, even in her frantic state of mind, she realized to be unspeakable.

Iris Young tucked the parcel under her arm, drew on one glove, took her first stride towards the door.

At this — almost, but not quite too late, words leapt to Alexandra's lips.

'*What* is it like to fly, Miss Young?' she cried, her voice loud with her desperation. This was asked not from any interest in the answer. The words had formed themselves with no help from her will. They were produced by the sort of instinct which comes to the aid of a desperate woman determined to retain in her company, at whatever cost, a man who shows plain signs of finding it irksome.

Iris Young stopped, and came back to the bedside. 'So you *are* capable of an interest outside yourself?' she remarked curiously. Alexandra, too shaken to reply, nodded silently, whereupon the other smiled and sat down on her bed.

'What is it like to fly?' she said thoughtfully; then laughed a little. 'My goodness, that's a question if you like! It's like asking somebody, "What is it like to be in love?" At least — to me it is — perhaps because I *am* in love — with flying! But . . . what is it like?

'Well, I must admit, not in the least what I thought it would be. You see, you look up at the birds, and you envy and covet their lovely effortless floating and looping and soaring (or what you imagine to be effortless floating, for probably even birds don't fly without a terrific muscular effort) and you imagine that when you get up in a glider or an aeroplane it will feel exactly what the birds look like. But it isn't. You have to fight all the time — not physically, of course, but mentally.

'At least, in a glider you have to. I'm told that once a man has learnt to fly a plane it is almost boringly easy. I believe it is quite possible to read while the plane flies on in the course you have set it in. But a glider's different. You have to be on the qui vive the whole time. And that, I think, is the glory of it. You feel so absolutely alive — consciously alive. You feel as if you are really and truly in charge of yourself — it's a feeling of "I am master of my fate, the Captain of my — well no, not soul — but certainly of my body!" A very boastful, vainglorious feeling of course — but very satisfying. It's a feeling that civilized people can very rarely obtain — and — oh, you cannot imagine how exhilarating it is!

'Then there are other minor pleasures. It is a pretty sight to see a tilting white wing at either side of you (if you can spare the time to look!). You fancy it is the earth and not yourself that is tilting — like a huge slowly spinning top it seems. Then — seeing things diminished from above is very charming and fascinating. And I am told that the upper sides of the clouds are very strangely beautiful. But I haven't been above the clouds so far. I haven't done any real soaring yet. . . .'

Alexandra sat listening, and listening intently, to all this. Yet she scarcely heard a word that was said. What she did hear she mostly failed to understand. Like a lover, or a heroine-worshipping schoolgirl, she was too absorbed in her thrilling pride in the

68

thought that she was actually being spoken to by the object of her worship, that the goddess had come down from her glider in the clouds and was actually sitting on this bed, to attend to the full meaning of what the goddess was saying.

Perhaps this was detected eventually by Iris Young, for suddenly she broke off, laughed her rough-towelling laugh, and said:

'I should not talk like this. I shall be disturbing your, no doubt, hardly-won content!'

And she rose, and in another moment was gone.

CHAPTER II

FOR nine years Alexandra had been, from the point of view of her nurses, the perfect invalid; that is, she had been cheerful, docile, easily amused, with few wants and very few whims.

Now, almost overnight, she became the traditional invalid, morose, cantankerous, tyrannical, restless, easily bored, and full of inexplicable whims.

From now on she showed only a fitful, peevish interest in the life of Finn Street — that life which she had watched for nine years as if each new day of it had been a fresh scene in an everlasting drama. She showed as little interest in the comings and goings of customers, and still less in the pattern of her own daily life.

The change was very disconcerting to her nurses. They felt somewhat the same dismay as is felt by the parents of an infant who, up to a certain age, between six months and a year, has been 'as good as gold', eating, sleeping, and being bathed, with complete submission to the arbitrary rules of the world into which it is being initiated, but who then suddenly gives startling evidence of a will of its own. Like most parents, they much preferred the state of helpless docility and looked upon the first sproutings of self-will as so many signs of the original Adam — not perceiving that, however inconvenient to themselves, the growth of self-will is a necessary stage in any mental advance.

Alexandra herself was as far from understanding what was happening as her brothers were. She accepted their verdict upon her actions — and yet could do nothing to control those actions. But, like a very young child, she did not attribute this change to something within herself, but to a mysterious deterioration in all about her.

Finn Street now seemed, and to her infantile perceptions therefore *was*, a mean little street of dirty brick; housing dull and tiresome people; containing nothing of fresh interest for months at a time; hot and garbage-scented; and littered in the evening with ugly, shrill-voiced children. Sam was stupid, and Peter irritatingly precise. Their oddities, she came to the conclusion, were evidently hardening with age into positive vices. The customers were all exactly the same, and even the firelight shadow-shows were becoming stereotyped.

All these changes appeared to her to result not from a shifting in her own focus point, but from some unseen, malevolent power outside herself, directing its spite deliberately against her, and her alone. On the days when, through long hours spent lying or sitting in bed, her buttocks or shoulder-blades were sore, it was no longer the result of a simple physical cause, to be remedied by a bed-bath and talcum powder, but a torment deliberately devised by fiends especially adapted for the art, with long, lean, flame-tempered, skeleton-like claws tipped with fiery poison, claws whose malice dug deeper than the flesh they bruised and scratched, poisoning her whole system with their spite.

It is natural to return malice for malice. But as these devil fingers were invisible and impersonal, her returning malice had to find some other object. Frequently this was Sam or Peter. Thus, on these days of torment she no longer endured it all with her one-time admirable courage, but passed on her torment to her nurses, by demanding first to be placed upright, then to be laid down, now to be laid on her left, now out of bed and propped in her chair, now to be bathed; and whatever they did for her, complaining bitterly that they hurt her.

At such times, even the level-tempered Peter became exasperated with her. His more explosive twin was moved one day to smack her arm quite stingingly — a procedure which cured her for that day by its unexpectedness.

But the cause of her peevishness lay too deep for such correction to cure it permanently. Two days later she was behaving in exactly the same fashion. In other ways, too, she was like a growing child, this time a child at some later period. She began to exhibit shame and annoyance at the necessity for certain services which they performed for her. She also refused to have her face and hands washed for her, or her hair brushed, the irritability which had been confined to Sam, when doing her this service being now extended to Peter also.

When either approached her with a brush or sponge, she would fend it off with a frown and a quick infantile flush of anger.

'I *hate* to be touched!' she would cry rudely, and, like nurses with a self-willed child, they would be compelled to give way, even though her self-will was frequently the cause of a great deal of extra work, since her efforts usually ended in her spilling soapy water over the bed-clothes.

So much for external changes.

Internally, she existed for these five months in a condition of spiritual dyspepsia. Spurts of bilious-coloured malice leaped into her consciousness from some deep-seated internal manufactory. There was an obscure but incessant burning sensation somewhere in the middle of her, which continually puzzled her. Like the physical dyspeptic, she was eternally uncertain whether she had eaten too much or too little, whether this sensation was the result of undigested past experiences, or of craving for future experiences.

There was also a strange obscurity in her senses. The world appeared to her as if it had stepped back several paces. It seemed veiled from her eyes, as if by a net of those maddening little dancing specks of silver and green which appear when the liver is out of order; veiled from her ears by the din of some tremendous cataract secreted in her aural passages; and veiled from her touch by the chronic pins and needles of her new-found irritability.

All through the summer and autumn following the visit of that disturbing creature with the long eager thighs and the helmet of fire, Alexandra stared at the sky between the sooty coroneted chimney pots of Finn Street, partly in the acid petulance of surfeit, but partly with the obscure sensation of waiting for something, of craving, feebly and ambiguously, but incessantly, for something unknown, but glorious, to step out to her.

Nothing ever happened but the usual trivialities of summer; the shrieking lines of gossip hung across the street from morning to night, like festoons of smutty washing; the notes of children — piercing the garbage-dreaming air like works' sirens; a whip-like swish alternating with a soft thud, indicating that Molly Blackhurst was at her favourite pastime of skipping; the mystic counting game 'one ptairter, two ptairter, three ptairter, *four*! Five ptairter, six ptairter, seven ptairter, *more*!' — concluding with a vindictive feminine shriek 'Yourron!', the sudden spattering of nailed boots, followed by comparative silence with a single voice under the window muttering and gasping up to one hundred; then more excited shrieks; and sometimes a high-pitched, long-drawn, singing call of 'Arl een! Arl een!' on cuckoo-notes, signifying the end of the summer-evening's game; these were the scanty food offered for the appeasing of her ravening hunger for astonishment.

In previous summers this fare had contented her appetite for life, yet now it filled her with nothing but unreasonable and inexplicable fury — sulky, silent, ice-cold fury that caused her to refuse even to look into Finn Street, or even to make the small effort necessary to lie and listen to sounds. On one such day of cold sulking she suddenly asked Sam to bring her a mirror. It was a request unprecedented in all her nine years of invalidism. Indeed, at first Sam could not think how to gratify this new outlandish whim. There were two big mirrors in the house, but they were fixed, one over the mantelpiece, the other in the wardrobe door. After some searching however he found an old cracked and mildewed hand-mirror of his mother's.

'Here you are, Miss Vanity!' he said, throwing it into her lap rather spitefully, for she had kept him from an urgent piece of work.

She took it up, ungraciously, and, for the first time for nine years, looked at herself.

To look in a mirror is always a surprising experience, even to those who look in one very frequently. The mirror image of a face never quite tallies with the impression built up by living inside it, looking out through its mask. A fairly accurate knowledge of the front and sides of the body can be obtained without a mirror, but the face, being necessarily hidden from its owner, is comparatively unknown territory. Frequent visits will wear away to some extent the discrepancy between the real and the imagined face, but there usually persists enough of the discrepancy to make each visit to the mirror a surprise.

Surprise however is far too mild a term for Alexandra's reactions on this her first meeting with her own face for nine years.

Out of the dull, speckly circle of glass there looked up at her a face that was pale, heavy in shape, a square rounded off at the corners, with a low, upright forehead, and black emphatic eyebrows, very much overhanging the eye-sockets, and shaped harshly in a series of jerks. The nose of this face was wide, and the lines running from its corners outlining the cheeks were sullen in a childish way. Its mouth was very full and red, set also in sullen lines. Its upper lip was rather comically short, the distance between the nostrils and the lips being less than half an inch — giving a curious look of childish distress. Its eyes were black, large, hot and heavy. Its hair, black and shining like newly-broken coal, was parted in the centre, looped back at the ears, falling again in a thick plait over each shoulder.

Alexandra was amazed, bewildered, repelled and absorbed in wonder at this face. What she had expected to see she could not have said. But it was certainly nothing like this.

Infatuated, though not in admiration, she bent over the image for the rest of the afternoon, gazing into those strange, heavy, tar-black eyes, so still, and yet so evasive, so magnificently liquid, yet seeming as if their real power were shut off by an invisible film. Those eyes, she felt, were hiding; hiding some secret from the world, and hiding themselves behind that invisible film. Whatever change came over the rest of that square, mobile mask, those eyes, which in most masks are the sole living things, seemed most mask-like of all — secret, unchanging, like disks of dark velvet, two small dominoes concealing a somehow frightening personality.

When Alexandra broke silence for the first time since she had demanded the mirror, it was to make a fresh demand.

'Sam! — get me some hairpins, will you?' she said in her new, tyrannical invalid voice.

Sam pushed an exasperated hand through his curls. 'What the dickens do you think *I* should want with hairpins! And, anyway, what do *you* want with hairpins. You've managed without such things very well so far!'

'I'm twenty-two! It's time I put my hair up!' said Alexandra sullenly, lifting her heavy plaits and twisting them one each way round her head, like a double-stranded crown.

The effect gave her a deep satisfaction, and also increased her restlessness. 'You *must* get me some hairpins!' she repeated imperiously.

Sam blew down his nose noisily like an impatient dog. 'Very well, miss spoilt! But you'll have to wait till I go out next time, and you'll have to pin it up yourself. Peter's enough to do without turning lady's hairdresser!'

'I don't *want* him to!' retorted Alexandra, and again in a voice new to her brothers — a voice of rude, childish independence.

She had her way. Henceforth, she laboriously pinned up her own hair in a heavy crown every morning.

The summer passed by, and in the heart of it there lay always that ambiguous discomfort, either of hunger or of surfeit. The hot garbage-and-dust smell peculiar to Finn Street air in July and August wafted in at the top of the window day after day. An occasional bee, and many bluebottles, came burring against the window-pane like miniature aeroplanes. Once or twice they adventured into the room, and then they burred and zoomed and blundered about the walls seeming like tiny symbols of her own restless, futile hunger. In the distance she could hear tramcars, dragging what sounded like heavy lengths of iron chains along the main road. These also, with the long, husky alto wail of trains, seemed like an expression of something in herself.

The grimy washing-lines of the women's gossip sagged in the listless air. The children dragged their boots in the peppery dust, trailing listlessly from hot stuffy homes to hot stuffy school-rooms and back again, four times a day.

Every evening the swallows screeched in the sky like whistling kettles. And sometimes Alexandra could see their young ones poking their bunched heads out of the nests under the gutters, peering this way and that as if looking along the street for that anonymous glory that Alexandra too was expecting. It was the hottest summer that Alexandra ever remembered. Her brothers

74

worked all day with their collars off, and their shirts unbuttoned, tucked back at the necks to show their potato-coloured chests. And Alexandra hated them, because they were not burned with her acid restlessness, but sat patiently, panting only with the heat, their spectacled eyes and minds bent docilely over their interminable work.

It must be conceded that they were justified. They cut their spiritual coats according to their meagre cloth. They expected nothing; and they received nothing; Alexandra expected and longed for heaven knows what; and she also received nothing. It exasperated her the more to see how their patience seemed so much more meet to the occasion than her own impatience.

The only outstanding event of this dreary summer was a dream. It was a night in August, when stars were beginning to come into their own again, as the blackness of the autumn dark deepened as a ground for them. Alexandra, as usual, lay awake often until five o'clock in the morning. But whereas until now she had watched the long, slow-turning arches of those stars with placid, unwearying eyes, it was now a torment to her to lie awake so long. She craved sleep with an intensity which mounted with every wakeful hour to the pitch of despairing tears. Wearing herself out, not so much by lack of sleep as by her frantic efforts to attain it, she would sink into it exhausted at last, and wake, nearly as exhausted, three hours later, to find it day again. For the first time in her nine years she began to dream. And during the day, she would continually be coming across broken fragments of these dreams, and would pick them up, turn them over, and wonder what sort of creatures they had been when whole, and from what mysterious depths they had come.

Most of her dreams were of common things. But this particular dream was so strange and so terrifying, and so beautiful, that it remained in her mind in its entirety when she awoke, not smashed into intriguing fragments like the majority of her dreams.

She had been sitting on the neck of a huge white bird, one leg hanging each side of its head. Sensation was so clear that she could feel the softness and warmth of its feathers, and of the body under those feathers, against the inside of her thighs.

Looking to right and left, she could see the huge white wings wafting lazily, and the air fluffing gently at the edge of its wing-plumes. A gentle breeze smoothed back her own hair from her temples and forehead. The bird was flying right over the town. Looking down Alexandra could see, as small as toys, but very clear, and without perspective, row upon row of Finn Streets, all exactly like her own Finn Street, all of dull mulberry brick, with brown doors, iron railings, yellow-ochred steps, with coroneted sooty chimneys out of every one of which floated a rag of violet-coloured smoke.

At every door in this toy town stood a woman staring up under her shading hand at Alexandra, and the magnificent white bird she rode. One house was a school; and as she drifted above this, the children all put their heads out of the windows like bunches of baby swallows, and screamed at her. One of the boys threw a blue cap up at her, and the bird caught it in its beak and tossed it still higher, right over a cloud.

'I would rather *fly*, than *dream* of flying!' it remarked in a voice agreeably rough, like a good towel. And with that it turned upside-down, and Alexandra began to fall off its back. It was a ghastly fall. Through clouds made of whipped white of egg, and a sky of wedgwood blue, she fell, lying horizontally on the air, and twirling over and over like a rolling-pin.

She fell at asphyxiating speed, yet for so long that it must have been a gradual fall. Whether gradual or not, she felt as if her guts were being unravelled and sent streaming from her stomach up into the clouds. At last she touched earth. But it was not earth after all, but something soft, feathered, warm, and smelling putrid. It was her bird, she found. But, by the smell of decay, it must be dead. That no doubt was why it had turned upside-down. She struggled frantically to rise from this disgustingly smelly feather-bed, but something held her back.

Sweating horribly, she gradually awoke — to a universal and utter darkness, and worse, and most unusual with her, to utter disorientation. The terror of waking and not knowing where the door is, where the window, where the bed, or even which way up one is lying, had been virtually unknown to Alexandra, who used to sleep so lightly. She struggled therefore, almost hysterically, to set this dislocation right.

At last her world was righted. She was lying on her left side; the

76

window was behind her, the door at her feet, the fireplace at her head, the table where her brothers worked in front of her, the ceiling above her, and the floor below her. These things set in their places again, she sighed with deep relief, wiped her sweating face and neck with a corner of the sheet, and began to think over her strange dream. But presently, as the light crept out in a grey patch on the wall opposite, a baffling sensation of something that was still wrong began to creep into her consciousness. Something was still dislocated. A very early cyclist purred softly by, and stimulated by this sound, the vague feeling of dislocation clarified into the thought, 'Oughtn't I to be *facing* the window?'

She pondered long upon the idea, concluding, over and over again, that she must have been mistaken. She lay on her left side now. Therefore she must have been laid on her left side last night. For it was of course impossible for her to turn of her own accord. That was a proved fact. But still her mind persisted in remembering, or misremembering, that she had been laid on her *right* side last night.

Sam and Peter made no comment on her position when they came down that morning. Her memory was evidently at fault therefore. Yet still, timidly, fainter and fainter, it persisted in its mistaken impression that when she went to sleep she had faced the window, not the room.

The obvious way to solve the mystery, which troubled her for many days afterwards, was by asking Sam or Peter. Yet somehow she could not bring herself to do so.

Nor did she speak to anyone, for nearly two years afterwards, about her strange dream of the white bird.

CHAPTER III

SEPTEMBER came, and October and November, and still nothing had happened to justify this new discontent of Alexandra's. And gradually through continual fasting, her hunger died down to a vague, fretful despondency — a new mood less troublesome physically to her nurses than her summer mood of tyrannies and sudden passionate whims, but more worrying to them mentally, as

77

she was subject to long fits of weeping, for apparently no cause at all. For hours at a time she would sit staring through a fog of slow-welling tears at the eternal flat façade of sad-coloured brick with its crests of jagged, sooty chimneys and its dispirited yellow steps. She never spoke of passers-by, or of the five families who lived behind that sad façade. What interest she had for anything was now kept for the sky, clouds and birds. But even here her interest was tepid.

To have vivid interest in any part of nature it is necessary to have some practical contact with it. The farmer, the sailor, the airman, the poet, the painter, the novelist, the explorer, the 'hiker', the picnicker, all have this practical point of contact which quickens the eye for the shape and quality of clouds, winds, birds, and landscape generally.

But how could Alexandra, incapable even of taking an afternoon stroll and thus endangering a new hat, possibly have any deep interest in these things? She gazed past the chimney-pots, therefore, in the desultory, languid fashion of passengers in trains looking through their windows at moving landscapes with which they have no concern whatever.

Her faculty for idle, rootless observation had been cultivated by her strange life however, and she noted, without attaching any meaning to the facts, the change from flat thin bluish clouds, pasted like coloured tissue paper on to a flat blue sky, to the solid sculptured clouds of September, and thence to the fleecy, grey wool pelt that completely covered the blue in October, with many exceptions of course, with the frequent harking back and looking forward to other seasons characteristic of English weather.

Bees and bluebottles thrummed against the window less and less. The screams of children and swifts filled the evenings for shorter and shorter periods, but grew more strident and more frenzied as they shortened. Then for a week she noticed a party of swallows lined up on a telegraph wire that ran obliquely across the street, pegged along it neatly like a row of little navy-blue socks hung out to dry. There they collected at intervals for seven or nine days, twiddling their long wings and tails, and arguing incessantly. Then one day she suddenly noticed that they no longer came to argue on the wire.

78

About the same time the children sang 'Arl een!' for the last time, and the rainy and foggy days of November began.

The day on which the miracle happened was the last day on which you would have expected anything of its kind.

It was a day of thin fog — a cold, yellow, sooty-smelling fog, through which the brick wall opposite looked the colour of bad meat. All sounds were lacking in resonance. The faces of passers-by looked like the faces of sick Chinamen. Their hair lay flat with damp over their temples.

When Winifred came with the washing, even she appeared to be affected by the dismal air. Her laugh rang like a cracked cup. The front crisps of her hair were dank, and dewed with discoloured drops of fog-water. Even the indomitable side-curl did not spring to her cheek with its usual resilience.

When she had gone Alexandra felt even more dispirited. Before the afternoon was over she had sunk into one of her long fits of silent, slow-welling tears. These continued to gather and trickle down her face until teatime, when a sort of muffled foggy cheerfulness returned to her. Teatime was always the best hour of a November day. Then the sad, sick Chinaman-coloured fog would be tinted by the gaslight to the colour and texture of blue chiffon. Behind it for a brief space the bricks opposite would be unsubstantial, indigo shadows. Still further lessening their reality came squares of firelight where the windows should be — some quite still, like squares of golden candied peel, others pulsing fitfully like warm agitated hearts.

Looking out of a window upon such a scene, it was possible once more to hope for something impossible to happen.

With this idea vaguely in mind, Alexandra besought her brothers to prolong the enchanted hour, by having tea by firelight and leaving the curtains undrawn. As they had noticed, with distress but no comments, her fit of silent and spiritless weeping during the afternoon, they consented.

Nibbling without appetite at her bread and jam, she sat with her eyes fixed mournfully upon the window-squares of golden candied peel, and ached for her nameless miracle. For the hundredth time she was disappointed. One by one the magical squares of firelight were dimmed by the sudden flaring of greenish yellow gaslight in each room. This woman and that came to each window and twitched the curtains across. Now there were only patches of tinted fog — foggy blue, foggy brown, foggy yellow, according to the curtain-colour, with here and there a pin-prick of light where the stuff was worn to a hole. Presently even these muddy colours were smudged out completely by the raw damp night. And at last their own green plush curtain was drawn, and there existed only a room with flowered, faded wall-paper, a pomponed mantel-frill, austere wooden chairs and table, plush-framed photographs, a pair of blue and white porcelain boys, and dangling pink glass prisms, all of which had never changed their positions by half an inch ever since she could remember — a room, therefore, in which nothing could *ever* change.

Alexandra relapsed once more into despair, and stared at her industrious brothers, side by side, cross-legged on their table, their heads bent and almost identical from this viewpoint.

And suddenly it seemed to her as if they might as well be the pair of blue and white porcelain boys on the mantelpiece — might as well be their own table or chairs — might as well never exist at all. Did they never want anything beyond their needles and their thimbles and their eating and their going to bed and their getting up again? Did they never weary of the days that followed one after the other like soldiers in uniform? Did they never stare across the dreary street or up at the shifting, restless flocks of the clouds, and ache for something nameless but unimaginably splendid to come by? Had they ever even wept in the whole length of their busy, futile lives? Gradually her exasperation gathered pace, until she wanted to scream at them, to leap out of bed, to take them by the hair and shake them, until their heads were splitting.

A sound from beyond the drawn plush curtains caught her attention. It was a sound rare in Finn Street, the sound of music — the sound of *original* music that is. Wirelesses and gramophones were common enough. But in fresh, first-hand music Finn Street was poverty-stricken. It was too poor to attract street musicians, who naturally will only display their talents in streets where coppers may be expected; and on the other hand not poor enough for the visitations of the Salvation Army.

The high, sweet but husky notes of trumpets, which now reached Alexandra's ears were, therefore, as powerful in effect as a few drops of raw spirits upon the unaccustomed drinker. She could trace no tune at first, but only impudent sparks of sound.

Other, non-musical noises, made a kind of sibilant background to these, noises which Alexandra could not liken to the sea because she had never heard the sea, nor to wind in full-fledged trees, which, if she had ever heard, she had forgotten these nine years. The only sound they resembled in her experience was the rustling of lining sateen, but these sounds were far more vast, more elemental, more deeply exciting, than the noise of textiles. She was sharply aware of the difference.

As the leaping trumpet notes came clearer, less broken, more coherently joined into melodic pattern, this sibilance gathered in body and depth. Now doors in Finn Street began to fling open. Shrill women's voices interrupted the trumpet patterns. One or two people went running past the shuttered window. The commotion had roused Sam and Peter by now. Sam was listening with his mouth ajar; Peter had removed his spectacles, as if to improve his hearing, and sat holding them before him like a lecturer answering a very knotty question.

Other sounds were contributory to the mainstream of noise now; the sharp, ripping sounds of trombones; the shrill swallow-like shrieks of fifes; the brassy whine of cornets; the deep moo of a tuba; the drill of small drums; the rhythmic boom of a big drum; and, background to all these distinct, musical sounds, a hollow, toneless sound, pulsing, like the rhythmic fall of handfulls of pebbles, together with a louder development of that first distant sibilance, which was now distinctly human in character, and in which could be detected separate voices, rising gustily as if lost in the flarings of a wind.

Steadily the uproar increased in weight, and in distinctness, and in the marking of its rhythm. More and more sounds in the confused murmurous background seemed to step out to join in the insistence of the main rhythm. But there was always more confused background to take their place.

Whatever was making this unprecedented uproar, Alexandra judged, must be going along the main road at the bottom of Finn

Street. What — oh what could it be? Something evidently of unbearable glory, for the excitement in Finn Street surpassed anything
she had ever heard in all her nine years of listening. Women were
chattering like hordes of jackdaws and rooks, children screamed as if
they were being scalded, men shouted as if somebody was fighting;
and all were rushing madly down Finn Street to the main road.
A tram ground down the main road, and for a moment its brutal
voice suppressed even the steady torrent of inexplicable sound and
excitement. When the tram had passed the torrent was so startlingly
loud that Alexandra realized that whatever it was, was coming
down Finn Street itself.

'Oh Sam! Peter! *What* is it?' she cried. But before the words
were finished the pair were off the table in a concerted leap and were
standing at the open door, so absorbed themselves in watching whatever was coming down the road that they neither heard nor answered
her.

'Brash! brash! brash! brash!' came the sound, closer and closer.
Suddenly she knew out of some forgotten knowledge in a previous
existence that it was the sound of many shoes striking the cobbles,
approximately, but not precisely, together. A word leaped up in
her mind — out of the same forgotten life.

'It's a procession!' she said aloud. Trombones ripped the world
into scarlet tatters of glory; trumpets pierced it with silver lightning; human laughter fell like an orgy of smashed crockery; human
tongues bubbled and roared like rain-water in turgid gutters; and
now a new sound lurched in and out of all the old ones; a voice in a
megaphone, which, like all megaphone voices, came out blurred,
distorted, enormous and quite senseless.

In her mind Alexandra cried out to Sam to carry her to the door.
But her throat made not a sound. It seemed like a dry stick of wood.
Her heart was thudding like a live animal inside her. Suddenly she
found herself sobbing loudly, not from distress, not even with the
rage of impotence, but from sheer excitement, unbearable excitement, engendered by the direct impact of this magnificent uproar
upon her ignorant mind. Confusedly she felt that the whole world
was in surging, boiling, brass-lunged revolution. Everything in the
world was churning past that darkened window — but she must lie
in bed, unable even to see it pass.

82

'Sam! Sam! Peter! Peeeter!' she sobbed in the agony of her frustrated longing. But they paid no attention. They were down on the second step, prevented from seeing her by the inward-swinging door, and from hearing her by the 'brash-brash-brash-brash' of feet, the leaping, husky, intoxicated notes of trumpets, the blurred roar of the megaphone voice, the high eunuch-whine of cornets, and the boom of the drum beating like the noise of a multitude's communal heart.

Her torment was driving all reason out of her.

'Sam! Saaam!' she yelled again. But again they could not, or would not, hear her. And suddenly she began to scream and to bounce in her bed with convulsive arching movements of her back, like a baby convulsed with rage at repeated frustrations of its will.

For a second or two she was blind — all but unconscious. She was nothing but the paroxysms of her rage. When she again became comparatively conscious, she discovered herself on the floor beside the bed. Even now, however, she was scarcely a quarter-conscious. She knew only what she wanted. She was certainly quite deaf now to the uproar outside. Yet this uproar was the unnoticed driving force behind her as she dragged her body, trailing its shrunken, all but useless legs behind her, in an agony of sweat and heart-thuds, across the limitless flat world of worn linoleum.

Writhing like a cut worm, sobbing for breath, pulling with all her arms' strength at the table legs, and the legs of her bed, and, though she was unaware of it, pushing, very feebly, against the ground with her thighs and knees, she reached her goal at last, collapsed on the doorstep, and lay, greasy with sweat, panting like an exhausted dog, her nightdress ripped across the thighs by her dragging progress, her thick plaits loosened, one looped like a black halter round her throat, the other trailing over the doorstep. She could see nothing for some seconds. Her sight was blacked out by the violent pulse of blood into her head. Then, for the space of a moment her sight cleared. She saw rank upon rank of dark figures — their legs swinging in syncopated time with the 'brash-brash-brash-brash' of their boots upon the granite sets; their faces jumping yellow and black in the fitful light of the naked torches they held before them as they marched. Other gamboge and black faces, carved grotesquely by the leaping flares, looked out of bedroom

83

windows or from the opposite steps. The small prancing shapes of little boys and girls flickered alongside of the dark mass of synchronized figures with their bouquets of fire. . . .

Her sight went out. A second later her consciousness failed also. The brothers, absorbed with the fervour of simplicity in the marching of the torchbearers, stood staring down Finn Street, unaware that at their backs a miracle had taken place.

Even when the torchlight procession had passed by, and, released from their spell, they turned to go back to their work, they did not recognize the bedraggled, unconscious figure sprawled across the top step as the central figure in a miracle. They mistook it for something they were much more familiar with — a calamity.

But Alexandra knew better. When she came back to the world of Finn Street, she found it once more sane, silent, apparently arranged in the immemorial fashion. But she knew that it was changed forever for her. Somehow — she argued, lying in a freshly made bed, her clean nightdress covering a newly washed and powdered body that felt limp and bruised as if beaten all over with rubber truncheons — somehow, she had transported herself out of this bed to that door.

How she had gone she did not know. But as it is impossible even to writhe along the ground without using at least the upper muscles of the legs, then it was clear that she was not, after all, so helpless as she had assumed herself to be.

The peculiar thing was that this discovery somehow failed to astound her as it should have done. It seemed as natural to her mind as a forgotten name seems, once it has returned. 'Of course!' was the unacknowledged response of her secret mind, 'I knew all the time!' And now she remembered the strange, persistent illusion she had had after that terrible dream — that she had turned in the night. Was it, after all, an illusion?

The conviction that she had after all proved capable of self-movement once, if not twice, gave rise to the timid corollary that she might perhaps move again. She found herself making feeble, almost imperceptible, movements with her legs as she lay in bed.

What had been accomplished in a hundred seconds under the compelling excitement of the torchlight procession, and, perhaps, under the anaesthetic of sleep, was not to be repeated, in cold blood, by conscious will-power, in less than a hundred days. Nevertheless, in a hundred days or so, it *was* repeated. Dr. Stuart, who had retired baffled from her case nearly eight years ago, was now summoned again, and suggested a graded series of exercises which she followed, and which eventually restored to her the power to walk across the room to a chair and sit down in it unaided.

After this her progress was much more rapid. In a few more months she was able to walk anywhere on the ground floor. And in just under a year the stairs were conquered, and the whole house was her kingdom. The bed that had been the centre of her world for nine years was banished from the ground floor. A third easy chair was bought to take its place. She slept now, like ordinary people, upstairs in a bedroom.

But there was one curious feature of this miraculous recovery which she herself accepted, however, as perfectly natural. This was that her life previous to the nine years of her paralysis was still shut off as if by a high wall from her present memory. The cause of her paralysis was, therefore, still as much of a mystery as her recovery was a miracle.

PART THREE

CHAPTER I

In little more than twelve months after the inception of her miracle, Alexandra had ceased to be grateful for it. Doubtless Lazarus showed no gratitude, after a time, for being brought back to this life from the blessed peace of the grave. Doubtless Jairus's daughter gave no thanks for being miraculously enabled once more to minister to her father and mother. Dr. Freud or one of his myriad of pupils assures us that the child yearns nostalgically for the warmth and comfort of the womb, and certainly the world must seem at first a poor substitute for those cramped but cosy quarters.

Similarly Alexandra soon began to look back with a certain nostalgia to her warm comfortable bed (she forgot now the bed-sores and the boredom), to the firelight shadow-shows after everybody else had gone to bed, to the satisfaction of being the centre of her world, of lying static, like the medieval earth, while the sun and the moon and the stars and all Finn Street revolved about her for her benefit and delight. Her new-found freedom, once the excitement of attaining it was over, seemed not to add to her happiness. On the contrary it seemed to wash out the intensity of her interest in events. Now that she could walk into the kitchen and see Sam at work there, there was no fascination in listening to his juggling with the pans. Now that she could walk to the door if she liked and see the whole of any passers-by, walking the whole length of Finn Street, there was no fascination in guessing their lower quarters by their heads. Upstairs was no longer an undiscovered country. The world seemed to have shrunk by the increase in her freedom to go about in it — a phenomenon common to all expansions in locomotion, but always surprising to the disappointed innovators.

By the end of her second January she began to feel almost as bored as she had done immediately before the miracle happened — a state of mind assisted, perhaps, by a falling off in the number of her visitors. At first they had come almost daily, as to the site of a fallen meteor, or to a bomb-crater, or a house where there has been

86

a murder. People who had never thought about her in her nine years of invalidism came now, their curiosity barely cloaked in kindliness. One or two doctors came from professional curiosity, and a few journalists from local papers from a different professional curiosity.

The Reverend Revell came from a third species of professional curiosity, but from a more personal interest also. For he felt that perhaps after all his prayers had played some part in the working of this miracle, though he was too modest and, fundamentally, too sceptical, to claim the credit for it openly. But by the end of a year Alexandra was near enough to normality to cease to be an object of interest to anyone, even to the Reverend Revell. This indifference, after excessive interest, naturally added to her discontent, which arose, however, chiefly from deeper causes than that of snubbed vanity.

In this mood of discontent she was lying on her bed one afternoon, in the second February after her recovery, when she heard footsteps stop at the door below; a knock, and then the sound of the door being opened and somebody stepping in.

Suddenly she sat upright. Somebody was speaking in the room below, in a voice low-pitched, and agreeably rough, stimulating to the nerves like a rough towel to the skin. The next minute she was hurrying downstairs. She still had to bring both feet together on each stair before lowering herself to the next. Nevertheless, she reached the bottom in a remarkably short time, and flinging open the door to the living-room, stepped forward, crying, 'Miss Young! Oh Miss Young! I *knew* it was you!'

Iris Young turned and smiled. 'Oh — hullo!' she responded. 'I was just being told about your wonderful recovery. You *do* look well.'

It was true. Alexandra had lost by now much unhealthy fat about her shoulders and stomach. Her figure, built in a sturdy concentrated style, was attractive because suggestive of immense stores of vitality, only just begun to be tapped. Such vitality is usually to be seen only in schoolgirls of sixteen or so, and is then offset by the willowy, fragile build of youth. But in Alexandra it was combined with the lines of maturity, with very unusual effect. There was the same change in her face. Broad, black-browed and square-jawed, it was a face built either for complacency or for excessive passions. Complacency had sagged its lines for nine years. Now it was quickened and fined, as she smiled eagerly at the visitor, by a passion of admiration.

'Yes — you really *do* look wonderfully well!' repeated Iris Young, after staring in the cool leisurely fashion peculiar to her. 'I see you've put your hair up too!' she added. 'It looks magnificent. It looks just as if it were carved out of coal! Just that glitter and weight — I don't know when I've seen hair so utterly black!' She turned abruptly from Alexandra and continued with her interrupted explanation of her requirements. It seemed that she had torn the skirt of the costume they had made for her a year last June, and had come back hoping they could find a piece of the material to mend it invisibly.

Alexandra stood watching her intently, confused by two opposing feelings, one a sensation of having found at last her home on earth, lost aeons ago, and sought forever since, the other an immense astonishment at something unique, something visitant from another and more radiant world. She noted every detail of this being's movements — vividly as if they came from her own flesh — the quick sensitive bucklings of the long upper lip as she spoke; the way she shook her head every now and then, as if to shake back an annoying lock from her face, although her hair was as perfectly polished as the hair of a bronze statue. She noted, too, with the microscopic eye of a lover, every detail of her texture — the golden down on her temples and chin, the faint bluish shadows of her concave cheeks, her pale stubble-like eyelashes, the greenish-brown freckles spangling the bridge of her nose.

At the same time, she experienced a distressing sensation of not being able to see clearly enough, as if some invisible veil hung between them. She longed to snatch this down, yet could not. She did not know that the veil was created by her own passionate desire to be closer to this wonderful being than it is ever possible for one being to be to another.

Presently Peter ran upstairs to search in his 'piece-box' for a scrap of the cloth she wanted. Iris Young turned back to Alexandra, looking her over with her characteristic half-smile of unoffending curiosity.

'Well — and what do you think of the world nowadays?' she

asked, with a faint suggestion of mockery which puzzled Alexandra and made her uneasy.

'I haven't seen it all yet!' she answered. 'I've only been to the end of Finn Street.'

Iris Young tossed back the non-existent lock of hair and laughed. 'Why? — How unenterprising of you!' she exclaimed. 'Or is it that your *legs* are unenterprising? Perhaps they're not strong enough for much yet?'

'Of course they're strong enough!' cried Alexandra, with sudden childlike indignation, 'but Dr. Stuart said I wasn't to go out of Finn Street without somebody going with me. And Sam and Peter haven't had time to go out with me yet!'

The older woman stared in silence for a while. The wording and manner of this reply had made her realize the anomaly before her. Here was a creature who combined the narrow experience (but eager thirst for experience) of a child, with the body of an adult woman, and with the uncertain, ill-directed passions of an adolescent. It would be interesting to watch the reactions of this queer creature to the modern world — or what part of the modern world was to be seen in Colebridge. It would be rather like conducting a survivor of the present about the world of 2000, in one of those Utopian stories — more amusing in fact, seeing that the guide in this case had no moral or political axe to grind on the way.

Ten minutes later, therefore, Alexandra stood with Iris Young at the foot of the steps, laughing up into the anxious faces of Peter and Sam, who hovered on the top step, as nervous as a couple of foster hens watching a duckling topple into its native element.

'Goodbye,' she laughed excitedly, and forgot them the moment her back was turned on them.

As they set off, Iris Young made as if to draw Alexandra's arm through her own. She snatched it away. 'I don't need *that*!' she cried, passionately independent.

They walked down the street separately therefore, and rather slowly, going at Alexandra's pace. After a moment Alexandra looked back at the house they had left: 'Do you know, Miss Young,' she said confidingly, 'I was terribly disappointed when I saw the outside of our house for the first time!'

Iris frowned, thinking the girl was in need of flattery to soothe some snobbery or other about her surroundings.

'It's no worse than the others,' she told her, rather uncomfortably, for she disliked giving flattery, but also disliked giving wounds to the vanity of others, however stupid the vanity seemed to her.

'Yes! I know,' persisted the girl, 'but that's just it. I thought it would be quite different. It gave me a shock — the same as when I looked in the mirror and saw what *I* looked like from the outside!'

At this Iris looked round at her in quickened interest. There was more in this anomaly of a creature than she had thought, it seemed. 'I see now what you were driving at!' she apologized. 'To see our house as others see it! as the poet didn't say! By the way,' she added, 'don't call me Miss Young. It reminds me of school. Call me Iris.'

'School?' said Alexandra blankly. But at this point they reached the main road, and a gawky, rectangular-visaged vehicle with a high, intellectual, but stupid red forehead containing one Cyclopian eye, came shuddering towards them.

'Oh! a tram! Oh let's have a ride!' cried Alexandra eagerly — and 'let's go upstairs, shall we? I always like it best upstairs!' The tram, grinding its teeth like an exasperated dragon, came to a stop, and allowed them to mount its platform. Thence they climbed, with some difficulty, the twisted stairs. Alexandra's lively delight in this exploit brought back to the older woman her twenty-year distant childhood, when those twisted stairs had seemed, as they still seemed to Alexandra, the spiral stairs of a castle turret, leading to scenes of romantic adventure; when the lurchings of a tram had seemed like the lurching of a sportive father pretending to be a monster shaking you from its back, to which you clung with shrieks of merriment and pretended terror. The tram was one of the oldest models in Colebridge. The centre of it was covered, but the ends were open and ringed by one long curved wooden seat with holes punched in it as if it were a hardened crumpet. Alexandra made straight for the front end. It was not until they were seated there, Alexandra sideways, her arm thrown over the brass rail, and her face hanging over like a black and cream sunflower, that a thought suddenly occurred to Iris.

90

'So you remember *trams* at any rate?' she remarked. Alexandra turned her broad sunflower face. 'No!' she said hesitatingly, 'I don't remember ever being on one before!'

'Then how did you know you liked the top best?'

'Oh — I dunno! I just *knew*!' replied Alexandra aggravatingly. She refused to consider the matter further, being too enthralled in looking down on the street.

There was, thought Iris, something grotesque in the extreme — yet at the same time something magnificent — about a tram's progress. It was like a cardboard stage monster come alive. Shuddering epileptically, pitching longitudinally like a boat, bouncing you on your seats like a couple of marionettes, hurling your ribs against the brass rail, it nevertheless managed to retain somehow a certain stateliness, possessing an almost medieval power to disregard its own absurdity.

As alive as Iris to all these sensations, Alexandra was unable to capture them in words and was, therefore, hopelessly entangled by them.

Over the brass rail that lurched against her open mouth with a violence sufficient to knock out her front teeth, she stared down bewitched into the gorge of the street. It was narrow, containing only one track, with an occasional pass-loop. The February sun was unable to reach the bottom of it, so that the lower half of the walls of the gorge were dark and solid, while the top half was unsubstantial, as if composed of pale gold and violet smoke. Windows in this upper layer flashed in her eyes as they hurtled past. And down in the dark bottom of the canyon, people, slightly diminished, and therefore made more lovable, swarmed ceaselessly and without apparent purpose. Sometimes they crossed in front of the tram, and then it would roar, shake its head at them, stamp a metallic foot 'Clang *Clang*!' and cause them to scurry fearfully out of its way.

The conductor came clattering up the stairs. Iris paid the fare, and this seemed quite natural to Alexandra.

The trolly clashed over their heads, making a bright green flare, translucent against the pale sunset clouds. Then Alexandra, leaning over her rail, watched the conductor run out in front of the monster, and poke the lines into position for the manœuvring of it round a corner. Off they lurched again, with a jerk which knocked her chin up and made her bite her tongue. A few minutes later came the terminus. Alexandra sighed deeply.

'Ah well!' she said in mixed regret and gratitude, as they climbed down the stairs, no longer an exploit, because they no longer lurched. 'Ah well, it was a lovely ride!'

Iris laughed, and agreed with her. Quickened by the intensity of interest shown by the girl, a mere means of transport had been transformed even for Iris into an adventure.

'I think I'll take you to the market first,' she said, drawing Alexandra's arm once more within her own. This time it was not snatched away, for Alexandra felt a little intimidated by the number of people she now saw about her. With her arm pressed firmly against Iris's warm ribs, however, she felt sheltered. From this shelter she was able to look out, giving her whole mind to the novel scenes about her. As they walked along, the first items of interest were the shop windows. These her eyes devoured without system, without personal or ulterior interest. Iris's eyes, for instance, went instinctively to the clothing shops. The eyes of the house-keeping women went to those containing food.

But Alexandra's eyes went equally to the electricity showroom windows, where a cardboard housewife, all smiles and check pinafore, demonstrated the pleasant results of cooking without looking; to a chemist's window, where a grimacing, bronzed young man, also of cardboard, perpetually stropped a safety razor, showing how to save and yet still shave; to a grocer's window, piled with red ball-cheeses like polished red ivory, jars of trans-lucent jams, and pyramids of dried fruit; to a U.C.P. restaurant, where a plump black cat was dozing between a dish of creamy tripe and a plate of scarlet tomatoes; and to a long window behind which a fat pink man, a sporty gentleman, a dapper man in pin-striped trousers, and a little boy in a blue hairy tweed suit, all stood about in absurd attitudes, all pink and smiling fatuously in the conscious-ness of their new clothes.

She perceived after a while that they were made of wax, and that they had been clothed by 'Everyman's Tailor'. She supposed contemptuously that the suits were so badly made that no living person would wear them, and so they had to put them on dolls.

They were now approaching the market place. Baskets were beginning to be replaced by string bags, and furs and gloves by shawls and red hands. A few stalls of greengroceries were set in the roadway. Coloured scraps of tissue paper and dirty little boys blew about together in the gutter. Several seedy camp-followers of the main army of commerce stood by the footpath; a red-faced man selling coloured celluloid windmills; a wizened one selling little gold and silver eggs which mysteriously 'walked' across his tilted tray; a little man with a purple, withered-looking nose who sold paper birds on sticks; and an old woman selling matches who might have been the Little Match Girl grown ancient and embittered.

Alexandra would have liked to buy a paper bird. But she was sufficiently aware of her adult body to know that this would not do. In any case, she had no money. And now they were caught in the maelstrom of the market proper. In five minutes Alexandra was utterly bemused, as if lost in a fog. Indeed, in a very solid way, the crowd resembled a fog, eddying slowly and powerfully, thickening and drifting away again, and suddenly opening before them in brief rifts of tantalizing glory.

Now they would find themselves confronted suddenly by a great mound of crumpled prints, sateens and lace, in which a crowd of women were scrabbling like dogs after bones. Now they would find themselves on the verge of stepping into a bed of flowery crockery. Dogs, the warm bodies of little boys, and bags knobbly with onions and potatoes, rammed their legs from unexpected quarters. Noises like a pack of variegated dogs pounded their ears. They were packed so tightly that Alexandra had to look under people's hats and over their shoulders to see anything. Yet, alarmed by the sudden quacking of a motor horn, this apparently compact mass of people compressed itself still more, opening a midway lane for the car, as if they and the stalls were made of rubber. Oozing along in the eddyings of this rubber mass they ultimately were squeezed into a narrow neck of the square, and so out into a long narrow appendix of the market called York Street.

Here the uproar was damped down, and the voices of salesmen were separable. Alexandra recovered her wits, and lost her somewhat strained and hunted look. The stalls here were poor relations of those in the main market.

93

A man with lank black hair and a birth-mark across his face was threatening to smash a plate which (excusably enough) nobody would buy. Next to him an old man with a beard like a dirty waterfall was selling packets of coloured powder guaranteed to cure every disorder you liked to name. He challenged you in fact to find one it could *not* deal with. Next was a man who combined goldfish and tin jewellery. And after him came a stall so degenerate that it was impossible to tell what was being offered upon it.

Alexandra stared about her in a puzzled sort of way, different from her interest as they entered the market. These lean dejected stalls were lit by old-fashioned, naked flares of gas, hissing like yellow paper streamers. They troubled her with something more than curiosity. So did the soot-encrusted church on the left, with its treeless graveyard crazy-paved with gravestones. So did the bumpilly-cobbled street with its single row of under-nourished-looking cottages.

It was not until they came to the last stall of all, and she saw lying in a flannel-lined box five tiny black and beige puppies, that she knew what had been troubling her.

'Why!' she cried, coming to a standstill. 'I've *been* in this street before! My dad brought us here once — Sam and Peter and me — and he bought us a puppy each, just like these. And he carried them all the way home inside his jacket in front. They kept popping their heads out and whining. And that made him so mad! He kept punching their heads and shouting 'Gerrin! gerrin, yer little fools! Dyer want to make me look like a blasted female kangaroo!'

Alexandra suddenly stopped laughing as a vivid image bobbed into her mind of a thick, squat, slightly bow-legged man, with hair like black stubble, frowning upon the three soft, timid little faces that peered out of his breast, and shouting so that even in the din of the market everybody turned to stare.

So that was her father, she thought, and wondered why for so many years she had been unable to remember how he looked, since the image had come now unsought and with such instant ease.

By this time they had come to the verge of a very steep, narrow chute, running down to another street a hundred feet lower, at an angle that was certainly more than 45 degrees and was more suitable for steps than for a street.

Alexandra stopped again, and clutched Iris's arm. She was trembling violently. 'Oh — don't take me down there! I can't go down there! I . . . I . . . I don't think I'm strong enough yet — it's so steep!' she pleaded, her voice full of a terror so utterly out of proportion to the cause of it that Iris looked at her uneasily, wondering if after all this strange medley of a creature was quite sane. She soothed her, and they turned back along York Street.

'We can go down the steps instead,' added Alexandra, belatedly, with an instant subsidence in her terror as soon as they had left Warner's Brow.'

Iris looked narrowly at her. '*What* steps,' she said, with intent to test.

'Why — Brewery Steps, of course!' said Alexandra with instant contempt. Then she stopped dead for the third time during their walk. 'That's funny!' she said wonderingly. 'I didn't *know* I knew that name. It just *came*. I believe — I believe,' she added in a rather anxious tone, 'I believe I'm getting my memory back at last. That's two things I've remembered to-day!'

They descended Brewery Steps, and turned along Under Market and into a little side street where there was a bridge over the River Cole. They stopped for a moment to look down at the river, fifty feet below, where slimy dark rocks and sooty warehouses made a narrow gorge for thick yellowish water, from which crept up a foul, chemical-and-sewerage smell which proved to be a key to a third portion of Alexandra's walled-up memory.

'Oh look!' she cried in her deep rather plangent voice, so that a passer-by turned in disapproving astonishment at her lack of reserve. 'This is where we used to come to see the rats!'

It was quite evident from her delighted tone that to see the rats had been one of the outstanding joys of her childhood.

And that, mused Iris, as they resumed their way, that surely implied things about Alexandra's childhood that were not pleasant to think upon. Perhaps after all it would be as well not to stir the stagnant water of her memory, lest something worse than rats, some putrefying or obscene horror, should be disclosed.

They threaded and shouldered their way, both of them silent, to Cobden Square. Here there was another bridge over the river, a new bridge of white concrete, looking very incongruous among

95

the thick-sooted buildings about it. They leaned over the white parapet and looked again into the river. The thick lentil-soup-coloured water coiled out from the arches below them, and crawled away over the black feet of a derelict factory with rows of broken windows, past two breweries, and a working mill which poured hot chemicals into the river through a rusty pipe, then slid under three more bridges, and so under the great brick viaduct. This, by straddling over all other buildings, dwarfing houses and making even factories seem insignificant, seemed to frame this view of the town, to give it style, to pull its anarchy of sooty, meanly built independencies into some sort of pattern.

So thought Iris, who had seen many other towns, beautiful, ugly or indifferent, and who felt Colebridge as a dreary prison from which she did not yet despair of escaping.

But this was Alexandra's first and only town. She stood and stared down dizzily at the furtive yet formidable water, over which a large sea-gull was looping powerfully. She stood and stared across at the great giant bridge with more than twenty legs, straddling the town, so that three factory chimneys had to look between its thighs, and mere houses huddled at its toes. To her it seemed splendidly black against the pale translucent clouds. As she stared there swept along the top of it a long, low, reptilian creature perforated all along with windows through which the gold sky showed, and crowned by a curling ostrich plume of grey and violet.

'A train,' whispered Alexandra reverently as this creature emitted the cry which she had heard so often, without seeing this picture, or any picture, in her wakeful nights. She roused reluctantly and turned to Iris. 'What a beautiful town!' she said.

But Iris, though she could acknowledge a certain brutal grandeur, a rightness and nobility of proportion in the viaduct, could not forget the miserable slums which huddled at its feet. It was typical, she thought indignantly, of this machine-ridden, engineer-made world, that the machine which was after all only a means of taking human beings from one place to another should be given so magnificent a roadway by which to cross the town, while the human beings it was supposed to serve must grovel in squalid slums at its feet, and be smothered daily in its filthy discharges.

She opened her mouth to say as much. But seeing Alexandra

caught in wonder again, her eyes glistening with the still tears of rapture, she closed it again. The girl would not understand.

And suddenly Iris felt weary of her charge — as even the most patient of adults must ultimately feel weary of the most charming of children, weary because there are so many things that must be left unsaid, the child's mind being not fit to receive them. It was time, she decided, to take this girl home. Nevertheless, the expedition had deepened her interest in Alexandra. To her original cool curiosity was now added a definite liking for her vitality, her simplicity, her fresh, child's eyes, a genuine compassion for what she guessed must have been a narrow and bitter childhood, and lastly, a new curiosity as to how far the frozen memory of that childhood might now, by reassociation with its scenes, be thawed again.

When therefore they reached the foot of number 12 Finn Street, and Alexandra, seizing Iris's hand in both hers, begged her to take her into the town again, she was willing enough to promise to do so.

'But what about a walk up on the moors for a change,' she suggested.

Alexandra assented eagerly. She had not the slightest notion what moors might be, but she was to have what she wanted; that is, more of Iris Young's companionship, and a promise of further explorations of this new and ravishing world that had lain, unsuspected, all these years about her bed.

CHAPTER II

It was about a month later when Iris Young first took Alexandra beyond the town. They rode first in a number 19 tram. This, waggling its behind like an 'eccentric' dancer, carried them along the narrow road that followed the way of the river, then turned at right angles, and rashly attempted a steep hill, made a great pothering smell of hot metal and oil in the effort, and discouraged, stopped half-way up.

They got out, and saw a row of cottages which, though black with the town's livery, had also a faint look of the country, on account of the strip of grass about three feet wide which lay between their feet and the road. They were quaint, too, in Alexandra's eyes because their front rooms opened level with the pavement, instead of being mounted to the height of three yellow steps, like most of the poorer houses in Colebridge.

She began to feel the peculiar glee that is to be obtained by travelling abroad and seeing other customs, a glee spontaneous in all who are not stiffened with insular pride.

They climbed the part of the hill which had baulked the tram. Gradually the regular, rectangular 'sets' gave place to real country cobbles, irregular and rounded. The cottages grew progressively cleaner, and crouched lower, in country fashion, to the sheltering hill. Then there were no more cottages, and here they turned to the right, along a road that was not paved at all but floored with soft dark sand.

Alexandra kicked her toes in it as they walked, with a primitive delight which should have been satisfied (thought Iris with a pang of indignation) ten years before on a seashore. She also raised her nose in the air, like a dog in a new country, determined to miss not a single scent.

'What a rum smell!' she remarked presently.

'Rum? I think it's delicious! But whether it's the gorse, or the heather, or the peat, or last year's bracken, or next year's bracken, I can never quite make up my mind!' said Iris.

Alexandra was silent. All these names were devoid of meaning to her. But she was not going to admit it. Already, in so short a period, she had mentally grown out of childhood, when there is no shame in confessing ignorance, to adolescence, when to do so seems almost an indecency. She tried to note the new names therefore, and made up her mind to listen, to find out their meaning by cunning and devious ways, and meanwhile to cover up the gaps of her ignorance with false looks of comprehension. She was still too young mentally to realize that Iris Young was not in the least deceived by her bright empty smile, and, understanding her shame, had decided to educate her by cunning and devious ways — to tell her the names of things in such a way that she would not know she was being told.

They climbed the steep lane slowly, side by side. On either hand there were steep banks, on which grew bushes, prickly brown, and apparently dead, but with little spurts of gold that looked like the last flickerings of the fire that had burnt the branches to this colour. But when Alexandra touched these little spurts of fire, they were as cool as water to the touch, and as soft as only flowers can be. She longed to know what these living flames were called, and, as if in accidental answer to that longing Iris murmured, laughing: 'When the gorse is not in flower, then kissing's out of season.'

On they plodded, the sand as soft as clouds under their feet. The sun softly dimmed and dilated, its dimming hardly less bright than its dilating, so softly misted was the sky. The wind coming crossways, gently ruffled Iris's hair, clouding it like a breathed-on mirror of bronze. But with Alexandra's heavy, tar-black crown the wind could do no mischief. Once a bird threw itself straight up into the air, and when half-way up began to shriek excitedly. They stopped to watch it rise as if lifted on the fountain-jet of its own song, until it was almost out of sight. Alexandra began to see millions of silver specks instead of one black speck, and sat down abruptly.

Iris sat down beside her, plucked a grass blade and began to nibble the tender end, remarking casually, 'That's the first lark I've heard this year. Disgraceful! Because if I had troubled to come out I could have heard one in February or even January!'

Alexandra noted the name of this fountain-like bird, and congratulated herself on her luck in obtaining this knowledge without asking for it. Soon after this they passed through a wooden gate, upon which was nailed a yellow tin notice saying, 'Shut this Gate and Use Cooper's Dip'. Alexandra assisted to obey the first order, but was somewhat puzzled by the second order. After a while her curiosity grew to such an extent that it overcame her new shame of exposing her ignorance.

'Is Cooper's Dip the place we are going to?' she asked at last, having revolved all possible interpretations of the word 'Dip' and picked out what seemed to her the most reasonable one.

Iris stared a moment. She had walked over the moors by this path so often that for her the tin plate no longer existed. Then she remembered it, and began to laugh.

'Don't laugh at me! How could *I* know what it meant?' cried Alexandra with a vehemence that astonished Iris. Accustomed though she was to schoolgirls at the ridiculously touchy, over-emotional period of life, she had never encountered so vehement a touchiness as this. She was indeed rather at a loss to know how to soothe the passionate resentment she had evoked.

'Silly girl!' she said, rather awkwardly therefore. 'I wasn't laughing at you! I was laughing at that advertisement. Cooper's Dip, I think, is some disinfectant they wash sheep with. I was only thinking how insulting they are to tell all and sundry to use it! "All we like sheep need Cooper's Dip!" ' she ended, intoning in a ridiculous imitation of a priest.

But Alexandra did not smile. Her first passionate resentment had lapsed as quickly as it had flared out, but she was still too humiliated to see Iris's joke.

And Iris, sensing the lingering smart, reached out impulsively, took her hand, patted the palm of it affectionately against her own thigh, and said, 'Don't brood so, Alex! Everybody makes mistakes — and the one you made was quite intelligent, you know!'

The soreness oozed miraculously away — more by the contact of her palm with the firm, warm, muscularly moving thigh of her goddess than by her words.

They went on in a contented silence. The lane had dwindled into a path now. On either hand stretched the open moor, fold upon fold of heather-coloured earth, like the folds in a thick coarse blanket (an army blanket, rough and harsh to the cheek), sad, brownish-mauve, right to the horizon. Here and there the bare earth protruded in miniature cliffs, the colour, Alexandra decided, of Christmas pudding. And indeed, when occasionally they had to stride across a small stream that crept along under these small cliffs, Alexandra found that they had also the consistency of Christmas pudding, sponging under her heels in an alarming fashion. Once Iris stooped, caught up a handful of this earth and crumbled it near her nose.

'I love the smell of peat!' she explained as she caught Alexandra's astonished eye.

At first Alexandra thought this folded tumbled blanket of moor-land would be very dreary. But though they seemed to walk for ever, exchanging old horizons for new ones exactly the same, she was surprised at the exhilaration which gradually began to mount in her. The little creeping watercourses talked without hope; the sun drifted tentatively like smoke over the folds of heather, browning it and purpling it as if it could not make up its mind between two such lifeless colours; the path wandered this way and that and ceased to care what happened to it; great heavy birds, uncertain whether to be black or white, circled over the melancholy place, crying dubiously 'peeeeee whee!' Yet the total effect of all these melancholy colours and sounds was to lift the spirit on a great wave of exhilaration — of gratitude, too, to some anonymous benefactor.

In Alexandra there was an additional astonishment that the world should be thus and not otherwise, that it should stretch so far, that its rim should be circular and so quietly shaped, and that the sky was so curved and so empty. A feeling of delicious power grew in her, as if she walked along the very roof-tops of creation, and could gather it all into the small burning-glass of her eye, and so focus it on her mind. Yet even she, in all her ignorance, knew that even this seemingly limitless moorland was not the entire world. She unconsciously began to increase her speed, pressed forward by a hunger to see more and yet more. Presently she did see more. Climbing over a long low thigh of the earth, they suddenly saw below them a long triangle of water, the sharpest point towards them.

'Ah! The reservoir!' cried Iris, in that tone of pleased surprise with which people always greet a sudden view of water, however often they have sighted it. Along the shortest side of the water was a wall with a battlemented tower at each end, and along the other two sides were scalloped beaches of ginger sand, moulded into several terraces by the different levels of the water. The dim sunlight moved over it like smoke, and some white birds bobbed in the middle, now and then taking wing with a sputter of water and high coarse cries. They found a hollow with a natural backrest of heather, spread their mackintoshes, and sat down to eat their lunch, their eyes stroking the water, more and more bewitched by it as they ate.

Alexandra was puzzled by the peculiar difference in their food. The lettuce, eaten in this quiet, with your eyes upon shifting sunlight on water, and your back against the prickly horsehair couch of the heather, seemed sweeter somehow than normal lettuce; the hard-boiled egg seemed spicy; the tomato (in which you bit a hole to suck out its juicy interior) was — what was it? — minty? Even the bread seemed half-way to cake. The tea from Iris's vacuum flask, on the other hand, had a flat metallic taste which was disagreeable.

After they had eaten Alexandra found that the shifting light on the water was too heavy for her eyes. She leaned back, trying hard to keep them open, but merely increasing the weight of her eyelids by the effort. Gradually she ceased to try, and lay listening to the quiet sounds — the papery whisper of last year's heather flowers, the long falling cries of the sea-birds, and, mingled with them, the cries of peewits, seeming by comparison almost cheerful, because they ended with an upcurling note. Then even the sounds ebbed away, leaving her consciousness quite empty.

When she awoke it was with a terrific nervous jolt, and the instant knowledge that Iris was not there. She sat up, terrified, and then saw by her side a note weighted by a stone, which said:

'Dear Alex,

If you wake before I am back, don't be frightened. *And don't go away from here*. It is easy to be lost on these moors. I shall not be away long. I got restless, and yet I wanted you to have your sleep out, for you are not used to long walks yet.

Iris.'

It was all very well for Iris to tell her not to be frightened, thought Alexandra when she had read through this note, but she *was* frightened. She felt exposed, vulnerable, sitting alone in this empty world. Instinctively she pulled up her knees to her chin, and drew her skirt down over them by way of protecting herself from the invisible and universal enemy which she felt about her.

A little speckled spider ran onto the back of her hand, and for a moment she forgot her uneasiness in making it race from one hand to the other and back again. But at length it decided to end the farce, and suddenly launched itself into freedom on a fine gleam of silk. Her deep uneasiness returned — coupled with a queer doubt of her own reality which was induced purely by the lack of anyone to speak to her and so convince her of her existence. Then, born out of her uneasiness and her loneliness, came a peevishness against Iris. She found herself plucking at the little rags of dead bracken to allay her peevishness and, perceiving the likeness of its colour to that of Iris's hair, found a spiteful pleasure in pretending that she was plucking at that hair instead of at bracken.

At the beginning of an attachment there is often a period of complete unselfconsciousness. New lovers and new friends will find themselves unusually content in each other's company without knowing why. This period may last only for a day or an hour, or may stretch into years, according to the experience or temperament of those concerned. It will be broken when the absence of one of the pair suddenly sharpens the perceptions of the other, as a fire draws attention to itself by going out, or a clock by stopping. So now, her perceptions sharpened by unexpected deprivation, Alexandra after a while began to be aware of a third reaction to Iris's absence.

Sitting there in the empty moors, she felt in herself an alternation of emotion — like a succession of waves running forward to break into an exquisite fan-foam of tenderness, then drawing back with a long-drawn snarl of resentment. And for the first time since she had set eyes on Iris Young, she not only loved her, but knew that she loved her.

It seemed to her that she sat there forever, though in actual fact she had slept for over two hours, and had only waited awake for twenty minutes. So absorbed was she in her terror, her solitude, her alternating tenderness and fury, that when she heard a sudden hoarse cry behind her that sound like 'Goback! goback! goback!' she paid no attention. It was a complete surprise to her when Iris, who had startled the grouse into this protest, came creaking over the last few strides of heather and sat down beside her with a quiet 'Hullo, Alex! Been awake long?'

Instantly the alternating waves of the girl's tenderness and hatred resolved themselves into a clear pool of happiness. She looked at Iris and then looked quickly away again, for she felt that the new love was too naked in her eyes yet to be decent. She was in any case unable to speak for the happiness of having Iris back again.

As yet, however, Iris was unaware of the increase in her self-consciousness. She thought Alexandra's silence and averted face were signs of sulkiness, and said, a little guilty at having left her,

'You didn't mind me leaving you, Alex, did you? You were fast asleep, and I knew that you would not be strong enough to climb up to the Gyll. Someday I *will* take you up there!'

Alexandra looked up, radiantly gratified. 'Oh *will* you?' she said eagerly, then, as an afterthought, not of great importance, 'What *is* it?'

Thus do children and lovers receive a present, delighted because it *is* a present, and concerned only secondarily with what is in it.

'Oh — just a waterfall!' said Iris. 'I'll bring you up when there's a hard frost; it looks lovely turned into a long beard of icicles. Well — are you rested enough to get back home now?'

They circled back by another route across the moors which might just as well have been the same path for all the difference in the horizon. Once a small bird flew up 'ttt — ttt — tting', from Alexandra's toe, it seemed, as if she had kicked it up out of the tussock of grass. She looked at her feet, and there, framed by a beautiful little arch of grass-blades, bent over as if for a doorway, she saw a hollow, lined with scraps of hay and a few soft buff feathers, in which lay three small eggs, of a speckled putty colour. She knelt down with a soft exclamation, and took one of the eggs out and put it in the palm of her hand. It was quite warm, and this, together with the delicious smallness of it as it lay in the centre of her palm, gave her a sensuous pleasure.

'I never knew eggs could be so tiny,' she murmured in astonishment. 'Why! It's like a doll's hen's egg! Is it real?'

Iris laughed. 'Yes — quite real! And tiny as it is, it contains all the essentials of a lark packed away in it!'

And she too knelt down, and took out a second egg, crooking her fingers carefully round the mysterious warm oval. A faint warmth, more subtle even than that from the bird's egg, reached Alexandra from her cheek, which was leaned now very close to hers, and this somehow doubled the sensuous pleasure she already felt in the bird's egg, and her sense of its mystery. 'What do you mean?' she asked in a sacramentally lowered voice. "*Essentials* of a lark?"'

'Well — put it this way. In this tiny thing there is a mysterious something which makes it certain that some day it will crack open and let out a baby lark!'

'Oh!' said Alexandra, bewildered by a sudden cloudy enlightenment as to the object of eggs — which had hitherto seemed to her to exist merely to be eaten at breakfast.

'At least, I *think* it's a lark's egg!' ended Iris, putting back her treasure, and rising briskly. Alexandra copied her, and they went on their way.

For many hours now their ears had been tuned down to the quietness of birds and water and sunshine drifting over papery heatherbells. Towards evening, they climbed a long rise in the folded moors, and when they reached its summit, a sudden noise burst out, which seemed as loud and multitudinous as a sudden cheering from a football crowd.

Startled, Alexandra looked below her. And there, many hundred feet below, lay what seemed to her a gigantic city. Piled in terrace after terrace, tumbled and tilted madly at all angles like the walls of some lunatic's multiple castle, were more houses than she had dreamed existed in all the world. From a million chimneys rose a warm confusion of smoke-spirals, softly plum coloured in the evening light. Up through this smoke came the throaty growl peculiar to towns containing trams. The horizontal light gave a look of unreality to the terraced and crenellated roofs of the town, so that it looked like a great castle of frozen smoke, translucent in places, opaque in others. Here and there a tower or a chimney shot out of the plum-coloured mist like the naked arms of sooty-skinned swimmers — gilded by the low sun. Over the whole town was spread a wide sky, against the brim of which were laid soft flat feather-clouds of dull peach and smoky lavender.

Alexandra, enraptured and amazed, thought for a bewildered moment that she must be looking down on London. For what city but London could be so vast and so beautiful? But just as she was about to say so, she suddenly perceived a great powerfully curving bridge with twenty black legs striding across the bottom of the valley. It seemed familiar. Surely it was the viaduct? But then, surely, on the other hand, this incredible city could not be Colebridge? Fearful of exposing ignorance, whatever notion was correct, she was kept silent. She began to note the details of the wonderful scene. She traced the crooked narrow grooves of the streets between the climbing houses, crowded each with its chin to the lower one's shoulder like spectators in the old-fashioned galleries of theatres. She followed the traffic, slipping like black enamelled beetles in and out of sight in these crooked grooves. She watched a train come sweeping with a bold scythe-movement along the viaduct, leaving behind a long tress of white which gradually became absorbed into the damson-coloured breath of the town. She even traced the river as it threaded under numberless bridges like a silver ribbon through a black slotted waistband. And as she stared, the sun, astonishingly and rather alarmingly swift, as if it had suddenly found its own weight too much for it, sank behind the low keel-shaped moors on the other side of the valley. The great sprawling castle of frozen smoke became a solidified castle of indigo and soot. Alexandra sighed.

And at this sound, Iris, who had been studying her intent face rather than the town, laughed a little and said, 'Well? And what do you think of Colebridge *now*?'

So it *was* Colebridge after all, thought Alexandra, and answered, softly passionate, 'I think it is the most beautiful town in the world.' She then looked doubtfully at Iris, expecting to be laughed at. But Iris did not laugh, though there was a crinkle or two of irony about her mouth as she considered the town for a moment.

'Well,' she said at last, 'they say every woman is beautiful once in her life at least. I suppose every town also may be beautiful once in its life!'

'When is that?' asked Alexandra.

'When she — or it — is loved,' said Iris.

Alexandra struggled with the implications of this. She did at length, rather cleverly, see one of the less obvious of them and replied almost reproachfully, 'Don't you love this one then?'

'Love it? I would give my very soul to get out of it!' declared Iris bitterly.

'But *why*?'

Iris turned and studied her a little anxiously, ending by taking her hand and patting it between her two palms as if it were a coin she were debating whether to spend.

'It seems a shame to douche your enthusiasms!' she said at last. 'But I like to say what I think about things you know. Colebridge certainly did look quite passable to-night. But for all that it's only a poky little Lancashire townlet, dirty, sooty, slummy, ugly, cold, filled with out-of-works and out-at-elbows, and down-at-heels, with fish and chip shops for restaurants, posters for art, cheap wirelesses for music, Cobden and Queen Victoria for sculpture, W.E.A. classes for culture — what can there *be* to love about such a town?'

Alexandra was silent. With her mind full of the glory she had seen, she could not accept this description, yet was too diffident of her own judgment to stand up against this schoolmistress who seemed to her the well of all wisdom.

Seeing this, Iris became remorseful. Excessive truthfulness, she told herself, can be a vice, like any other excess. She went on, therefore: 'But perhaps I'm prejudiced. I may be blind. Perhaps if my eyes were as fresh as yours I might see beauty in it after all. But to me it seems a dreary little prison.'

Alexandra was silent again, striving, and failing, to imagine how anyone could stand before the glory that she had seen, and feel imprisoned.

'Come on!' said Iris, pulling her by the hand. 'You're beginning to be chilly. And so am I.'

They bumped down the steep hillside to the town, the coarse grass growing darker as they descended, partly with a deposit of soot, partly with a deposit of darkness. Lights in the town were reflected and purified in the sky above, which was cool and clear as a sheet of water, with clouds like dim blue weeds drifting in it. Sparse cottages thickened into the dense brick jungle of the town. From doorways, from groups about the streets, from behind worn fabric across the lighted windows, came multiplying the discord of humanity — a discord enchanting to Alexandra. And even to Iris, now that her mind had been soothed by solitude and the thin, crystal, threefold harmony of birds, water, and wind, the voice of provincial humanity now had a certain rough charm.

CHAPTER III

ALEXANDRA's mental growth, in these first few months after her emergence from her long hibernation, was very rapid, almost visible by the minute, like the extraordinary growth of a moth's wings just after emergence from its cramped pupa. It was a growth chiefly in breadth of imagination and in richness of experience, much like the growth, that is, of the normal adolescent, but tele-scoped into a much shorter period on account of her late start. Perhaps the rapidity of growth may be also accounted for by the fact that, apart from growing, she had very little to do.

Because of her prolonged withdrawal from the world she had made no friends. She found now that all her contemporaries were already fixed in their spheres, in whose pattern there was no room for a newcomer. The pattern of the Gollen household was also stiffened by long use, and would admit of no interpolations. Sam was so harnessed to the cooking that he could not be persuaded to leave the shafts, which appeared to have grown into his very soul. Alexandra's first timid but impetuous efforts to assist led only to inexpressible confusion. Their tailoring was also tight against amateur assistance. Nor could Mrs. Tyler be induced to relinquish the weekly baking, a kindly impulse long since petrified by habit.

Alexandra therefore, restless, charged with the energy of her delayed youth, released that energy by exploring, mostly alone, the streets of Colebridge, an exploration at first almost completely dis-interested and almost purely objective. She went alone because the only friends she had were otherwise occupied. Sam and Peter worked as incessantly as ever. Winifred Bell had only Wednesday afternoons free, when her shop closed. And Iris Young had only Saturday free, and, moreover, had only a limited appetite for the company of one so immature as Alexandra.

She never again beheld Colebridge in the full splendour of that first view from the moors. But that impression lingered in her mind and dyed with rich colour all her subsequent impressions, so that the mean streets, steep and narrow and squalid, as even she could now perceive, still seemed to her parts of a magnificent whole. Not that the mean sad streets themselves were devoid of minor splendours. There were shops for instance: the fishmongers' shops — with their treasures of silver cod, smoky-golden kippers, sunset cuts of salmon, heaps of pink coral shrimps, and crimson-spotted, porcelain-bellied plaice; or the greengrocers' with their pyramids of waxen oranges or crimson polished Canadian apples, cabbages, great tiered flounces of green-blue taffeta shot with purple, cauliflowers like cream lace, onions made into knobbly plaits like the auburn tails of horses, and daffodils, tossing their long yellow muzzles like midget ponies.

Then there were funerals, processions of shining black and silver cars, purring reverently along the narrow streets, preceded by a splendid chariot of glass and silver, bearing a pyre of flowers, only real no doubt, but looking like an extravagant selection from a milliner's stock of trimmings.

Weddings also were splendid. First came a car bound to its bonnet with white ribbons lest it should fly to pieces in excitement, with flowers spraying out like pink, mauve, and white music from silver trumpets fixed by the windows. Within this sat the white bride and the black bridegroom smiling like dolls. After them came another car, undecorated except for its squash of bridesmaids like a crowded cottage bouquet.

And of course there were the posters. These Iris had condemned, but with guilty delight Alexandra continued to admire the lovely curly-headed mothers with their plump pink babies, the bronzed young heroes with impossible pipes and incredibly golden beers, the fruit that never was on earth or in heaven, or even under glass bell; the jellies, custards and blanc-manges that were like a child's dream of a party. None of these pictures, of course, tallied with her experience of reality. But she assumed that somewhere there *was* a Reality with which they tallied, and wondered only where it might be. Perhaps in London, or Paris, or one of the other great cities which Iris did not despise.

Despite her loneliness she was happy in these first few months after Iris's return. It was not until April that her happiness began to be troubled by a whiff or two from behind the wall which still shut off the first twelve years of her life. On a Friday afternoon, tired of trying to assist Mrs. Tyler in her baking, and being permitted only to fetch basins and wash them when finished with, Alexandra suddenly decided to go out.

It was not an inviting day. A sluttish version of a traditional April shower had just ceased, and as Alexandra stumped along Finn Street, the wet pavement was slimy with combined soot and rain, shining like the skin of black slugs, and the usual litter of tram-tickets and chip-papers and cigarette packets had been swept in sodden puddings over the grids in the gutters. However, beyond the sooty chimney-crowns smiled a sky of impudent blue, like the eyes of a slum beauty. Alexandra was pleased with the sunshine, but at the same time hoped that it was not going to last all the afternoon, for she wished to keep her mackintosh on, it being new, bright scarlet, flowered, and given to her by Iris Young. Very conscious of the brilliant contrast of this scarlet coat with her glittering black crown of hair, and also of the distinction of this heavy coiffure over her broad, slightly sullen face, she insisted upon going out hatless even in the rain. However, rain did her hair little harm, for she had no waves or curls to be cherished, and the oily sheen of its texture made it as waterproof as a duck's plumage.

Her walk was rapidly acquiring personality. From resembling the staggering trot of a baby, it was becoming more and more a part of Alexandra — rather thumping, the ball of the foot being placed on the ground almost simultaneously with the heel, giving her a passionate, all-or-nothing appearance, even when seen in the distance.

A tram came along just as she reached the end of Finn Street. She mounted it and clattered up the stairs, for she had by no means outgrown yet her delight in these lurching howdah rides on the back of a tram. Half-way down the hill to Cobden Square, the sky began once more to pelt the streets with rain. Everybody except Alexandra retreated from the open prow of the tram. She remained leaning over the railing, as indifferent as a mermaid on a spray-drenched rock.

This, the ninth shower of the day, was over by the time the tram reached the terminus. Alexandra stumped cautiously along the slimy streets to the market — her favourite haunt in these solitary explorations. Whether on market day or not, this square, and the streets immediately about it, had a curious and not entirely healthy fascination for her. To-day was a Market Day. But those stallsmen whose goods were liable to be ruined by rain had grown weary of rushing every fifteen minutes to put them under cover, only to uncover them again in five more minutes. In final disgust they had cleared their stalls.

The Market Place in consequence had a restless, impermanent look, like houses on a day of 'flitting'. The sluttish, unwashed light from between the ever-moving rags of cloud gave the minimum of colour to fruit and vegetables. The general effect was of a badly executed sepia sketch, with dabs of faded, muddy, amateurish colour here and there. The cobbles were treacherous with a litter of sodden cabbage leaves and pale pink paper wrappings, and Alexandra's high spirits soon began to flag.

There was little pleasure, she soon saw, to be got from the market to-day. Yet the secret fascination of this place drew her, as the baffling reek of a strange smell will draw a dog. Aware of the pull of it, but not able to understand it, she lingered, wandering more and more unhappily about the dismal stalls.

And at last she came, as she invariably did, to Warner's Brow — the steep cobbled chute of a hill down into Under Market where she had stopped with such terror the day she first went forth with Iris Young. Even yet she had not ventured down this place, though every time she visited the market she would come and stare down Warner's Brow.

Having stared long enough to induce a certain familiar nausea, she turned away and stumped slowly along York Street, the narrow neck of the market where her father had once bought the puppies.

Usually, when she reached the squalid stalls where this incident had occurred she turned back. But to-day that same compelling force that drew her to the market drew her farther on still.

The street grew rapidly and incredibly meaner the farther she went. Finn Street, she now knew, was a street of poverty. But it was a self-respecting poverty. This street was quite different. Doors were blistered; gutters wrenched off; slates missing; windows broken and stopped up with rags several years weather-beaten, or with cardboard sodden with rain; and just inside an open door she could see a great black greasy smear on the paper where countless filthy shoulders and behinds had rubbed in and out.

If this glimpsed room were a fair example of all the others, it was no wonder, thought Alexandra, that the people preferred to live chiefly in the street. For here old men shuffled aimlessly about, prodding the cobbles and spitting at them alternately. Youths clustered at corners, with faces that looked as if the bones, trying to push through the skin, had bruised the flesh; these had nothing better to do than to produce a number of raucous cat-calls as Alexandra passed. Dirty grinning little boys rode about on trollies made out of old prams. Old women perched on the steps of the houses chewing their withered lips. Middle-aged women, with arms folded upon bosoms either like slatted blinds, or like well-filled balloons, shrieked venomously from their doorways. Little girls, in cotton frocks that seemed to hang straight over their naked bones, dragged along and slapped generously their baby brothers or sisters — practising for motherhood, Alexandra supposed. Other babies crawled on the greasy pavements, black as if they had crawled along the tunnels of a coalmine; they had nothing to cover their bottoms, which were red and sore and marked by the grit of the pavement. This sight was the one which shocked Alexandra most of all. She longed to pick them all up, bath them and powder them and clothe them in soft clean napkins. Her inability to interfere, and the magnitude of the business if she had had the right to interfere, distressed her exceedingly.

In a growing passion of social indignation she stumped along loathing all she saw, yet unable to turn back, driven perhaps by a curiosity akin to that which compels some people to continue poking in the loathsome contents of a blocked sink. Presently she turned from the main conduit of this squalor into lesser drains even squalider, though this had seemed impossible. Among these lesser streets she tacked this way and that, walking without compass, and without purpose, yet impelled to go on, down back 'entries' giving her a view of lean-to privies and dustbins, in backyards built only to contain these two sops to civilized standards, compelled to walk with her handkerchief clapped to her nose, on account of the combined reek of them.

At last, as if she had walked in her sleep to the centre of a tangled labyrinth and was now brutally awakened, she came to a sudden stop, and stared about her, bewildered, yet with a baffling sense of familiar territory. Across the road was a public house faced with brown glazed tiles, and called by the dismal name of the 'Railway Arms' — a title inspired by the railway which ran slantwise across the road on a bridge built of that peculiarly depressing type of small bluish brick beloved of railway engineers.

As Alexandra stood at that street corner she was attacked by three separate and equally appalling smells — the warm sooty sulphureous smell of railway smoke; the sickly, sweet, yet acid smell from a street latrine under the bridge; and the thick muddy smell of cheap beer from the public house. Whether these fumes were possessed of slightly anaesthetic qualities, as they might very well be, or whether the nausea produced by them released some catch in her brain, who can tell? But as she stood there, it seemed to her that a man came out of the swing door of the 'Railway Arms'; a man squat, thick at the waist, heavy in the shoulders, slightly bow-legged, short necked, the head bent forward between the shoulder blades like a miner's, the hair cropped so that it looked like worn dark velvet, the jaw powerful, thrust forward, the equally prominent brow-ridges marked roughly by angular black eyebrows — a man with only one anomaly in his physical aspect: his fine, rather repulsively flexible hands.

This man paused a second on the top step of the 'Railway Arms' to spit in a contemptuous trajectory into the road, then waddled hurriedly down the steps and across to the latrine. A few moments later he came out again, in such a hurry that he was still buttoning himself up as he went. The door of the 'Railway Arms' swung behind him again.

Alexandra stood frozen still with terror. She had understood that her father was dead — dead nearly ten years ago. What then was he doing walking in and out of the 'Railway Arms'? The doubt that he was not, after all, safely dead was intolerable. To put an end to it she marched, stricken with terror as she was, across to the door of the public house.

The door was locked! In a sudden frenzy of even greater terror, she rattled the handle. After a while a window screeched and a woman's face looked down at her malevolently.

'It's naw yuse yu jigglin' that dooor! It'll awpen at regulairtion hower an not a minute afore! Ah'd be ashairmed an arl, a girl of yure airge with the crairvin' that bad yu af ter coom jigglin' dooors at this time of dair!' The window slammed down again. Alexandra hurriedly retreated.

So absorbed was her mind in battling with this terrifying experience of a man who had come out and gone in again through a locked door, and who had seemed to be her father, ten years dead, that she wandered as purposelessly as before in the labyrinthine squalor, but this time quite unconscious of disgusting sights and smells. When she next came to full consciousness, she found herself once more in the Market Square.

'Why — it's as if my *feet* knew the way to that pub!' she said in amazement, and also in some fear. For, not being in the least introspective, she was not very familiar with the uncanny way in which the body will at times perform a complicated set of actions without the interference and, indeed, without the permission of the conscious mind. What frightened her still more than this uncanny return of memory to her body, was the mysterious and terrifying figure which had emerged from the 'Railway Arms'. Was he a suddenly revived memory also? Or was he an evil spirit? Her direct, materialistic temper rejected the superstitious explanation, while the solid realism of the apparition kept her in doubt of the other.

That evening she asked Peter if their father had ever been in a place called the 'Railway Arms'. He looked at her uneasily, and at last replied, in the stiff manner usual to him when referring to this part of the past: 'I'm afraid, Allie, he was very seldom *out* of it.' The reply brought little to the solution of her problem. But some deep distaste prevented her from disclosing to anyone her strange experience.

From this time, however, though never again with such startling realism, fragments of those blank thirteen years began to be vomited from time to time into her present memory. These fragments came when she least expected them. When she deliberately fished for them they easily evaded her hooks.

One morning, for instance, while helping Sam to make the beds, she became suddenly aware of a figure lying in the double bed in which Sam and Peter slept. This impression could not be described as a hallucination, for there was nothing actually visible; but she was so vitally aware of the mass, weight and contour of the figure that it seemed as though it would in another instant become visible also. She hesitated to turn the bottom sheet back, lest it should rip under his weight, so certain was she of the existence of this figure, which she knew was pinned to the bed by the dead weight of the utterly helpless. Speechless and motionless, his black eyes horribly crossed, his mouth twisted and dribbling ceaselessly, his hands crooked and feeble as a baby's, he lay there for eight days. . . .

'Now then John-o'-dreams!' said Sam indulgently, and the figure silently melted away, thus enabling her to turn back the bottom sheet. 'What did our Dad die of?' she asked as they struggled with the clean top sheet.

'Stroke — brought on by drink,' said Sam gruffly.

'Doesn't it worry you to sleep in the bed he died in?' Alexandra pursued — with a cunning intention to test the truth of that recent conviction without betraying it to Sam, for he might think she was going mad.

Sam laughed, as grimly as he had spoken. 'Old Man Gollen stopped worrying *us* the day he died,' was his ugly comment. 'And anyway,' he went on, more in his usual tolerant voice, '*Somebody's* died in *most* beds if you come to think of it!'

The next fragment was turned up about a week later, on Baking Day. Mrs. Tyler began to tell Alexandra about some neighbour whose husband had just died.

'Ah dawn't want to seem 'ard,' she remarked, as she moulded the dough with her elastic, dough-coloured fists, 'Boot it were a merciful release, an' that's flat!' (blap blap! echoed the dough).

'For — for Mrs. Harrison?' suggested Alexandra innocently.

'Ah'm nairmin' naw nairmes!' (blap-blap-blap!) 'Ah dair sair as it were a merciful release for '*im* an arl, boot (ah dawn't want to be 'ard mind yu), Ah can't 'elp thinkin' as 'e didn't desurve neither murcy *nor* release!' This time the moulding of the dough continued without interruption. Alexandra was struggling with a sort of doubling of her hearing. The words spoke by Mrs. Tyler seemed to exist in two planes at once.

'Am I going cross-eared?' she asked herself, for the effect was analogous to that produced by crossed eyes. As she struggled to re-focus, a fresh fragment of those harsh forgotten years was flung up into her mind. For a lightening space of time she was twelve years old, hearing almost precisely these same words spoken, this time of her own father. And at the sound of the word 'release' a great pothering black cloud of joy surged out of her, like an evil genii out of a bottle, and she ran upstairs to the room where that stiff body lay, and stood in the doorway, grinning at it and dancing a malignant hop or two of triumph — a small sturdy malevolence with streaming black hair like treacle.

So that was how it had been, she thought — but as she formed the words, time shifted again, and she was standing on the pavement, biting her nails, and watching with cold curiosity seasoned with terror, while two strangers extracted a stiff Guy Fawkes effigy of her father from their car and struggled up the stairs with the burden, awkward and slippery after the fashion of the dead or the unconscious. . . .

A slight shift in time again, and she stood at the door of the front bedroom, watching Mrs. Tyler and her two brothers (gawky youths of twenty-two) battling with that same ludicrous effigy in an attempt to take off its clothes, and being told by Mrs. Tyler to 'git out — if yu'd any sense of decency yud not *need* tellin'!' But she obstinately remained, bound there by curiosity and horror, until they had stripped that short broad body, the chest and legs covered with a dark crinkly pelt, and laid it between the sheets.

Mrs. Tyler seemed to run through all this portion of the past. Wasn't it Mrs. Tyler who had paid for the funeral ten days later? She was not sure, for remembrance was ceasing now to be spontaneous. She felt that she was correct, however, though why Mrs. Tyler should have sacrificed her own Burial Club money for a man whom she denounced daily as a devil out of hell, his daughter could not well imagine. Her memories of this period ceased, submerged by too much effort.

Three days later Alexandra was putting up some clean lace curtains at the front-room window, that window which had been her only gate into the world for so long, and which was still a more significant window than any other. As she raised her arm to fix the rod from which the crisp clean curtains hung, she tottered a little, for her sense of balance was still not quite perfect, and the brass end of the rod struck the window. However, the glass was not broken, thank goodness. And then she saw that it *was* broken, but curiously enough, not where she had tapped it, but in the upper pane.

Very puzzled, she let fall her arm and looked about her. For a second she wondered if by some strange translation of the senses she had been dropped in a house in that labyrinth of squalor near the Market Place. Where her bed used to be was an old horsehair couch, the black covering gashed to let out obscene offal-like lumps of grey stuff. A filthy wool cushion, of indescribable colour, lay ruckled at the head of this, and on it two fleas sat waiting for their next prey.

A horsehair arm-chair in similar condition, two wooden chairs, one with a broken back, the other with a broken leg, another chair, once rush-bottomed, and a long trestle table marked with rings of greasy brown, completed the furniture. The floor was carpeted with crumpled newspaper stained with the grease of fish and chips. And bottles of all denominations stood and lay about like skittles half-way through a wild and ruleless game. Dirty clothes and snippings of dark cloth filled up any remaining spaces. The tall gas-chimney was cracked in half. A candle was stuck by its own grease to the mantelpiece. By the door the dingy yellow and pink striped wall-paper was black with memories of passing shoulders. Elsewhere it was spotted with small red smears, whose origin was explained by other smaller, but moving spots.

Beyond these things, however, worse because not physical and not definable, was a sort of creeping smell of stale evil — evil that seemed to bubble and ooze oilily from the very floor, like marsh gas out of a bog. Filth and stale sweat, and fleas and bugs may be cleaned away. But this stink of nameless evil could not be touched by the strongest of disinfectants. She shuddered, and looked down at her feet. Without surprise, she saw that the old ruptured couch was now replaced by a spectre of itself in which her body stood like a tree in a mist. A second later and even the spectre had disappeared.

The room she knew and until now had known always and only, was returned, clean, bare, neat, and even a little gay, with its wall-paper like a flowered, pastel-coloured print, its blue and white china-boys, and its pink glass prisms. But now, having seen that other room, it was as if she looked at a green putrefying corpse dressed in a pretty print frock. As if her eyes were X-rays she saw through the fresh covering to the horror beneath. Moreover, no print, however flowery, could keep in the creeping, nauseating reek of evil that emanated from that other room.

So strong was her conviction that the visionary room really

underlay the present one, that she went scratching at the wall-paper to see if there lay under it a yellow and pink striped filthiness. There did not. Only plaster lay between the present paper and the bricks.

A dim, unhalucinatory memory came now to her, of a day when she had come home from school to find in yellow paint across the door-step, 'Gas! Keep out'; of another which she and Sam and Peter had spent in scraping the old pink and yellow filth off these walls; of a third on which Sam had stood on the trestle-table with a length of paste-sodden ceiling-paper about his neck, like a clown just emerging from a broken hoop. How they had laughed! She could remember sitting on the floor, rocking like a boat, and Peter staggering with laughter against the paste bucket and tipping it over; a rare piece of clumsiness that brought all three to the verge of hysteria.

So that was how the room had been reclothed. But where had the disgusting couch gone to? When had the new windsor chair and the rocking chair appeared? The broken-legged chair she recognized as the one with a patched leg in her bedroom. The broken-backed chair served, she suddenly remembered, as a stool in the kitchen. She supposed that all these changes, like the papering and cleaning of the house, were brought about by the energy of her brothers.

She began to ponder on that cleansing energy, and also upon their long and patient devotion to herself — a devotion hitherto accepted without question, like the movements of the sun and the moon, and the appearance of her daily food.

CHAPTER IV

'They're not ready yet. They've been three-quarters of an hour already!' said Alexandra as she opened the door to Winifred Bell.

Winifred laughed and tossed her curl mischievously. 'Only three-quarters of an hour?' she said mockingly.

Alexandra smiled her slow, slightly sullen smile. 'I don't know *how* you persuaded them!' she replied with only outward irrelevance.

'A fluke! — I couldn't repeat it if you paid me a fortune. But for goodness' sake hurry them up. The First House starts at half-past six you know.'

Alexandra ran upstairs and looked in at her brothers' wide open door. Peter was standing in front of the looking-glass with a brush in each hand, smoothing his hair at either temple alternately, with light finicking wrist movements, turning his head this way and that to see the result like a thin exacting bird. In the exigencies of vanity he had completely lost his characteristic unselfishness — forgotten even the existence of Sam, who stood impatiently behind him, dodging his head this way and that in a vain effort to get an uninterrupted view of his necktie over Peter's shoulder.

'Winifred's here!' cried Alexandra, selecting quite innocently the only statement likely to rouse the pair from their tranced vanity.

A certain flurry now appeared in their movements, even in those of Peter, whom she observed trying to stuff a clean handkerchief into his breast pocket, where he had already disposed one with its corner carefully puffed out.

'Buck up — or you'll miss the Walt Disney!' came Winifred's voice up the stairs, like a tune on glass tumblers.

The brothers started violently, shied towards the door like a pair of nervous horses, and were off — but not without a wild leap back on Sam's part to retrieve the money he had emptied out of his trouser pockets onto the dressing-table, under the impression, Alexandra supposed, that he was going to bed.

Five minutes later the front door slammed behind them and off they went down Finn Street, two by two, the short cortège an object of interest to several spies concealed behind lace curtains, for never before had Sam and Peter Gollen been known to go forth on a pleasure-jaunt on a week-day evening.

Why they should have suddenly succumbed to Winifred's invitation, Alexandra did not know. Winifred had been entreating them to try the pictures for years but with no success. Perhaps, she thought, the shock of her own sudden rousing had shaken them out of their ten-year-old groove.

They rode down to the Square inside the tram because Winifred would not bother to climb stairs. They sat in a row, Sam's and Alexandra's feet dangling just off the floor, Peter's and Winifred's crossed neatly at the ankles. The sun shone slantwise on the dusty window opposite, transforming it to a dim mirror, so that behind the row of faces opposite Alexandra could see dusty uncoloured reflections of their own four faces. She thought how happy these dim faces looked compared with the real ones. Perhaps these people were not going to the pictures, she thought compassionately — then with a burst of childish worldly wisdom, decided that perhaps they were, but had been too often and so had become 'mardy'. Yet this again could not be the cause of their look of glazed boredom, for Winifred went to the pictures at least once a week, and just look at her, leaning her pretty shoulders first towards Peter, then towards Alexandra, laughing like a canary, and now and then leaning over across Peter to say something to Sam, so that he should not feel left in the cold.

Alexandra could hear little of what she said, however, for the tram groaned as it lurched down the steep long hill to the Square. Presently the dusty reflections of their four happy faces vanished. They had come to the bottom of the hill, and the dark houses which had been the mirror-back gave place to an open space over which you could look to the viaduct. It was not black against the sky, as Alexandra would have wished. The sun was not yet low enough. But it slanted sufficiently to produce the misted unsubstantial look that preceded the silhouetting of its form against the west. The great multi-legged giant striding the huddled town looked as if it were made of violet smoke liable to dissolve at any moment into nothing at all.

But here was the terminus. And there, at the other side of the Square, was 'The Pictures', a large, flat-faced erection of dazzling white which Alexandra had often admired in her explorations, but had so far never entered. Round its veranda a row of lights like a necklace of coloured pearls ran round and round. On the wall above was pasted a huge picture, coloured pink, blue and brown, showing a lady and gentleman tilted backwards at a perilous angle, the gentleman uppermost, trying eternally and in vain to kiss the lady.

'Where shall we sit?' said Winifred as they mounted the shallow steps under the chasing pearls of the veranda.

'Oh — er — *you'd* better choose — you know more about it than we do,' cried Peter hurriedly. Whereupon she laughed, and exclaimed, 'My goodness — talk about the Innocents Abroad! Well, I say the back stalls, the balcony's so smoky and hot.'

They passed through heavy glass doors, guarded by two men in green and gold, and came to a glass cage with two little holes like the doors to beehives, in which was imprisoned a girl who certainly looked exotic enough to be preserved under glass. Over one hole were the figures 1s. 6d., 1s. 3d., and 1s. od., over the other 9d. and 6d.

Before this glass case the party halted. In a certain agitation the brothers looked from each other to the glass case, and back to each other again. They then started simultaneously to move towards the cage, only to stop short, again simultaneously — with the sidling, bowing movement of people uncertain who ought to go first through a door.

'Er — what about — which of us . . .?' said Peter brokenly, with a sideways nod of his head towards Winifred.

'Well — I *was* intending — but it doesn't matter, of course!' replied Sam, evidently able to comprehend this allusive question.

'I don't mind in the least!' declared Peter bravely. 'It's a mere formality of course!'

'Six of one and half a dozen of the other!' agreed Sam heartily.

Doubtless this exchange of knightly civilities would have gone on forever. But a small crowd of impatient people had by this time collected behind the Gollens.

'If you don't stop arguing I shall treat you all *myself*!' threatened Winifred.

That thrust them forward, again simultaneously. But this time Sam was victorious, because he kept his money loose in his pocket, whereas Peter had to fumble with the stiff fastening of a heart-shaped leather purse.

Sam was so flushed with this victory that he forgot to pay for Alexandra, and had to rush back again, much to the contempt of the painted humming-bird of a young lady in the glass case.

At last, however, they passed through into a long room with a dark blue carpet soft as a feather bed, cream-coloured walls with gilt panels, huge dark blue arm-chairs and settees, and rows of big golden studs in the ceiling. It was so splendid that Alexandra thought the pictures must be shown here, and wondered why the

seats were so few. On the wall the same moustached young gentleman was again attempting to kiss the perilously tilted lady, but on a
smaller scale than on the outside wall.

But Alexandra was soon undeceived. Another door swung open
before them, and they passed through into a tobacco-smelling
obscurity, with a square of blinding light in the distance, and a
smothering din.

Somebody snatched the tickets out of Sam's hand. 'Ay!' he cried
indignantly, under the impression that he was being robbed, but
she took no notice, tore them in half and gave him four halves back.
She then switched on a long jet of light and motioned them to
follow down a gangway. 'This way,' she said, peremptorily, turning
the jet of light along an empty row of seats.

They shuffled meekly to the places she had indicated. Then, after
a tempestuous period during which they poked as many people as
possible with their umbrellas, pushed their hats too far under the
seats, and instructed Sam, who was trying to perch on the edge of
his without first tipping it down, exactly how to manage this
peculiar object, they sat back and began to look about them.

Sam and Peter had the advantage over Alexandra, in that they
had at least attended church lantern lectures. They had, so to speak,
got the idea of the place. They were chiefly awestricken by its size
and luxury.

But Alexandra looked about her as the dreaming Dante might
have looked about his Dream of Heaven, or Hell. She gazed in
solemn wonder at the great curved phalanx of dark heads, sloping
gently down from before her. She raised her head and saw the bold
curve of the balcony supported apparently upon the smoky air, and
black against the reflected light from that distant oblong. She tilted
her head back and followed the line of the long beam of white
transparent light, in which smoke was dancing and curling — back
to its source in a tiny square at the back of the theatre. This beam of
gauzy light seemed to her the most beautiful thing she had ever seen.
But presently there came a loud pompous roar, from nowhere and
from everywhere, like the voice of a god. And a pair of wonderful
curtains came swinging down in two lovely, stately, symmetrical
arcs across the oblong of light. Blue and gold they were, and gauzy
as summer sunshine, yet they swung in heavy sensuous measure,

and when they met, swung back again, and met a second time, and a third, before they came to rest. Their movement was even more beautiful than the beam of light, and her eyes filled with tears of sensuous pleasure.

When they were dry the great oblong of light behind the heavy gauze curtains had vanished. The curtains now were seen to be of solid velvet and brocade, not transparent at all, and the beam of light had also disappeared. Then, all over the place, other lights opened out, like magic flowers, all in perfect synchronization.

Alexandra looked round at this bewilderingly changeful heaven. Its domed ceiling was blue, painted with large golden stars. On the panels on the walls were painted gentlemen in coloured coats, white breeches and white stockings, and ladies with heads like snowy lettuces and frocks like huge parasols. The walls between the pictures were stippled with gold. So these at last, thought Alexandra, were the pictures! ('We must have just missed the News, thank goodness,' said a voice, sweet as glass-tumbler notes but a long way off.)

Alexandra gazed with all her might at the pictures, passionately determined to learn every inch of them. But before she had examined more than four of the panels, and just as she was beginning to suppress a faint, reluctant disappointment at a certain monotony in subject and style, the lights began to go down again.

Oh, thought Alexandra, they've forgotten to put enough pennies in the meter. And she felt somewhat vexed at this abrupt termination to her worship. The next instant she thought of nothing at all. It was impossible to think against the sudden god-like roar that now burst into the air.

'Oh, good! An organ interlude! Look, Allie — look! The new organ!' cried Winifred, shaking Alexandra's elbow excitedly.

Just in time Alexandra looked. And behold, just in front of the blue and gold curtains, a sort of horseless chariot rose majestically out of the ground — a chariot alight with coloured fire, whose unconsuming and translucent flames chased over its surface unceasingly. It must be like Elijah's chariot of fire, thought Alexandra, suffocated with wonder. But the man who rode in this chariot was not dressed like Elijah. He wore an ordinary evening suit, and instead of standing gazing up to heaven with his arms lifted, he sat with his back to everybody, his legs dangling, she had to admit, in a foolish manner which marred somewhat the dignity of his ascent. She suppressed a faint giggle as unsuitable to the solemnity of the moment.

The chariot came to a slightly bouncing standstill, just above the level of their heads. This gentleman, it seemed, was not like the Elijah of the Bible, destined for heaven. And now she perceived that the succulent god-like roar which had accompanied the ascent was no mere coincidence, but an integral part of the phenomena — that in fact 'Elijah' or whatever his real name might be, was making all that noise himself, simply by moving his arms up and down the front of the chariot, and twiddling his dangling legs. Sometimes it appeared to be necessary to bounce on his seat, as if he were riding a horse, roughly in time to the roars.

These were at first quite stupefying. Presently however, the chariot, which had been burning with clear vermilion fire, faded to a pretty pale rose. And as if in sympathy the din faded also, and presently clarified into a nasal whine, accompanied by thick throbbings.

Suddenly Alexandra recognized a tune. She nudged Winifred excitedly. 'He's playing that thing Peter plays on the whistle!' she cried loudly, so that several people turned their grinning faces to her.

'Sh! It's Schubert's Serenade!' Winifred reproved her.

Alexandra did not see why it should not be Schubert's Serenade. But there was no time to say so. For now the fire in the organ had changed again — this time to blue, violet and green, like salt flames; mysterious dithering music came forth as a result of this change. From this Elijah modulated into orange and rose, with sounds sweet and glutinous as burnt sugar, thence to crimson and purple with heart-searing passion; to scarlet and blue, and a swaggering military march; to pale pink for sentimental yearnings.

It was all very beautiful, Alexandra thought — but especially when she recognized a tune that Peter could play too — even though he had no fiery chariot to sit in. At length, amid clapping that extinguished even his own Olympian thunder, Elijah descended into the bowels of the earth in a rainbow glory of coloured fires. As he sank, however, he tried to acknowledge the applause, without rising and without turning round, producing as a result a number

124

of ridiculous, ill-directed bobbings of his head and shoulder which marred somewhat an otherwise magnificent departure.

Now the curtains were made to seem gauzy again. Some writing showed behind them. Presently they parted with that slow voluptuous swing, and drew back to show clearly the dazzling oblong of light behind. Before she could read a single word the writing was whisked away, to be replaced by a list of names in fancy writing. This also was whisked away just as she had settled down to read the first word in it. But after this had happened several more times, the pictures at last began.

And after all —thought Alexandra, they were not a new idea. She had watched the same sort of things for years, thrown on her orange firelight screen by her old friend the Shadow Showman. She had to admit, however, that *these* shadows were more real. They had faces, voices as well as shape.

Solemnly and rather critically she watched the antics of the two workmen, one very fat, the other very lean, both equally gormless, as they struggled to deliver a large and awkward case containing a piano to a house at the top of a very long flight of steps. When the piano escaped and bumped down these twenty steps, swooping like a Juggernaut over the prostrate fat man, giving vent to unearthly twangling noises as it swept along, Alexandra was more terrified than amused. But when the process had been repeated three times she began to see that a comedy and not a tragedy was intended. The fourth time she was ready for the joke and, when it came, greeted it with loud and lengthy laughter, as children greet the climax of a familiar story. Her brothers were already laughing — so heartily that the audience about them was infected, although they had as a matter of fact begun to be bored by the over emphasis of these comedians. From this point the Gollens laughed without a break almost. Stupidity and destructiveness, which in real life would have shocked all three, seemed to them in this shadow-show almost as funny as *Three Men in a Boat*. The incompetent workmen, by the end of the film, had reduced the Gollens, as well as the house of their labours, to a sodden ruin.

Next came the Micky Mouse (not, reflected Alexandra, between two showers of tears, very much like a mouse, or indeed very much like anything at all). They knew now that films were to make you laugh. And laugh they did, from the first appearance of Micky pedalling an ice-cream bicycle, through the chase by a brutal work-man in a steam-roller, ending by the steam-roller rolling out its driver like a pool of pastry, right to the final succulent kiss, with very much everted lips, between Micky and his sweetheart, a daintier replica of himself in a short frock and an enormous spotted bow.

Hard on the heels of this satisfactory denouement came 'The Real Picture', as Winifred called it. Alexandra never knew what its true name was, and she was not very sure either, what it was all about. It was not quite so funny as the Micky Mouse and the piano-film, but they did their best to laugh at it, and certainly succeeded better than most of the audience who seemed, if not reproachful, at least surprised at their merriment.

The conclusion came at last, a protracted kiss, not unlike Micky's kiss, Alexandra thought, and wondered if films always had to end thus, as hymns she knew, must always end with an 'Amen'.

In a cloud of smudgy, solemn, amen-like music the kiss dissolved, and the lights slowly brightened. The phalanx of dark, still heads became a tumultuous sea of waving coat-sleeves. Then, as this sea gradually calmed and poured itself up the gangways, the smudgy kiss-music ceased abruptly and some dance-music began, fiercely cheerful, as if impatient to clear up the sodden mess deposited by the last picture in the minds of the audience.

The Gollens oozed into the gangway with the rest of their row, Alexandra in an exalted, yet tremulous state of feeling. A sharp word, or a very kind one, would have been enough to set her weep-ing. A fly settling on her hand would have killed her with laughter. She felt that she was capable of the most heroic deeds, as yet un-specified, and that she was on the verge of some obscure and tremendous mystery, that she held, almost, the secret of existence in her hands, that she walked burdened by some great, some universal sorrow, nobly borne as a crown.

When they came out into the neon-lit night she thought she had never seen anything so wonderful as Cobden Square.

The trams moving through the glassy dark like huge elliptical bubbles of light, the lamps, trailing long reflections like kites' tails in the shining ebony road, the jagged coxcomb of the roofs against a sky glowing faintly with the pinkish reflection of the town's neon tubing, some new cube-shaped lamps, giving a pale diluted version of the peacock flash of tram-trollies — all these seemed to her more wonderful than anything she had seen at the pictures. That had been only Shadows. This was Reality. And this, she felt, was the thing for which those magnificent, voluptuous swinging curtains had been made. To reveal this scene, and not those funny shadow-shows, they should have parted. And indeed, for her, so they had parted.

A sob of excitement lay couched in her throat as she walked across this magnificent scene with Sam. As they crossed the bridge, she heard the furtive gabblings of the water under it, and, looking up, she saw the negative image of a train come rushing over the viaduct, its whole length jewelled with windows, and a great rolling plume of smoke underlit with vermilion fire flying back over its shoulder. As it rushed along, it let out a long husky cry, that seemed to speak for her mood of tremulous exaltation and heroic sorrow.

The sob sprang out of her throat.

'What on earth's up with you *now*?' said Sam crossly, and at his voice, her exaltation subsided with a quick sigh like a balloon.

Why was Sam so cross? And why did he keep on glancing back so anxiously at Peter and Winifred? Was he afraid that they would be lost? This might well be so, she decided, for the Square was positively alive with people. Until Sam spoke she had seemed to be alone in a paradise of light. But now she was rather frightened at the number of people about her, particularly when they reached the tram-stop and the people began to press into actual physical contact with her. There would never be room enough for all these in all the trams in the world, she thought.

It seemed a similar idea was in other heads. When the first tram drew up alongside the 'island', the mass of people made such a frantic rush for it that Alexandra was almost trampled under. Some man with a hand like iron pincers seized her and held her up, and by the thrust of the crowd Alexandra was forced forward and up the step, helpless as a stone in a glacier.

She staggered to the foot of the stairs and clung to the brass rail, and, looking back from this refuge, caught sight of Sam, shouting inaudibly and gesticulating madly in the thick of the crowd. She thought he seemed to be wanting her to get out of the tram. But this she could not do — streams of people were buffeting past her as they thrust into the tram. It was impossible to get out. Poor Sam, she thought, seemed torn by conflicting forces. He was afraid of losing Peter and Winifred, whom Alexandra could not see at all. And he was afraid of losing Alexandra. He could not save them both. He could not make up his mind which to save.

The tram lurched and made as if to move off. Sam's face buckled up with his agony. Then, with a last glance of despair, he leapt for the platform. 'You silly little donkey! Why didn't you *wait* for us?' he cried instantly, and his sharp tone surprised Alexandra so much that she began to laugh. So they rode home, she laughing, helplessly, quite unable even to think what she was laughing at, he scowling at her, for people about were beginning to exchange the shamefaced, amused glances which say 'Drunk!'

When they left the tram to walk down Finn Street she became more sober, and began to chatter about the film. 'Wasn't it lovely when the piano went into the fish pond, Sam? — Oh, and when Micky was riding along the telegraph wires! Oh, I thought he'd be killed! But how can they do such things, Sam? I didn't know even a tight-rope walker could ride an ice-cream bicycle along a wire — *and* bounce into the air every time he came to a telegraph pole! I didn't understand the 'Real Picture' very well, did you, Sam? I don't see why Winifred calls it Real do you? Why did that man always have to be bending that lady backwards onto beds and things? . . .'

She became aware that Sam had not answered a single question. There was something peculiar about Sam to-night.

'What's the matter, Sam?' she said anxiously, putting her hand on his arm. Like a sulky boy he stiffened it so that it was impossible for them to link.

'Nothing!' he answered, in a tone which contradicted what he said.

'Didn't you enjoy the pictures?' she said wistfully, then added, 'but, of course, you did. I heard you laughing like anything!' A thought struck her. 'Did you laugh too much? Aren't you well?'

'*Nothing's* the matter, I tell you!' he cried peevishly.

They reached their home in silence, Alexandra still unenlightened as to the cause of this unprecedented mood. He went straight upstairs, and after a short interlude of bumps rather subdued for Sam, came down again with his best tie and collar removed and his shirt unbuttoned at the neck. Alexandra thought he looked rather nice in this unregalia'd state, noting, for the first time, how slender and boyish his neck was, and how white his throat and the beginning of his shoulders.

He went grimly to the door as soon as he came down, and opening it, stood on the top step, gazing down the road intently. It was cold with the door open, but he took no notice of her complaints.

Alexandra decided to prepare the supper. When bread and cheese, and some fancy biscuits, and three cups, were laid out, and the kettle was nearly boiling, she went to Sam.

'Shall I make the cocoa or shall we wait for Peter?' she said, for she was hungry, and nearly half an hour had now passed since they reached home.

Sam suddenly sprang to life. 'Oh be *blowed* to Peter!' he cried, and banged the door so that the house shook like cardboard.

'Sam!' said Alexandra, shocked, for though she had heard much worse words spoken in the street by other men, never before had she heard so mild an expletive as 'blowed' spoken by her brother. Sam had shocked himself also. And now he came shamefaced to the table, his eyes shifting uneasily just below the level of hers.

'Well — they should have kept with us! Dawdling behind like that!' he said, as if by extending the expression of his annoyance he could excuse it.

And as he spoke, a suspicion crept quietly into Alexandra's mind — a suspicion which explained certain age-long rivalries between her brothers — rivalries hitherto accepted by her as a meaningless part of the comedy of her daily life. 'Oh, dear — I hope it isn't true!' she thought, staring at Sam hard. 'I must ask Winifred. I wonder if she knows?'

They sat in silence, so quiet that they could hear a tram grind to the end of Finn Street and start off again.

'Perhaps they're on *that* one!' said Alexandra, trying to comfort him.

'Who?' retorted Sam, and working his pathetic attempt at deception like a creaking old mill-wheel — added, 'D'you mean Peter? I wasn't thinking about him at the moment! Let's have our supper!'

I   129

'Oh! Poor Sam!' thought Alexandra. 'It *must* be true! He's jealous all right!' Silently she made the cocoa.

They had almost finished drinking it when Peter came home. It was more than an hour now since they had left him in the Square.

As soon as he opened the door, Alexandra knew that in his case, too, her suspicions were true.

He could not meet their eyes. And on his face was a curious expression; a thin veil of badly made unconcern, beneath which lay a very patent self-satisfaction; a thin scum of self-control, quite inadequate to conceal the exaltation bubbling beneath.

Something had happened to Peter on the way home, something beautiful and precious to him, which he longed to tell and longed at the same time to keep secret. What could it have been?

Sam's mind was working at the same question.

'Whatever have you been doing all this time?' he demanded of his brother. Alexandra wished he would not show what he felt so crudely.

Peter walked to the fireplace to warm his hands. Quite oblivious of the fact that there was no fire there he stood spreading his hands to the empty grate. It must have been something very lovely to warm him still so that he needed no earthly fires.

'Well — *someone* had to see Winifred home!' he said at last, as if accusing Sam of neglecting her deliberately.

'Yes! But it doesn't take an hour and a quarter to do that!' retorted Sam, resenting this implication fiercely.

'We waited for the next tram quite a while. And when it came Winifred wouldn't push, and we didn't get on it. She said she was not going back to savagery for a ride on a tram. So we walked it. It's a beautiful night. Did you notice the stars?' finished Peter, dropping altogether now the thin veil that had failed to hide his exaltation.

'No — we came straight home!' said Sam, with a stinging, unpleasant wit very unusual for him.

If he expected the remark to sting Peter into further revelations he was disappointed. In silence Peter made himself a cup of cocoa, sipped it, nibbled absently a sugared biscuit, and went quietly up to bed. Soon Sam stumbled up after him.

How upset they both were was proved by the fact that neither remembered to lock the door. Feeling protective, wise, burdened like a mother by this newly-discovered folly of her brothers, Alexandra locked it for them, and went herself to bed. To-day, she thought, as she blew out her candle, had brought her a rich store of new experience.

Being over-excited by these new experiences, it was a long time before she slept, and she was troubled by certain illusions which were apt to trouble her after such days. As she lay there, flat on her back, her legs fully stretched, she felt as if she were floating backwards through the air. She also had the curious sensation that her hands and head were enormously swollen. Yet she was fully aware that these were illusions. It was as if another self in her were being floated and had these enormous hands, and merely reported the sensations to her.

The sensations were on the whole rather pleasant. She lay in a serene detachment from them and, meanwhile, bobbing and drifting and diving and spinning, came fragments of the evening's richness, elusive as wreckage in a still-heaving sea.

Among this wreckage came an image of a woman being dragged across the floor by her long brown hair. Had this been a scene in the 'Real Picture'? she wondered vaguely. She thought not — yet it seemed to associate very easily with other images, which had been she knew in the 'Real Picture' — those scenes where the man with the little black moustache bent the woman over beds and things! Yet if this image had *not* been part of to-night's shadow show — where *had* it come from?

CHAPTER V

ONE Saturday morning when Alexandra was making the beds, she heard a new sound coming along Finn Street, a sound reminiscent of Sam's saucepan and gas-exploding symphonies. She ran to the window, and pressed her face sideways against the glass. An old and shattered-looking car was panting by the kerb, and Iris Young was just ducking her head to get out of the driving seat. Alexandra rushed downstairs. She liked to open the door herself for Iris.

Iris gave her a smile like a kingfisher flashing in and out of sight. 'Would you like to come and see some gliding at the club? The attractions include a ride in this old dustbin first, and a night at an inn with me!'

Alexandra was speechless with happiness. 'Well?' said Iris, smiling patiently.

'Peter? . . .' said Alexandra, still inarticulate in her joy.

Peter looked rather bewildered. Such sudden invitations were hardly decent to his mind. Besides — 'How much would it cost, Miss Young?' he said awkwardly, resenting this necessary exposure of a poverty he and Sam generally contrived to forget.

'My dear fellow!' cried Iris Young, 'it's an *invitation*! You don't invite people to take a ride and then charge them for their transport!'

'Oh well — I suppose there's nothing to stop you if you want to go!' stammered Peter.

'Right!' flashed Iris. 'You don't want anything but a nightie, Allie! — And your mackintosh, of course!'

Still silent, still breathless, Alexandra ducked her head and contorted her spine, and settled herself back into the soft body-dented upholstery, that trembled under her as if the car were as violently excited as herself.

Over the railings peered the dubious faces of her brothers. Never before had a member of the Gollen family ventured into one of these new-fangled contraptions, and with their obvious pleasure at their sister's happiness was mingled equally obvious doubt as to the end of such a bold experiment.

'Wouldn't you like to come, too?' shouted Iris in an impulse of mischief.

'Oh no! No! No!' cried the pair in unison, retreating a little from the railing as if they suspected this disconcerting woman of planning to abduct them.

Iris laughed, stooped to pull a stick with a knob at the end, and with a few preliminary roars, a few snorts, two abortive jerks forward, and a terrifying fit of epilepsy, they were off.

Alexandra relaxed into the soft friendly leather, giving herself up to the sensations of riding in a car. At first she was rather disappointed. It was not, after all, very different from riding in a tram. You were flung about in the same boisterous manner. Your ears were afflicted by the same loud, rude hawking as of some monstrous iron throat. There was the same burring up the scale, with the same unexpected stops, followed by fresh beginnings at a lower pitch. And the low vantage-point of her seat was inferior in her opinion to the princely, howdah-pride of the top of a tram.

But when with a lurch, which flung up Alexandra's right foot into the air, they turned into a wide straight road with no tram-lines, but with trees along each side, Alexandra decided that cars had their compensations. She began to perceive, as she had never perceived in a tram, the strange effect of fluidity which speed can have upon usually static objects. The road, for instance, which she had thought to be an unyielding switchback of granite, now began to buckle slowly under the devouring wheels of the car, as if it were a long carpet, billowing slowly in a wind that crept underneath it. This carpet, though it appeared in the distance to be too narrow for their passage, seemed to be opened out by the nose of the car, like a seam being pressed open by the nose of her brother's irons.

She was so fascinated by these phenomena that if Peter had asked her to give an account of the first ten miles of her first journey in a car, his opinion of motorists would have been confirmed. For a time she even forgot the existence of Iris herself, so that her nerves twitched when the latter suddenly asked, 'Enjoying yourself?'

'Oh yes!' she replied in her deep, tense voice. Then, the hypnotic spell of the billowing, opening road being broken by Iris's voice, she set herself to watch the passing countryside.

Her first amazement was at the softness of it all. Her eye and mind were accustomed to the unyielding brutal patterns of slates, bricks, cobbles, chimneys and street vehicles. In all her walks with Iris, she had seen only the moors to the east of Colebridge. And these in effect were almost as harsh, as unyielding, as grimy, as the town itself.

But this was different. Here were soft cushiony fields of brown corduroy; or of delicate green-striped silk; or of green and buff taffeta; here were trees and hedges like flocks of soft green-feathered birds; here were froths of white blossom, like great clouds of milk boiling over the edge of a saucepan. How deliciously soft it all was! She wanted to stroke the passing fields; to jump out and bury her face in them. Even the hills away to the right looked soft, scarcely more substantial than the cloud-shadows that blew gently over them. Even the houses looked soft — like things to eat almost. The low sheds round the farm-houses had roofs crusted with gold powder like fried bread-crumbs; the farm-houses themselves were either a soft thick pink colour, like pressed tongue, or a rich creamy, sugary colour, like marzipan. They were all so delicious looking that they must belong to witches, for the purpose of attracting silly and greedy children, like Hansel and Gretel.

On they went — faster and faster billowed the long carpet of the road. And after a while Alexandra's amazement at the softness of the country was forgotten in her even greater amazement at the vastness of the world. She had begun by thinking that the world was Finn Street; then it had expanded to the boundaries of Colebridge; next she had been confounded by the extent of the moors; and now once again the world was stretched into unimaginable amplitudes.

'Iris — how big *is* the world?' she said suddenly — moved by a sudden impulse to put a limit somewhere to this eternal expansion.

Iris did not answer at first. 'Well,' she said at last. 'That's a difficult question to answer. It depends so much upon who is looking at it. In figures, if figures mean anything to you, they say it is twenty-five thousand miles round.'

'Oh!' said Alexandra. 'That doesn't sound very big! I thought it would be a lot bigger than that!'

Iris laughed. 'Some people are hard to satisfy!' she said teasingly. And she thought, as they drove on in silence, 'I often notice a disappointment in *children* when I tell them that figure. Whether there's something small about the sound of it — or whether a child's imagination is too big for reality to satisfy I don't know. I suppose, as a matter of fact, the older we get, the smaller the world grows . . . I wonder if I'm shrinking the world for Alexandra — instead of widening her imagination as I would like to think?'

But she did not dwell long on this uneasy notion, for though intellectually capable of questioning her actions, fundamentally she was not of the hesitating, self-doubting temperament.

They ate their lunch by the roadside, drawing the car onto a verge of rough grass, and sitting with their legs swinging from a stone bridge over a little stream — whose voice was like the quiet scattering of beads from a broken necklace.

Alexandra swung her legs in space and was so happy that she did not know she was eating. She swung her legs and stared at the beech woods opposite, bursting into green fire; and at the rooks, wafting out of the fire and in again, like smutty flakes of burnt paper. She was so happy that everything seemed to happen within her, slightly magnified; the sunlight, the incantations of a distant cuckoo, the blackness of the rooks, and the greenness of the new beech leaves, were all within her — the result, not the cause, of her happiness.

She could not have said all this. She could not, indeed, even say that she was happy. She could only repeat over and over to herself like a song

'I am sitting on this bridge, with Iris!'

At about six o'clock they purred gently down into a village of green-grey stone set in a triangle about a piece of cropped grass. The houses round this grass were gardenless at the front, except for one, a little more sprawling than the others, which had a frieze of yellow and brown gillyflowers at the base of its walls, set in a narrow strip of soil unfenced from the road. There was a board swinging above the door of this house, on which was a picture of a yellow beehive with some very large bees buzzing out in a curved file.

'Jump out!' commanded Iris, stopping the car in front of this house.

A few moments later they were in a narrow hall, so dark that Alexandra could see nothing but a blurred white shape at the far end. This shape stirred and advanced upon them, and resolved itself into a large round-bellied man in a white overall.

'Good afternoon, Mr. Downes,' said Iris. 'This is my friend Miss Gollen. Is my usual room empty?'

Mr. Downes rotated slowly in order to look at Alexandra, then bowed, as far as a globe may safely allow itself to bow. 'Pleased to make her acquaintance,' he said in a smothered sounding voice, as well he might, thought Alexandra.

Then he rotated solemnly back to Iris, like a large ball twirling slowly in mid air by a string. 'Yes! I think we can manage it! Does your friend want a separate room, or will she share yours?'

Iris looked at Alexandra. 'What do you say?'

Alexandra's cheeks warmed. 'Oh — I should like to share yours!' she said, and felt that if more were added she would die, heartbroken with joy. To be called Iris's friend — and now to be allowed to sleep with her!

Mr. Downes, with the puff-ball lightness of very fat people, floated up the dark narrow stairs before them, opened a door, compressed himself against the lintel until Alexandra thought he would pop, remarked, 'All as usual you see, Miss Young!' and drifted down the stairs again.

Iris walked into the room. 'It's rather pokey,' she apologized, 'but it's incredibly clean, and the bed is well sprung despite its ribbon bows!'

Alexandra stared at the bed, and thought that it looked like the bed of a princess. Its foot was oval, without a rail. At the head was one tall post, from which hung two curtains of spotted muslin, drawn back slantwise and fastened with pink satin bows. Muslin frilled the sides all round down to the ground. And a wonderful eiderdown lapped like a fairy sea of ruched pink satin wavelets up to the snowy banks of the pillows.

'It's *too* beautiful!' she said at last. 'It's too beautiful to sleep in!'

Iris laughed at her. 'The only thing that's worrying me is whether there is enough room for our four feet at the bottom!' she said.

When they had spread their few possessions about the room and so made it theirs, and had washed, and tidied their hair, they went down to the sitting-room — a dim room with a small square window, a picture of a girl, swinging, in what seemed to be her nightdress, a case with a little red-brown animal in it which Iris said was a squirrel, and a fire of quarter-logs of wood, which burnt very red, and made a great quantity of beautiful, soft white ashes.

Here they ate a meal which the clock called supper, but which by its ingredients seemed to Alexandra to be a dinner.

Afterwards they played for a time with a queer mechanism with a slot into which you put a penny, when a large brass disk with holes in it began jerkily to revolve, producing music, so jerky and so twangy, that it made Alexandra weep with laughing.

In the midst of this the host's wife came in, a little woman with a halo of black hair. 'Oh!' she remarked, 'that thing used to go a lot better than that till the gentlemen fooled with it too rough. But there! Gentlemen *will* be gentlemen I suppose!' — a remark which seemed to amuse Iris nearly as much as the twangling musical disk had amused Alexandra.

When they were tired of this amusement, they went for a stroll up a steep hill. They sat on a stile at the top of the hill, watching the light wither out of the lucent sky, and listening to the stealthy hands of the wind in the leaves over their heads. And Alexandra wondered, helplessly, achingly, what Iris was thinking of. There she sat — so near that her shoulder just touched Alexandra's with each breath she drew. Yet her thoughts were as much out of reach as the thoughts of a picture-book princess — more so — for the book told you what the princess was thinking about. But there was no book to tell what Iris thought about. And into her happiness fell the single drop of bitterness necessary to perfect that happiness.

When it was almost dark, a great soft, wood-ash coloured creature looped up to a branch of the tree above them. There it folded down its broad noiseless wings and sat looking over their heads with eyes like faint pennies of light.

'A white owl'! whispered Iris. 'Lovely thing!'

But softly as she whispered, the owl seemed to hear. Unhurriedly it spread its great ash-coloured sails and floated noiselessly away.

'It must be getting late. Come home to bed,' said Iris. Arm in arm, not speaking, walking thoughtfully, they went down to the 'Beehive' Inn, between the hawthorns whose whiteness was muted in the darkness, but whose scent was not. Alexandra's mind reached forward and backward — but chiefly forward, to the bed fit for a princess, and to the night she would soon spend, in that bed, with the princess by her side — the strange, lovely, remote, yet friendly princess who had come from nowhere to call her from her living death, who had a helmet of gold, and eyes like the wings of dragon flies, who knew everything, and who showed her the great and wonderful world. At the thought of lying in the same bed with this miraculous creature, her skin thrilled and her pulse accelerated.

Alexandra was in bed first by a long time. She pulled the soft satin eiderdown up to her chin, and lay straight and still, her eyes fixed upon Iris, for perhaps never again would she be allowed to sleep with her princess — and to watch her undress. Such things are for once in a lifetime. She must treasure the smallest details.

She had never realized that the act of undressing could be so beautiful. It was more like the paces of a lovely and deliberate dance than what Alexandra understood by undressing. Deliberate, but swift, and perfectly timed, were all her movements.

First her blouse — which she removed by crossing her arms over her breasts in a momentarily virginal posture, then sweeping them up over her head in a sort of laughing contempt. Now her shoulders were revealed — and how beautiful they were, creamy as milk, and smooth as eggs, each curving in a shallow wave to her spine, where there lay a gleam of golden down. And instead of a vest she wore the prettiest garment Alexandra had ever seen — consisting of two pink inverted cups, like satin flowers, over her breasts, and a number of narrow criss-crossing strips, like trellis-work across her bare back.

One by one her other garments slipped from her to the floor, and were folded, and hung neatly over the chair back, or on her small silk-padded hanger in the wardrobe. This flower-like garment of pale shining pink silk alone remained. But at last, with a small click, this too was unfastened, slipped from her body, and hung carefully over the chair back. The princess stood in the shifting, whispering candlelight, straight, spare and naked. How beautiful she was! Flat, slender, shallowly curved and hard, as if carved out of bone, the whiteness of her warmed in the hollows of her form to the colour of old ivory, her eyes looking black and glittering from under her helmet of bronze — ah, how beautiful she was! Happiness, which had reared like a smooth gliding wave all day above Alexandra's heart curled over now, and crashed upon it in a prolonged seething of passionate delight.

When it was spent, sliding back into tranquillity to gather up its force for another advance — the princess, clad now in peacock blue pyjamas, was slipping down into bed beside her. A dim, sweet scent came to Alexandra, and an even dimmer, sweeter emanation of warmth stole across the bed to her. The wave crashed upon her heart a second time. When it retreated once more, Iris was blowing out the candle.

There was a silence. In the dark, jazzy with imaginary lights still, Alexandra lay rigid, terrified of moving lest she should touch the warm scented body of her princess. She could hardly bear the joy of her nearness; how then could she endure the terrible joy of actually touching her? But presently Iris put out one foot and felt cautiously to find Alexandra's.

'Good heavens child!' she exclaimed, when she found it, 'what are you lying on the edge of the bed for?' She pushed a warm bare arm under Alexandra's neck, and over her shoulder, and pulled her close.

The third wave crashed down upon her heart, and this time washed her completely under. For the rest of the night she remained half-submerged in her passion of sensuous joy — which broke and foamed over her afresh whenever Iris's cold toes, or silken knee, touched any part of her body. And whether it was this submerging joy, or whether it was that unravelling of the heart which is so often effected by proximity to a loved and friendly companion in the warmth and darkness of bed, who can tell? But something that night opened many rooms of Alexandra's mind — dark and musty rooms, locked up since her childhood.

Iris unconsciously began it all by asking, after a soft explosive yawn, if she had enjoyed the day.

'Oh yes! But I wish Sam and Peter could have come too!' replied Alexandra — then added, 'But I doubt if they would have — even if they could! They don't think anything of motor cars!'

'Your brothers', said Iris, in the low dreamy voice peculiar to conversations in bed, 'are the most simple-minded pair of men I have ever met. And the happiest — or at any rate the most content. I suppose they are survivals really — out of place in this world — they belong to the age of craftsmen — they are anachronisms I suppose. But oh! What a pity that we ever grew out of the world *they* belong to! . . . Not long ago I went over a tailoring factory — where they turn out hundreds of suits in a day, all in stock sizes, by mass-production methods of course — well enough made suits I suppose. But the workers! Why! they were so bored and so unhappy that they had to turn a wireless on all day, so that they would not be able to think how unhappy they were. If I had to work there, I should go mad before I could receive my first wage-packet. The world *is* slowly going mad, I think!

'Now, if we could get back to your brothers' world and could put
our hearts into our work — perhaps we should all be as good and
contented as your brothers!'

'No!' said Alexandra, after her usual pause to think this out.
'No! I think my brothers must have been *born* happy, just as they
were born *good*. My father was a very good tailor. He didn't
work in a factory. He was a better tailor than either Sam or Peter.
He was as good a tailor drunk as he was sober! But he was the
wickedest man ever born! And I don't think he was very happy
either. Not that *I* care about that!' Her vehemence astounded
Iris, and so did her sudden independence, for as a rule she showed
herself deferent to Iris's opinions, humble and docile indeed to a
dangerous degree. Something in her early experiences had bitten
deep and bitterly into her mind. That was plain.

'What was he like — to look at, Alex?' she asked, alive with
curiosity, but uncertain how much she ought to probe into this
troubled and probably unwholesome part of the girl's life.

Instantly — at these words, like a dark, inky cloud-genii out of a
magic bottle, there rose up before the eyes of his daughter the squat,
powerful form of Henry Gollen, as vivid against the darkness of
the bedroom as if he were floodlit, as vivid almost as on the day
when she saw him outside the 'Railway Arms'.

Black-browed, with his head like a hard rock, scarcely softened
by the dry close-bitten moss that served him for hair, his lower lip
thrust out loose and wet, but caught in at one corner by a gleam of
teeth, his repulsively small fists clenched at his waistcoat armpits,
he stood there and leered at her. He seemed like a gorilla — made
more horrible, more obscene, by being dressed in human clothes.
But though she saw him so vividly, so vividly that her pulse
quickened with an ancient, all-but forgotten terror, she could
not describe what she saw. 'He was very ugly — black and strong
and ugly as sin!' was all she could find to say.

The tone of this remark made some amends for the poverty of
the words. But Iris had not a strong visual imagination, and the
genii who rose before her, conjured out of his bottle by Alexandra's
description, was scarcely visible against the dark.

'Did he die before you were ill or after?' she inquired in an effort
to reach the secret of this strange girl's childhood by some other route.

'Oh before!' answered Alexandra instantly.

'What did he die of?'

'A stroke — he drank too much!'

'Oh — is that what made you say just now that he was wicked?'

'No,' replied Alexandra indifferently. 'Lots of people drink too much. It doesn't make them wicked — only silly!' she explained, in the tone of pathetic, because premature, worldly-wisdom of a child, thought Iris compassionately as she asked.

'How *was* he wicked then?'

There was a very long pause this time. Iris began to think she had asked too much — stirred too deeply in these mysterious and stagnant memories. But at last Alexandra answered, and now there was more than a child's wisdom in her answer.

'He wasn't always *doing* wicked things. But even if he was doing nothing at all he was still wicked. You could feel it, coming out of him like a *smell* . . . I don't know really what he did, because he always used to lock us in the kitchen — that is, after my mother died.'

As she spoke these words there was resurrected in her mind, instantaneous, yet nightmare-long, in the paradoxical manner of a dream, in which an eternity of horror is telescoped into an instant, that time after her mother's death, but before her father's, when Sam and Peter and herself seemed to be huddled for ever before a microscopic fire in the kitchen, she with two pairs of their big socks on her feet to warm their bitterness, and another pair on her hands. Even the bitter cold, however, froze her blood less than the sounds coming from the next room. Those sounds! Oh those sounds! Of her father, or of some beast he had let loose in that room! — low, guttural, half-animal some of them; storms of crazy laughter; shrieks — a woman's shrieks! — half of extreme terror — half of an excitement which the girl in the icy kitchen, ignorant as she was, half-crazed with imagination as she was, recognized as obscene; splinterings of wood; ripping of cloth; the long snail, like waves on pebbles, of breaking glass. These sounds she could interpret, with a certainty which robbed them of three parts of their terror. But what were those other sounds? And what was that staggering of feet backwards and forwards across the room — that thud as of something soft and heavy — that rusty sounding screech — those terrible sobs, accompanied by more of the low, guttural, half-animal sounds — and followed, most terrible of all, by silence, a silence that crept with obscenity as surely as those walls in there crept with bugs.

Even now — at the slow faint echo of that terrible silence, across nearly twelve years of forgetfulness, her blood crept and chilled.

'And your mother — what was *she* like?'

Iris's voice crashed into these creeping and crinkling spicules of horror like a stone into a freezing pool.

'She had very long hair!' replied Alexandra, with a prompt inadequacy that caused them both to laugh.

'Is that all you can remember?' asked Iris. But she received no answer. Alexandra was no longer there. She was being swept away on an avalanche of remembrance — set tumbling by her own words.

She was nine years old, lying in the small bumpy bed which she shared then with Sam and Peter. It was a summer night, and the air was so hot that it seemed like your own sweat, and the swallows were screaming above the black crowns of the chimneys.

Suddenly came other screams — screams that dragged her up in bed and left her trembling all over as if she had just been sick — screams from downstairs — screams she had heard before, but which she had never dared to find the meaning of. They were worse to-night than they had ever been. She could not endure them, as she had managed to endure them always before. Trembling and sweating and cold, she crept downstairs in the ragged old striped shirt of Peter's that served her for a nightdress, and went into the kitchen to get comfort from her brothers.

The kitchen was empty! Still those screams continued. Were Sam and Peter being murdered in there? Trembling, she stood barefooted on the black rag hearthrug and listened. Words were tangled in the screams.

"'Arry! Let me go you ——! 'Arry!'

Then it was her mother in there — being murdered, and her father the murderer! She ran to the door and flung it open violently, because she was so terrified.

On her knees, with her hands to her head, was her mother, screaming piercingly without a stop.

142

Over her stood her father, with both fists clenched in a great knot of her mother's brown hair, yanking her from side to side, with a vicious laugh at each wrench.

'Let *that* larn yer!' he shouted, over and over again. And her mother shrieked.

And suddenly Alexandra's terror dissolved and reformed into rage. 'Let go of 'er!' she shouted so loud that he started and nearly did so in his surprise. The next moment, however, he gave a loud and savage laugh, and a still more vicious wrench to the knot of brown hair.

'Listen to your bloody little champion!' he mocked.

The next instant Alexandra had snatched up a pair of his tailor's scissors, and with one grinding snip, had freed her mother's hair from his grip. There was an astounded pause. Then her mother sprang up, and backed behind the table, her eyes blazing with terror, hatred — heaven knows what beside, staring at Alexandra standing there in her ragged shirt, panting, the huge scissors trembling in her two hands.

And at last she spoke. 'You silly little fool! Look what a bloody mess you've made of my hair!' she cried furiously — and suddenly darted out to Alexandra, snatched away the scissors, and gave her a stinging blow on one cheek. '*That'll* teach you to poke your nose into my business! Get back to bed!' she shouted, and burst into tears. And her father leaned against the wall, the brown knot of severed hair still in his repulsive fists, and laughed till it seemed the house must fall. . . .

How could she tell all this? The passions of that far off night eluded words — as well try to tie up smoke with a string.

'No!' she therefore replied. 'I don't remember my mother. She died when I was ten. Mrs. Tyler says she was pretty — when he married her!'

Iris grimaced in the dark at this unconscious condemnation of the man who was 'ugly as sin' and who 'smelt of wickedness'. 'Did he marry again?' she asked after a pause — with an eye to the locked door Alexandra had mentioned previously.

'No. Mrs. Tyler used to tell him he ought to, for the sake of the children. But he wouldn't. "Why should ah bother wi' parson when t'bitches coom roonin' fast enoogh wi'out im? Coom roonin' like flies to t'mook 'eap!" — That's what he answered, she told me not long ago.'

And now, at these words, the first direct quotation of this creature's speech, Iris began to feel something of that which his daughter had said you could smell coming out of him. There was more than plain brutality, more than plain sensuality, in the man who could speak those words. A bitter recognition of his own degradation — a twisted, malicious pleasure in his own obscenity, and a contempt for those who were drawn irresistibly by the sinister power of that obscenity — all these things were implicit in those few words of his. Smelt of wickedness? The man positively stank of it!

Stirred by a sudden gust of compassion for the child who had been born to live in the house of such a man, she leaned across, found Alexandra's cheek, and kissed it.

'I think we'd better go to sleep. Good night my dear!' she said gently, and turning over on her side, fell asleep in a very few moments.

But Alexandra could not sleep. She lay, stupefied at first by the impact of this most shattering happiness of all. Then, recovered a little, but still languid, she lay helplessly, while the delicious foam of remembered pleasure washed over and over her heart. The shape of those warm lips on her cheek still lingered there, as the shape of some brilliant object will linger on the eyeballs after it has actually withdrawn. The illusion came and went and each recurrence produced a new seething of that delicious foam of sensuous pleasure. It was not for over an hour that the last whispers of this foamy pleasure died into silence, ... d she was able to sleep at last. She did not know that in this hour of rapturous joy, she had reached the culminating point of her relationship with Iris, that after this night there would be disintegration — adulteration of the fierce purity of her worship with other less admirable emotions.

The next day was like its predecessor, a dappled day, with light downy clouds puffed before the wind like thistledown. It was still a new and very lively delight to Alexandra to stand on the hill-top and watch their shadows blowing along, even more downy than themselves, pale violet on the far hills, dark green on the near fields.

144

But there was a great deal more to look at to-day than cloud-shadows — more than enough to sweep out the dark and sultry shapes of her memories of the night before.

On the hill-top, covered with short grass tipped with feathery brown flower, ruffled in sheeny waves by the wind, were three curious objects, white, fragile-looking, like great angular birds of cardboard.

'There's my "Kittiwake"!' said Iris affectionately, pointing to one of these as they came in sight of them. 'At least — *not* mine exactly. But, I feel as though she is. I've been up in her so often now.'

Alexandra felt very alarmed at the thought of even Iris going up in one of these inadequate-looking structures. She could not conceive how it could possibly be lifted into the air.

But so eventually it was. There was a great deal to happen before this, however.

First of all, Alexandra had to encounter a bewildering collection of strangers. Somehow she had never thought of Iris as possessing any friends. She had seemed to her a unique and solitary creature — god-like in her isolation.

Now, however, a tall lean man with a shock of dark hair, a large mouth and protruding dark eyes, strolled up with his hands in the pockets of a very ill-shapen sports-jacket, and, ignoring Alexandra, began to talk to Iris in a way that indicated a well-established friendship.

Alexandra developed an instant and unreasonable dislike for this man, whose name, it seemed, was Gordon.

Then three more men, rather weathered, in khaki shorts, a withered-looking young man in dirty flannels, a large loose limbed elderly man in plus-fours of unfashionable exaggeration, and a woman in a tweed coat, with a very highly-coloured face as bright as a mask, gathered round Iris, laughing and talking at her all at once.

Alexandra had the satisfaction at least of seeing that this Gordon creature looked very annoyed at this incursion of the general public into his friendship. It was poor consolation. He could, after all, understand what they were talking about, and make his own contribution to the talk. This was impossible to Alexandra.

She stood apart, silent and sullen, her eyes alternately black and hard as she looked at Gordon and all these other men, brown and liquid, as they moved to Iris herself.

At last yet another man came to the group, a man with a face red and polished as if he had been pumice-stoned all over; even his bald pate was polished scarlet.

'Well Miss Young — you couldn't have picked a better day!' he remarked. The chatter died down to a murmur.

'Gordon — will you look after Alex?' said Iris over her shoulder as she strolled across the field with this man.

The rest of the circle turned itself into knots of twos and threes, and Alexandra found herself left alone with this lanky, ugly, shock-headed and detestable young man.

Refusing to answer more than yes or no to his conventional remarks, she watched how Iris and the bald, polished-pated man wandered about the 'Kittiwake', he flapping his arm towards this part and that, Iris nodding repeatedly. Evidently he was giving her a few last words of advice.

'That's our instructor,' the Gordon creature told her. 'Wonderful fellow — much more patient than Job!'

'Oh!' grunted Alexandra rudely.

Presently she saw Iris climb into a hole just between the wings of the glider, which rocked under her weight, and still further alarmed Alexandra by this proof of its flimsiness.

Two men in shirt-sleeves stood by the wing-tips of it, holding them level; the instructor flapped his arms a few more times; Iris's rough voice, but not her words, drifted across the field.

Then suddenly a loud rattling and chugging began in another direction. Alexandra saw a group of men about what looked like the broken-down interior of a very old-fashioned car, and wondering what on earth they were doing she forgot to look at the 'Kitti-wake' until a sudden bark from Gordon — 'She's off!' — jerked her eyes back.

Very deliberately, like a lazy sea-gull, it was lifting from the ground, and as it lifted, something slipped from it and thudded softly to the ground.

'She's loosed!' said Gordon by way of explanation.

And now the 'Kittywake' began to climb, in a lovely lifting

curve, tilting slightly in a pendulum motion at first, then steadying. Then it swept easily like a great white bird with rather thick angular wings, right out over the steep scarp of the hill.

Alexandra held her breath. How could it possibly hold up? She had watched sea-gulls turning and drifting over the River Cole, and noticed how seldom came their wing-strokes, in this unlike crows, who work hard all the time. But this thing did not, could not, move its wings at all. Powerfully it swept out, then hesitated, then tilted until the near wing was pointing almost to the earth, swooped back at them, but high above their heads, tilted on the opposite wing, and swept away, seeming to edge sidelong, a little awkwardly, like a sea-gull blown in a gale. When it reached the far end of the hill, it tilted again, circled in a wide **C** shape and came edging back in that strange, slightly awkward, yet contemptuously confident manner, a little lower this time. As it passed over them it seemed to increase speed with a rush, and they could hear the wind creaking under its wings. The next instant it was passed — and silent as a bird.

Alexandra's eyes filled with tears at the beauty of its passing.

'Lovely things, aren't they?' said Gordon, who seemed to have a detestable knack of guessing other people's secret feelings. She would not answer.

Again the 'Kittiwake' was tilting, circling lazily, awkwardly, with serene confidence in its power to afford being lazy and awkward. And — whoosh! It was over their heads again — drifting contemptuously to the far end of the hill. Twice more the pattern was repeated. Each time the 'Kittywake' passed a little nearer to their heads.

'How lovely it must feel up there,' cried Alexandra, carried all at once out of her sullen antagonism by the thrill of that lazy powerful swoop past. 'It must feel as if you are dead — and your soul is let out of your body!'

Gordon looked at her curiously, and gave a somewhat discomforting laugh.

'Well — you put it a little ghoulishly, but I get your idea!' he said, and his tone caused Alexandra to redden, and set her face once more in its heavy lines of sullen antagonism.

'As a matter of fact,' he went on, 'it doesn't feel nearly so effortless

147

as it looks. In fact, I should say you are screwed even more tightly than ever into your five senses. If you aren't, you may look for disaster!'

Alexandra refused to answer.

The 'Kittiwake' came over again—whoosh! drifted to the nearer end of the hill, and this time curved back not in a C shape, but in the shape of a writing L, rushed so low over their heads that they both instinctively ducked (though needlessly), and gently, in a series of curved steps, came to earth, with a final long slide, a bounce and a rocking sideways, so like a sea-bird, that Alexandra almost expected to see it fold back its wings and tuck them neatly to its sides with the quaint little twiddling movements of a gull.

Everybody ran across the field, laughing and cheering. Gordon was the first, the instructor second, and Alexandra the last, to reach the 'Kittiwake'. In the general hullabaloo there was not a single cranny for Alexandra's voice.

But afterwards, when they walked, unfortunately with this Gordon fellow, down the hill to the 'Beehive', Iris said, with a smile which instantly melted away her sulky pain at this exclusion, 'Well — and what do you think of gliding, Alex?'

Alexandra smiled back at her passionately, 'I think I should never want to fly an aeroplane if I could fly in one of *those* lovely things!' she said.

Iris gave a delighted laugh, and turned to Gordon on her other side. 'There now. You see! An instinctive agreement with what I always say — gliding is poetry, but machine flight is only prose!'

'Oh, I agree—I agree entirely. But all the same, your glider is a toy — whereas a machine is real life. But there is a place for toys, just as there is a place for poetry!'

'Poetry and toys are ends in themselves! Aeroplanes are only a *means* — a means of transport. But, of course, men always prefer means to ends. That's why our civilization is in such a ghastly mess! Anyway, give me poetry — give me and Alexandra poetry every time — eh, Alex?' And in her excitement and triumph she squeezed Alexandra's arm tight against her warm breast.

Alexandra thrilled with pleasure — but it was not now purely sensual pleasure as from the kiss in the darkness. It was a mixed pleasure, with a strong flavour in it of the joy of conflict. She felt that Iris had been with her, and against this Gordon fellow, and that for once at least he had been worsted.

When, outside the 'Beehive', he mounted a rusty old motor bicycle, and departed explosively in clouds of dust, she felt that he was routed indeed.

CHAPTER VI

But Gordon Bridges was not routed on that dappled morning in May. On the contrary, as May turned into June, and June danced on towards July, he became a more and more prominent obstacle in the course of Alexandra's love for Iris. And, piled up against that obstacle, like water by a great boulder in its path, her love became more and more violently troubled.

One evening, towards the end of June, she suddenly realized that she had walked from Finn Street to the Public Library without noticing a single object on the way. She was startled. She remembered her intense eagerness for sights and sounds and sensations when she first came back into the world, and she was horrified to think that in so short a time the world could have become of so little importance to her. For this was not the first time she had walked through the streets blind and deaf and without delight. Was she abnormal, she wondered? Was there something fundamentally lacking in her make-up? She could not know that it was her previous intensity of vision, her previous almost complete objectivity, which had been abnormal, and that now she was coming into line with the majority of mankind, whose ears are for the most part stopped up with the music of what they wish they were hearing, and whose eyes turn (except for practical purposes) chiefly inward upon what may be, or what might have been.

During this walk, her mind, like the mind of all those who are too violently, too jealously in love, whether with some ambition, or with some fellow-being, had been building its own impossible world of brilliant colour, simplified emotion and complete docility to her will.

In that world, Iris Young did things she would never do in the real world—she fell over one hundred-foot precipices, was threatened by bulls, was drowned, crashed in her glider, set her clothes on fire. And Alexandra existed purely in order to save her from these variable deaths. The accidents and the manner of the rescues, were all vague, rapidly sketched pictures, soon tossed aside. The important scene — always the same, contained a white, exhausted Iris, lying with closed eyes and bleeding forehead. Kneeling beside her was Alexandra, her heart wrung with terror and grief — unable even to whisper her name, loosening her blouse, gently rubbing her hands, moistening her forehead. After a long time the white, auburn fringed eyelids would lift weakly, and the beloved blue-green eyes dwelt on her gravely. And Alexandra kissed her hand and wept, and again could say nothing. But she would tear off a strip of her underskirt and stop the bleeding of Iris's forehead, and give her her coat for a pillow. And at last Iris would smile weakly, and say with her own peculiar mixture of affection and irony, 'I believe you've been saving my life Alex! Have you?'

'Oh I *hope* so!' Alexandra would say fervently.

Whereat Iris would smile again. 'I believe you love me better than anyone else in the world!' she would say.

'Oh I *do*, Iris! I *do*!'

'It's funny it should be *you* and not Gordon that has saved my life!'

'He doesn't love you like *I* do, Iris! He doesn't really!'

In this and similar scenes she had lived all the way from home to the library, and when someone said 'Hullo' at the library steps, she stared stupidly for several seconds, unable to think who she was, or what she had to do with the drama within. Then she remembered that it was Winifred Bell, who lived in the real world. That world of tears and sweet confessions within her had not been real.

'Oh, hullo!' she said nervously, wondering just how long the pause had been before she answered, and whether Winifred was suspicious of her sanity. If she was, she made neither sign nor comment. They stood in the queue together and chatted, as if Alexandra had never had to be recalled to reality.

'What have you been reading?' said Winifred, twisting her face upside down to read the title of Alexandra's book.

'*Gliding and Soaring*! What on earth is the idea? Are you after being another Amy — *wonderful* Amy?' Wrinkling her small white nose mischievously, Winifred fluttered the pages.

' "If the angle of incidence is 5° the lift force is 1.8 lbs per square foot, and the drag load is . . ." Crumbs! It's Greek to me! And I bet it's Greek to you!' she teased.

Alexandra flushed in the rapid febrile way that was now the only visible remnant of her invalid years.

'I know I'm an ignoramus,' she retorted hotly. 'But you shouldn't make fun of me for trying not to be!'

Winifred laughed in her sweetest bell-tones — very soothing to the temper. 'Now spitfire!' she said. Then she looked at Alexandra more thoughtfully.

'You know, Allie, all the time you were in bed I never knew you lose your temper once. You *used* to have a pig of a temper at school, of course. Now it's come back again it seems! You must have kept it in your legs!' she ended playfully.

Discussion of one's character is always a delicious piece of flattery. Alexandra's temper was not long in abating. And as they moved slowly forward in the queue, she was moved to confide in Winifred quite rashly.

'You see, Win,' she explained, 'when I'm with Iris and her friends — especially that Gordon fellow I told you about — I feel I might as well be in a foreign country. I can't understand a single thing they say, let alone join in with them, and so, of course, they forget all about me. Gordon Bridges calls me "Silent Night". I *hate* him! . . . It's mostly flying they talk about. So I thought I would get a book about it. But I can't understand *this* book a bit,' she ended despairingly.

Winifred was sympathetic now. 'Why don't you get Iris to advise you what to read?' she suggested.

Alexandra flushed again. 'I wanted to surprise her one day by suddenly joining in. But I think I will *have* to ask her. I shall never get anywhere by myself,' she said mournfully.

'I'll see if I can help you to find something — a bit easier,' promised Winifred trying to console her.

As they passed through the gate into the library, a woman was going out at the other side of the counter — a woman built on old-fashioned barmaid lines, with a high, extravagant bosom, a pinched waist, dumpy, sensible-looking hips and legs, and tawny hair, puffed out over combs at each temple, and piled on top like a cottage loaf.

This woman looked across at them, staring at Alexandra as if she thought she knew her, and then averting her eye in an embarrassed way, as if she had mistaken her for someone else.

Winifred waited until this woman had gone, then turned to Alexandra and began to laugh. 'Good heavens! Did you see who that was? Miss Smedley! I haven't seen her for years. Good heavens! Not an inch off her bust, and not a comb of her head altered!' she cried mischievously.

'Who is Miss Smedley?' asked Alexandra — rather absently, for she was still half haunted by that other more satisfactory world of her own arranging.

Winifred looked shocked. 'Miss Smedley? Why, surely you remember Miss Smedley? She was the only decent teacher at St. Saviour's. The only one who was ever kind to us. And to *you* especially. *You* were a proper teacher's pet with her!'

'Oh!' said Alexandra, too surprised to attempt the pretence of a memory she did not possess. Then, seeing Winifred still incredulous, she gave way to a sudden impulse to confess. 'I suppose you think it is very ungrateful to forget her. But you know Win, I don't remember *anything* hardly about school. When I was ill I pretended I *could*, I don't know why. I used to listen to what you said, and remember it to say next time so that it seemed as if I remembered. But I *didn't*. Not a single thing, Win!'

Winifred wound her curl about her forefinger. 'Do you know,' she said, half thoughtful and half teasing, 'I always *had* my suspicions? Womanly intuition again you see!'

It was their turn at last. The attendant's fingers rippled up and down the card index like ten playful pink flames, snatched out their cards from hundreds of others precisely the same, and laid them on the counter.

They passed through the barrier into the pastures of print.

Alexandra stood for a moment with her head slowly swinging from side to side, filled with a devouring greed at the sight of so many thousands of books, and at the same time with a feeling not far from terror. How — how in God's name to choose *one* only out of all these? Winifred had left her, darting towards a column of wall shelves labelled mysteriously 'Far — Ell'. Alexandra felt a surging increase in her terror. She must act. To stand still would be fatal. Terror was closing in on her like walls of water. Only incessant movement could keep off its menace.

She hurried between two mid-floor cases and looked up at the rows of oblong, schoolmasterish faces, those on the right labelled 'Sociology' those on the left 'Rabbit Farming', 'Basket Work', 'Dressmaking', 'Fretwork', and so on. Those on the left she partly understood. Those on the right meant nothing at all. She therefore concluded that the right would furnish most improvement for the mind.

And to these she clung persistently. Once Winifred reappeared, remarked, 'What on earth are you prowling round here for? What you want is fiction! This is *non*-fiction!' Her tone suggested that it was practically poison, and she led Alexandra peremptorily to the side cases, mysteriously labelled with bits of words. However, Alexandra soon found that she could more or less understand these books, and, obstinate as a cat with young, returned to the incomprehensible middle shelves — finally choosing a book on fungi, because she had heard Iris mention that word on one of their walks.

When they stood on the steps outside the library again Winifred looked at her watch — 'Five to eight,' she said. 'I don't feel like going in yet. What about a coffee in the Savoy? I don't think there's a decent picture on anywhere or else I'd suggest that!'

Alexandra began to look flushed. 'I'm — I'm sorry, Win — I'd like to — but I haven't any money!'

Winifred bounced her curl. 'Oh, but I'm treating you, of course!' she said. But though her carelessness was the essence of tact, and though Alexandra succumbed to it, yet she felt humiliated, as she would not have done if Iris had made this proposal.

They paused at the door of the café, looking round for an attractive position. As they stood there, a sudden memory came to Alexandra, of the curtains which she had watched, a month — two months ago, in this same cinema; miraculous curtains, moving her to tears by their heavy sensuous swinging. Here, she thought, was a scene fit to be played in by such a prelude.

Like an embossed design in gold thread upon the dark blue background of the carpet were sprinkled innumerable little gilded tables, and painted gold basket-work chairs. The tables reminded her of some fairy story which she had read and forgotten, for they were topped with glass. There was a great deal of glass in this room. One side of it was made up of long windows framed in long dark blue curtains. The other wall was hung with long narrow mirrors which reflected the windows and the room between.

Transformed by this elegance, the people who lolled in the gold woven chairs, with their elbows on the glass-topped tables, seemed kings and queens. Alexandra, following in Winifred's swift, dancing wake to a table by one of the long windows, felt that she also was royal. The slim, naked blue figures on the walls, dancing upon three wavy blue lines of water, the beautiful circular gold pattern which lay under the glass of the table, like lovely weeds under water, these and all other details of this splendour were created, she felt, for her especial delight. And for a few moments she responded with the quick, easy gratitude of a child, as she would have done a month ago.

But by the time the waitress had brought their coffees, her mood was again troubled — her response to the splendour of the café muddied and obscured by her new self-absorption.

Next to lying in bed together in warmth and darkness, there is probably nothing so apt to promote egotism, and to begin a flow of dangerous and delicious confession, as the drinking of coffee together at a small café table. The spell began to work upon Alexandra in a very short time. As she sipped her coffee, she was reminded that she had not been able to pay for it, and this reminder in turn awaked a distress that had raised its head in her more and more frequently in the last few weeks. She put her cup thoughtfully into its saucer. Then, instinctively adopting the café attitude, elbows on the table, chin cupped in her hands, she said to Winifred, 'Win — do you think I'm too old to learn to earn my own living?'

Winifred got her own elbows into position — with deliberation due to the pleasant conviction that a long and confidential talk was brewing. 'That depends on what you want to learn!' she replied invitingly.

'Oh, I don't know. I haven't thought yet. It's just that I'm so

154

tired of having no money — of having to ask Sam and Peter for every penny I need . . . I never used to think about *them*, all those years I was in bed. I must have been just like a baby, I think. I took everything they did for me as my *right*. I'm only now beginning to see how good they are. How hard they have had to work to keep me alive — to be just a nuisance to everyone!'

She stopped, and looked rather hesitatingly, but with curiosity, into the face of her companion. Finding the high cheek-bones and slanted eyes full of attentive, serious sweetness, she was encouraged to go on.

'You know, Win, I have been thinking just lately that if I were out of the way, or at any rate could keep myself, my brothers would be able to think of marrying!'

A look of mischief darted into the slanted eyes at this. 'And how do you know,' asked Winifred, poking her finger carefully up the middle of her curl, 'how do you know they would *want* to marry?'

But before Alexandra could frame an answer to this question delicate enough to shield her brothers, yet plain enough to elicit from Winifred the truth concerning what she suspected, mischief ran out of the grey slanting eyes again, and sweet seriousness came to take its place.

'I don't think you should blame yourself too much for that!' said Winifred earnestly. 'If anyone is to blame for keeping your brothers single it's me!'

'But . . . ,' began Alexandra, meaning to say, 'it is *you* they both want to marry', but as usual too slow in framing her words, so that Winifred was there before her.

'I expect you've guessed that they're both in love with me,' she said, removing the crinkling skin of her coffee. 'I didn't mean to make them be. Honestly, I didn't realize till it was too late. With knowing them all my life nearly, I never dreamed it would happen! And now I don't know what on earth to do with them!'

'*Do* with them?' echoed Alexandra.

'Yes! — you see — I like them both — they're both absolute dears, of course. But I'm not in love with either of them. I couldn't *ever* be in love with either of them I'm sure. There'd be something quite indecent about it somehow — like those marriages you read

155

about in eastern countries, India or China or somewhere — where people get married to tiny boys or girls, you know! I feel as though Sam and Peter are only little boys!'

'Oh dear!' said Alexandra in dismay. 'And do they know?'

'What?'

'That you can't love either of them?'

Winifred looked troubled, but also a little mischievous. 'I'm not . . . sure,' she said. There was a short silence, during which the subtle forces of the intimacy induced by cafés worked upon Winifred. She succumbed, of course.

'I don't know whether I ought to tell you this,' she began at last, a prelude which is invariably a sign that the speaker has already decided to do so. 'You promise *never* to let them know that I told you?'

Alexandra promised. It would be interesting to know if anyone about to receive an indiscretion has ever refused to promise not to repeat it.

'Well . . . ,' went on Winifred, having received the assurance, 'you know that evening when we went to the pictures, and Peter and I were left behind at the tram-stop? Well, something happened on the way home!'

'That was written all over Peter when he came in, but I couldn't tell what it was,' commented Alexandra.

'Oh! How did he look?' asked Winifred, curious in her turn.

Alexandra considered an invisible Peter just behind Winifred's shoulder. 'He looked,' she said slowly, 'as if he had been walking up in the clouds — but as if he had been trespassing! He looked as if he wanted to tell a lovely secret, but wanted to *keep* it too!'

Winifred laughed. 'That's just what he had been doing,' she cried. 'Trespassing in the clouds! I could tell that something was coming, all the way home, for he never spoke a word, and his face was very set and dreamy and several times he nearly got run over, and I had to put my hand on his arm to keep him back. When I did that he closed his eyes, like people do when they can scarcely bear a pain . . . I suppose you won't believe me, Allie, but until that night I never seriously thought he loved me, or Sam either.'

'Why shouldn't I believe you?'

'Well — women are supposed to know always, aren't they? And

after all they're not the first men to fall in love with me. I really *ought* to have known! ... Well — when we got to our garden gate, he suddenly said, in a queer woolly kind of voice, "Ah no, Win! Don't go yet, Win! I want to ... to ask you something!"

'Well Allie, when a man says a thing like that in a voice like that he doesn't need to say any more! You know what to think — or you think you do! But I was wrong! — though I was right in a way. It *was* a proposal, of course, but believe it or not — it was not for himself — it was for Sam. It was queer, I can tell you. He sounded quite sincere. I do really believe he wanted me to marry Sam. And yet there were times when I began to think my ears had deceived me, and that he wasn't asking for Sam but for himself, only in the third person as they say! He actually took hold of my hand once, and I think it was *that* that made me think he was speaking for himself after all — not *knowing* he was meaning himself though, of course ... There was something *about* the way he held my hand — *his* was trembling — Oh, and when I told him I was quite, quite sure I could never care for Sam, he gave such a sigh! Terrific! I swear it was a sigh of relief, though I know he thought it was a sigh for Sam's hard luck. Then there was a silence. And then, Allie — I felt a tiny, timid pull at my hand, and I fancied I felt a sort of power coming out of him — it's a queer sort of feeling, I can't describe it, Allie — but I've felt it before with men. And I thought "Good heavens! he's going to kiss me!" For Sam? Or for himself? I wondered, and I couldn't help but laugh a bit — but I was very sorry too, of course. Anyway — he *didn't* kiss me after all. He hadn't the courage. If it had been anyone else I'd have kissed him myself. But you couldn't flirt with Peter. It would be absolute cruelty. Anyway, at last I could feel the impulse to kiss me dying out of him, and he said, in a voice all tangled up in yards of wool, "Win, is it because you ... you care for somebody else that you can't care for Sam?"

'And then I *knew* he'd really been asking for himself all along — but thinking he was hiding it — really *meaning* to give Sam the first chance — and you know, Allie, it was very noble of him, of course, absolutely splendid, but somehow it gave me such a queer feeling. It wasn't *natural* to do that — do you think so? I can't explain myself very well. I'm not clever enough. But I think I felt like I do with a cripple — or somebody with a horrid birthmark — sorry and yet disgusted — *repelled* by them somehow! Do *you* think it was a natural way for man to act?'

Alexandra was silent. Her experience was not wide enough to enable her to answer. And besides, the whole thing seemed unreal, almost fantastic. The blood tie, and the familiarity of daily life, is apt to hamper the imagination, so that to picture a brother or a sister, or one's parents, or one's children, in the acts of love, is either impossible or distasteful.

'What I'm interested to see *now*,' went on Winifred, the mischief in her hardening as she spoke so that it came perilously near to cruelty, 'is whether *Sam* will come pleading for *Peter*! Wouldn't it be a scream if he did?'

Alexandra smiled unwillingly, forced to do so by the absurdity of the idea, yet feeling heartless and disloyal.

The conversation lapsed. They turned their heads and stared out of the window, Alexandra a little alienated because Winifred had made her feel disloyal.

While they had been talking the light had been sifting away. They looked down now into a square filled with the lavender-tinged mist which is the breath of coming darkness. The sky was like a clear glass dish with a few shreds of transparent marmalade at the rim. Human lights were still unnecessary. But they were lit. In the misty Square they looked like drops of water refracting the clear light of the sky into electric-green, amber and vermilion.

Alexandra had never looked down into the Square before. Already she had so far matured, or deteriorated, that she needed to look on things from a new angle before they were as vivid to her as everything had seemed when she first saw the world. Seen from the level of its own cobbles the Square was now commonplace. Seen from this café window, it was as magical as ever.

The new concrete bridge, curling like a great arm round a glimpse of the river, looked like a snow bridge in this muted light, its lines bold and strangely curved like the lines of wind-sculped snow. Through the crook of this arm slid the river, thick and green as train-oil, as viscous in movement, and as silent. Across the Square was the Town Hall, like a large dusty wedding cake in both form and colour. And behind this sloped a gallery of common houses, unified by the evening light into the likeness of one great complicated castle.

Just behind the second tier of the wedding cake vermilion lights spelled the words 'Bile Beans'. Alexandra thought what a pity it was to spell so unpleasant a word in so beautiful a colour.

Across the misty Square, moving leisurely or leaning over the bridge to look into the river of oil, were little smudged figures, like rough charcoal sketches.

Alexandra watched them, with an agreeable feeling of detachment, an idle, lordly curiosity quite new to her. This feeling was increased when, as she stared, a sea-gull came wafting in a long upward catenary curve from under the arch of the bridge, and with an occasional and contemptuous wing-stroke, circled the Square, almost on a level with the café windows. By being on its level, above the level of the human figures below, she was imbued with something of its easy power, its indifferent, lordly contempt for things that grovel or strut upon the mere earth.

After one slow, wafting, perfect circle, it looped under the bridge again and disappeared down the river. But Alexandra remained in spirit where it had been — circling with easy, dreamlike power above the heads of reality. And suddenly she looked out of the present altogether, as the sea-gull had looped under the white bridge.

She was standing in front of a banked room of little children. Her short thick legs were wide apart, her hands defiantly snatched behind her back, her two thick stumpy little pigtails sticking out from her ears like some strange African coiffure.

At the side of the room stood Miss Smedley, her arms struggling to fold across her large barmaid-like bosom, her eyes helplessly compassionate.

Miss Brittain, also fat, but solid and hard like a saubot ball, stood near her, with eyes like blue 'glasseys', and a polished round nose.

'How much longer are you going to keep me waiting?' she was saying in a voice that bruised and humiliated as surely as her own 'poking stick'.

Alexandra was furiously silent.

Miss Brittain tried again, every word a spiteful jab. 'Alexandra Gollen! Everybody else has come out and said something. *You* will say something if we stay here till doomsday! *What did you do on Sunday?*'

Still the small creature with the heavy sullen face and coal-black brows was furiously silent.

'For the last time. Alexandra Gollen! What did you do on *Sunday*!' The fury could not be kept within any longer.

'Nowt! Blast you! Nowt!' cried the rebel savagely, glaring with all the power of her tar-black eyes.

There was a shocked stir, followed by sycophantic giggles and 'oohs' during the public torment to which Alexandra had condemned herself by this outrageous defiance.

She was taking it well. At each vicious impact of the long bamboo pole against her ribs, she gave a little gasp it is true, but she refused to budge an inch. And though her heart was near to bursting with its charge of passionate hatred, shame, and sense of injustice, the only change in the square little face was a tightening of the obstinate lips. She was not going to cry for Miss Brittain!

'*Now* will you speak,' barked Miss Brittain between each vicious prod. Alexandra remained furiously silent.

But she was, after all, only seven, and at last her child's body betrayed her will. To her unspeakable, unforgettable horror she began to make a small pool at her feet. She stood clenched into a knot of agony that every second dragged tighter. For those few seconds Miss Brittain was so absorbed in her part as inquisitor that she did not notice the growing pool. But ultimately, of course, she was bound to see. . . .

'Disgusting little brat! — But of course — we can expect nothing better out of the slums!' she cried when she did. And Alexandra was hurried out of the room, crying at last, not because of the poking stick — not even because of the disgraceful pool, but because of the unforgettable insult of that word 'slums'.

She was nearly twice as old. Her stumpy plaits had grown to waist length. Her square, dark, brooding face had changed scarcely at all. She was holding a little boy by the hand — a little boy with springy dark hair, brown mischievous eyes, and a nose that looked as if it were constantly being squashed against shop windows.

160

Opposite to her, sitting at his desk, with his long striped legs crossed, and one bony hand ruffling in perplexity a horn of grey hair, was Mr. Snaithe, the headmaster of the Council School.

'How is it your mother did not bring him?' he was saying.

''Aven't *got* a mother!' was the stony reply.

'And, er — no father?'

'Yes!' more stonily still.

'I suppose he's too busy?'

'Ay! At the pub!' said the eleven-year-old brutally.

Mr. Snaithe looked embarrassed. 'Mmm! Which school have you been attending until now?'

'St. Saviour's.'

'And why do you wish your little brother to come here, and to come here yourself?'

Then at last Alexandra unlocked herself.

'I wouldn't let Nick go into that place for a thousand pounds!' she declared violently. 'I'd *never* forgive myself if that Miss Brittain did to Nick what she did to *me*! It's all right for me now. It's not so bad when you get into the Big School. It's the Infant School that's so bad. I'd as soon send Nick to *Hell* as to Miss Brittain — the old bitch!'

'My dear child!'

They faced each other, the furious, stumpy girl of eleven, her face virulent with a hate no child should have cause to feel, heavy also with a brooding maternal love, called forth too early and too completely; and the man, lean, shocked, but compassionate, and admiring the spirit which triumphed over home conditions apparently very bad indeed, to judge by her language, the poverty of her clothes and her contempt for her father.

'You say the "Big School" is not so bad — yet you wish to come here as well as your brother — why?' he said at last.

'Well — it's not for myself — honestly it isn't. I can stand it all right now. I got through Miss Brittain, so I can stand anything now! But Nick's only a boy, you see. They can't put up with what a woman can, can they? So I thought I would like to be where I could look after him.'

The schoolmaster was polishing his glasses, for the third time during this interview.

'Does your father approve of this transference, my dear?'

'Don't know, and don't care!' was the retort; then with the sudden gush of passion as characteristic as her stolidity: '*I* look after Nick. And Sam and Peter (them's my half-brothers) bring all the money in what comes into *our* house. It isn't nothing to *do* with my father!'

The polishing increased in fervour. 'Mmm — mmm!' murmured Mr. Snaithe for an exasperating length of time. 'It's all very irregular!' he cried at last, 'but I suppose I shall have to let you have your way!'

Thus was Nick saved from the inquisitorial terrors, and the festering insults of Miss Brittain.

Thus far she had done her duty. Why then this hazy little cloud of uneasiness in the corner of her mind during the whole course of this remembered scene? What had happened to Nick, eventually? How strange, she thought suddenly, that she had never wondered this before! She did not even know what he had died of — if indeed he had died at all. He might have run away to sea — or have been lost, or had to be sent to a home, for all she knew.

The Square was bluer now, almost as blue as the curtains. In the blue the new lamps shone, pale, electric-green, translucent cubes of glass.

She looked suddenly at Winifred. She, too, was staring out into the Square, as silent as herself. Her face was fluid and remote with dreams, whose passage, like birds in their passage through the air, left behind no impression of their shape — no clue to their character, scarcely a ripple to indicate that something had passed through.

An impulse to ask a question about Nick died away as Alexandra looked at that face — neither mischievous nor sweet, but something quite apart from Winifred's ordinary face.

She had become aware, just lately, of the extent to which human beings are insulated from each other by the flesh and its egotism. Her association with Iris Young had taught her this. But she had never before been made aware of the fact by Winifred Bell. And even now there was a difference. With Iris she longed frantically to tear away the insulating stuff which shut her out from Iris. With Winifred she was only mildly curious.

The next instant Winifred, perhaps feeling her eyes' intensity, turned and smiled.

'Well — have you had enough of the view yet?' she said, rather meanly making it seem as though it was Alexandra only who had stared in silence at the Square.

'It's lovely,' said Alexandra, 'but I'd better be getting home now. They'll be anxious.'

They strolled across the Square, both in a half-dream still. Their minds were in the state of peculiarly dreamy exaltation induced by an evening spent in intimate conversation, full of a sense of the tragical comedy of life, full of a sense of the complexity and mystery of human beings, feeling warm, vital, as if they had sat for a while in the very heart of life.

CHAPTER VII

ALEXANDRA stood alone on the crowded platform and stared at Iris and Gordon Bridges. They were strolling away from her, out of the hot, heliotrope shade cast by the dirty glass roof, into the even hotter heliotrope of the dusty, mote-filled sunshine.

Far beyond Alexandra's hearing, they paused, turned half towards each other, gazing at their toes, and talking.

Two pigeons waddled in contrary directions about their feet, jerking their clockwork heads, pecking at the dusty platform as if laying an enchanted circle about the two figures, isolating them from the world, rendering all else invisible to them. They had forgotten her very existence, thought Alexandra.

But she was wrong. If she could have heard them she would have been surprised to learn that, far from forgetting her, they spoke of nothing else but her.

Iris was confiding in Gordon how troubled she felt. 'I've tried in vain,' she was saying, 'to throw her on her own resources. I've brought her amongst people of her own age. I've deserted her, in order to *make* her make other friends. I've pretended to be a lot more absorbed in you than I really am, in order ...' ['Thanks!' interjected her companion ironically] 'in order to force her to make

163

more suitable friends than me. But it's no good. Look at her now! The rest of this party are absolutely invisible to that child!'

'I wouldn't worry yourself into the grave!' returned the young man, kicking one toe with the heel of the other brogue, a characteristic gesture of his.

'But I *do* worry myself into the grave! I consider myself responsible for this — this unhealthy "fixation". I was too interested in her when she first began to recover the use of her legs. I showed my interest too much, and she's returned it with this unhealthy passion for me. I thought I could help her cramped mind to grow — show her the world a bit more than her relatives could do — they are so cramped themselves. Now, I feel as if I'm *distorting* her mind instead. I've done my uttermost to cut her free, but — well, look at her now!'

Gordon Bridges obeyed. 'Yes! She's got it pretty badly,' he admitted, turning back with a shrug of his wide, flat, rather bony shoulders. 'But these infatuations are quite a normal feature of adolescence, aren't they? Especially female adolescence, I believe. A secondary schoolteacher should be well used to such problems,' he ended teasingly.

'Yes, but Alexandra doesn't happen to *be* an adolescent schoolgirl. That's the point!' said Iris. 'She's getting on for twenty-two, and what is normal in a girl of sixteen is decidedly beastly in a young woman of twenty-two.'

'Mental adolescence doesn't stop short at the school-leaving age. In some people it lasts all their lives. And with some people it begins much later than with others — that's true even of people who have had a more or less normal upbringing. But this girl, from what you've told me, has had a most extraordinary time. I should imagine from the bits she's told you, and you've passed on to me, that her childhood was really appalling. I'll tell you how the whole thing strikes me, Iris. You know that certain kinds of fish who live in the Arctic Sea are able to survive a winter frozen into a block of sea-ice, and when it melts, are able to resume their physical processes where they left off?

'Well — I should imagine that emotionally, and mentally, this girl has had a similar experience. For nine years — is it? — her mind has been frozen, almost static, at the twelve-year-old level. Some

164

extraordinary emotional crisis, preceded by excessive emotional strain perhaps, caused this state of paralysis, physical and mental. Then suddenly, for some reason unknown, there came a release. The ordinary human line of development is resumed. She is now struggling with certain adolescent upheavals. Leave her alone — that's all you can do. She'll grow *through* it. Mark my words — the first young man to pay court to that young woman will drive you instantly out of her heart!'

'There speaks the conceited male!' said Iris, laughing for the first time that morning.

And then the train came in. And Gordon began one of his characteristic extravagances, upon the locomotive and its essential maleness.

'Look at its flat bosom for a start,' he said. 'Then of course, the emphasis upon locomotion — the restless seeking after movement for movement's sake, rather than living for living's sake, betrays the male. And the absurd self-importance of the creature! The portentous breathing, the alderman-like humming and hawing! And that implacable, logic-bound revolving of coupling-rods! Oh it's easy to see no woman ever had a finger in the making of the monster!'

'Oh, but surely that scream was feminine,' protested Iris, laughing, as with a lurch and a screech the monster set their carriage into motion. 'Definitely feminine! Dangerously and perpetually on the verge of hysteria!' she went on.

'And what about the voluptuous curves of its sides. What about the smug, comfortable, domesticated, bumpetty-bump of its progress — and most feminine of all, the docility with which it runs along its man-appointed rails!'

So they disputed, laughing and extravagant, yet half in earnest, in the fashion of those who, in love with one of the opposite sex, are temporarily out of love with their own.

So absorbed were they in their railing that neither of them noticed Alexandra sitting in the opposite corner, staring enough to bruise her eyes.

This carriage was crammed with members of the Labour Youth Movement Rambling Club. Two girls sat on their friends' knees for lack of other seats. But to Alexandra it was empty except for the lean young man with the ugly mouth and the shock of dark hair, and the vivid young woman with dragonfly blue eyes. The carriage was crammed with noises; three young men singing 'Riding Down to Bangor'; a tangle of private conversations; holiday laughter; the scraping of hiking-boots; and the oily rumble of invisible wheels under the floor. But to Alexandra it contained two voices only; one soft, woolly, male, and detestable; the other rough, like a hard towel, but agonizingly dear.

To these two voices and their torment she clung all day. Over the hot birdless moors she followed them. Up the stony hill paths, and down into the valleys of withered ferns, across the gelded streams, and under the brittle, burnt-paper leaves of late summer, she followed perversely after her torment.

In this portable hell there were no other souls. In her bed that night she could recall no other human face or figure but these two. Yet strangely, though at the time she was also unconscious of the scenes about her, afterwards she found them vividly impressed upon her memory.

These rough, shaggy-coated moorlands, flecked with little white tails of cotton grass; those distant hills, thin, flat as if cut out of paper, blue as sloes in the morning, dusty amethyst in the evening; and the grasshoppers, dry like blowing grains of sand; and the dancing veil of hot air over the grass — they were all there printed indelibly on her mind by her torment.

Doggedly she tramped on the heels of her misery all that swelter- ing day, keeping just behind the only other people in the world, or just ahead of them, or a yard or so to their side, listening, always listening, yet hearing not a word they said, only how they said it, tracing, with the passion almost of insanity, every small concavity in their tones, exquisitely sensitive to the minutest shades of their feeling.

She could detect, beneath the sophisticated, mock-indifference of Bridges's tones, the adoration that was so insultingly akin to her own. She detected the proprietary warmth that lay behind his apparently malicious teasing. She divined the desire to touch that itched in the palms of his hands and at the corners of his extravagant mouth.

Even more was she aware of Iris's responsive vibrations. Under

166

the rough texture of that now-familiar voice she heard, all too plainly, the subtle overtones of triumph and surrender, of tender pride and of proprietary teasing. Lingering in the air at the close of each word sounded a faint, unresolved, sweet discord, a questioning, an invitation, a longing, that ripened Iris's lips to the same curves as the man's.

It was as if the perceptive senses of the jealous girl lay raw, skinless, to these torments. And yet, in the strange masochistic fervour of the jealous, she sought out more torment, as if one newly skinned were to roll deliberately in a bed of gravel.

At lunch-time, when Iris and Gordon seated themselves a little apart from the others, she went and sat near them, knowing she was not wanted, taking perverse pleasure in the misery this knowledge and her defiance of it caused her.

They tried at times to break their chain of talk, and re-link it to include Alexandra. But her mind was choked in the tangles of her jealous misery. She was so long in struggling to drag her answers out through this jungle that they had passed to some other thought by the time her mouth opened.

The great shaggy back of moorland on which they sat seemed to pant like a huge animal in the heat of July. Down at its foot the cars passing along a main road glittered and hummed distantly. The horizon was so hot and misted that it was fused and welded into the sky. An aeroplane burred somewhere incessantly. Half-way down the slope was a single small bent tree which reminded Alexandra of old Miss Hope who used to pass by the window in Finn Street, in the dream-far time when Alexandra lay in bed and was happy, and innocent of jealousy. From this tree came the hesitant broken notes of a cuckoo. 'Cu-cuckoo' it kept saying, as if it had the hiccups.

One by one the Labour League of Youth succumbed to the heat, and lay back with their heads in the rough grasses, till only Alexandra was left sitting upright, kept raw and wakeful by her jealous misery. She sat with her hands clasped about her drawn-up knees, her black eyes fixed upon the figures slightly in front of her, vigilant for new torments.

Gordon lay on his back, his hands clasped under his head, his bony knees wafting continually out and together again.

Iris lay on her stomach; with her head pillowed on one arm, her

167

face turned away from Alexandra, who stared at that helmet of warm, living bronze, and ached with the crushed desire to touch it. So intense was this desire that she could almost feel the slight magnetic pull of the burnished hair against the palm of her hand.

As if it came vibrating across to her on the hot air, she became aware of a precisely similar desire in Gordon Bridges. And she hated him for this, with the venom peculiar to those who discover their most cherished feelings reproduced in other people.

Suddenly he rolled over on to his stomach, so that his hips almost touched Iris's. Alexandra's throat tightened. She thought he was about to do what she dared not do. She was mistaken, however. His hand shot out, not to that burnished living helmet, but beyond his own head. At the same time Alexandra became aware of a pervasive and ubiquitous chirring sound in the grass — like salt rubbed between finger and thumb.

Gordon Bridges opened his hand cautiously. And there, hooded by his fingers, perched a tiny green creature with a long foolish face, and long crooked back-legs.

Iris's head leaned over to see what he held, thus stabbing the watcher with a fresh jag of exquisite misery. For her cheek was now so near to Gordon's that he must feel the warmth of it, and be wafted by the faint human-scented breath coming between her parted lips. Alexandra remembered the day when Iris had bent her cheek by *her* cheek, as they looked together at a lark's nest and its putty-coloured eggs. She would never be happy again like that.

'There is something quite archaic about a grasshopper, don't you think,' Bridges was saying, low into Iris's ear. 'Something *frighteningly* archaic. It's so absurdly primeval that it baffles the imagination. We can put ourselves in the place of a bird (or we *think* we can). Even a reptile isn't quite an enigma. It is possible to feel sympathy even with a snake. But this little creature, with its head like a medieval pageant mask, and its unbelievable legs — what *can* it possibly be thinking?'

'This one is probably thinking that it has got to an Extension Lecture by mistake!' said Iris mockingly — with that proprietary undercurrent of warmth which hurt the listener so excruciatingly.

But Gordon paid no attention to the gibe.

'I don't believe they can think or feel anything. These creatures

168

are living fossils — relics of a time when thought and feeling were yet to be evolved. They preceded the true insects. And the true insects themselves were one of the first branches of life to emerge from the sea. Even the true insects are baffling — cold, repulsive, green-blooded creatures devoid of almost every human-like feature. Of course they have the instinct of reproduction. Even there they seem totally devoid of even temporary tenderness to their mates — such as you see in some mammals. But these pre-insect creatures are one degree worse. Do you know, Iris, that according to Fabre, the "praying" mantis, a sort of cousin to this fellow, will devour her mate even in the very act of coupling?'

Though the mental content of most of this speech had meant nothing to Alexandra, the warm, silent intercourse of man and woman that went on behind his garrulity was as vivid as if she had inhabited one or other, or both, of those recumbent forms.

She felt now, like an internal blow, the shock of this concluding remark upon both man and woman.

A silence followed the shock. And this also she felt as if in her own body. She felt the hush of self-consciousness, and consciousness of each other. She felt the exquisite embarrassment that slowly flooded them. She felt the delicious pain of longing, like two flames stretching out to touch each other.

Savage with jealous pain, she grew like a high wall round Iris, trying to shut the rival lover out, and crying in silent passion.

'You shan't have her! You shan't have her!' Her eyes filled with scalding tears. When she could see again, she saw that Iris and Gordon were now both lying on their backs, with their faces to the hot sky. And both were smiling strangely. The flames had touched after all. She thought she would die with the pain of it.

But she did not die. She rose with the rest of the party, now reshouldering its rucksacks, and toiled on under the savage sun in pursuit of fresh torments.

But there is a limit even to the endurance of a self-torturer. Towards evening Alexandra reached that limit. Obeying a sudden impulse she began to run. The startled party laughed as she passed, and shouted humorously after her. She scarcely heard them. She had some obscure feeling that if she ran long enough she might leave her torment behind. For a time it seemed indeed as if she might.

There was silence all about her. The moors, growing opaque in the dying light, held nothing but the thud of her feet on the grassy track, and the creaky pumping of blood up her throat.

On she ran — until her consciousness narrowed, and she was a creature with no past and no future, running in a void, nothing in fact but an exhausted mechanism for running, her breath coming in loud whoops, her heart thudding louder than her feet, the blood in her throat hurting at every pulse. At last she could run no more. She lay down on the path, and discovered that after all her running she had brought her misery with her.

In addition she had put herself into a pitiable condition physically. Sweat was oozing out all over her body. Her crown of hair was fallen over one shoulder. Her throat was so dry she thought she would never speak again. Her head throbbed so that she could see nothing. She wiped her face despairingly, then, hearing the distant voices of the party, crawled in a sudden instinctive shame into the bracken.

Her sight was clearing, and she was just beginning to cope with her flow of perspiration, when the first of the party passed by. She lay hidden, ashamed of her bedraggled condition. In twos, threes and fours the Labour Youth passed by. She watched them climb the stile, in their various ways — some frisky, some primly guarding their skirts, some vaulting inexpertly — one by one they passed, their voices immediately cut off as if by a closing door, as they dropped down behind the high stone wall.

A good deal after them came Gordon and Iris.

At the sight of them Alexandra's heart began to sound again in her ears, and the bracken near her began to rustle faintly, moved by her excessive tremblings. They were walking very slowly, reluctantly almost. They walked as if to some unimaginably lovely music, music which only they could hear, music which hung about them like an invisible bell, and shut them out from the world into a world of their own. Alexandra, as if temporarily endowed with an extra octave of hearing, seemed to catch snatches of that music, snatches that filled her with unspeakable pain.

As they reached the stile Gordon took Iris's hand in his, and swung her round gently, so that Alexandra could see her face over his shoulder. A deep and agonizing shame welled up in Alexandra as she watched that face. It was marvellously alive, alive to the words of that man as water is alive to the wind. It seemed to the watching girl an indecency that it should be so. But there was worse to come.

'Iris,' the man was saying softly, 'now that our "chaperone" has disappeared for a moment, I want to ask you something.' He paused, and watched, as Alexandra watched, the lovely, changing, expectant gravity of that face. Then, after a faint and curious forward movement which brought Alexandra's heart up into her throat, he went on: 'I feel silly asking it, because I think you know already what it is . . . *do* you?'

The lovely, grave face stirred and broke like ruffled water into a smile — deathly to Alexandra — and the eyelids lifted from eyes that were softer, and less blue, than Alexandra had ever seen them.

'I think I do!' she said. 'And I think you know the answer! *Do* you?'

There was a poised silence, an ecstatic pause of interrogation.

Then Iris laughed, and in harmony, at the same moment, the man murmured 'Iris!' and drew her body close to his.

At the moment when their mouths came together, Alexandra's consciousness flickered out.

She regained consciousness reluctantly, becoming aware first of the bitter smell of bracken above her head, and next of the insistent thrumming of a whole string orchestra of flies. Then something tickled her ear. Attempting to brush it away she found she had been lying on her crossed arms long enough to paralyse them temporarily.

She sat up to rub them. All about her, beyond the veil of thrumming flies, lay silence, and an empty moorland.

Gordon and Iris had gone. This fact, and the memory of what had happened in front of that stile found her numb, with the same sort of prickly cold which was gradually thawing out of her arms now.

She sat there, rubbing mechanically, her heart cold and her mind empty, so long that she forgot why she was rubbing, or how she came to be there.

She was neither surprised nor interested when a head appeared over the stile, a boy's head, with brown tufted hair, and rather large ears, pink with the sunset behind them.

He paused on the top of the stile, and looked down on her.

'So here you are!' he said reflectively, and came slowly towards her.

Alexandra opened her mouth, found that she could make no sound, cleared her throat violently, and produced a gritty, unfamiliar voice demanding 'Who are *you*?'

He raised his eyebrows, carelessly marked eyebrows, of light brown. 'I've spoken to you several times to-day. But I had the *impression* that I didn't exist for you!' he told her reproachfully. 'But never mind me — what have *you* been doing to yourself? How was it we left you behind? We thought you ran *ahead*!'

Alexandra winced. Sensation was returning at last to her numbed mind, as painfully as it had to her numbed arms.

'I think I must have fainted,' she said, then, with an effort which betrayed more than she knew — 'Where are — where is Iris?'

'They are looking for you, too!' he answered, tactfully exchanging the disagreeable name for the more impersonal pronoun. 'They went along the road to Rawsley, thinking you might have turned down there by mistake. All the others caught the train. We had better be going, I think, or we shall miss the *last* train.'

Without a word she got to her feet. Without a word she waved his arm away, and climbed the stile, shaky but independent. And without a word, in a cold and dogged despair, she walked beside him all the way to the railway station, not even hearing his timid attempts to lighten her trouble with his talk.

CHAPTER VIII

IRIS YOUNG hurried along in a drizzle so cold, so colourless, that you might have fancied it to be the pale dripping blood of November itself. She disliked the 'Waist', the narrow canyon of foul smells, which led to one of the many iron bridges across the Cole. But it was a short cut to Under Market, and the aim to which her whole body and soul were devoted was to finish her shopping and get home to her fire. But half-way across the bridge she hesitated, for there, leaning with her elbows on the iron balustrade, was Alexandra

Gollen. She had not seen her for some weeks now. And their last meeting had been so uncomfortable that Iris did not feel eager to encounter her again. The girl had become queerly elusive, and even more queerly antagonistic ever since that ramble in July, when something, she was not quite sure what, but something evidently catastrophic, had occurred in her emotional development.

She came and stood beside Alexandra, without speaking. She could hardly turn back now, she thought, for Alexandra might have seen her. Not that she gave any sign of this, thought Iris, as she studied the left half of Alexandra's face.

Profiles are not, of course, very expressive of mood. The groundwork of a character may be guessed from them but not the subtler shades; for these you must look into the full face. But Iris thought even from Alexandra's profile that she must be under some strange repulsive fascination. Her eyelids were half-lowered, heavy and still, the natural rhythm of their blinking completely arrested. Her whole face indeed was still, heavy, frozen; and her sallow skin looked an unhealthy greenish mud-colour in the light of the gas lamps at the corner of the bridge.

After a while Iris too leaned her elbows on the iron coping, and looked down to see what absorbed her so. Swirls of greenish-brown oil appeared to be oozing along below. The sour, half-chemical, half human-refuse, smell, peculiar to these degraded rivers of industrial towns, came creeping up as oilily as the river itself crept along.

Iris Young's nostrils and lips contracted with disgust, and she spoke suddenly, forgetting that she had not yet announced her presence.

'Thank God they are covering all this filth up soon — so they say!'

The terrific start of the girl's body betrayed the depth to which her consciousness had shrunk. If the genuineness of this start were in doubt, the expression of her eyes as she turned to look at this disturbing noise of another being, in a world that had obviously contained only herself, was beyond doubt.

How those eyes had changed! For a second Iris Young fancied that the filthy river below had thrown out two large drops, like muddy blots, upon this square, sallow face. For within those eyes, as in that greasy water below, seemed to creep, just hidden beneath the vicious surface, things indescribably foul, things *best* hidden, since they could never be made clean.

These large dull disks stared at Iris for a long time, struggling slowly and heavily to redirect the brain behind to some sort of contact with reality. In some fashion they seemed to succeed at last. Recognition showed in them, and the full, sullen lips curved stiffly, as if cracked by cold winds, into a reluctant and bitter smile.

'Oh, it's *you*, is it,' said Alexandra resentfully.

This resentment, this sullen, guarded antagonism, Iris reflected, was the usual greeting now. It was, she supposed, the reaction, the unlovely reverse face, of the foolish unmeasured adoration which had preceded it. She felt uncomfortably remorseful, for she considered that she had herself provoked that extravagance by her own unconsidered actions, before she had realized fully the immaturity behind Alexandra's mature physique.

She wanted very much to put right her mistake if it was hers indeed, but how to set about it was beyond her psychological skill.

Gordon's reiterated advice was, 'Leave her alone'. Well, she had followed this, to a great extent, for the last four months. If those eyes, and that cracked, tormented smile, were the result, was it good, was it safe, indeed, to follow it any further? Nevertheless, she followed it now, for want of better council.

'Sorry I made you jump!' she said in a tone as indifferently friendly as she could make it. 'But it came over me so suddenly what a blessing it will be when they get the new road built over all this, that I forgot you didn't know I was here.'

Alexandra turned, slowly, and looked again at what had recently been absorbing her whole attention. 'What's the good of covering it up? It'll be there just the same underneath!' she said, with such an explosion of despairing passion that Iris began to wonder if, having recovered bodily sanity, the unhappy creature had now lost mental sanity.

But still she could think of nothing better than to ignore the dark emotional background of the words, pretending to have heard only the words themselves. 'Well—what of that; *we* shall not see it!' she argued, laughing with quiet care.

The dark disks of oily liquid turned blazing on her. 'But we shall *know* it is there all the time. And knowing is *seeing*!' she cried.

Still, Iris tried to ignore the dark undercurrent of passion.

'I thought you had pleasant memories of this bridge? Isn't it where you used to come to see the rats when you were little? I remember, the first day I brought you out, how pleased you were to remember it!'

Alexandra turned again at this, unsmiling, her eyes dull oil disks again now, so heavily curtained with despair that Iris suddenly thought of some words from a poem of John Donne:

> 'For I am every dead thing,
> In whom love wrought new alchemy.
> For his art did express
> A quintessence even from nothingness,
> From dull privations, and lean emptiness:
> He ruined me, and I am rebegot
> Of absence, darkness, death; things which are not.'

So plainly did those despairing eyes speak, that there was no need for Alexandra herself to add:

'Yes — I *was* pleased! But I've remembered a lot more since then. A lot too much. And now I wish somebody had thrown me down to those rats — when I was little! It would have saved a lot of trouble and hard work for my brothers!'

Iris began to feel cold at the stomach. Suddenly she felt that if they were to stay any longer looking at that oily, craftily swirling stuff below, that distillation of all the filth and wickedness in the world, she, as well as this unhappy creature, would lose all sanity.

'Have you had any tea yet?' she cried desperately.

'No!' came the rude reply.

'Then come and have some with me at the Regal Cinema Café. They do very nice cosy fish and chip teas!' urged Iris, putting her hand with most unusual timidity, on the bend of Alexandra's arm. She felt she had lost the clue to Alexandra's heart. She could not tell now, as she could so easily when she first became interested in her, what would be her reactions.

However, though Alexandra tore away her arm, as if from fire, she ungraciously assented to the invitation.

In the Regal Café, cosily underground, wrapped in warm air and the fuzzy angora of the softly booming wireless, Alexandra's eyes lost the greater part of their terrifying likeness to the disgustingly polluted river. Across the steam of the fish and chips, they looked dark, heavy indeed, but with a merely human quantity of misery.

Iris's heart melted to her, and she set to work with a passion that surprised herself to ease that misery. For a time she thought she was succeeding. That painful, cracked-lipped smile was creaking less at every attempt. Iris began to fancy she felt faint ghostly emanation of the old, embarrassing adoration coming across to her, when suddenly she saw that Alexandra was staring fixedly somewhere behind her shoulder. Her round dark eyes, which had warmed to something of their old look of warm velvet, were cold black ice now, and somewhere below the ice swam a repellent glint of cunning.

'What are you staring at?' asked Iris uneasily.

'That man behind *you*!' answered the disconcerting creature, in a strange voice, almost, Iris fancied, as if she had waited for this question, had compelled it to be asked in fact, in order to answer it. There was, too, a definite twang of almost savage anticipation of triumph.

Iris turned to look, and laughed. 'That fellow with a mouth like a cod-fish? What about him?' she asked.

Anticipation flashed into crude, naked exultation. Evidently Iris had fallen beautifully into her snare.

'Well — he reminded me of that — that Gordon Bridges,' Alexandra said, almost savagely.

Iris flushed faintly, a rare occurrence with her. And for a moment her eyes glittered with anger at this crude insult.

Then she remembered that the insult had come from one not quite sane in mind, at any rate not fully set in the balance of maturity, destined by birth, perhaps, to spiritual disorder. She stroked down her anger in silence, therefore, and contented herself at last with the grave, faintly reproachful reply: 'Oh! I gather from that then that you, like myself, think ugly faces are far more interesting than pretty ones!'

What was it moving in the cunning, watchful face across the table? A contraction of pain — even at this mild reproach, there certainly was. But something else — almost a look of fanatical satisfaction in the pain, such as might appear in the face of a self-flagellating saint?

'I believe she *wants* me to hurt her. She's in love with her own jealousy, I think. There isn't a scrap of love left in her, yet she's still

176

jealous of Gordon — fanatically jealous; and it gives her pleasure to torment herself with it. Jealousy, of course, is always its own Iago, expert in the art of torturing insinuation!'

She did not think it good, however, to indulge the girl's morbid craving for pain. To feed that craving would only be to increase it. Therefore, when Alexandra leaned forward, with that new repulsive glitter of cunning in her eyes, and asked Iris to describe her ideal man, she recognized the question as a trap to snare torment for the questioner, and said gently:

'I'm too old to demand an ideal, Alex! After all, I'm over thirty, you know — far too old to pick and choose. I prefer reality, anyway, to ideals! Besides,' she said more earnestly; 'Besides, Alex, love isn't like that a bit. You don't make up your ideal pattern of a man and then go searching the world for him. Or if you do you'll never find him. No — you fall in love with the most unlikely man in the world. And afterwards you find that somehow he fits something in you, as a key fits a lock!' She stopped, aware that in her earnest pity she had run on into exactly what the self-flagellator wanted. She had spoken, indirectly it is true, but too warmly, of her love for Gordon Bridges. She watched, cursing herself, the malevolent, bitter rings of joy spreading over Alexandra's face; saw how the girl almost licked her lips to taste the last drops of the delicious, searing poison.

And at last, when the last dreg had vanished, the licked lips parted in a rich line of malice.

'I know *one* thing!' cried Alexandra harshly, 'I know I could *never* love a man with a mouth like a great fish, who talked *clever* all the time, showing-off! I *detest* clever men with ugly faces and soft woolly voices like old sheep! I don't care how many locks they fit!'

She stopped, and cowered back, terrified of what she had done — obscenely terrified, like a cat that knows it has scratched its mistress too maliciously at last. But even to this incredible insult, Iris refused to retort in kind. Remembering the vital sickness of the other, she replied with gentle dignity, only a very little acid: 'I tell you, Alex, you don't know *who* you will love. Wait and see, child! Don't try to *dictate* to life!'

Laughing carefully, she rose, and attracted the eye of the waitress. Outside the café, Iris, rather awkwardly for her, asked if Alexandra could find her own way home.

'I have a friend coming to see me, and I have only just time to get back as it is,' she explained, and her tone, dismissing Alexandra, firm but embarrassed, gave her thereby a fresh lash or two of the pleasurable whip she craved.

'Oh yes! Don't let me keep you from your *friend!*' cried Alexandra, spitefully emphasizing the word friend to show whom she suspected the word to indicate. And she turned abruptly away to the tram-stop.

Iris, watching her stumpy, solid figure melt into the drizzling cold veil of November dark, smiled a little achingly to herself at the crude sarcasm, which nevertheless had hurt a little, as the crude thrusts of children can often hurt.

But like most spite, it had hurt its author far more than the intended victim. As Alexandra walked down the long hill to the Square, the words she had just spoken cracked over and over in her brain, raising fresh weals across her unhealed misery. As she marched along, she thought, in an ecstasy of torment:

'She was going back to Gordon Bridges! She was only filling in time with *my* company. She only wants me when she has nothing better to do. Well, at any rate, I've done with her now. Our friendship's finished for ever. We can never look each other in the face again after what I've said to-day. I don't know how she kept her temper. She *must* have been furious underneath. She can never forgive me!'

Behind her verbal thought was an unexpressed terror — or defiance perhaps, a *daring* of Iris Young to forgive her. She found pleasure in the thought of not being forgiven. Something in her at this time violently repudiated the one-time idol, but pretended the while that it was the idol who had repudiated her.

For the rest of that evening she slammed the door on the thought of Iris, talked with hard laborious gaiety to Sam and Peter, and despised them for being deceived by the hard sham.

But in sleep, slammed doors are apt to burst wide open again. All night long, over hot birdless moors, up stony hill paths, and down into valleys of withered fern, across the gelded streams of late summer, accompanied by the dry insistent chirring of the grasshoppers, she was condemned to tramp after two figures, who walked with their fingers intertwined, their feet moving to some

178

unimaginably lovely music, which hung over them like an invisible bell, shutting them into their private paradise, their lips ripened into sweet, rich curves of longing, their eyes hazed with tenderness, their speech hazed with faint overtones of unspoken harmony.

These figures, and these moors, were pervaded throughout by the bitter, slightly medicinal reek of bracken, like the persistent reek of anaesthetic through the visions of an anaesthetized patient.

Then suddenly the moors vanished. Instead there was a fairy sea of pale pink silk, ruched into little waves that lapped at a beach of lawn. Instead of the anaesthetic reek of bracken there hung over this sea a scent cool, fresh, yet velvet soft — like the scent of violets. 'It looks like the bed of a princess,' whispered someone, over and over again, until the words were mesmerically forgotten, and the sound became like the whisper of that pink, fairy sea breaking in small neat waves on the snowy beach.

Half on the beach, half submerged in the silky sea, lay a beautiful creature with eyes of turquoise, a helmet of burnished gold hair, and one shoulder, round like an egg, smooth and creamy as milk, flung up out of the pink foam, the long warm creamy arm trailing loosely over the surface. 'The princess!' whispered the invisible somebody.

But what was this hideous nightmare, this deep-sea monstrosity, this cod-mouthed, mop-headed, prickly-cheeked, elephant-eared fish-head that gaped on the pillow beside the lovely princess?

'Who is it? Who *is* it?' whispered the invisible onlooker. But it could not answer, and so it went on whispering until it forgot its own meaning, and became again the voice of the fairy sea of silk.

Suddenly, the princess stirred, and turned to the fish-head beside her. Soundlessly the cream-smooth arm looped like a crest of foam, over the hideous creature's shoulder.

At this point the dream ceased to be visual; it became tactile instead. She felt, in darkness, the warm scented satin of that arm as it curled over her neck, felt the smooth, egg-cool cheek laid gently to her own cheek, felt the warmth beat softly through the cool skin to hers, and at last felt warm lips press the spot the cheek had already warmed.

With that a great wave reared above her, curled cruelly over, and plunged, in a prolonged seething of pain, across her heart, obliterating all consciousness, even dream consciousness.

But though these things seemed part of her own self, she knew that they were not happening to herself, but to that hideous fish-head with the dark, cold, clever eyes. Therein indeed lay the pain.

When the great fan of delicious agony had snarled back and left her exposed to consciousness again, she saw again, instead of feeling, the fairy sea of silk and the lovely sleeper and the hideous sleeper, cheek by cheek on the snow-white pillow.

Suddenly the palms of her hands itched with intense hate. And next, they ceased to be her own hands at all. They were the hands of Murder: long, sharp-nailed, green-fleshed, claw-like hands, motionless in the air above the sleepers like an eagle's talons.

At last, with a savage whistling screech, they swooped. They grasped the lean, corded neck and squeezed — squeezed — squeezed again. Then they thrust it down, down, through fathoms of pink translucent water. Out of the gaping cod-mouth snarled great ropes of bubbles. As the hideous thing sank, the clear sea was churned into a pink milk jelly by its choking breath. Relentless the talons squeezed. At last the neck became limp, and the monster fell unresisting to the sea-bottom.

Wafting effortlessly to the surface, the hands waited for the milky froth to subside. Clearer and clearer grew the fairy sea, and at last it became the light shining through her closed eyelids, and Sam was calling to know if she was ever going to get up to-day.

Ten minutes later her dream had vanished. But its mood — savage, sensual, perverse, tormented, vindictive, persisted in the core of her all day. And all day her body, like a sleep-walker's, performed an accurate copy of her usual daily actions, while her mind wandered over moors of hot misery, which though no longer visualized, were identical with those moors of her dreams. She was still in this sleep-walking state when she went in the evening to call on Winifred.

'Win's bathing the baby,' said Judy Bell, opening the door.

'*What* baby?' demanded Alexandra, though she knew quite well that Winifred's sister Doreen had come home for a time with her year-old baby.

Judy Bell looked at her with the tremendous contempt of the

twelve-year old. 'Why — our Rene's, of course!' she jeered, and led the visitor, disgraced, into the kitchen.

Winifred was the only member of the family there. She was kneeling on the hearthrug, leaning over a white enamel bath, from which a faint mistiness, not definite enough to be called steam, crept up over her head and shoulders like a saint's halo, of a very doubtful, low-caste, earthbound quality, tinted faintly by the firelight.

She looked up at Alexandra, and smiled, bobbing her curl against her cheek by swinging her head, for her hands were both occupied.

Alexandra sat down, carefully, yet indifferently, in her sleep-walker fashion, as if it did not matter whether there were a chair there or not. And she stared hard at Winifred and the baby, and saw nothing, for her mind still trudged on the heels of its own torment.

Suddenly Winifred's voice thrust through her blank mind so that her eyes came dimly alive. 'Damn it,' she was saying, 'I've forgotten the talcum! Here, Allie, catch hold a minute while I get it!'

The next instant not only her eyes but all her five senses leapt into sudden intensity.

She was suddenly aware as she had not been aware for months, of every detail of the moment — of the wet, slippery, rather chilly skin of the small creature she was supporting, one hand across its soft boneless back, the other clasped in the water over one knee, of the winking glittering eyes of the suds gaily dying about its pink flesh; of the flat feathers of its hair, auburn, and so thin that the skin showed through; of its hands like tiny soft starfish, patting aimlessly at the water and throwing up a pathetically small splash; of the sheen of the firelight on its wet skin; of the narrow shoulders, and of the pathos of the soft, bag-shaped body; of the stealthy movements of the fire, echoed even more stealthily by the water.

And why were all these things — so intense, also so familiar? Why this distressing tenderness in her heart, almost as if it were bruised, as she knelt stooping her shoulders over the wet, helpless child? Suddenly — like an electric shock through her system, the tenderness was wiped out. In its place was a murderous hate.

Her hands seemed under an intense compulsion to let that small, soft, bag-shaped body slip forward, to push back the feathered wobbly head, until it lay under the soapsuds.

Cold with horror, she knelt there, staring. She saw a small pink body feebly struggling, waving soft starfish hands, vaguely for a second, then limp, collapsed, along the bottom of the bath.

She saw the limp body laid out, face downwards on a towel on the hearthrug, water trickling from its open mouth, while a pair of woman's hands, dough-coloured, gentle, pressed rhythmically on the soft curve of its back.

Nightmarishly — she saw the soft, formless features change — the mouth grew large as a cod's, and as bony, the eyes grew dark, clever and cold, the neck masculine and corded and lean, the sparsely feathered head thickly tousled with dark hair. Lastly, instead of horror, a savage triumph danced naked in Alexandra's heart.

When Winifred returned Alexandra was kneeling, livid as a statue, with the year-old baby still in her hands.

'Good heavens, girl, I thought you'd have had him out by now — half dry! He'll catch his death of cold. Here — give him to me!' cried the voice of reality.

Alexandra roused from her hideous trance, looked dazedly at this miraculously resurrected baby, and surrendered it into Winifred's hands.

She stared as Winifred, a towel across her knees, and another in her hands, patted gently, expertly, at the pink skin (fading as it dried to shell colour) tipped the small victim ridiculously with its legs in the air, lifted its unprotesting limbs and fiddled between its miniature toes, finally powdered all cracks with talcum, and folded it up in a clean nappie, as rapidly as if it were a parcel in her shop, chattering all the time like a chime of sledge-bells.

But of her chatter Alexandra heard not a word. White and deaf and dumb, she sat, wrestling with her recent visions, and their discrepancy with the present fact of the baby's continued life.

When the baby was at last clothed, kissed and taken up to bed, Winifred became aware of her strange abstraction. Instead of emptying the bath, she sat smoothing the towels over her knees, and stared at Alexandra thoughtfully — 'What's troubling you, Allie?' she said at last.

Alexandra sat with her hands clenched on her knees, and her face tightly sullen upon its trouble.

'Nothing!' she said — but her obstinacy sounded strangely hollow, as if it were a door swung-to against its own will, against the will of the prisoner within, by some relentless weight upon its hinges.

'Is it that Iris Young?' persisted Winifred.

The sullen face tightened into a false sneer. 'Is *what* that Iris Young?' she said tiresomely.

Winifred was silent. Her light-fingered, faintly inquisitive sympathy was helpless as a butterfly to open that heavy door.

Behind it sat Alexandra, beating weakly at the entombing stone to get out, and unburden the terrifying visions of a few moments ago.

She wanted to say to Winifred, 'Win! Just now I thought the baby had slipped out of my hands and drowned!'

She would never be happy again until she had said these words. But she could not say them. The door was too heavy; too ponderously it swung back upon her.

Supposing it were true that she had drowned the baby? — But that was silly. Of course she had not. With her own eyes she had seen him dried, powdered, kissed, wrapped up, and carried to bed.

But with her own eyes she had also seen him drowned!

How could she know which was the truth, which illusion? Even if that nightmare on the hearth was the illusion, how could she account for the hideous reality stamped upon it, except that, like those other hallucinations, of her father at the 'Railway Arms', of that loathsome room behind the present flowery papered room — except that, like these, it was a *memory?* — Something out of that mysterious, unsavoury, pre-paralytic time — something a thousand times worse than all the rest of the squalid broken fragments hitherto washed up in her mind.

She made an effort to shake off this horror by facing it. Supposing it *was* true that some time she *had* let Nick (yes, let her face the name, once and for all, for this was what she was so afraid of, wasn't it?) slip into the bath? Well — babies were notoriously slippery, boneless almost, you would think. Quite a number of people must have let babies slip by accident into the bath.

By accident! she repeated despairingly, several times, for she knew well that if the vision was a true memory at all, it had been no accident. For what of that convulsion of murderous hate?

Deliberately — yes, *deliberately*, she had held that phantom baby

183

under the water until it choked to death. Then if that phantom baby had been Nick, she had . . .

All at once she remembered a later part of the visions. A pair of heavy, dough-coloured hands kneading the limp narrow shoulders, a faint blown bubble between the parted lips, a trickle of water, an almost imperceptible stir between the shoulder-blades — surely that phantom child had been brought to life again?

Even so . . . that did not rid her of the hideous evidence brought against her by that convulsive flash of murderous intention.

With a deep shuddering sigh she came back to reality. Winifred was still staring at her helplessly, sweetness and curiosity struggling like two butterflies in her face.

Alexandra looked away in the fire to hide whatever of her recent thoughts might lie exposed in her eyes. She departed soon afterwards, with her confession still unsaid. For a time she clung desperately to that last scene in her nightmare visions. If any of it were true, *that* must be true, she told herself with a defiance born of still lurking doubt. She may perhaps have meant, once, in a strange fit of temper, to have drowned Nick. But she had not done so. He had been saved.

It was a full week later that she woke one night with a violent start that rattled the brass knobs of her bed. Somebody had whispered in the dark room, 'But Nick is *dead*! If he wasn't drowned — *how*?'

Henceforth began a new prowling in the streets of Colebridge — not in search of life this time, but in search of something which she was terrified of finding — in search of a nightmare dread, which slipped, as she searched, behind every street-lamp, door, gutter, window, tram — which peered covertly out at her, but could never be caught by the throat. Up and down the steep hills, cobbled and narrow and greasy black with a mixture of November rain and perennial soot, she hunted evidence for her own damnation. Several times she thought she had found it.

One day, for instance, she was about to cross a road which ran parallel to Finn Street, a road which was distinguished by a tree at one end, grimy and thwarted and very much wounded by boys, with a ricketty old iron seat under it. Just as she put her foot down into this road, something caused her to pause, and look at this tree.

And in that pause, she recognized in the arrangement of a round iron drainage lid, a hydrant, and the gutter, a pattern that seemed to have a sinister significance.

The next instant up leapt the occurrence which had invested all these things with that significance.

There was a pram tipped carelessly by one wheel down the kerb, a small girl, with two stiff pig-tails of black hair, struggling to right it, and a baby hanging by the strap upside down over the road, face purpling, tongue hanging out, and slobber dripping from its choking mouth. Up rushed a fat woman with crossed brown eyes.

'Silly little fool — can't yer see yer 'alf *murderin*' 'im?' she screeched, and righted the choking baby with a bump into the seat of the pram.

The incident, however, was by no means conclusive. It proved carelessness — 'gormlessness' even perhaps — but not an intent to murder, despite the fat woman's words.

More worrying than this was another incident. One day, coming downstairs in her now usual dream, she caught her foot, and only just escaped a fall down the last five stairs. Up rose the remembrance of a morning when she had fallen down the whole flight of these very same stairs, covered then with a dirty foul-smelling carpet, instead of with scrubbed lino, and she fell clutching Nick in her arms. Somehow, as she sprawled at the bottom, she had managed to hold Nick's head just, but only just, off the stone flags there. And she had wrenched her arm and something in her side in the effort. And as she picked herself up, sobbing from the shock, the kitchen door switched open and her mother's face, pale, thin, sucked in at the cheeks, surrounded with brown puffs of hair, like a ragged faded sunflower, looked round.

'My God, girl — do yer *want* to kill that kid?'

'Yes! Sometimes I *do*,' bawled the unnerved child through her tears, and rushed into the street, leaving the howling baby to its mother.

This again was not decisive. Was that reply, for instance, the wild extravagance of a crisis of nerves? Or was it the sudden explosion of a secret and permanent hate? In either case, of course, the incident was not evidence of murder. But the town was littered with similar incidents. They would turn up, like skulls in an old battlefield, wherever she went in these months of ceaseless prowling. Surely she must have been an extremely careless girl? Or was the multitude of such incidents an indication of a secret desire to be rid of that small burden, a desire which cropped out in seeming accidents to him?

To offset this ghastly dread, there were those other very different scenes. Had she not valiantly defended Nick from Miss Brittain and her array of tortures? Had she not mended his clothes, wiped his nose, dried his tears, tucked him in bed, tied up his wounds in her own handkerchief? How could she reconcile such things with the suspicious frequency of accidents to him? Had there been some evil thing in her, working against her undoubted love for Nick, producing these seeming accidents?

She could neither solve the problem nor give it up. Ceaselessly she padded through the dirty streets, yellow-green with fog, littered with children, dogs, smells, and her own unsavoury memories.

With one exception, there was not a street in the steep queerly built little town of grime, which she had not searched a dozen times over during the winter of this year.

But when Christmas came she still had not found the thing she dreaded and yet craved to run to earth — that is, the evidence of the true manner of her brother's death.

CHAPTER IX

CHRISTMAS was over in the Gollen household. It had consisted of a strict two days' holiday, for the Gollen brothers were as orderly in their merrymaking as in their daily work. Christmas Day was according to pattern: church in the morning for Peter, while Alexandra and Sam prepared the dinner; a period of torpor in the afternoon for the digestion of pork, apple sauce, stuffing, plum-pudding and custard and hot mince pies; and church in the evening for all three of them, followed by the cracking of nuts, and the perfuming of the air with tangerines, to the music of Peter's celluloid whistle.

Boxing Day had been filled by leisurely walks to the houses of various friends, seldom visited except at this time, there to exchange presents.

The 27th of December saw the two brothers once more side by side on their work-table, quite undisturbed by this yearly break in their routine.

Not so Alexandra. Her temperament and her brothers' were as like as Cape Horn and a Cheshire Mere. She was imaginative and, therefore, subject to discontent. Her life was a procession of troughs of passionate despair and crests of equally passionate exultation. She did not know how to be level.

Christmas Day had been one of the troughs. Weary of her long pilgrimage after torturing half memories, she had craved in violent reaction an impossible gaiety. She had visualized dancing, feasting, a gaiety like broken lights in water, laughter like all the bells in the world, a tree festooned with the magic of Hans Andersen, rooms tangerine and rose with an improbable firelight, rooms with windows whose other cheek was turned to blue twilit landscapes, of crystal and white snow. The real Christmas had contained no dancing, no feasting, only eating, and a mundane fire looking out upon Finn Street and a curtain of warm gentle rain. The simplicity of her brothers' festival appeared to her as poverty — poverty of purse and poverty of soul.

As she stood now, glaring moodily at the same dreary scene, curtained with the same gentle rain, she felt that if a barrel of gunpowder were in the room she would without hesitation put a spill to it and blow those busy little tailors and herself and the neat bare room into a thousand pieces. . . .

A head of burnished copper under a transparent green silk umbrella bobbed past the window, and a once familiar knock roused her out of her angry gloom.

She opened the door and stepped back to allow Iris Young to enter, clad in a glossy coat of green oiled silk that looked like coloured cellophane paper.

Alexandra had not seen Iris since the middle of November, when she had insulted her, as she thought, so finally. The fact that Iris had not been to see her confirmed her conviction that she had, by those final impossible insults to Gordon, cut herself off for ever from Iris's friendship. This notion had given her a savage pleasure, and had also added to the bleakness of her state of mind during the last two months.

'What had she come for now?' she wondered with a sultry recrudescence of her antagonism to Iris, as she helped her to remove her oilskin coat. It gave her a sort of acrid pleasure to observe that to do this no longer gave her the sensual pleasure it would once have afforded her.

She took the oilskin and umbrella to the kitchen to drip, returned, unsmiling and said sullenly, 'Well?'

Iris laughed and seated herself, with the energetic precision characteristic of her, in the rocking chair.

'You sound like a sentry barking out "Who goes there?" ' she remarked. Alexandra, flushing deeply, sat down on the other side of the fire.

'I suppose it *is* rather a shock to see me after so long,' continued Iris after a pause, 'but I've been so busy, what with a play at school, Christmas presents, and so forth, that I've been neglecting my friends shockingly. What a fascinating little tree!' she broke off, looking across Alexandra's shoulder at the little bamboo table by the window.

Alexandra flushed again, but this time with simple pleasure. For the tree was a creation of her own, consisting of a large branching spray of mistletoe, set upright in a jar, and fruited with a number of gold and scarlet crackers, of the midget kind. The colours – the pale green gold of the mistletoe, with its pearly berries, and the coloured crackers – were an unusual and pleasing combination. But everybody else had laughed at her tree, preferring the normality of the paper festoons hung by her brothers diagonally across the room.

This sudden appreciation by her one-time idol warmed her heart with gratitude, shot with a little of the old worship.

'You know, Alex, I think you have an instinct for colours and shapes – you're a bit of an artist, I think! You should do something with your gift!' said Iris, casually but sincerely.

Then, before Alexandra had thought of any answer to this, she returned to her previous subject. 'Now – I don't know whether I told you, but I had arranged to spend the New Year week-end with a party of young people at Corvar Hall, a Youth Hostel in Derbyshire, you know. I was looking forward to it quite a lot; it's

188

glorious country round there, wild and yet rich — and it's jolly at these Youth Hostels. But now I find I can't go. My father has been taken ill, rather seriously. At any rate my mother can't be left to wrestle with the business alone. I shall have to go home to help — not that I'm much of a nurse, but still I can give mother some valuable moral support! However (to cut short this Mrs. Nicklebyish rigmarole), I wondered whether you would like to go in my place. You see my fees are all paid, my railway ticket booked and everything. I daresay I could get my money back, but it's more trouble than it's worth. These Youth Hostel week-ends are very cheap ... Now will you go, Alex ... to do me a favour?'

The blue eyes flashed imperiously, rather than pleadingly, as she concluded. Alexandra immediately suspected that the whole business had been carefully planned, that it was another of Iris Young's many efforts to thrust her among a crowd of contemporaries, with a view to releasing herself from the burden of her love and jealousy.

If the offer had been made two months ago, when jealousy had festered at its worst, she would probably have refused it.

But recently her jealousy had been crushed down under the pressure of her ghastly suspicions concerning her dead brother.

From this obsession she had still more recently revolted into a state of morbid craving for gaiety. This week-end in Corvar Hall seemed to offer hope of that gaiety. And lastly, the praise given to her tree of mistletoe had warmed her into a more gracious attitude to Iris than she had felt for many months.

Whether Iris had originally schemed this week-end for her, or whether it really had fallen to her by accident, Alexandra never knew. But she was always to be thankful that she had accepted the offer. For it was during this New Year week-end that the brooding clouds of her self-suspicion were finally dispersed.

The 31st of December was a raw bitter day. The sky was of exactly the same colour and quality as the grimy glass of Colebridge Lower Station. And the air lay against one's flesh like cold cast iron.

Alexandra had never felt so alone in her life. And never had the world appeared so utterly outside herself as now. Never had she despised the show so bitterly. Never had she been less amused. She stood among twenty-five or so of her fellow travellers, and stared, and with the burning cold of frozen metal, seared them all with her scorn. She seared thus, with her contempt, a young man whose mammoth boots were stuck like a pair of St. Sebastians with nails, and whose immense hairy socks were rolled over his ankles so that they looked like the huge fore fetlocks of a shire cart horse. Could he *never* keep still, she thought with cold vindictive temper, watching him executing his ceaseless and deafening clog dance on the granite edge of the platform, from which he occasionally struck blue sparks.

Equally seared with her scorn was another young man — very thin, very drooping, like a sapling just transplanted and not doing very well, who had a green trilby pulled dejectedly over his eyes, long lean legs like strips of raw meat, and a very limp rucksack hanging, apparently empty, to the hem of his shorts.

This revolting creature was surrounded by a billowing ring of short-clad, pantomime 'boys'. And though he spoke in a limp, lugubrious voice, either his remarks were very funny or the girls were exceedingly foolish, for the cast-iron air vibrated with the thin empty cymbal-like clash of their reiterated laughter.

A little way off was another group — also a central figure ringed with a half moon of audience, but with the sexes reversed. This central figure was a girl, trying, Alexandra thought with sour amusement, very hard to be charming — a girl with cheeks like painted Canadian apples, eyes like brown stones, and a flat, slight figure like a whip.

The audience, mostly youths, though one was grey-haired and ought to have grown out of it, thought Alexandra contemptuously, called her unanimously 'She'. This reminded Alexandra of Miss Brittain, who had once barked at her, on a reference to her mother as 'she', 'OO's she? Mother *pig?*'

The thought of Miss Brittain led, like a train of gunpowder, to the thought of Nick. In a second, with a terrific detonation, her world of cast-iron air, grimy-glass, and cold contempt collapsed into a chaotic heap of terror and remorse.

When the shattered debris of this sudden cataclym had settled about her again she became aware that someone had spoken to her.

She crawled out from the dreary ruins of her mind, to find herself looking at a pair of eyes that reminded her of something. They were eyes of a peculiarly clouded grey, soft as feathers, shifting and friendly as a rainy sky, warm as smoke.

She stared into them, and as she stared, the earth-bitter smell of bracken came dimly into her mind. But the link would not join with anything else in her memory.

A smile moved gently in the watchful grey eyes, like a shifting of grey clouds, and the boy said, teasing yet reproachful, 'No! You can't remember me, can you?'

'No,' admitted Alexandra, with ungarnished truth.

At that the smile spread until it lost is subtlety and became merely a boyish grin. 'You don't go *in* for flattery, do you?' said the boy. But suddenly he had thrust through her clouded memory.

'I *do* remember you now!' she said. 'You're the boy who found me — the day . . . the day I fainted!'

The grin was repeated. 'Quite correct so far! But I bet you can't remember my name?'

'No!'

'Yates — Donald Yates.'

When the train at last drew negligently out of Colebridge station, she found him sitting by her side in the corner of the carriage. She liked his company. He did not speak to her throughout the hour's journey. Yet his silence somehow conveyed friendship. She was no longer a bitterly contemptuous observer, as she had been on the platform. She was a traveller, a traveller with an unobtrusive companion at her side, travelling in a world that began, faintly, to seem her home again. Though nobody spoke to her, and she to nobody, she was allowed to feel, by the silent friend beside her, that she was one of the company. This feeling gave her security (a security she had not felt since Iris had betrayed her) and released her mind and eyes and heart for the exploration of the world.

She looked out at the slowly turning landscape, at the bare fields, patterned by plough and harrow like brown hair showing the marks of the comb; at the winter-sour green of the pastures; at the thin black trees, stamped like steel engravings on the discoloured paper of the sky; and at the hedges, bloomed faintly with sloe-colour, too dark ever to bud again.

And all this stringent beauty came to her pure and cold, uncoloured by emotion, save that of the pleasure of the eyes.

With similar wonder, still and impersonal, she watched the antics of Sheila and her half-moon of admirers. There were one too many of them for the seating capacity of the carriage. The half-moon of admirers, therefore, competed for the honour of seating Sheila on their knees.

'Don't go to Jack — he's a bag of bones, Shee!'

'Shee! You know what you promised!'

'Ah Shee!'

'Shee!'

'I'll guarantee *these* to be equal to any Lilo, Shee!'

Thus they contended. And 'Shee', rosy and chuckling like a baby, was tossed and tugged about from knee to knee, eventually lying stretched across the knees of four, who pulled at her ends like a quartet of medieval rack-attendants.

Alexandra looked round at the boy sitting beside her, and received back a smile of tolerant contempt for these antics and their central figure. The smile was vaguely flattering to herself, she found.

At Dalehead she lost Donald Yates in the swirls and rapids of the exit from the station. But they had not been walking long down a gentle slope of chalk-white road, when he appeared again at her side. She soon found that she could talk to him as if he were one of her brothers, but that without alarming her, he was more exciting than they were. He knew more than they did, at least about country things. And he had a faculty, which they had not, of understanding things that she was not able to say completely, for lack of vocabulary.

Thus, perceiving the lovely fashion in which the earth, at each side of the road, reared itself into long shallow, tranquil-looking waves, at the crest of each of which was flung up, like a beautiful iron-grey spray, a cluster of slim trees, she had only to say, 'Aren't those trees lovely?' Whereat he would reply, 'Yes! beeches are the loveliest of all, I think!' in such a way that she felt he had understood all that she could not say about the lift and fall of those exquisitely broken waves.

Later, they left the soft waves of earth crested with beech trees, and walked along a broad grass track between two parallel walls of faintly heliotrope limestone. Beyond lay sour moors where groups of silky green-grey birds with white bibs and long slender crests strutted and pecked at the reedy grass. Donald told her that the grass-track was an old Roman road, and that the birds were peewits. And she felt, immensely out of proportion to the value of this information, that her store of knowledge was being tremendously widened.

Once he sprang suddenly up to the top of the wall and clapped his hands like a couple of pistol-shots. The silky grey birds rose, and became instantly black and white, clumsy as flying shawls, no longer dapper and prim. She was amazed at the transformation.

'You wouldn't think they were the same birds would you?' she remarked, then added, 'but peewits are queer. In winter they sound so sad. Yet in spring they don't! They only put an extra little bit in their song. But it makes a lot of difference!'

Donald had to admit that he had never observed the extra little bit. She had the pleasant feeling that she in her turn had enlarged *his* store of knowledge.

Later in the morning they came to an old stone signpost, at the junction of three moor-top ways. One side of the stone was carved with the word 'Eyam'. They did not take this track. But as they moved off again, Donald remarked, 'Eyam is where they had the plague, you know, years after it was all over in the rest of the country. But I suppose you know all about that?'

'No! I'm afraid I'm very ignorant,' confessed Alexandra, but with no sense of shame at all.

'They say it all began through some men digging in a field and unearthing some old clothes. These clothes were infected clothes belonging to someone who had died of the plague years before. Personally I don't believe it. In the first place, surely the clothes would have been burnt, not buried. And in the second place the germs would surely not live all that time in the earth. However, that's the tale. I think about half the village caught it and died, and the whole lot would have been wiped out if it hadn't been for a heroic parson and his family. If you ever want a gruesome afternoon, and can't get to Madame Tussaud's, you want to go down to Eyam and visit the churchyard there. It tells you all about it. There's a churchyard full of plague graves, and lots of postcards, etc.!'

Alexandra was struggling with a number of fragments drifting up from the muddy bottom of her stagnant memory.

'I think I can remember something being said about the plague at school!' she said at last, frowning with the effort; 'I think I used to enjoy it rather!'

Donald laughed. 'Oh, I think it's usually a popular part of the elementary school history scheme!' he replied. 'It's those carts, rumbling through the narrow dirty streets, and the bells and that "Bring out your dead" business, that captures the imagination!' he explained.

'Yes! — And the crosses on the doors — and people locked up in plague-stricken houses!' added Alexandra eagerly.

'And people breaking out, running naked down the street, to roll in the river to ease their agonizing boils!' returned Donald.

'And something about a little girl being handed out through a window, without anything on, and being taken secretly to the country,' cried Alexandra.

'And communal graves in limepits!'

'And that Abracadabra business?'

They laughed.

'My word — You did learn your lesson well!' teased Donald, his teasing muffled by the smile in his gentle cloudy eyes so that there was no sting in it at all.

'What a *bond* the elementary school tie can be!' he continued, still teasingly.

But Alexandra did not respond. For she felt quite seriously that her returning memory of these old trivial school lessons did constitute a bond between herself and this boy. What was a commonplace to him was to her an intense pleasure, because it seemed to establish, after all, her normality.

After lunch the feminine half of the party gathered in an outhouse for toilet repairs. Alexandra washed her hands and face in the bucket of cold water. Then not thinking anything else necessary, she stood gazing in astonishment at the varied preenings of this flock of restless birds, feeling as if she were of a distinct and alien species, heavy and uncharming as a great crow. She watched them powder their faces, lacquer their lips, colour their cheeks, tweak and fluff their curls, tie ribbons and adjust hair-nets, and fuss with scarfs and berets as if they were on the threshold of a ball-room instead of on the edge of the moors. When she finally emerged with them into the bleak light of the farmyard, and found Donald waiting for her, it was as if she were welcomed back home.

The afternoon darkened quickly, the sky gathering cold into itself until it was the colour of a yellow bruise, of which the moors beneath seemed a muddy reflection. And now she felt so close to this long-legged, tufty-haired, gentle-eyed boy that she found herself telling him of the strange hiatus in her life, even now only partially mended.

'I seem to be like a battered old book!' she said. 'All the front pages have been ripped off, and some of the first of those left are very tattered. You know how aggravating books like that are! Well, I feel aggravated about myself! I can't understand things a bit, because the beginning of me is lost for ever!'

'Well,' said Donald cheerfully, 'if it comes to that we're all of us much of a muchness. *I* can't remember much further back than about my sixth year.'

'Ah, yes — but I stop short at *twelve* years old — *absolutely* short. At least, it *was* absolutely until a little while ago. Now bits keep coming back . . . And I'm not sure that it wasn't better *before* they started to come back!' she added sombrely.

He looked at her, with so genuine and so simple an interest, that she found herself telling him, in brief, all that she had recovered, with such pain to herself, of her unsavoury childhood — the brutalities and obscenities of her father, the filth and discomfort of the house, of her mother's death, her brothers' goodness, the heroic struggle they had had to rescue the house in Finn Street, and to maintain her in helpless invalidism, her own premature maternal cares, her efforts to protect her young brother Nick from the terrors of St. Saviour's Infant School.

She almost told of the terrible suspicion that so far she had dared tell to no one, lest it should be true — the suspicion that despite her proved love for her brother she had also, in some mysterious fashion, hated him so much that she had murdered him. Only in the nick of time did she draw back from the fatal, alluring edge of this confession.

Trembling physically from the shock of her narrow escape, she shrank back into silence. The terror of finding herself so near to this disastrous piece of self-exposure destroyed a large part of her new-found serenity in the company of Donald Yates.

The world, in any case, was now decidedly more unfriendly than when they had set out after lunch.

The bruised yellow of the sky had now begun to vent its pain in a heavy fall of sleet. The party paused, slung off its packs, crouched down by walls, and presently went on transformed into a troop of monsters; some in large bell-shaped capes, swimming through the watery gloom like huge black or yellow jellyfish; others with lumps on their backs like gigantic toy camels of unnatural-coloured cloths; some of the girls in inadequate-looking coats of coloured cellophane.

All but Alexandra had some sort of hideous, but waterproof, headgear. Donald offered her his sou'wester. She assured him that her hair was waterproof in itself. But she was not proof against his gentle persistence, and finally they went on, Alexandra watching remorsefully how his brown tufty hair gradually blackened and flattened in the sleet, until his face looked quite a different shape.

Doggedly the mirth-quenched party tramped on, gradually descending to tree-crested country, wilder but richer than that of the morning, climbing over walls like waterfalls, squelching through lanes of mud, squeezing through hedges like fountains, and at last reaching, with the relief of the civilized, roads prepared for the shoes of the civilized with stones and tar. At last, through a rift in a plantation of larches, dripping like hair just emerging from the baths, they saw Corvar Hall.

It looked, through the veil of sleet, like a house submerged in wavering water. You almost expected to see fish swimming out of the windows, or shooting between the tall elaborate chimneys. And the green with which its walls and roof were encrusted seemed the green of water weeds.

They passed over a narrow stone bridge, arching its back like an angry cat over a river the colour of boiling coffee, then through some wide gates, guarded by old crumbling stone posts, on which sat a pair of stone birds, and so up a short wide drive. And now the Hall came into complete view, a low, lounging building of stone, of a quiet green-grey almost the colour of ash bark, with long windows of stone, a roof of large greenish stone flags, and a door to which you climbed by a shallow flight of semicircular steps, cracked and greened by time, worn concave by feet laid long since in their graves. The garden was mostly lawn, sourly green through the mush of sleet, and set with a group of black yews, old and branched and unkempt, like savage upward-growing beards.

Alexandra was ignorant of history, except for broken memories of the Plague, the Fire of London, and so on, ignorant of the long tradition behind this house, ignorant too of the reasons for its present decay into Youth Hostelry. But she felt vaguely the sadness of its state. And though, unlike others of the party, she saw no ghosts, in historical fancy dress, pacing the garden of yews, or climbing silently the broken fan of steps, she nevertheless felt a discordance when they stepped into a room which resembled the Corner Shop in Finn Street, being furnished with a deal counter, cases of picture postcards, bars and slabs of chocolate, bags of nuts and raisins, guide books, pamphlets, and postage stamps. This room, lit by a storm-lantern and warmed by an oil stove with a perforated circular top, depressed her so that she became miserably conscious that her skirt was soaked with sleet, that her shoes were walking baths for her feet, and that her neck and bosom were chilled by the drips from her hair.

They showed their Youth Hostel cards to the rough-faced, uneven-toothed man behind the counter, signed a book, clattered out, and gradually sorting themselves out into Male and Female, parted company.

Alexandra lost Donald for the first time since lunch, and found herself, with a host of unknown girls and women, climbing some bare wooden stairs and entering a low long room, dark and furnished with nothing but ranks of the most peculiar beds that she had ever seen — if indeed they *were* beds.

They seemed to have two layers, like double-decker buses. On each layer was a wire-mattress, covered by a flock-mattress, and piled with rough dark brown blankets.

Alexandra felt vaguely some sort of indecency in these sleeping arrangements — an indecency which she could not form into words, however.

The host of unknown feminity moved about her, chattering, clattering on the bare unstained boards, unpacking their rucksacks, stepping out of sodden skirts, or shorts, and into dry garments, powdering their pink rain-polished faces, pressing crinkles into their rain-straightened hair, laying blankets over their bunk-like beds, disputing amiably as to upper or lower deck.

Alexandra copied them, as far as she could, miserably aware of her lack of spontaneity. Then, finished long before the others, she stood at the low window, whose sill was only just above the floor level, and looked into the garden. It was bitterly cold, and she felt very near to tears as she stood with her arms folded across her damp jumper, trying to keep her knees from touching her sodden skirt.

It was not until their own comfort was achieved that any of the girls noticed her. One of them called to her to go down with them. And as she obeyed, silently, another suddenly reached out and squeezed her skirt-hem. A small pool of water dribbled on to the stair — 'Good heavens, child! Why haven't you changed!' she cried.

'I haven't anything to change into!' said Alexandra harshly, ashamed of her threatening tears.

'Oh — hard luck — oh well — you'll have to steam it dry in front of the fire downstairs. They usually have a good roaring fire here.'

A wisp of comfort crept into Alexandra's misery at this friendliness — casual though it was.

And when they reached the hall — at one end of which there was indeed a splendid fire, she began to recover her spirits. The casual sympathizer pushed a place for Alexandra in the crowd of men and women about the fire, and soon she began to steam like a Christmas pudding.

Presently she felt that sufficient of her misery was melted out of her eyes to allow her to look into the faces of others. She lifted her rain-heavy eyelids and looked round the circle. At the other side of the wide fireplace stood Donald, smiling his gentle, cloudy smile at her. And immediately she was at home again. From the shelter of that smile she peeped out at her new surroundings as if from a tent — her movable home, pitched now in a new field.

Presently she became aware that the eyes, besides sheltering her, were trying to send some message to her. But what it was she could not tell, and finally Donald gave it up, and came across to her.

'Come out into the passage with me — I want to make a suggestion — not fit for the ears of the vulgar,' he said in her ear.

Reluctantly, for her skirt, though still soaked, was now warm at any rate, she followed him into the draughty passage.

'Can't any of the girls lend you something to change into?' said Donald when they were there.

'I don't know — I don't think so . . . I . . . I don't like to ask them because I don't know them yet!' she stammered.

'Well — if you wouldn't object to the idea — I could lend you some shorts,' he said, rather shyly, avoiding her direct stare, for the first time since she had known him.

But Alexandra by her long illness had been rendered innocent of the fussy sexual self-consciousness that cheapens a good many relationships, and she accepted the offer with a simple pleasure and gratitude which astonished and delighted the boy, slightly more sophisticated than she, despite the direct and simple friendliness of his nature.

But when she returned to the hall, warm and rather tightly encased in her borrowed corduroy, she realized that a new and intimate turn had been taken in this new friendship. It was as if, in wearing garments which he had worn, a remote sort of physical contact had been made between them. Warming her with his corduroys was next door to warming her with his own body. And beyond her gratitude for the mere comfort, there lay the kind of warmth, much more mysterious, which is only to be kindled by intimate personal contact — either of body or of mind.

The rest of the evening was lit by this secret and mysterious warmth. She began to enjoy herself, as she had never yet done in a large party of human beings. After dinner, which they fetched each for himself from a hatch looking into the kitchen, and ate on long clothless tables of unpolished wood, afterwards joining in a communal washing of the plates, they sat round the roaring fire of logs, in a double semicircle, the outer ring seated on chairs, the inner ring crosslegged on the floor. Four people played table-tennis behind this fire circle; two hard-bitten-looking elderly men studied maps and papers sternly in a corner; but the rest were all about the fire.

Alexandra had a chair to sit on. And at her feet, sitting cross-legged between her knees, with his head leaning back against one of them, sat this boy who had made himself so rapidly her friend. She found that the feathery warmth of his hair against her bare knee gave her the most delicate and unfamiliar sensations of pleasure. She also experienced quite powerful urges to thrust her hands into this tufty brown warmth, and to stroke between a finger and thumb the velvet skin of his ear which she could feel against her knee. But she was afraid to give way to these urges — not being sure whether it was a recognized thing to do in this society.

The orange firelight dilated and flapped and rippled over the long gloomy room. Behind the wide square cavern of the fireplace roared the wind. Behind the long low window-panes, deepening from dark blue to the indigo of night, whispered the cold sleet. Within, huddled behind walls from these primitive noises, the human noises mounted more and more impertinently as the sense of security grew deeper. The light, foolish patter of ping-pong balls seemed like the putting out of urchin tongues at the now impotent sleet. The confused surge of human laughter and human chatter rose above the breakers of the wind and overwhelmed them. Firelight leaped in the gloom like a school of orange porpoises, more and more gaily as the uncurtained windows grew more indigo.

Alexandra sat in a trance, staring at the firelight, staring at the pictures (some old, made in needlework long since faded, great wheel-like patterns of fantastic flowers and birds, never seen on this or any other planet, some new, crudely-coloured railway posters of mountains in purple and green with sunlight falling in shafts like the light shafts at the 'Pictures'), staring at the ring of nailed boots crossed on the floor, staring at the faces, cut into bold facets of purple-brown shadow and tangerine light, their bone-formation thereby quite changed, staring at the antlers hung above the stone chimney, bold as the branches of ash trees.

She scarcely heard the talk of this double circle of fire gazers, scarcely realized that they had begun to sing, uproariously and sentimentally in turns. When they began to play games she joined in with the surface of her mind. But the under-fathoms of her being were still absorbed in her trancelike staring. And below everything, stirring faintly yet thrillingly like a deep-sea flower, was this strange, delicate, yet persistent pleasure in the touch of the boy's light warm tufty hair against her bare knee.

Some of the talk must have penetrated into the lower fathoms of her mind, however. For as she lay in bed at last, in the upper deck of one of the queer double beds, a curious fancy came growing in her.

The darkness of the room was absolute. She could see nothing as she craned her neck to look out of the window, whose top reached just above the level of her head. The girls about her had long since fallen asleep. The silence was so complete that it seemed a positive thing, not a negative. Surely such silence could never exist on earth? Surely it was a silence such as could be heard only in the deepest valleys of the ocean bed?

Suddenly there came back to her her first fancy when she saw this house between the dripping larches, wavering behind the veil of sleet as shapes waver through fathoms of water. She remembered also that during the evening someone had said that it would not be long before this house was submerged. The owner, it seemed, had been offered the alternative of seeing the stones of his ancestors transported to America, or of seeing them drowned under 150 feet of reservoir. He preferred to see them drowned.

There fastened upon Alexandra now the persistent fancy that the drowning had taken place, that evening, as they sat round the fire.

Had she not heard the water slapping its heavy cold flanks against the dark window-panes? Had she not heard the waves roaring as they filled the wide chimney? And now all was still — deathly still as only drowned things can be.

In the garden, in fancy, she saw the strange black growth of the yews stirring, groping in the green water like the thick, unseeing fingers of strange aquatic creatures, neither plant nor animal, while among them swam strange fish with eyes like cold lamps and mouths like monstrous flowers. Anchored to the chimneys, there wavered broad bands of weed, transparent, but tough, like smoke solidified. And far above them, separated by fathoms of still water, floated the shapes of birds, like tubby boats, dipping their orange and rosy feet, but only succeeding in sending a few spreading circular scratches over the surface of those fathoms.

From this incredibly distant surface came down the muted cries of sea birds and peewits.

It was the muted, dream-far quality of these voices that finally convinced her that Corvar Hall was drowned.

CHAPTER X

TOWARDS morning the weight of green water upon the Hall thrust a way into the bedroom where Alexandra was still sleeping. Snorting and glugging through the small panes of the broken windows it gradually filled the room, welling higher and higher until its surface lay just under the bed in which Alexandra lay, and finally, rising a few inches higher still, rocked the bed from its feet and lifted it unsteadily towards the ceiling.

Alexandra lay, placidly watching the whiteness of the ceiling grow as it came nearer and nearer to her upturned face. But before it crushed down upon her there came a sudden sideways drag in the current of green water. Her fantastic boat sidled and wobbled towards the window — and in another second or two, with a muted splintering of glass, she had swept clean through it, and was shooting up, up, in a swirl of bubbles and small astonished fish-faces, through the fathoms of still cold water. The light grew more and more intense. From the sombre green opacity of the depths she swept on towards the sparkling diamond clarity of the surface water. Up . . . up . . . up . . . and out she came. . . .

She opened her eyes, but quickly shut them again in the searing pain of the whiteness that met them. After a second she tried again, cautiously this time, beginning with a cat-like slit.

When they were wide open again she looked down through the window, and saw now what had seared her eyes so painfully.

The garden of the Hall was bewitched. In place of the sour struggling green of the wintry lawn was spread a thick cloth of crystal, perfectly matt in the even light that falls before sunrise. Out of this cloth of crystal grew strange fantastically branched growths of white sponge. The shadows of these, so tenuous they hardly existed at all, breathed upon the cloth of crystal like faint clouds of smoke.

For a moment Alexandra thought her dream was reality after all — that the old Hall really was drowned under fathoms of water; that these strange growths were really aquatic; that the cloth of thick crystal was white sea-sand.

But a blackbird, hopping gingerly at the foot of one of the white sponge-like growths, startlingly black, dispelled the illusion. Who ever heard of blackbirds under water? Presently he took wing, dropping a shattered icicle of sound as he went, but the black image of him kept her anchored, slenderly, to reality.

It became imperative to get out of bed. From all around her came snores and deep-breathing, a desecration of the enchanted world below. She climbed carefully down from her high iron tower and dressed hurriedly, tiptoed along the old see-sawing boards to the stairs, and there suddenly took fire and ran like a black flame down and out into the garden. Once there she became a frozen flame, rooted with wonder, in that snow-hung enchantment, to the path near the door.

Now and then, as she lay in her bed in Finn Street, she had watched snow falling. She had admired it too as it iced the roofs and footpaths and gave them transient beauty. But this was an altogether different thing. This was not a garden merely painted with snow. This was a garden bewitched, unable to grow anything but snow itself.

In the neglected border bent tall tassels of snow-grass, springy trailers weighted with thick bunches of snow-roses, and spikes blooming with hexagonal, lacy wheels of crystal. Snow-bells and snow-stars bordered the path, and the wall was covered with snow-creeper.

The air, and the sky, above these strange blooms seemed a thick solid dome of grey glass; and the garden itself seemed as if it had grown, like glass-crystals, within this grey glass dome.

She stood as bewitched as the garden of strange flowers, as still as if she were herself a crystal within that grey glass dome.

In her ears sang the cold xylophone tinkle of the river, the voice of enchantment itself.

Suddenly, she became aware that out of the clear solid grey glass of the sky more crystals were growing — but these were falling crystals, small, cold and thin. They came very sparsely at first, but gradually thicker and faster.

And at last, as she stood there, one, bigger than the rest, fell on the palm of her hand, stung it delicately, and slowly vanished.

Delicious thing!

As if stung into life, the next second Alexandra was leaping like a midnight rabbit, back and forth over the crystal lawn — stretching out her hands to catch the lovely stinging flakes in her palms, and laughing aloud with the pleasure of its mysterious disappearance on her warm skin. Oh, the delicious lightness of it! She wanted to gather it all into her arms and toss it up again to the grey glass sky like a million little white shuttlecocks. Oh, the grace of it as it fell! The exquisite silence of it! The delicious creak of it under her feet as she danced! Oh, that it might snow for ever!

'Hullo!' said a voice from the doorway. Coming abruptly out of her ecstasy she saw that Donald was watching her. As she turned her head and stood suddenly motionless, he came running across the lawn to her in five long crunching bounds.

They stood face to face, uncertain and embarrassed; she because she had been caught unmasked for a moment, and feared that a fool had been revealed; he because there was something in her eyes that he could not understand, something which frightened him a little.

She would not look directly at him. Her eyes strayed continually to the snowflakes, falling and falling with them as if each flake were a parachute to float her eyes to the ground. But in the glimpses he had of her shifting eyes, he fancied he saw strange things. In those heavy dark globes, brightly polished by the snow-light, things seemed to stir that were darker even than the eyes, uneasy, bitter things, things best forgotten perhaps, things, maybe, out of that ugly childhood at which she had hinted the day before.

Whenever her eyes returned from the snow to him they seemed to him to be dilated with some private terror, and to plead with him to release them of that terror. And he longed to do so, and chafed at his impotence, for how could he banish a terror he did not understand?

Thus they stood, silent, tranced by each other's eyes, and by the veil of spotted muslin that curtained them thickly into this twofold solitude. And Time was measured only by the falling snow and their own drifting thoughts, both so formless, so softly homogeneous, that they were utterly unreliable.

Suddenly Alexandra saw that the boy's head was no longer tufty brown, but capped with a round cap of snowy feathers. For one wild moment she fanced that they had stood so long that now they were old.

Then common sense, common Time, and common eyes returned. With a long sigh, tailed with a queer little laugh, she roused, and looked around her at a garden that was after all, to her peculiar relief, only snow-covered, not enchanted at all. And she said, 'It's lovely — but there's something frightening about snow. Does it frighten *you*?'

'No — I don't think so. It might in other countries. But in England it seems more of a decoration, and a plaything, than a reality!'

At this answer Alexandra looked rather dejected, so that he added hastily, 'But even in England it can be dangerous, sometimes. Perhaps something once happened to you to make you afraid of it?'

He was amazed and intimidated by the result of this question.

'I've never been out in the snow in my life!' she cried. The terror that had lurked, uneasily smouldering, in her dark glittering eyes ever since he came out to her, now flared up as she spoke into a dark fire. And in her voice was the hard, passionate defiance of the deliberate and terrified liar.

Yet he would have sworn that those eyes, black with terror as they were, were conscious of nothing but truth in the assertion just made. He stared, unhappy, unable to think what to answer. Then, just as his embarrassment was becoming too great to be borne, the sullen face lightened with one of her rare smiles. Her eyes, less black, less glittering, had shifted their focus.

'Well?' he said, his own eyes smiling instantly in sympathy.

'There's a snowflake caught in your eyelash,' she said softly. 'Ah! Now it's melted!'

Donald laughed awkwardly. He was young, and therefore embarrassed by admiration. 'Come in to breakfast,' he said, roughly for him, and awkwardly pulling at her hand, drew her across the lawn to the house.

Terror was temporarily driven back. Whatever it was due to, it did not venture out again that morning.

After breakfast the party stood in the brown, low hall and watched the thickening curtain of white chenille that wavered down endlessly past the window. The old uneven glass of the panes gave a further twist of unreality to that silent falling music. Alexandra fancied soon that the whole house was drifting upwards, an illusion which seemed fostered by the flames in the wide fireplace, flickering up transparently in the reflected brilliance, as weightlessly as the snow flickered down.

The walk of twenty miles which had been planned for this day was abandoned. But half of the party, including Donald and Alexandra, went for a short morning walk up the valley, across the reservoir, and down the other side of the valley.

It was like a walk on the moon. By the roadside the dry skeletons of last year's hedge parsley hung out like umbrellas of thick white lace, whiter and lacier than its real flowers had ever been. All the trees wore high white powdered wigs like court ladies. Sometimes, like the more extravagant court ladies, they wore birds, real birds, perching in their false hair. And whenever a bird took wing from its strange perch, it shook down some of the white powder on the walkers beneath. Over a low wall, thick as an ermine muff, they could see the still water of the reservoir, like dark smoked glass. It was curious how each thick flake came drifting nonchalantly down to this glassy surface, poised a moment with one wing touching, then vanished silently, without even a water ring to show where it had alighted.

The party walked hatless, for as Donald had said, snow in England seems, unlike rain, not one of the unkinder elements, but an incredible plaything.

Half-way through the morning one of the men caught up a handful of snow and threw it so that it stuck in a soft rough star in the middle of Sheila Herne's back. A general conflict ensued. The wall's white muff was torn to shreds, the road was churned like a half-frozen sea, and everybody became starred and blotched with the soft missiles. Cheeks glowed with cyclamen and magenta, hands became small fires contained in skins of ice, and every breath turned into a laugh. Alexandra, an obvious target for all in her scarlet mackintosh and head of jet against the white road, could hit nobody in return. But the wilder her aim grew, the louder she laughed, until the stolid, stumpy figure with the sullen face of repressed passion that had been Alexandra was vanished. Instead there now flew out a creature that had been there all the time, but locked down tightly under hatches, a vivid, bright-feathered, bright-eyed, bird-like creature whose vitality and dark beauty eclipsed for a time even that of Sheila Herne.

When the party returned home they were decorated one and all with camellias of snow, laid flat against their temples, their eyes, under these snow wreaths, clear and merry, coloured still with the excitement of the snow battle.

But Alexandra, more than the rest, retained her new look of bird-like freedom. Her plaited crown had caught the snow in a different way from the bobbed hair of the other girls. She came back wearing a crown of plaited ermine. As they came through the gateway, whose stone birds seemed twice their normal size, as if their white feathers were fluffed out against the cold, Donald and Alexandra paused for a second and looked at each other.

Alexandra noticed that the light, upthrown from the ground, had changed the cloudy grey of the boy's eyes to a clear, jewel-like brilliancy. She also saw something in them that made her breathe a little faster and look away.

'What are you staring at?' she demanded, harshly, to cover her intense pleasure.

'You!' said Donald exultantly; then, softly and eagerly, 'I was just going to tell you that you look like a Russian Princess in that fur crown and your red coat!'

'Oh!' said Alexandra. She could speak no more, and, silent under great drifts of happiness, crisp and beautiful as the snow, she went before him into the Hall.

During dinner the snow ceased to fall. A weak sunlight patterned what had already fallen with smoke-coloured shadows. Those who had been frightened indoors during the morning were now eager to go out. Those who had already been out were eager for more exhilaration. They all went together up to the moors to the east of Corvar Hall.

They climbed quickly, their blood thrilling with the iced air and the pale sunlight which crept through its meshes without warming it, yet struck warmly on their cheeks.

As they climbed, fold after fold of hills came up from the horizon, long, low wave-forms, soft and pure, and classically shaped, like drifts of snow sculped into cold lines by the wind, rather than like hills. On these classic folds trees and the few farms seemed untidy litter, dark and mean, but nevertheless could not spoil their pure beauty. Below them lay the long narrow glass of the reservoir, shaped like a hand-mirror, with the river forming the handle. Two sea-gulls were circling above the water, and at the sight of them, below their level, Alexandra felt a second faint stirring of the uneasiness she had felt in the morning, the vague terror of heaven knows what that Donald had seen in her eyes, and failed to understand, as she also failed to understand.

At last they panted to the summit of the long, bony-backed ridge of moorland. As their heads rose over the summit there burst upon them like a sudden clash of bells, or a sudden shower of broken glass, the sound of laughter. A moment later, the cause of the laughter came into view, a crowd of school-children tobogganing on the further slope.

Up and down the steep hillside they went, small, snow-diminished figures in woollen caps and scarves, toiling up, and shooting down again endlessly, like very earthy angels on a solidified Jacob's Ladder. Alexandra stood with Donald, a little apart from the rest of their party. And as she watched, the dark flame of terror which had been driven back that morning stirred for the third time in her heart and eyes.

Something about the polished trackway, its slope, its bony humps, where the toboggans jumped and scraped, its yellow ivory lights and its violet shadows; something about the thin cries of the children; something about their bent, wiry, dark bodies as they toiled up the powdery side of the track dragging their wooden chariots; something in the quality of the air itself stirred up this terror, making the skin of her throat tighten and thrill and her heart thud woodenly against her ribs. There was a double bend half-way down the track, a sharp bend to the left and back again. Every time a toboggan swished round this double bend the passengers let out a piercing shriek, hysterical as the shriek of a railway engine. This shriek seemed to Alexandra to strike into her very blood — to be the very voice of terror itself.

She felt, as she stood on the summit of this snow-padded moor, that there was something ugly, something incomprehensible, something poisonous, lying behind all this beauty. She had felt it that morning in the garden, and had tried to express it to Donald, and failed. He thought she had meant there was some tangible terror about snow, that she feared the cold of it, or the depth of it, or the isolating power of it. But what she feared had no connection at all with the physical nature of snow.

Two girls, their faces like crimson anemones, their hair bursting like spluttering fireworks out of their blue berets, their eyes and lips moist with excitement, came toiling up to where Donald and Alexandra stood, their toboggan running hoarsely behind them.

'Want a try, mister?' one of them cried to Donald.

Donald laughed. 'How on earth did you guess?' he asked.

Whereupon they giggled, and the bolder of the two declared that she was a thought reader.

'Come on then!' said the other, and, ignoring Alexandra, they seated themselves with Donald sandwiched between them, his arms round the front girl's waist and his waist encircled by the girl behind. The back girl, who was steering, swung out her black-stockinged legs, and with a leap and a hoarse cough of the runners the thing was off.

Alexandra felt faintly sick as it lurched forward. As it reached the double twist her sickness doubled; it was as if something sharp gave a double twisting jab at her stomach. And when the toboggan slid, a little sidelong, to a safe standstill, she discovered that she was trembling violently from head to foot.

What was the matter with her? She sat down weak and shivering as if she really had been physically sick, and buried her face in her hands. After a short interval she heard Donald's voice, close to where she sat.

o   209

'Will you let my friend have a try?' he was saying.

Instantly she was on her feet. 'Oh, no! No! Donald—No! I couldn't really!' she implored him.

'Rubbish, girl!' he cried gaily. 'It'll be a new experience for you. If you've never been out in snow before, you won't have been in a toboggan. Everybody ought to try it once. It's glorious! Come on! *I'll* take care of you. There's nothing dangerous about it, is there now?' he appealed to the girls, who added their persuasions to his, though with enthusiasm markedly less.

Alexandra submitted. Sick and cold as if about to be shot in a rocket to the moon, she took her place between Donald and the blowsier of the two girls.

Whoosh! — They were off — her stomach left behind at the top of the track. Immediately, it seemed to her, they were at the double-bend. It was here that her trembling arms finally lost grip of Donald's waist.

Before her head reached the track she was unconscious. One foot trailed across the knees of the shrieking girl behind her. The toboggan rushed on without her, while her unconscious body rolled, over and over to the bottom of the hill, finally coming to rest against a stone wall.

But her spirit still shot, sick with horror, down a hill. At the top of the hill was the Market Place, floored with rotted snow, trodden by yesterday's crowds into a choppy sea, then refrozen with the market litter imbedded in it like archaeological refuse. It was silent as only a Sunday market place can be silent, and occasional footsteps across it sounded like the feet of a few persistent ghosts. At the bottom of the hill was Under Market, flowing like a brown river of scored and littered ice through a dark blue gorge of closed shops.

The hill hung down to this gorge, a tributary tongue of ice; lolled down between tumbling, dirty little shops, unglassed, and unshuttered, stinking of fish and meat.

Down the lolling glacier tongue they shot, so swiftly they should have been down in a second, yet continued to shoot down for a period of time only to be measured in nightmares.

The snow was thin, scarcely covering the cobbles, more a coating of ice than of snow, hard, treacherously polished. The toboggan danced and skidded all the way down. Nick was terrified, screaming all the while, but laughing at the tail of every scream because after all he was enjoying his terror.

Their breath came clouding from their open mouths, condensing into little fogs upon the cold fishy air. Once one of her heavy plaits flew round her shoulder and thumped Nick's head, and he screamed louder than ever. On — on — they shot, at asphyxiating speed, and yet at that nightmare length, like an old-fashioned motion picture held up indefinitely and excruciatingly at the climax.

In this eternal second she had time to see many times over the car which came crackling along the frozen ruts in the crawling brown glacier of Under Market. She had time to realize, many times over, with a heave of her stomach into her throat, that it would arrive at the foot of the hill at exactly the same moment as the toboggan.

'Nooooo! No! No! No!' she screamed, piercingly, yet somehow a long way off. And that car screamed too — like a stuck pig, made of metal, with blood of oil.

She tried to dig her toes into the iced cobbles. In reply the toboggan gave a last sudden spurt. The car vanished. Instead a monstrous wheel swelled up before her. The wheel vanished. Now it was a huge wave of patterned grey rubber rearing over her eyes. Something screamed again. Then Nick lurched out of her arms and was gone. The next thing was a world unbelievably still, frozen into unlikely, unmeaning attitudes, like the 'Still' of a moving picture.

The car stood motionless with its wheels wrenched at right angles to its body. The sky was still, yellow, echoing the ache of her own bruised flesh. The closed shop-windows were glazed with dark blue like blind men's eyes. Kneeling by her was a motionless figure in a black overcoat like a wax tailor's model. She herself was still — held stiffly prone as if the air were a casing of plaster of paris about her body.

And Nick — just beyond the wheels of the car — Nick was more still than anything else — stiller than anything in the world — except for a narrow dark thing creeping out of his head into a furrow of the rotted snow.

She opened her eyes and found a pair of warm cloudy grey eyes looking anxiously down at her, and a warm arm crooked under her head. She stared. She had no strength for the struggle necessary to identify them. All her being was occupied with one question. At last it rose, reluctant as a foetid marsh bubble, to her lips, exploding there in a whispered, 'Is he dead?'

The forehead between the grey eyes puckered. 'Who?' asked their owner.

But the need for an answer had burst as the question itself had burst into speech.

Of course Nick was dead — long ago Nick was dead. What had possessed her to ask a stupid question like that? Once more she had very nearly betrayed everything.

She took another quick look, with half averted mind, at that last 'Still' of the scene in Under Market. It was becoming a little smudgy already — beginning to go back into the past to which it belonged. Like an exorcized ghost it was becoming bleary in the light of the present. It was still plain enough, however, to make it certain that at last she had discovered her secret. This, then, was the terror that had brooded within her for so many months. This was why she had feared so sickeningly to go down that steep cobbled hill into Under Market. This was what snow had meant. This was the horror behind the beauty which she had felt all day.

Suddenly she identified the grey cloudy eyes still looking down at her so anxiously as Donald's. For the first time since she had first come in sight of the toboggan run she smiled.

He smiled waveringly back. 'Do you realize what you were saying a minute ago?' he asked slowly.

She closed her eyes. Her first instinct was to deny any responsibility for that question. After all, people often say silly things when they are 'coming-to' she reflected. Now that she knew exactly what it was, she would be able to keep her secret more easily. Nothing is more exhausting, more terrifying, than to have to keep a secret you yourself only suspect — to *feel* your guilt, without knowing the precise reason for it. Now that she knew exactly what she had done she did not feel herself to be the horrible monster she had suspected. Without precisely forgiving herself, the bitterness

212

of her self-condemnation was eased, the horror of her self-suspicion lightened.

Then suddenly, it did not seem nearly so important to keep her secret — and after all, this was only Donald, her friend.

'Yes,' she said therefore at last, and left the door ajar for his inevitable further questioning. Yet when, after a long, searching silence he said:

'I wish you'd tell me what it is that's troubling you!' she turned her head peevishly, like a wilful child refusing medicine at its very lips.

'I can't!' she declared. But the next minute she added, significantly pleading, 'Not yet, at any rate, Donald!'

He smiled. 'I shall take that as a promise,' he told her.

CHAPTER XI

THEY were walking behind a shepherd along a narrow grass foot-path climbing diagonally the flank of the valley. The shepherd was accompanied by a sheep whose long grey fleece flounced against her legs like a gown as she trotted, and a tiny lamb, its umbilical cord still dangling, its wool so close-curled and its legs and flanks so thin that it looked like a toy made of pipe-cleaners. Its cry was as thin as its legs.

'Ah!' cried Alexandra, 'Isn't it a darling? I'd love to pick it up and cuddle it!'

Donald laughed at her. 'It's funny,' he remarked, 'how girls always say "Ah!" when they see a lamb. I suppose it must be the maternal instinct!'

He glanced at her, more thoughtfully, and added: 'I guess it has always been pretty strong in you. In fact, from what you've told me about that little brother of yours, I guess it was *too* strong. I should think that that was probably the cause of all the trouble. I think it was a wicked shame for a girl of your age to have to shoulder such a burden. You should have been playing hopscotch, not caring for a baby. I hate to see little girls from poor homes

213

lugging babies about, nearly as big as themselves. It's not good for them — physically or mentally!'

'It wouldn't have hurt me, if I hadn't been so thoughtless and taken him tobogganing down that hill, and so killed him,' said Alexandra.

'No!' said Donald obstinately. 'The fact that his death had such a disastrous effect on you proves that your feeling for him had already become unhealthy. Naturally such an awful accident would have been a terrible shock to any sister. Of course, any decent girl would blame herself bitterly — though I can't see that there was much to blame yourself for. After all, cars don't go along Under Market all that much on a Sunday. Anyway, I think the normal healthy-minded sister would have got over it a lot sooner than you did. And I've certainly never heard of a sister — or anyone else — who was made ill by such a thing for nine years!'

'Perhaps you're right,' agreed Alexandra meekly. Even now she did not understand the cause of her nine years' collapse, nor the exact mode of her miraculous recovery. She had never been of an introspective nature. And now, though the scenes and inner emotions of her once walled-off childhood were returned to her, vivid, and almost intact, her own character and motives were still as mysterious as ever to her. She therefore accepted Donald's explanation meekly, as those who cannot generalize must always accept the theories of those who can.

She was a little ashamed sometimes of the ease with which she now spoke of the once terrible secret. She was also glad. There was a calm grown over the whole episode that astonished her, when she thought of her nightmare of horror and suspicion, only two months ago.

She was very conscious of her returned well-being as they paused at the top of the sloping hill-path and looked across the valley.

How beautiful the world was in February, she thought. Perhaps she would always love February best, for it was in February that Iris had first taken her into Colebridge to see the world after her nine years' winter. She had been a year in that world now. And how she had wasted it! Jealousy and Love between them had completely blocked her vision.

Well — this year she would love nobody, be jealous of nobody.

214

She would work; learn dressmaking so that she would no longer be a burden to her brothers; and look at the world. Nothing should escape her. Every minute treasure of every month's bringing should be seized and enjoyed. Everybody's life was too short. But hers was shorter than most by nine years. She must live intensely to make up for those lost nine years. She would begin this instant.

Unconscious of her companion's watchful eyes, she stood on the hill-top, gazing with all her soul at the shallow valley below. How beautiful was the pale catkin-coloured sunlight on those woods opposite! How beautiful were the woods! Not black as in January when she last saw them, but a warm, light, cloudy brown made by millions of swelling buds. Beech woods, she thought, for she was beginning to learn some country names now, under Donald's guidance. And those solitary trees, half-way down the valley side, so bare, so pale, looking like freshly scrubbed deal in the sunlight — those were ash trees. And those knotted, tangled, faintly purplish, thin-twigged, difficult looking trees, those were hawthorns.

A cool February wind laid its invisible palms against her cheek. She could just detect the faint heat of the February sun on her hair. Catkins, green as the sunshine, wagged their tails feebly in the hedge, and a lamb, perhaps the one they had followed, pierced the thin air with its weak cry.

Her eyes filled with tears of gratitude for all these lovely things. And abruptly, lest Donald should see them, she turned and climbed the stile that led to their next path.

Silently Donald followed her. He had already seen her tears, but he asked no questions. He had the quality, rare in boys, and rarer still in men, of wordless divination of the moods of others — and, better still, when to make comment on those moods and when not.

Presently, when he judged the tears to be dried, he began to talk of other things.

'Did you know?' he remarked, 'that your friend Iris Young is to be married at Easter?'

'Of course I knew,' retorted Alexandra. '*All* her friends know about it!'

Donald was silent at that. Then, rather hesitatingly he said, 'You know, Alex, I used to think you were rather keen on that fellow she's marrying.'

Alexandra turned astonished eyes on him. 'Keen on Gordon Bridges! Why, I hated him like poison!' she cried, unaware, in her astonishment, of the relief these words, and the astonishment which guaranteed their truth, gave to the boy.

'Well — for one who hated him like poison, you followed him *about* somewhat!' he persisted, but without serious intent.

'I didn't follow *him* about. It was Iris!' she retorted, and began to tell him, as well as she could, the story of that half-year's infatuation. 'It's all over now,' she ended indifferently. 'I still like her, you know, but sensibly now — the other liking was out of all reason. I can see that now. I don't know what was the matter with me.'

'Girls *have* these infatuations quite often!' commented Donald, with the comical, yet somehow comforting air of worldly wisdom he had, which made her feel that after all she was not eccentric in her follies or her griefs.

'Everybody seems to be getting married this Easter,' said Alexandra, reverting to the remark that had led to her newest confession.

'Who else — besides your friend Iris?'

'Well — I was thinking of another friend of mine, called Winifred Bell.'

'I don't think you've told me about her.'

'Haven't I? Well — she's a girl I used to know at school. And Peter and Sam both wanted to marry her. But she isn't marrying either of them. It's very sad for them, of course. But in a way it's the best, I suppose. She couldn't have married them both. And if she'd chosen one, I think it would have broken the other one's heart. As it is they neither of them seem to care as much as I thought they would. I suppose it doesn't hurt so much if *neither* of them has lost. They'll get over it in time, I expect. But they won't go to her wedding!'

'And is her new name as pretty as her own name?' asked Donald.

'No — I think it's going to be Warner.'

'What a pity!' returned Donald, 'that women have to give up their names when they marry — though, of course, if your name happened to be Higginbottom or something indecent like that, you might be very glad!'

Alexandra did not hear the end of this reply. She was thinking of

216

something Peter had said, when they had discussed the idea of her learning to be a dressmaker.

'And when I'm trained,' she had said to him, 'you'll have to alter the notice in the window from GOLLIN BROS — TAILORS, to GOLLEN BROS & SISTER — TAILORS AND DRESSMAKER.'

Peter had smiled.

'What a mouthful! And besides, is it worth while? How long do you think you'll be likely to stay with the firm?' he had replied with a mischievous look.

'Always!' she had retorted passionately. 'I'll always stay with you and Sam!'

But Peter had continued to smile.

'What are you grinning at? I mean it!' she had cried, hurt by his scepticism.

'I know you do. I know you'll *continue* to mean it, as long as your name remains Alexandra Gollen!' he said aggravatingly.

Even now, after a good deal of meditation on these words, Alexandra was not quite sure what he had meant. She would have liked to have consulted Donald on the matter, but something held her back, which again was strange, for there were few subjects she could not speak of to Donald.

A little after this they came to a ruined farm-house. Although it looked strangely trim, as if the owners had just left, and had tidied up the garden before leaving, this was only due to the bareness of February.

The sunken roof, the fallen stones, the broken windows with their screens of ivy, and the wilful growth of the grey apple trees, betrayed the length of time the place had been empty.

They wandered into the orchard, in silence, for there is always something silencing about a ruin. A few golden brown, wizened apples, small and dry as oak apples, still clung to the furred grey branches; and in the rough grass lay scattered fruit, or rather the shells of fruit, containing the brown mush which had survived the wasps' feastings and the winter's rains.

But under one of the trees there grew something that brought them to a pause.

Out of a tuft of dark green leaves sprang four delicate and slenderly curved stems. Dangling from these were four exquisite little lanterns of an almost transparent whiteness, each suspended by a glossy green bead, each having three pointed slender lobes of pure white, within which hung a frilled shallow bell, streaked with a clear icy green.

The little lanterns swung, almost imperceptibly, in the faint wind creeping through the orchard wall. And as they swung, something swung with them in Alexandra's heart. She knelt to look closer, and presently put out a timid finger and tilted up one of them to see what hung inside. The lantern contained three candles of yellow, and one of pale waxen green. She let it fall. It swung with a sort of miniature joy for a while, in gentler and gentler arcs, until it was still.

Then she sighed, and rose to her feet, and smiled at Donald.

His eyes, greyer, cloudier, softer than usual even, were waiting for her. They did not smile back, but looked at her gravely, and seemed to tug at some inner part of her. She felt drawn — as a bubble is drawn to the edge of a cup, lightly, yet irresistibly, drawn by the tension of the liquid.

'Oh, what *is* it? What is happening?' she thought, in a sweet agitation, as she slid towards those grave, tugging eyes.

But he spoke — and then the tension was lifted. Like a bubble released, she swam back to her own centre.

'Would you like them?' he said seriously.

And immediately, though she had not until then considered the idea, she felt that there was nothing in the world she desired more than to be given those four snowdrops.

She nodded, as serious as he.

Whereat, with a swift, almost greedy stoop, he picked the small lanterns on their long slender handles, and put them into her hand.

She looked down at them, swinging them carefully, worshipping their fragility, and smiling her gratitude. For it seemed to her that in giving them to her he had almost made them.

Neither of them could speak for a time.

At last Alexandra spoke. But it was not to say what was in her heart.

'If *I* had named them, I wouldn't have called them snowdrops — I'd have called them "snow-lanterns",' she said.

'Why shouldn't you? Things are themselves whatever *we* call

218

them. I'll adopt *your* name if you like,' was what he answered, and this was not what was in his heart either. But they were neither of them ready to say that yet. After a pause they went on again, silent, and wondering at the bare stringent beauty of the February sun on the hills.